S0-BLV-291

96 -01

ACO

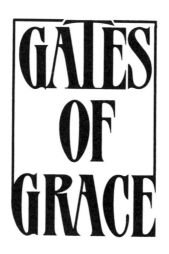

GATES OF GRACE

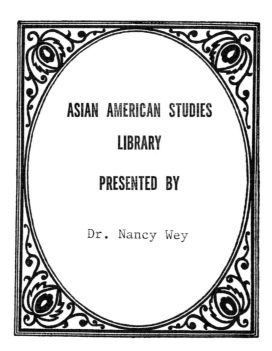

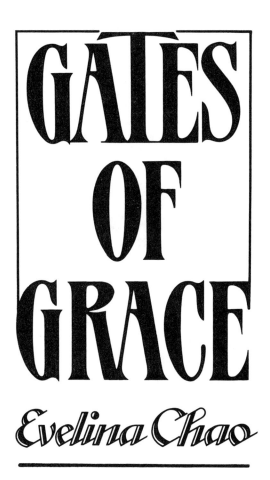

GATES OF GRACE

Evelina Chao

WARNER BOOKS

A Warner Communications Company

This is a work of fiction. The events and characters that it describes are fictitious and are not intended to represent or are not based on real people or events.

Copyright © 1985 by Evelina Chao
All rights reserved.
Warner Books, Inc., 75 Rockefeller Plaza, New York, NY 10019
W A Warner Communications Company

Printed in the United States of America
First Printing: September 1985
10 9 8 7 6 5 4 3 2 1

Library of Congress Cataloging in Publication Data

Chao, Evelina.
  Gates of grace.

  I. Title.
PS3553.H276G3   1985   813'.54   85-40006
ISBN 0-446-51303-2

Designed by Giorgetta Bell McRee

For my mother and father

Acknowledgments

I would like to thank the following people for helping me see this book through: my dear friend Zdena Heller, who was the first to suggest that I write the book and whose encouragement helped sustain me throughout; my mother, Vera, father, Edward, brother, Daniel, and sister, Katherine, for helping me select Chinese names for characters and for sharing family stories that inspired scenes in the book; my agent and friend Jonathon Lazear, for having believed in me from the first; my editor, Ed Breslin, for having seen promise and who inspired, with his wisdom, sensitivity, and tact, confidence on my part to finish; Pinchas Zukerman and the management of the Saint Paul Chamber Orchestra for granting me leave, which enabled me to meet my deadline; my dear friend Mimi Zweig, who sent me the map from San Francisco; my friends and colleagues in the SPCO for their interest and support; and finally, to Fred, who was there the entire time providing space, light, and warmth.

Author's Note

I have chosen to use a modified version of the Wade-Giles system of transliteration (Romanization) of the Chinese names in this book in an attempt to make their pronunciation as simple as possible. I have also chosen to use the modified Wade-Giles system rather than the pinyin system, because the Wade-Giles was the system most widely in use at the time during which the novel is set.

PROLOGUE

THE LAST BOAT

1949

Mei-yu stood in the shadow of the ship. The ship lay low in the water, the gentle waves of Canton harbor lapping at the rusting scars of her hull. People milled everywhere around the base of the gangway, pushing forward even though it was already sagging under full weight. Mei-yu found herself among those straining against the chain that separated them from the people up ahead; those already on the gangway clung to it with the grip of barnacles, waiting impatiently for the captain's whistle to signal the advance of the next shift to board. She turned to look for Kung-chiao, her husband, who had gone to get water. She saw the line of people snaking behind her in endless loops, the clusters of families waiting restlessly, the cloth bags containing their belongings lying at their feet. They turned often to look over their shoulders, shielding their eyes from the sun, straining to see beyond the edge of the city. There, in the distance, muted by the curve of the hills, the bugles could be heard, bleating the tattoo of the red flags. She saw the white dust cloud made by the marching feet rising up into the sky—a sign as terrible as the black-sky approach of locusts. The army was getting closer.

She turned again to look for Kung-chiao, fearful that he might miss the next group of people allowed up the gangway. Why had he left her now, when they had gotten so close? It was true, they needed extra water, and he hadn't known the line would press forward as it had, the officers of the boat motioning the people on with increasing urgency, sometimes reaching to pull on a sleeve. At the railing of the ship Mei-yu could see the captain, looking out over the city through binoculars. She saw him lower them. The army was near enough now that he could see it with his own eyes.

A family stood close to Mei-yu; a man and a woman and their daughter, who was about twelve. The woman stood watch over their pile of bags, a satchel clutched close to her chest, her back turned against the sun. The man held his daughter close to him and lifted his arm over her face, like a shield. The girl looked back at Mei-yu with wide eyes, leaning against her father as she would a tree. Her father was tall, thin, and wore faded blue trousers bound at the ankles with twine, dressed like the other commoners standing around him in the crowd. His hand, however, the one shielding his daughter from the sun, was smooth, uncallused, the hand of a scholar, perhaps a poet. So there were those, too, standing disguised in the line among the others, Mei-yu thought. Her father had had smooth hands, once. She had watched him practice calligraphy, the brush held aslant in his hand in the crook between thumb and forefinger, rotating and weaving its slow dance on the surface of the rice paper, leaving its twisting traces of ink. She had watched him plant the chrysanthemums in their courtyard, carefully lifting up the handfuls of dirt, placing the stems in the furrows, dusting his hands of every fragment of earth. And then she remembered when he had stood in front of her, his hands grasped tight together under the folds of his robe, pronouncing that she was no longer his daughter.

"I admonished you," he had said, his voice dead. "I had forbidden your marriage to this peasant's son. Now that you have eloped with Wong Kung-chiao, you must accept the consequences of your action. I forbid you to enter my house ever again, and I instruct those who remain in my house to refrain from ever speaking your name. You have brought me pain and dishonor by disobeying me, and by disobeying me, you relinquish all right to the title of daughter."

He had looked ill then. He had never regained his health after his release from the Japanese prison four years earlier, and as he stood before her, stooped, his sparse beard turned completely white, Mei-yu thought the maggots had already had their feast of him, and that he was now hollow inside, eaten away.

"Please, Father," she begged.

He turned away from her abruptly, his hand sweeping out from under the folds of his gown in a gesture of dismissal. Mei-yu saw that what had once been his smooth-fleshed hand had become a dried fist, as brittle as the bones of a bird.

She turned away at last. "Good-bye, Father," she said.

Outside, in the courtyard, Kung-chiao was waiting. "I see by your face that he has not reconsidered," he said. Then, seeing that she could not speak in her grief, he walked with her silently to the gate leading from the courtyard. There, Mei-yu turned and saw the figures of her mother and her old nursemaid standing at the opposite end of the house. They had already said their farewells, for they knew the resolve of the father, and knew that Mei-yu would leave. Her mother was still, as impassive as the wall behind her. Hsiao Pei, Mei-yu's nursemaid, rocked on her heels, her arms hugging her body, and from across the courtyard Mei-yu could hear her weeping.

"Come, let us go now," Kung-chiao said, taking Mei-yu's arm. Outside the gate she looked at him as if startled and said, "But where are we going?"

He avoided her eyes. "Tonight we will stay at an inn. And then, after that . . . we will have to talk about that later."

Later, in the dark, Mei-yu whispered again to Kung-chiao. "Where are we to go?"

"To America."

She had known he had been thinking of America. But now, severed from her father, her father's house, the thought of America frightened her. They had little choice, she knew. With the defeat of Japan and the clashing of the two armies of China, people everywhere were forced to move, to go. But where?

"We must leave China," Kung-chiao had said even five years ago, when they had met. "The old regime is collapsing, and I do not trust our future with the new one."

He spoke of the old guard, the Kuomintang, which scrambled in retreat, croaking its defiance as it moved its remaining forces and wealth to safety. The Communist People's Liberation Army, its leaders emboldened and backed by swelling ranks of men born of bitter poverty, marched throughout the cities and countryside, searching out and hanging those it judged to be aligned with the old regime. Those of the intellectual class were particularly at risk. Even so, many of the older intellectuals, professors and academic leaders, chose to remain at the side of China, regardless of which army ruled her. Mei-yu's father was among those patriots, remaining in his house like the legendary man by the river, refusing to abandon his home to the flood. The younger ones, Kung-chiao included, feared the new regime, feared the new policies that jeopardized their future in education, their freedom as individuals.

"We must leave China," Kung-chiao repeated in the dark.

Mei-yu clung to her husband. She felt the fusion of strength between herself and Kung-chiao, but still her fear did not give way. She thought of her father, remembered the sight of his back turned to her, the sight of the house of her childhood. Her father's grip remained strong, hidden as it had been under the folds of his gown. She struggled to accept Kung-chiao's decision, resolved to make it her own. America, she had heard, was a land of promises. Mei-yu had grown wary of promises, but she knew that she, like the countless others, had nothing left in China now, not even promises. The decision became hers as well. They were to go to America, then, she and Kung-chiao.

Now, waiting at the bottom of the gangway of the ship that was bound for America, Mei-yu turned her face away when the man who had reminded her of her father looked up, seeing that she had been staring at him. He did not look like her father after all, she thought. Her father's eyes were set wide apart, his brow broad. This man had a narrow, closed face. She turned her back to him, surprised at the feeling of revulsion that suddenly overtook her.

The ship blasted a column of gray-black smoke from its stack on the upper deck. People standing on the gangway surged forward at the sound. An official dropped the chain in front of Mei-yu and she felt herself being pushed by the hundreds in back of her. She stumbled forward, looking frantically above the heads in the crowd around her for Kung-chiao.

The dust cloud of the army had drawn nearer, and now Mei-yu could see the tiny pinpoints of the red flags waving above the column of soldiers that wobbled toward them like a great worm. The bugles continued to bleat, louder now. The boat signaled another blast into the air, and the people around Mei-yu cried in one voice, panicking, pressing forward.

"Mei-yu!"

She turned and saw Kung-chiao pushing his way through the crowd, two water bags slung over his shoulder. Bodies pressed on all sides of her now. She groped with her foot for the edge of the gangway and felt the planks of wood. She struggled to keep Kung-chiao in her sight as his head bobbed up in the wave of faces and then disappeared again. The woman in front of her screamed in Cantonese dialect, her child held up high in front of her above the crush of people. The child's face was crumpled with crying, its eyes rolling as it struggled against its mother's grip. Mei-yu lost sight of Kung-chiao completely. People around her were scrambling for a foothold on the gangway, fists with tickets for passage waved in front of her face, and families in different sections of the line called to one another to hold their places. A man with a live chicken under his arm thrust his head under the side rope and screamed for his son up ahead. Mei-yu looked behind her again, searching for Kung-chiao. She saw only the line of waiting people curving far into the distance. She knew hundreds had already made their way up the gangway, thought that the boat seemed to lie lower in the water. Mei-yu knew this was the last one, the last boat that would be able to leave before the arrival of the army, before the harbor would be closed.

"Kung-chiao!" she screamed, not able to hear her own voice in the crowd. She felt herself moving forward, struggling to keep her balance on the uneven planks. She was reaching the side of the boat now, and in front of her were the outstretched hands of people waiting to pull her aboard.

"Hurry! Hurry!" she heard them shout. "We can see the army entering the city! We must leave the harbor now!"

Mei-yu felt hands pulling on her arms, felt herself hoisted over the edge and onto the deck of the ship. The captain, seeing her condition, motioned for an officer to escort her below.

"No!" Mei-yu cried. "My husband has not come on board yet! I must look for him!"

She made her way to the side of the ship. Below, people were surging up the gangway, the line behind them having collapsed, transformed now into a mass of bodies crushing forward. She thought she saw Kung-chiao struggling midway up the planks. Someone pushed her aside. It was the captain.

"No more! There is no more room! Pull up the gangway, we must sail immediately!"

Mei-yu could hear the blare of the bugles clearly now. The army was streaming through the city, approaching the harbor. Sailors began winching up the chains, hoisting up the gangway. People at the bottom fell backward, immediately surrounded by their companions, who came forward with a roar to grab onto the end of the plank. Those at the top clung to the ropes dangling at the sides of the gangway, crying out in fear of falling, in agony of leaving those behind them. Mei-yu saw people losing their grip, falling, hitting the water. Sailors threw ropes overboard for them to cling to; others continued to work at the winch. The gangway continued to groan upward, people dangling from the end of it as from the lip of a sated beast. Mei-yu pushed her way to the front of the plank and searched the faces that plunged toward her, refusing to obey the shouts of the sailors to stand back. The ship seemed to roll, loosed from its tether to the harbor, and Mei-yu saw that they were moving, the dark gray smoke roiling from the stacks above.

"My mother!" cried a young man behind Mei-yu, grabbing onto her skirt. "She has fallen into the water!"

Mei-yu looked down and saw the people who had fallen, flailing now amidst the flotsam of their cloth bags and other belongings. She searched the water for Kung-chiao, but the figures below were tiny, splashing beneath the high arcing bow of the boat, and she could not tell one face from another. Their voices, coming to her amidst the cacophony of the harbor, sounded faint, and Mei-yu turned away in horror as she saw one white face after another slip down beneath the waves.

The boat drew steadily away from the shore. Those left on land set up a wail, answered by their relatives who had managed to board, those who were standing now against the railing, reaching for them with out-stretched arms. Then a shout rose out of the crowd. The army had reached the harbor! The people on the boat watched, some stunned into silence, others crying out warnings, as the soldiers carrying the red flags ran toward the people at the edge of the water.

Now the crowd swirled in upon itself in confusion, like a serpent swallowing its own tail, as people rushed back from the edge of the water in an attempt to reach the sheltered areas of the city. The khaki uniforms of the Liberation Army closed upon the blue-clothed bodies of the people, and Mei-yu saw the clubs beating down, saw those in blue falling in still heaps. She fought her way to the open edge of the boat again, searching for Kung-chiao, fending off the tangle of arms that reached for a hold. Had he fallen into the water? The boy whose mother had fallen threw himself at the opening at the side of the ship and tried to climb over the edge. An officer grabbed him and pulled him backward, slapping him. The boy fainted. Suddenly Mei-yu saw Kung-chiao, just below the edge of the opening, his mouth twisting grotesquely as he strained to pull himself up. Mei-yu screamed for the officer to help her. Together they pulled her husband onto the deck. He lay there sprawled, gasping. "He's all right," the officer said, then left them to tend to others still struggling from the now hoisted gang-way. Mei-yu helped Kung-chiao over to the inner wall of the boat, away from the crowd of people still rushing around the deck in confusion. The officers were now gradually gaining control, calming people, sending them down below. They reassured them they were safely beyond the reach of the army. Mei-yu and Kung-chiao clung to each other on the deck of the boat, knowing that people had died in the panic created by the advance of the army. They stroked each other's hands, reassuring themselves that they remained alive, together. As the deck gradually began to clear they could hear in the distance the cries of those on shore; the people retreating, the army. They listened until the sound of the bugles was drowned by the blasts from the boat. Then, when the echoes of the ship's voice had died away, they listened again, and heard only the sound of seawater rushing against the prow of the boat as it cut its way out of the harbor, and out into the open sea.

Later, below deck, in a roped-off area that contained forty berths placed close together, Mei-yu lay down as Kung-chiao unpacked their knapsacks. She lay on her back with her knees up, seeking to relieve the aching in her spine. When Kung-chiao had finishing unpacking their few belongings, he poured water on a cloth and gently bathed her face.

"Are you all right?" he asked. "And the child?"

Mei-yu nodded. He placed his hand on her belly.

"We're safe now," he said. "You must rest."

"How long will we be at sea?"

"Two weeks. We make a stop in Honolulu."

"Where will we stay in America?"

"Shh. Be quiet now. Try to sleep."

But Mei-yu continued to look into his face as he pressed the damp cloth against her skin. She knew he did not know what it would be like either, where they were going. She listened to the sounds of the other people on all sides of them, moving quietly about as they arranged their belongings in the racks suspended over their berths. They laughed nervously as they sought to keep their balance with the gently rolling motion of the boat. The air was close. Kung-chiao lay in the berth next to Mei-yu's, his arms underneath his head. He had hidden the water bags under his blanket. She hoped their small trunk had been brought on board earlier, as the men on shore had promised. The motion of the boat was of a gentle swaying. She placed her hand on her abdomen. The child had kicked, a good sign. They were safe, for now. She closed her eyes.

Fifteen days later their ship steamed into San Francisco harbor. Mei-yu and Kung-chiao stood in line with the others, allowing doctors to look into their mouths as if they were horses, grimacing as the needles pricked their arms, filling their bloodstreams with innoculants to protect them from the strange American diseases.

But nothing protected them from the shock of their arrival in their new country, from the bruises that appeared on their limbs as they were shunted from place to place and squeezed into rooms filled with their own people. Those already in the rooms regarded them with eyes clouded with fatigue and illness. Mei-yu sucked in her breath at the stench. But with the passing of several weeks she and Kung-chiao became as the others, and the feelings of shame and embarrassment dropped away, meaningless now.

As Mei-yu's time drew near, Kung-chiao demanded to see the officials and grabbed their arms, begging for help; a place to bathe, a quiet corner for his wife to rest. The officials wrested themselves away from Kung-chiao and cursed him, saying there were too many of them already for the immigration authorities to deal with. The hospital was already overfull with people more needy of medical attention than his wife. But Kung-chiao persisted. Finally, someone told him of a mission near the building where they were staying. Perhaps he would find a room there, perhaps they would summon a midwife. He went to the mission and knocked on the door, standing away from the woman who answered, afraid that she would smell him.

"Please," he said. "My name is Wong Kung-chiao. My wife and I are waiting for our papers to be cleared by the Immigration Bureau. My wife is going to give birth very soon, and I am looking . . . I am hoping that perhaps you would have room for her here?"

"Where did you learn to speak English?" the woman asked.

"In China."

She stared at him, seeing how he held his hands together in front of him, folding his fingers underneath the palms to conceal his nails. She knew he had been deloused and innoculated as part of the disembarkment procedure, but still, she regarded him as she would vermin. There was the fact that he spoke fluent English, however, and he did stand humbly enough before her now, waiting patiently. "Where is your wife?"

"There." Kung-chiao pointed to the detention center near the wharf. "We are waiting for our papers, as I said, or until I hear from my cousin in New York."

They were always waiting, the woman thought. They all had cousins or uncles or nieces who would eventually send for them. There were so many of them, and so many more bound to arrive. But there, in front of her, this one, this different one, continued to stand, waiting for her to answer.

"We are a charity. We are very full, but you may bring your wife tomorrow. She may stay until after the baby is born."

"Will there be a doctor?"

"I said, we are a charity. We cannot afford to keep a doctor on the staff. . . ."

"I can pay."

The woman hesitated.

"I will pay for the doctor. Your charity will not be at any risk."

The woman stared at the thin yellow man before her. His eyes met hers. She could not imagine what he was thinking, what was happening in the mind behind the slit-shaped eyes.

"Very well. Bring your wife tomorrow. I will see about a doctor."

"Thank you. I am very grateful."

She pulled the door toward her, then saw that he had not moved. "Is there anything else?"

"Yes." He hesitated. "Would it be possible . . . I would like very much to . . . bathe. In hot water. My wife, too. Before tomorrow? I will pay for the water."

It was then that she caught the scent of him. She stepped farther inside behind the door. It suddenly became too much for her, this man, his slanted eyes, his outrageous requests.

"No! I told you we were full! Tomorrow! Bring your wife tomorrow!"

She slammed the door.

Mei-yu gave birth to their daughter four days later. Kung-chiao held the infant and, looking into her tiny face, forgot that he had wanted a son.

"Sing-hua," he said, looking at his wife. "We will call her Sing-hua, new flower, for the new planting we have made here in America."

Mei-yu nodded her approval.

"Now we must give her an American name as well," Kung-chiao said. Mei-yu lay back on the bed, exhausted, but held her arms out for her daughter. She saw no need to give her daughter another name; Wong Sing-hua was beautiful enough.

"She is in America now, and she must have an American name," she heard her husband say. The only American names she knew were the names of film stars she had seen in the movies that had been shown in

Peking and Shanghai, names such as Dorothy, Elizabeth, Rosalind. Then there were the names from the novels she had read in school: Jane, Anne, Emma. She preferred the name Sing-hua.

Kung-chiao was thinking. He had looked through the magazines lying on the tables in the foyer of the mission, searching for names suitable for his son or daughter. For a son he found the name William. For a daughter he searched for a name that was beautiful, sonorous, and strong. He found photographs of a benefit event, a dance. There was a picture of a dancer, a ballerina. She was held aloft by her partner and seemed weightless, like a spirit, yet Kung-chiao could see that she was strong from the way she arched her back, held her head. The caption underneath the photograph said the ballerina's name was Fernadina. She looked exotic, non-Caucasian, but she had an American last name. Kung-chiao liked the looks of her, liked the sound of her name.

"Her American name will be Fernadina," he told his wife.

Mei-yu held her daughter close to her, feeling the warmth from the tiny body. "Sing-hua, Fernadina," she murmured, feeling herself drifting toward sleep. "Wong Sing-hua, Fernadina." It wasn't so bad. The Fernadina part was unnecessary, but if Kung-chiao wanted it, she would not disagree.

PART ONE

NEW YORK, 1954

Fernadina herself had no recollection of San Francisco, the rooming house near the wharf, or the stink of fish heads in the street. She did not know when her father finally received the letter from his second cousin in New York, or how they managed to find the right train there. Her memories were of Mott Street in Chinatown. Perhaps the first memory was the stack of crates filled with turtles and pigeons and crabs piled in front of the restaurant next to the apartment building where they lived. The eyes of the turtles and pigeons were identical; red, with scaly lids that blinked slowly. The turtles lay mostly with their heads sucked into the puckered skin within their carapaces, but occasionally the weight of the several bodies would shift, and one head would stretch out, the jaws agape with hissing, the throat throbbing. The throats of the pigeons worked, too, as they lay on their sides or backs, their feet bound by twine. Their red-and-orange eyes peered over the skin growth of their beaks, blinking as they swiveled their heads like owls. The crabs lay in their crate, blowing bubbles from their mouths and gills. Fernadina remembered how Bao, the cook, came out with a cardboard box and thrust a turtle into it, then several crabs and pigeons. The box seemed to fly as the pigeons flapped their wings wildly, and Bao shut his eyes as he carried the box with his arms stretched out in front. Blinded by the flapping wings, Bao dropped the box, and Fernadina caught sight of the turtle lying upside down, its shell cracked, its beak clamped tightly onto the bleeding leg of one of the pigeons.

The rooms they lived in were dark, hazy with the greasy smoke that rose from the restaurant to the left of and below them. Mei-yu scrubbed the linoleum floor twice a week but could not prevent the tacky layer of grease and soot from settling there. The smells of frying fat, garlic, scallions, and ginger hung like droplets in the air. Against the west wall in the main room stood Kung-chiao and Mei-yu's bed, and in the middle, the steel table covered with a cloth embroidered with red silk chrysanthemums. They ate at this table, and Kung-chiao studied at it, bringing over the one lamp from the windowsill next to the bed. In the southeast corner Mei-yu had her two-burner stove, and a wooden board that was hinged to the wall. Her blue-and-white ceramic bowls painted with encircling dragons and matching teapot and teacups were placed carefully on this board. A cheap cardboard wardrobe stood at the wall opposite their bed. On the door of the wardrobe hung a calendar with the picture of a Chinese opera dancer. On successive pages, above each month of days, were pictures of different opera actors and dancers, each in different attitudes. The month of June was smiling, curtseying, her pink rouge contrasting brightly against the white almond-paste makeup and black-lined eyes. October was a fierce warrior character, crouched and scowling, ready to grapple with ghosts.

The second room, Fernadina's room, was no bigger than a small foyer. Her parents' blue padded coats hung on pegs on the wall. Here, Fernadina slept in her bed made out of crates. Lying there at night, she could see the light under the door and dark shadows of neighbors' feet as they walked down the hall.

Bao the cook lived alone in the room above. Mei-yu could hear him every morning at six o'clock, putting his feet from his bed onto the floor with a thump, clearing his throat loudly of phlegm, spitting repeatedly. Kung-chiao slept noiselessly as Mei-yu rose at six thirty. Sometimes, when she went over to the box where Fernadina slept, she found the child awake, gazing at her expectantly, like a patient waiting for an attending doctor. Mei-yu had to smile at her solemn child.

Fernadina would sit up, looking at her mother. Her mother's face was long and smooth, her skin polished and white like a pearly grain of rice. Her narrow, wide-spaced eyes looked down from above high, mounded cheekbones. Every morning they shared a ritual. Mei-yu would bring Fernadina a single black lacquered chopstick. Then, winding her long thick hair up on her head and coiling it into a knot, she would bend her head and help Fernadina slip the chopstick in among the ropes of hair, securing them. Her long slender fingers guided the child's. When the chopstick was in place, Mei-yu would laugh, but the greatest moment for her was when Fernadina's face yielded her smile of solemn satisfaction, as if the child knew she had partaken of an intricate and ancient rite. Mei-yu lifted her five-year-old daughter from her bed and dressed her in a cotton shift. Then, wrapping her robe around herself, she took her daughter by the hand and went out into the hall and down to the bathroom.

Kung-chiao lay with his arm flung over his head. The chopping had begun. Bao and his helper boy, Shen, did the chopping every morning, hacking bits of chicken, beef, and pork in unrelenting rhythm in preparation for the opening of the Sun Wah Restaurant at eleven o'clock. Kung-chiao pulled the shade up. It was already warm outside. Sounds of the street came in the window, of barrels being dragged onto the sidewalk, of awnings being cranked down, of doors opening and slamming shut. He heard Bao complaining bitterly to Shen and to the old man, Kuo, who came by every day to sit in the restaurant. This was their morning ritual. Bao's barking in Cantonese dialect, Kung-chiao thought, assumed the outraged tone and character of a furious old baboon.

"Chicken up to twenty cents a pound, eh? Can you believe that?" Bao whacked his cleaver on the chicken, dividing the breastbone in half. "I should use snake meat instead of chicken, who would know the difference, eh? Except snake is even more expensive, ha hah! Celery, that's what. They want celery in everything, they'll get celery. What is it this week, how many, Kuo?"

Kuo showed his brown, stumpy teeth. He held up eight fingers.

"Eight!" Bao said. "Today it will be eleven, I bet you."

Eleven, the number of Americans who would come down to Chinatown for lunch and ask for chop suey. Bao made marks tallying the requests on a piece of paper taped next to the refrigerator.

"No, stupid boy! Dumb egg!" Kung-chiao heard a loud slap. "Across the grain, how many times have I told you? That's good meat! And smaller, smaller!"

Bao's voice continued its harangue, punctuated by the loud whacking noise of his cleaver and the cackling hoots that came out of Kuo's crack of a mouth. Kung-chiao could hear Shen's mumbles of protest underneath it all. He got out of bed and pulled on his trousers. Every day the same harangue, the same threats. Every day it was the same for him, too, the oppressive pressure to do well on the exams, to coddle his cousin in order to keep the monthly allowance forthcoming, to deflect the look in Mei-yu's eyes. There were still five days before the exams. He slipped his feet into his rubber thongs and went over to the sink to splash water on his face. Mei-yu came into the room with Fernadina. As soon as she saw her father awake, the little girl ran across the floor and threw her arms around his leg.

"Ai yah, little mouse," Kung-chiao said, laughing, and glancing at his wife, who held her robe closed with one hand, smiling thinly. Kung-chiao reached down and lifted Fernadina by the armpits, swinging her up so she peeped over his shoulder. The mother saw how the child already resembled her father, with her brown skin, little triangular face, and shining black eyes. Fernadina hardly ever laughed, but her face, held up against her father's shoulder, radiated a fierce happiness. Her hands gripped his undershirt as firmly as a young monkey clings to the fur of its parent. Mei-yu saw this and turned away, busying herself with Kung-chiao's breakfast instead.

Did he eat so loudly on purpose? Mei-yu tried not to hear Kung-chiao as he slurped his congee and scooped the preserved vegetables into his mouth with his chopsticks. Mei-yu listened as the wooden sticks struck the side of the ceramic bowl with rapid, ringing pings, her irritation growing with each stroke. Her husband ate with as much civility, as much decorum, as a dog, she thought. She saw a wet grain of rice sticking to his upper lip, stared at it with disgust, and knew an angry gladness that he went on eating as he did, oblivious of that blemish. He had become like all the others, those workmen sitting in the tiny restaurants on Mott Street, slurping their bowlful of noodles, letting the white strands slap against the sides of their cheeks as they sucked them into their mouths. He had not been like that in China. Even as a stranger to Mei-yu then, he had seemed to bear himself with care, with an awareness of all that was around him, all that related to him. In another it would have been self-consciousness. In Kung-chiao it was keenness, tempered, well tended. Throughout the days of their meeting, Mei-yu had been filled with this sense of his strength. These had been the days when the strength of men made its appearance in every guise, but in the face of real threat, often yielded, or vanished.

Mei-yu remembered what it had been like then, in Peking, in 1944. She had been a student at Yenching University. Despite the occupation by the Japanese, the university had managed to carry on. Following her morning classes, Mei-yu had often shared her lunch in the school court-yard with her friend Wen-chuan.

"Chiang Kai-shek is a corrupt elitist who sits in Chungking eating dainties while we starve under the eyes of the Japanese," Mei-yu re-membered Wen-chuan saying. Wen-chuan had cut her hair short, to make it easier to spot lice, she said, but Mei-yu knew that modern young women in Peking were affecting the bob to symbolize the chop-ping off of traditionalist ways. Wen-chuan was two grades ahead of Mei-yu in school. She had a round face, a wide mouth. She wore rimless spectacles that gave her a severe look, Mei-yu thought. They sat under the one tree in the yard, enjoying the warmth of the October sun.

"I think we should organize a group of students to go to Chungking and root out the old pig and roast him alive. He's fat enough to feed the entire country."

"Chungking is over a thousand miles away, Wen-chuan," Mei-yu said. "And Chiang Kai-shek, at least from the pictures I've seen of him, is a lean man. Not fat at all."

"What are you, a pacifist? I meant fat in the figurative sense, of course. He is wealthy enough to feed us all. He has grown fat from diverting Chinese and now American money into his private treasury."

"Be careful, Wen-chuan," Mei-yu said, laughing, looking around them. "The Kuomintang do not appreciate subversives like you. You know they are all around here at school."

"Our school is pro-Kuomintang only in that the administration says it is in order to continue receiving government money. But the students know better. You cannot deny that we need change, Mei-yu." She looked closely at her friend. "Don't you want to free your father from prison?"

Mei-yu imagined her father weak, sick. "Yes. I do."

"There, then! What has Chiang Kai-shek done to free your father? Nothing! And that is the problem! He is not concerned with the peo-ple. We need new leadership, a new government, a whole new mecha-nism."

Mei-yu knew her friend spoke of the Communist Party. They had had a conversation similar to this months ago, when Wen-chuan told her she had joined the Party. Mei-yu thought her friend had been un-wise in being so open about her affiliation with the Party, for everyone in the school knew of it. Now Wen-chuan leaned her face close to Mei-yu's.

"We are doing something about it, Mei-yu. You must not tell anyone, but we are planning a demonstration in the spring. Wu Teh-shan, Mao Tse-tung's chief deputy from the Shensi Province, is due here for talks with the Japanese commandant Fujiwara. We plan to gather a group of pro-Communist students together in a peaceful delegation to present a scroll to Wu Teh-shan to give to Fujiwara. The scroll will describe the many crimes the Japanese have committed against the people of China, including the imprisonment of several important elders such as your father. We also want to show that the Communist movement is growing. We hope to gather representatives from every province."

"From every province!" Mei-yu shook her head. "How can they come, when all the roads are patrolled by the Japanese?"

"They face great danger, that is for certain. My brother said a friend of his just arrived from Tientsin, south of here. He says the Japanese are checking passengers on the P'in Han railway, demanding proof of identification, proof of destination. He says the Kuomintang army can't feed its men, that hundreds are left by the road to die of starvation. Starving Kuomintang soldiers have been going over to the Japanese, helping them build bridges in exchange for a bowl of rice. My brother's friend says the roads were a terrible sight; men, looking like skeletons, dying everywhere. The youths who flee the cities to join the Kuomintang army, thinking to be fed and taken care of, are mistaken; there is no provision for them at all. So delegates coming to Peking must contend with both the Japanese and the Kuomintang. But they must get through. They must come. The demonstration is too important."

Wen-chuan looked at Mei-yu, her eyes shining. "We are not just a few students, a few peasants, Mei-yu. We are many, and we grow stronger every day. We must show the Japanese that we can organize and resist. There are reports that their forces are encountering difficulties at the hands of the American forces in the Pacific. They are being worried on all sides, like a leopard surrounded by dogs. They are still strong, but we can tire them out, outlast them. The Communist Party must unite China, and drive out all the foreign powers."

Mei-yu saw Wen-chuan's commitment, the fixedness of her gaze. The intensity of her friend frightened as well as thrilled her. Mei-yu tried to understand why she resisted looking into the eyes of her friend, why she felt that Wen-chuan drew too near. Was it the seemingly endless flow of her talk, her gestures that called attention to them? Looking at Wen-chuan reminded her of the actors in the Peking Opera—their faces made up to exaggerate their passions, their movements stylized into grotesque postures. She knew the need for change in their country was real, that the fact that her father remained in prison was real. But somehow the agitation by the new Party, by people like Wen-chuan, remained unreal, merely theatrical to her. Now she saw Wen-chuan had more to say.

"The plans for this demonstration were made by the student committee at the university, led by my brother, Tsien-tsung. I am the only woman member. More women must become involved. Mao Tse-tung has proclaimed women equal in the struggle to achieve independence for China, but still, the old mores exist. One day Chinese men will take Chinese women seriously." She took Mei-yu's arm. "Come with me to accompany the delegation, Mei-yu," she said, her voice urgent. "Let us show them that the women of China are committed and can be involved in effecting change as well."

"But I am not a Party member," Mei-yu said, looking down, amazed at the strength of Wen-chuan's grip on her arm. Then, in spite of herself, she glanced around her to see if anyone was watching.

"You don't have to be a Party member! Think of yourself as a patriot, wanting like everyone else to be free of the Japanese, free of the corrupt Kuomintang! Help us, Mei-yu!"

Mei-yu shook herself free of her friend's grip and gathered her books.

"I can't promise, Wen-chuan. I must think first." She stood there a moment, hesitating, then turned and walked away before Wen-chuan could make her change her mind.

Two months later, in December, Mei-yu was crossing the school courtyard on her way to a class. Her thick cotton shoes crunched on the icy crust of the snow. Suddenly she heard her name called out behind her. She turned to see Wen-chuan, who ran toward her awkwardly on the ice, her face red and chapped from the cold.

"Mei-yu," she said in a low voice when she had drawn near. "You have been avoiding me, I know. But there is something very important that I must ask you now."

"What is it?"

"Do you remember what I told you, about representatives coming to Peking from every province to take part in the demonstration we have been planning for the spring?"

"Yes." Mei-yu looked around. The other students hurried by on their way to class. She allowed herself to be pulled by her friend close against the outer wall of the courtyard. No one was near.

"I need your help. A man arrived from Chungking last week. He has been staying in the northern quarter of the city, but we're afraid the

Japanese are suspicious of his presence. They searched the house where he was staying last night. He had to climb onto a neighbor's rooftop and wait there for three hours. It is dangerous for him to remain there. We must move him tonight to my house."

Mei-yu stared at her friend.

"Mei-yu! I need your help! I cannot go fetch him alone; a single woman out on the streets at night is suspect . . . vulnerable in too many ways. Besides, you speak Japanese better than I. If a soldier or official stopped us, you could tell them we were late on our way home from visiting friends."

"What about your brother, Tsien-tsung? Wouldn't it be better if he went to meet this person?"

"Tsien-tsung must attend an emergency meeting with other students tonight. Besides, don't you think women can contribute to the cause as well?" She looked steadily at Mei-yu. "If you can't help me, say so," she said.

Mei-yu thought of the student in hiding. She remembered the night the Japanese took her father away. Then she saw the contempt in her friend's face. Wen-chuan was turning to leave.

"Wait," Mei-yu said, grabbing hold of her friend's arm. "I will help. Where shall I meet you, and when?"

Wen-chuan stared at Mei-yu, her eyes hard. "Are you certain you want to do this? Once we begin, you cannot change your mind."

"I said I will help you."

"Good. I will meet you in the alleyway in back of your house at nine thirty. I will be able to move unseen in the darkness between our houses. We will go together to the northern section of the city, not that far, maybe twenty blocks. You remember my friend, Huang Sung-lien, from our philosophy class?"

"Yes."

"It is behind her house where we will meet this student. The plan is to meet him at ten o'clock."

Wen-chuan's eyes protruded from her face, her mouth set in a nervous grimace. Mei-yu, continuing her walk across the courtyard, was relieved her friend was frightened, too.

At nine twenty-five that evening Mei-yu took off her hard-soled shoes and, carrying them in her hand, made her way quietly to the rear entrance of her house. There, she slipped her shoes back on. She cupped her hands over the brass hinges of the gate and blew into them, her warm breath thawing the hinges of ice. She noticed that the hinges had squealed loudly when she had tried the gate earlier in the afternoon. Now the gate swung open noiselessly. She walked into the alley, her eyes gradually becoming accustomed to the dark. All was black around her; the bright sliver of moon was shrouded by clouds.

She heard Wen-chuan's steps crunching on the surface of the snow before she saw her, five feet away. Wen-chuan had wrapped a black scarf around her face and handed a similar one to Mei-yu. Together they walked quickly down the alley, keeping close to the walls of the buildings, staying in shadows whenever they could.

They came to an intersection at the edge of their neighborhood. A restaurant was open, filled with Japanese soldiers who were eating and drinking inside. The men were laughing as they drank, raising their tin cups filled with warm sake. Steam rose thickly from the vent above the door. Here the aroma of frying fat was the strongest; neither Mei-yu nor Wen-chuan had eaten meat in over two years.

Two soldiers stood outside the restaurant, waiting for friends still inside. Their rifles were slung over their shoulders. They smoked, and occasionally pulled the door open to shout for their companions to hurry. The cold night air penetrated Mei-yu's thick cotton coat. She resisted stamping her feet, instead staring intently at the soldiers, hoping they would soon leave.

Finally two more soldiers came out of the restaurant. After lighting fresh cigarettes and belching loudly, the Japanese left, swaying and laughing, making their way toward their compound in the western section of the city.

Wen-chuan and Mei-yu crossed the intersection quickly. They had ten more blocks yet to go.

The alley was quiet, the gates to the neighboring courtyards shut tight. It seemed to Mei-yu that she passed between the walls of a deep frozen canyon. All of Peking seemed hushed. In times of peace people visited each other at night, sharing meals, playing cards and mahjongg, repeating old and favorite stories. Now people had stopped inviting guests, ashamed to have nothing to offer. The stories, which had formerly been many, had now dwindled to one. That one was the story of hunger, known by all the families now, a story that needed no telling.

Wen-chuan and Mei-yu finally reached the alley behind Huang Sung-lien's house. It was not yet ten o'clock. A few blocks away they saw the dark shapes of Japanese soldiers on patrol. They knew it was not often that Japanese searched the same house two nights in succession, but they could not be certain. They leaned against the wall opposite the alley of their friend's house, waiting, blowing softly on their hands, trying to warm them. Mei-yu's feet were cold. She tried wiggling her toes.

"Hey! You two! What are you doing here?"

The soldier appeared from the alley behind them.

Mei-yu looked beyond him; he seemed to be alone. She slipped her arm through Wen-chuan's, her mind racing to find a reply to give to the soldier.

"We are just resting," she said. "We are on our way back home from visiting friends."

"Oh, hah, visiting, this late at night?" The soldier spoke Chinese. He must have been stationed in Peking since the beginning of the occupation, Mei-yu thought.

"Where do you girls live?" He came close and looked Wen-chuan up and down, his face only inches away. He was short, stocky, dressed in the thickly padded winter uniform of the Japanese Army. He wore a fur cap, the ear flaps of which were unfastened, sticking up on either side of his head like the ears of a dog.

"Not far from here," Mei-yu said. Wen-chuan seemed to have been paralyzed by the nearness of the soldier, who began to circle her.

"How far from here?" he asked finally.

"Ten blocks," Mei-yu said.

"How do I know you're telling me the truth?" he said, raising his hand and pulling Wen-chuan's scarf aside. She moved away, grabbing her scarf from him.

"You girls could be in a lot of trouble, you know. I could take you in to the Commandant for questioning. I could even detain you overnight myself."

Mei-yu pulled Wen-chuan to her and gripped her arm tightly.

"Stop it!" she said. The sound of her voice startled her. She could feel Wen-chuan trembling inside her coat. "Leave us alone! We have done nothing wrong!"

The soldier drew in his breath with a hiss and stepped closer. Mei-yu felt herself tensing, getting ready to run. She pulled Wen-chuan closer to her. Then the gate to the courtyard behind them opened.

"What is all the commotion? Private, have you found my sisters?"

The man closed the gate behind him and approached the soldier. "I hope my sisters have not been too troublesome. We've been worried about them all evening."

"What?" the soldier said. "They live here?"

"Yes. They just escaped for the evening, bored from being kept inside so long. That is the problem with youth in Peking these days. When they're bored, they cause mischief. They don't realize the problems they create."

The soldier looked at the man and then at Mei-yu and Wen-chuan. The man turned to the young women. "Did you tell this soldier you lived elsewhere?" He shook his head. "Someday your mischief-making will get you into deep trouble. It is lucky he found you."

The soldier hesitated, confused. "I should see your papers," he said at last.

The man reached into his pocket. "My family is very grateful to you, Private. Please accept these."

The soldier stared at the gold earrings. He rubbed his nose vigorously with one gloved hand, seeming to consider. Then he held out his other hand.

"Foolish Chinese girls," he said, putting the earrings into his pocket.

Quickly the man took both Mei-yu and Wen-chuan by the arms and pushed them back through the gate. He closed the gate behind them. They listened, hardly daring to breathe. They heard the soldier's boot squeal in the snow as he pivoted on his heel, then turned to each other in relief as the footsteps grew more faint, then disappeared.

"Now." The man bent and picked up a knapsack leaning against the inner wall of the courtyard. "With luck we will make it to Wen-chuan's house without further incident." He looked at Mei-yu. "Are you Wen-chuan?"

"I am Wen-chuan." She stepped forward and offered her hand. "We are grateful to you for your help."

"It was nothing."

"What is your name?"

"I am Wong Kung-chiao, from Chungking."

"This is my friend, Chen Mei-yu."

He shook Mei-yu's hand. In the darkness Mei-yu could not see the features of his face but saw that he wore spectacles, which glinted faintly.

"Come, we must go quickly."

Wen-chuan looked down the alley. It was clear.

Twenty minutes later they reached Wen-chuan's house. She opened the door to the kitchen and startled her brother and another student, who were sitting at the round table, reading a piece of paper. At first Tsien-tsung, her brother, seemed irritated to see them, but then he caught sight of Kung-chiao in back of his sister.

"Friend, comrade!" he said, coming forward to grip Kung-chiao's hand warmly. "I am sorry not to have met you myself, but I was called to preside at an emergency meeting. A delegate was arrested in Sian-fu two weeks ago. We just got word today." Tsien-tsung looked at the paper in his hand. "I do not know him, but I hear he is a highly esteemed member of the Party. It does not look good for him." Tsientsung shrugged. "But let us not speak of that now." He looked up into Kung-chiao's face, smiling. "Welcome. I trust you had no difficulty in getting to our home?"

"None. Everything went very smoothly."

Wen-chuan looked quickly at Mei-yu, then pushed past her brother to put water on for tea. Mei-yu sat down at the table, exchanging nods with the other student, whom she recognized as one from her own class in school. They were the youngest present. She sat, her eyes lowered, her hands wound inside the scarf Wen-chuan had given her. She knew she did not belong, being outside of the Party. But the others did not seem to mind her presence. Kung-chiao sat down opposite her, and the others sat down on either side of him.

Ping-sung, the other student, leaned forward. "Tell me, Wong Kung-chiao . . . what was it like, your journey to Peking? You must have encountered much hardship."

Kung-chiao shrugged, nodding his head slowly. "It took me more than two months to travel from my city to Peking. It is a very long story, and I am sure you are all very tired." He smiled. Mei-yu could see that he was tired.

"No, please tell us," Ping-sung said. The others also urged Kung-chiao to tell his story. He held out one hand. "Truly, you will not want to hear the whole story. But I will say that as long as I live, I will be grateful that I survived that journey."

"Did you go on the train?" Ping-sung persisted.

Kung-chiao nodded wearily. His smile was faint. Mei-yu could see that although he was not much older than they, he seemed older, drawn. "I began on the train, but was discovered by the Japanese and had to jump off. I wandered for many weeks in the countryside, stumbling into villages, bartering for food, for rides in oxen carts. The villagers were suspicious at first, but they were anxious to hear the news I brought from Chungking. They also finally respected the fact that I was a student. I wrote letters, read a few things for them. Actually, I think the fact that I wore spectacles was what really impressed them." He laughed. His face was angular, his forehead broad, his high cheekbones tapering in sharp planes down to his jaw. His eyes were dark, black behind the lenses of his glasses. Mei-yu was struck by the intensity of his eyes. When he looked directly at her, she had to look away.

"I owe much to the people of the villages," he continued, sipping from his tea. "If it weren't for them, I would not have survived, I am sure."

The group was quiet, watching this man who had come all the way from Chungking.

"But now you are here, friend," Tsien-tsung said, "and we welcome your help in the planning of the demonstration. For it is the demonstration, the success of it, that will show the Japanese the growing strength of our Party."

"Yes," Wen-chuan said. "And when we have rid ourselves of the Japanese, we will unite to heal China, to make her strong, independent."

Kung-chiao swirled the tea leaves at the bottom of his cup.

"You are quiet, my friend," Tsien-tsung said. "Do you not believe the demonstration will achieve these ends?"

Kung-chiao smiled. "Certainly. If the demonstration is successful, we will have accomplished much along those lines. There is still much to do in the way of organization, though. We will have to wait and see."

"I have no doubt that we will succeed!" Ping-sung said.

Mei-yu saw the look of zeal on his face, his young, oversized hand gripping the back of Kung-chiao's chair. She looked again at the faces surrounding the table. Tsien-tsung sat back in his chair, looking up occasionally to smile at Ping-sung's outbursts. But Mei-yu saw that his eyes kept returning to the piece of paper he held in his hand. She saw that his eyes returned to read the lines repeatedly, flickering up and down, back and forth across the page, as if searching for the beginning, or the end; an answer. Her eyes left his face and rested on Wen-chuan. Wen-chuan returned her gaze, smiling brilliantly. Here Mei-yu saw the same fire, the same urgency that emanated from Ping-sung's face, and Mei-yu thought the two looked slightly mad. Wen-chuan nodded, reached over, and refilled Mei-yu's teacup. Mei-yu smiled her thanks but withdrew her hands, which had been holding the cup, tucking them back under the scarf that lay in her lap. She watched the steam rising from her cup, avoiding Wen-chuan's eyes. When she raised her eyes again, she looked directly into the gaze of Kung-chiao, who sat opposite her in the heart of the group. She knew suddenly that he had been looking at her for some time now, as she had been looking at the others. In the instant their eyes met, Mei-yu saw the core of Kung-chiao, the certainty of him, which lay in his knowledge that he would survive, no matter what happened around him. The instant she saw this, Mei-yu was forced to drop her eyes. But she knew he had seen her look into him, she knew he had seen into her as well. When she dared look up again, she found his eyes still upon her, and this time they stared at each other for a long moment, acknowledging their recognition of each other.

Now they were alone, and he sat across the table from her, slurping his congee. He did not look at her but read from his notebook spread open next to his bowl, his glasses steamed from the heat of the gruel. He continued to scrape at his bowl with rapid motions, eating as if it were his last meal, she thought. Mei-yu tried to disguise her disgust for him by being pleasant.

"Will you be at the library all day? Shall I pack you some rice buns?" She spoke in the Mandarin dialect. They all spoke Mandarin, those from Peking.

He looked up. She had her back to him, he knew, so he would not be able to see the look of reproach on her face. Did she speak to him merely to flaunt her native Mandarin? he wondered.

"No, don't bother," he said, conscious of his own accent. "I'll have something to eat at the school cafeteria."

He knew it cost more to eat in the cafeteria, but he did not want her to be able to do any more good deeds for him.

Didn't he know that while he indulged at the cafeteria, she thought, she and Fernadina ate the vegetable scrapings left from Bao's kitchen?

"Don't forget, Roger and Diana are coming over tonight," Kung-chiao said, buttoning up his shirt. His wife was ladling congee into a bowl for Fernadina. Fernadina sat rigid in her chair, watching her father as he picked up his books.

"I'll be back at six."

His wife turned and looked directly into his eyes for the first time that morning. His heart jumped. Which spirit looked at him so powerfully through her dark, narrow eyes, the spirit of misery, or that of reproof? he thought. She stood, leaning against the bedstead, her hair glossy and purple against the white of her skin.

"I'll have dinner ready, then," she said, her voice strangely vibrant. She knew she had won, this time.

At ten thirty Mott Street was fully awake, braced for the business to come at noon. Mei-yu, with Fernadina's hand in her own, skirted the baskets of mustard greens and bok choy brought in from New Jersey that morning. Shopkeepers stood on the steps of their stores with fistfuls of red-and-gold pennants, pleated paper fans strong with the scent of musk and sandalwood, plastic wind-up toys from Hong Kong. Wind chimes and dragon kites dangled from the frames of open bookstalls. The smells of meat roasting on hooks suspended over hot coals made the air seem heavier, and with the sudden, explosive sizzle of food thrown into hot fat, heard through windows open onto the street, Mei-yu thought that if she didn't escape Mott Street soon, she, too, would end up strung up or fried. But she hurried for another reason. She felt the eyes of the other women on the street upon her; she heard her name being spoken in the harsh Cantonese accent, openly, the words floating to her on the waves of air pushed by their rapidly fluttering fans. She held Fernadina's hand firmly in her own and walked quickly toward Pell Street.

Pell Street was narrower and cooler. Here, people sat on the stoops in front of their homes and read the Chinese newspaper, their heads bowed to the print. The restaurants had proper dining rooms, with menus and wallpaper, not tattered strips of script taped to the wall. They reached the tall red building. The cool, dark hallway smelled of incense. Fernadina trailed her hand along the nubbly plaster of the walls. She liked Madame Peng.

"Come in, come in!" The old lady motioned them into her apartment, her head bobbing up and down. She gathered Fernadina into her arms, pinching her playfully. Fernadina felt a strange comfort as she was pressed against the satiny bed jacket, smelling the familiar yet peculiar odors of camphor and incense. To her, Madame Peng's face was like a melon, round and smooth, with eyebrows penciled in as thin as wires.

"I have your coconut candy for you, little squirrel," Madame Peng said, stuffing the nuggets into Fernadina's pockets. "Go now, go play with Min-di, but come back later to talk to me."

Fernadina clutched the candy inside her pockets. She knew where the kitchen was, where Madame Peng's dun-colored pug could be heard snuffling eagerly through the gap under the swing door.

Mei-yu followed Madame Peng into the parlor. She was impressed again by the darkness of the room. At first she had difficulty adjusting to the absence of light, as if she found herself staring at a dark painting whose subjects revealed themselves only after moments of close scrutiny. But gradually she began to see the contents of the room. Several pieces of rosewood furniture were placed along the wall and grouped in the center. These were covered with dark green silk and embroidered with blue-and-gold dragons that coiled as if they were alive on the seats. The windows were shuttered against all natural light; a single lamp next to the sofa glowed softly under a pleated paper shade. A large, ornately carved screen stood in the center of the room, behind the chair opposite the sofa. Mei-yu admired its intricacy of design, its prime condition. The rug underneath her feet was dark blue, thick, and cushioned the sound within the room as did the heavy silk drapery. To Mei-yu the parlor was a nave of darkness and quiet, quite apart from the world outside. On first entering she felt cooled, soothed, her senses lulled. But after a few moments the room began to seem too dark, too quiet, infinite, and she strained to see into the shadows behind the blackwood chest against the wall, into the corner of the room farthest from the light.

Madame Peng sat down on the sofa and gestured for Mei-yu to sit in the chair across from her. Mei-yu sat, feeling the outer panels of the antique screen enfold her.

"I wanted to talk to you myself today because I have an important task for you, Mei-yu," she said. The old woman sat among the cushions, her large head seemingly balanced between the pillows as if her body were too frail to support it.

"I have an order from Colonel Chang's niece. She wishes to have a ceremonial jacket made. I thought of you straightaway." Madame Peng put her hand to her temple. "While I ordinarily do not go out of my way to do business with that . . . let us say . . . sector of Chinatown, Colonel Chang's niece is a beautiful and wealthy young woman and has promised a handsome sum. Besides"—Madame Peng laughed dryly—"I can hardly deny the wish of the niece of Colonel Chang, now, can I?"

Mei-yu nodded. She recognized the name that was whispered throughout the neighborhood. Colonel Chang, the man who reputedly owned Chinatown.

"I will leave the design up to you," Madame Peng went on. "It would be presumptuous of me to tell you how to make this jacket, only, I believe the young lady desires something elegant, simple, not like the gaudy stuff we are getting from Hong Kong these days."

"May I have premium silk, then?" Mei-yu asked.

"Yes. I've arranged for Mei-ling to show you our new silk for you to choose from at the Union." Madame Peng looked at Mei-yu, who was sitting less than five feet away from her. "I can see you are pleased by this commission, Mei-yu. That is good. This jacket is important, the most important commission of the year. Let it be your best work."

"Yes. I understand." Mei-yu could hardly contain the excitement that rose within her, the urge to rush to the Union to finger the silks, to choose the best piece with the most exquisite color and texture. But Madame Peng was not through with her.

"Now," the old lady said, ringing a little bell that would bring forth her maid with a tray of green tea and savory snacks, her voice becoming lighter, even gay, "tell me, are the other women at the Union as horrid to you as ever?"

Mei-yu sat, staring at the designs in the rug.

"Ai, peasants! Stupids! The best hands I give them, the most critical eye for line and color, and they spit in their own faces. What do they do, not talk, not acknowledge you?"

Mei-yu nodded.

"Did you finish that dress for the Moy wedding?"

"Yes."

"So, it was beautiful, a masterpiece, even when you first cut it out." She grunted with disgust.

"They think I think I am too good for them."

"Pah! Paranoid stupids! Dumb southern squash! You would think they would get over their idiotic notions about the north and south when they come to this country, but no, it's worse! Do you know why? They're envious of you and Kung-chiao because you already know English and have had college in China; because they know you will be able to leave Chinatown someday and become real Americans."

"But I am proud to be Chinese!" Mei-yu cried.

Madame Peng snorted. "Are you proud to be poor? Of eating pig parts thrown out by the restaurants? Think of Sing-hua, your daughter, Fernadina! Why did you give her an American name?"

"It was Kung-chiao's idea," Mei-yu said, her voice strangely hoarse.

"Don't deny your own pride, my naive girl!" Madame Peng's eyes shone under the high arch of her brows. She looked perpetually astonished. "Don't tell me, after living here in Chinatown for three years, that you haven't wished to die, that you haven't wished you had never come to this country, that you haven't blamed everyone you know for your circumstances."

Mei-yu was silent, her hand going up to touch the lacquer stick holding her coils of hair in place. Madame Peng leaned back against the silk-covered pillows of her sofa, satisfied. When she spoke again, her voice sounded suddenly tired. "How old are you, twenty-four, twenty-five? You are young to have suffered, but you really haven't known true suffering."

Her words stung Mei-yu. What was the nature of true suffering, then? she thought. Was the hunger she woke with every morning the kind of suffering Madame Peng understood as insignificant, as trivial as the tears caused by a cinder in the eye? It was true; she lived, still had her family, a place to return to. She suddenly felt ashamed of her preoccupation with her stomach, her acute sense of it as it seemed to shrivel within her daily. The maid came in then and placed a tray with a teapot, teacups, and a plate of custard tarts on the table in front of Mei-yu. Madame Peng leaned forward, sniffed, and shook her finger at her maid.

"Where are the almond tarts, Ya-mei? I went out myself this morning to get them."

"I did not see any almond tarts, Madame," Ya-mei said, her head bowed.

"I put them right on the counter in the kitchen!"

Ya-mei lowered her head but said nothing.

Madame Peng shook her head in annoyance. "Ah, well, I see I will have to go fetch them myself." She heaved herself up from the cushions.

"I am sorry, Madame," Ya-mei said, backing away toward the kitchen.

"Please don't bother, Madame," Mei-yu said, rising out of her chair.

But Madame Peng had already begun to shuffle in her silken slippers to the kitchen, her distraught maid at her heels.

Mei-yu sat and stared at the custard tarts. She smelled the vanilla, the sugar, the eggs. She had watched her friend Ah-chin make tarts such as these, in the bakery down the street. The crusts were made with lard, so crumbly and tender that they collapsed in one's hand. The delicate yellow surface of the custard shimmered and trembled when one brought it up to one's mouth. Mei-yu had not eaten a custard tart since Kung-chiao had brought one home for the New Year, last season. Back home, in China, custard tarts covered the table in her father's house when they celebrated the seasons with feasts. She licked her lips and leaned back in her chair, thinking, daring to think, that she could finish one of the tarts before Madame Peng returned. But immediately she felt shame at the thought, imagining herself caught in the act of stuffing the tart into her mouth. She braced herself in her chair, determined to wait. Her hand felt the smooth, polished wood underneath, traced the carved surfaces of the arm of the chair. Her family had had chairs such as this, with wood as lustrous, as smooth. She thought of the feasts, where members of her family and guests sat around the table and helped themselves to the bowls of lichees, oranges, and pears, and how she reached carefully across the table for her treats, fearing to soil the silk sleeve of her gown. Seated across from her at the table were her younger brothers, Hung-bao and Hung-chien. The older of the two, Hung-bao, who was two years younger than Mei-yu, stared greedily at the tarts. Mei-yu felt the slight tremor of the table as he kicked his feet underneath in impatience. The younger boy, Hung-chien, three years younger than Mei-yu, sat quietly, his eyes as round and big as those of a lemur, listening to the murmur of the adult talk, waiting for the signal when they could begin the sweets. Mei-yu, at twelve years the oldest, tried to preside among the children with dignity, looking at the tarts only occasionally. She listened to the adult talk, composing her face into a mask of seriousness, looking from the face of her mother to that of her father, and then to the family's guests, who nodded with sleepiness, for they had already eaten the main body of the feast. She looked around the table, saw the hands stretching from silk cuffs to shield the yawns, heard the intervals of quiet between soft laughter. Her mother poured more tea for the guests. Mei-yu admired her white hands, the delicate curve of her nails. Then, from the side of her eye, she saw her father reach for the plate of tarts and offer it to a guest. The guest laughed and passed the plate to her; sweets for the children first. The tremor of the table had stopped. She saw Hung-bao's face before her, watching her as she carefully picked up the tart in its paper cradle and laid it on her plate. Then, before she bit into it, she saw her brother take his tart and cram it into his mouth and, before her, and all the guests, transform his face into a mess of crumbled flakes and custard. Laughter rang around the table. Mei-yu's mother, her hands shaking with laughter, poured more tea for everyone.

Mei-yu stared at the tarts before her now as she sat in Madame Peng's parlor. They looked identical to the ones of her childhood, but no one passed her the plate; she knew they were not hers.

"Ai, on the counter all along, in plain sight!" Madame Peng said, coming into the parlor carrying a plate of almond tarts. Mei-yu smiled and watched as Madame Peng began to pour the fragrant light green tea into the porcelain cups. She saw the old lady's rings, brilliant with gems, on each finger. Where had Madame Peng come from? she wondered. Madame Peng was one of the few Mandarin-speaking persons of influence in Chinatown, but Mei-yu could not place her accent. Where had she gotten her wealth? Someone had said her husband had been a general in China, since disgraced, now dead. If she was indeed wealthy, why did she continue to work at her age, managing her garment-making business? Stories about her, gossip, were everywhere, and as full of holes as a paper cutting. She looked up. "Madame Peng," she began, hesitating.

Madame Peng looked up. She held out the plate of almond tarts to Mei-yu. "Go on. I think I know what you are going to ask."

Mei-yu took a tart, let it rest on its plate next to her teacup. "Madame Peng, if I may ask . . . why do you stay here in Chinatown?"

"Because I am too old to change," the old woman said promptly. She wiped her mouth on a silk napkin. "And because I am powerful here in Chinatown. People respect me here. What would I be elsewhere in this country? A wingless pigeon! I have my son, a lawyer, who lives in Washington, D.C. He is well-off. He is an American now."

Mei-yu heard Fernadina laughing in the kitchen, and the pug growling. "I am afraid, Madame Peng."

Madame Peng nodded.

"My English is not as good as Kung-chiao's."

"Study, then. Go to school."

Mei-yu shrugged. It was pointless to even think of school for her. Where would they get the money? Who would stay with Fernadina?

"You will find a way. You are gifted, Mei-yu. When I first saw your work, I knew you were more than a laborer, like the others, more even than a craftsman. And then when I found out you had gone to college, I thought, this is incredible, what is this gem doing here in Chinatown?" She waited, as if expecting an explanation.

"Kung-chiao has a second cousin who lives in Manhattan," Mei-yu said hurriedly. "He was the one who arranged for Kung-chiao to go to New York University. Chinatown was the cheapest place to live. This cousin is really very generous, Madame Peng. . . ."

Madame Peng waved her hand. "Tell me no more. I know all about second cousins."

The growling in the kitchen grew louder. Mei-yu could distinguish Fernadina's growls from the pug's. They were louder, more fierce. "I've taken up enough of your time, Madame Peng. I think I should rescue Min-di from Sing-hua."

"Don't worry, Mei-yu. Ai, you haven't eaten a thing! That is certainly not very polite, my dear!"

Mei-yu picked up the almond tart in front of her. She longed for a custard tart but imagined eating it in front of Madame Peng, seeing it collapse in a tumble of crumbs and custard all over her dress, Madame Peng's silk-covered chair. Madame Peng caught the direction of the young woman's eyes.

"You are very thin, Mei-yu. You must eat more."

Mei-yu nodded, chewing on a bite from the dry almond tart.

"Come, we will wrap these up." Madame Peng picked up the plate of custard tarts and rose from her chair. Mei-yu jumped to her feet.

"Oh, Madame Peng, please, you have already been so kind . . ."

"Nonsense," snapped the old woman, heading out to the kitchen. She turned, beckoning for Mei-yu to follow her. She paused before the door to the kitchen. "As for the other women, my dear, all they can do is talk. Let them talk. You must rise above that."

Mei-yu waited in the foyer while Madame Peng gave the tarts to Ya-mei to wrap. "I have tried to," she said when Madame Peng turned back to her. "I think that is why they dislike me so much."

"Well, then, you simply must be strong, isn't that so? Yes, I know you will be strong." She patted Mei-yu's arm. "Come see me again, and not too long from now. Give my greetings to Kung-chiao. I hear he is near the top of his class in school."

So talk circulated about Kung-chiao as well, Mei-yu thought. It really was no surprise. Fernadina came running from the kitchen, her cotton shift damp from her play with the dog. Madame Peng filled her pockets again with coconut candy. Fernadina allowed the old lady's heavily ringed hand to rest on her cheek for a moment, then, closing her fist around the candy in her pocket, followed her mother out the door.

Walking down Pell Street toward Mott, Mei-yu wondered if there was anything in Chinatown that Madame Peng did not know. If the old woman did not already know what went on in the labyrinthine society of close-knit and closemouthed families, she had her sources of information. Mei-yu remembered the first time Madame Peng had summoned her. It had been after she had finished tailoring a jacket for the wife of one of the import merchants on Mulberry Street. Her nursemaid in Peking, Hsiao Pei, had taught her well. Sewing had only been a hobby for Mei-yu, but she had a natural talent; her fingers seemed to be able to coax fabric into pleasing shapes, her scissors to cut material into pieces of symmetry and elegance. Her pieces had life, at least that was what Madame Peng had said. They sat that first time in her cool, dark parlor. It was in that parlor and parlors like it where information was exchanged, bargains struck, and decisions made. Mei-yu had to wonder why Madame Peng had made herself accessible to her, why she had in this instance stepped off the fulcrum of political balance in her, a Mandarin's, favor.

Mother and daughter made their way down Mott Street. Mei-yu held Fernadina's hand and smiled as she watched her daughter skip around the lettuce leaves lying in the oily puddles on the sidewalk. Fernadina's grip was strong, and sometimes she tugged impatiently on her mother's hand as she purposefully steered her around the puddles. Mei-yu saw the frown of concentration on her daughter's face, and impressed, as well as bemused, allowed herself to be towed home. They approached the entrance of the Sun Wah Restaurant next to the apartment building where they lived. Mei-yu looked in the window briefly before they went up to their rooms.

It was close to noon. Chinese workers and Americans from mid- and lower-Manhattan offices crowded the tables. For the Americans, Bao provided a menu printed in scrambled English. The Chinese needed no menu. They knew what they wanted and what Bao had; specials were written in Chinese on strips of paper and clipped to a long string suspended between the kitchen and the front doorway. The three waiters, young Chinese men with the waists of girls, wrote down the orders on their paper pads and scurried back and forth from the kitchen. Occasionally an American would want an explanation. His waiter would stand at a respectful distance, looking intently at his notepad.

"What is a spring roll, exactly?"

"Numbah fi, you like numbah fi?"

"Is that an eggroll?"

"Yeah, sure." He would point his pencil at the grease-streaked menu. "Take numbah fi, I know you like."

"Yes, but I thought I'd like to start with the spring roll, that is, if there's shrimp in it . . ." but his waiter had already nodded, scribbling sticklike figures onto his pad and disappearing, barking in the singsong dialect, toward the kitchen.

Here, Bao was throwing shrimp in with the frying noodles. His neck was becoming fused to his spine, he thought. To straighten up would be to snap himself in two. Up at six thirty, chop chop until nine o'clock, receive his baskets of produce from the vegetable grocer from New Jersey, and scrape vegetables until ten. Make sure the tables were set properly, put another ad in the Chinatown newspaper for another dishwasher; Tong had found better pay on Mulberry Street. Cuff the waiters for coming in with dirty shoes, decide what to give the health official this time so he would give him the precious piece of paper; a pair of roast ducks, a basket of salted eggs, a braised pig's head?

The steam and flying globules of hot fat filled the small kitchen. Bao and Shen moved in perfect synchrony in the cramped space, moving the blackened woks from the high-licking flames at precise moments, scooping bits of meat into the hot oil with their two-foot-long chopsticks. _Bend the knees to save the back,_ Bao chanted to himself. Three hours of this at lunch was the worst, because people were in a hurry. Sun Wah was open throughout the afternoon. Sometimes a Chinese would saunter in at three or four o'clock for a snack of pork bao or tea. Then the Americans would come at six and seven o'clock, the ones who knew to eat family style. Often, one man would explain the whole sharing concept to his eating companions and, with an air of command, place the orders, although his friends seemed to wince at the very idea. Mixing, sharing dishes?

Bao would bring the dishes to the table himself, proudly slapping down a large oval plate brimming with swirling squid tentacles and things with pouches and honeycomb membranes, or a long plate with a fish whose eyes stared. The host demonstrated the technique of using chopsticks. "See," he said, "let one stick balance on your fourth finger, then use the other on top to squeeze them together." He exuded confidence, picking up a cluster of squid tentacles. Pinching the two sticks together, he blinked in astonishment as the little clump of arms squirted onto the wall in back of him.

"Did we order this?" he demanded of Bao, who appeared at precisely the right moment with platters of egg foo young and chow mein, things the others had wanted all along.

Sun Wah closed at 2:00 A.M., six days a week. On Sundays, Bao went to Brooklyn to visit his second aunt. "Forget that your last one ran away," she told him, "you need a good Chinese wife to share your burden." At forty-six years of age, Bao ate the dinner she cooked for him, sipped his tea. He was too exhausted to argue.

Fernadina lay asleep. As the afternoon grew hotter, Mei-yu sat at the metal table, wiping the fine sweat from underneath her eyes. In front of her were her new sketches. The air was so heavy with humidity, it seemed to press down on her, weighing down her eyelids, dragging on the pencil she held in her hand. The pencil was stubborn today, refusing to move. She had wanted to capture a new line, a new design she had envisioned. Suddenly, even before he made a sound, she knew he was at her door. She moved quickly to the foyer and opened the door before he could knock and wake her daughter. Stepping out into the hall, she carefully shut the door behind her. She stood facing him, her back pressed against the door, her hand twisted in back of her, gripping the knob.

"I told you never to come here, I told you I did not want to see you ever again," she said.

"Mei-yu . . ." he began.

She turned her head. A door closed down the hall.

"The stairs." She left her post and walked ahead of him, halfway down the steep, winding stairs. She turned to face him. "You must leave. Now."

Why had she left her apartment? Why was she standing here with him? she wondered. He stood two steps above her. Yung-shan was dressed American style, wearing real leather shoes. His thick black hair was natural, not slicked down with oil like the hair of other Chinese men. Yung-shan was also not wasp-waisted, but compact, muscular. He filled his clothes. Mei-yu felt him looking at her, felt the heat creeping up within her, burning behind her eyes.

"Mei-yu," he insisted, reaching for her hand. She crossed her arms, grabbing her elbows.

"I've done nothing to encourage you," she said, her whisper hoarse with panic. "You know I cannot . . . I cannot do what you want."

He stood, patient. She saw that his eyes were lighter than Kung-chiao's. She saw the strength in his hands, the fine slender fingers, and the fleshy palms.

"I can give you everything you want," he said. "You know my position."

To Mei-yu's horror she felt her mind go dark with all the possibilities. Then, suddenly, her words rushed from her. "I am not afraid of you, Yung-shan. Colonel Chang may be your father, but you cannot buy me."

His voice was soft. "I had hoped . . . surely you know . . . buying was not what I had in mind."

He seemed gentle, even sorrowful to her. She felt pity for him. She did not like the feeling of pity for a man like him. This gave her strength.

"I must go back to my child." She wanted him to go down the stairs past her, not for her to have to move past him. She waited. He stood, immobile. She saw that she would have to move. She turned against the wall, away from the railing. Still hugging herself, she stepped past him quickly. He did not move.

"You are making a mistake," he said, his voice flat.

She crossed the hallway and opened the door to her apartment. When she turned to look back, he was gone.

Kung-chiao sat in the university library and listened to his stomach complain. He had deliberately skipped lunch. The smell of macaroni and cheese made him nauseated anyhow. Here, in the shadows of the book stacks, he savored the perverse satisfaction of his hunger. He would not even tell Mei-yu; let her go on thinking that he squandered their allowance and what little she earned with her designs and sewing. Let her serve him his supper with her lips pressed together; let her watch stone-faced as he bathed Fernadina and told her stories of how China began. Then, when it was dark and time for Mei-yu to slip off her chemise with her back toward him, he would give her the money; the money he had saved with his hunger.

He shook his head of the vision. He knew it was absurd, the lengths he went to to make Mei-yu's face break, either in weeping or a smile. It was easier to make her weep, only lately, he had not even succeeded in that. The smiles she allowed herself were flashes that burned briefly, yet brightly, with satisfaction. Her small but laserlike victories. These smiles seared his very insides. Where did they come from? he wondered. Had she learned to mimic the women who ignored her and then sniped at her behind her back as she walked by? "Your wife is too beautiful, she holds herself aloof ," his friends told him, as if to explain their wives' attitude toward Mei-yu. But he knew, from their eyes and voices, that his friends perceived Mei-yu differently. Kung-chiao himself had no trouble with the people of Chinatown; he was like one of them. Besides, a man who worked to better himself was looked upon favorably. Mei-yu worked, but she had the misfortune of having been born in another social stratum. And then, of course, she was a woman.

She had been different in China. She had been spirited, but soft, laughing, eager to please. She would have made any man the perfect wife.

Sometimes they happened to meet on the school grounds, at Yenching University in Peking. By then, in 1945, the Japanese had been defeated, and the city was free of them, waiting now for the stronger of the two forces in China to take the seat of government. Meanwhile, students continued to attend classes uneasily, for all knew change was imminent.

When they passed each other on the campus, she always acknowledged him with a nod of the head, and he responded by abruptly finding something else of interest to stare at.

"You know she will probably accept one of the men her father approves," Tsien-tsung told him one evening. "And there are many of them sniffing about the Chen house." The two of them had been discussing politics, and now suddenly Tsien-tsung had brought up Mei-yu's name. This was certainly not typical of his friend, Kung-chiao thought, scrutinizing Tsien-tsung's face. Normally Tsien-tsung's mind was focused, piercing in its probing of ideas, theory. If Tsien-tsung ever thought of women, Kung-chiao had never known it. Why would he bring up Mei-yu's name? He looked again at his friend's narrow face with its hooded lids. Tsien-tsung always looked so dour. It was not the face of a man who loved women.

"I know for a fact that Lee Ta-wei, the son of the dean at the university, who is a good friend of her father's, is madly in love with her and intends to ask for her hand," Tsien-tsung went on. "And soon, too. You know, the Lees are very well-off, an old family, long living here in Peking. I hear Ta-wei will probably be promoted to an assistant professor next year. . . ."

Kung-chiao pictured Ta-wei's tall figure, inches taller than his own, his unctuous smile. He heard the modulation of Ta-wei's voice, the elegant flow of words. Many times he had wondered how his rival had come by such white skin, such a lithe figure, and despaired of his own brown hide and sinewy, slight form. There were others, too, the brothers Chou, each wealthy, dealing in trade, gliding across the school grounds in their English leather shoes. He imagined Mei-yu standing with one of these favored young men, a bride.

"Ta-wei stands to inherit quite a bit of land as well," Tsien-tsung was saying.

"Why are you going on like this?" Kung-chiao said sharply.

"So that you will stop being such a turtle and move swiftly, or you will lose her."

Kung-chiao stared at Tsien-tsung.

"You are not very good at hiding, Kung-chiao. It is obvious to all of us how you feel about Mei-yu."

"How I feel . . . ?"

"Squirm all you like. Now I am positive."

Kung-chiao sighed, shook his head. "I am a fool. It is hopeless. My family is poor; I have nothing to offer. I know what contempt Professor Chen has for men like myself."

"Professor Chen is ill. He is a broken man, a totally changed man since his release from prison. He has turned around, gone back to embracing the old ways, grasping for certainty there. Mei-yu says it is breaking her heart, how changed he is."

"Mei-yu? Have you spoken to her?"

"My sister, Wen-chuan, is her good friend. They speak. My sister speaks to me."

Kung-chiao saw the mischievous smile creeping in at the corners of Tsien-tsung's mouth.

"Well?" he said finally, laughing, embarrassed, as his friend continued to smile, silent. "Must you enjoy your fun with me so thoroughly? Stop smiling like that! I give in! Does she speak of me, then? Mei-yu?"

Tsien-tsung looked down at the table where they sat. "Wen-chuan says Mei-yu admires you above all other men."

Kung-chiao burst out in laughter but felt his whole body begin to tremble. He waited.

"Wen-chuan says Mei-yu says you are not like all the others, fatuous, vain, full of bravado."

"Ha, ha," Kung-chiao heard himself laugh nervously. "She must think I am a pretty good fellow."

"She says you are serious, brilliant."

There may be some truth to that, Kung-chiao thought cautiously. After all, he had received the scholar's prize this year. He stood number one in the senior class. Did he really come across as being so serious? People said he smiled even less than Tsien-tsung. How could she have found that attractive? She must have thought he was something of a hermit; he had spent much time studying, reading, out of the sight of the others. But he had also come forth with the plans for the demonstration that was to take place in scant weeks to come. Everyone had said his plans were brilliant in concept, comprehensive. Everyone, that is, except for Ta-wei, who could not be bothered with political matters. Mere students' concerns, he had scoffed. Perhaps Mei-yu liked the serious, studious types. If she did, then perhaps he could see the logic, Kung-chiao thought. But still his mind protected him, insisting that Mei-yu could not love a bookworm. "You are crazy," he muttered to Tsien-tsung, secretly hoping that his friend was as sober as he looked.

"She says you are very attractive, that you don't look dough-faced like the rest of the young men here at school."

Kung-chiao put his face down to the surface of the table. He gripped the edge of it so that the shaking of his hands would not show. Tsien-tsung looked away. After several moments, he chuckled.

"She also said you were socially backward." Seeing the horrified look on Kung-chiao's face, Tsien-tsung quickly spread his hands palms out in front of him, as if to deny all responsibility for his previous remark. "I'm just telling you what Wen-chuan told me. You asked," he said.

Kung-chiao groaned. He stared at Tsien-tsung, wondering how long his friend had contained all this information. Then they both burst into laughter.

The next time Kung-chiao saw Mei-yu, she was standing with a group of her women friends outside the laboratory of the university. In spite of what he now knew, he still could not look at her directly, especially when all her friends stood so close. Yet, as he walked by, twenty feet beyond her group, he saw, from the side, how her eyes followed him. He felt her eyes and his eyes sliding in their sockets like magnets, and suddenly he knew the absurdity of it all. *We are like two fish in separate bowls, staring pop-eyed, gliding past each other, gulping with desire,* he thought. Everyone knew. It was a joke to everyone but them. Very well. He turned around suddenly and approached the group. Instead of titters he heard nothing, saw nothing but that the women politely made way for him, like a dividing school of mullet, and disappeared from view. Now Mei-yu's face alone was before him. He forgot what he had said to her, forgot what she had said to him, only that he touched her and she held his arm. They were in public, but she held his arm firmly, nevertheless. Her face had turned white, as white as it had been the evening he had first seen her, two years ago, during their confrontation with the Japanese soldier. Then, from the vantage of the gate, he had seen that in spite of the whiteness of her face, she had held onto Wen-chuan, had withstood the menace of the soldier. Afterward, sitting at the table with the other students, he had watched her as she sat quietly, looking into the faces surrounding her, and he knew what she was within, knew that she was for him. They walked together from the university grounds and entered a park, and talked, and discovered their plans together. They grew calmer with each hour. She released his arm, for they were among others again. But with each hour Kung-chiao's certainty grew, and at the end of the afternoon he told her he would speak to her father.

Her father refused to receive him. "Marry him, a peasant's son," her father said to her, "and you sever yourself from your family." After several months of appeal, anguish, and seeing that she would not be able to soften her father's resolve, she finally eloped with Kung-chiao. She had done that for him.

He had repaid her by bringing her to a strange country, this America, first to the squalid waterfront of San Francisco, and then here, to Chinatown. And then, of course, there was Sing-hua, their daughter, Fernadina, whose name gave expression to his hope. Hope that seemed elusive now. What had he brought Mei-yu, and his daughter, to?

Kung-chiao swept his books into his satchel. He looked at the library clock: five thirty. His head could not possibly contain any more facts or formulas. By this time on Friday he would be finished with his exams. He actually looked forward to them. Standing up, rubbing his neck, he noticed the brown-haired girl who was in his class; Janet, she had said, when she had introduced herself to him. He found her too forward, too large-boned. These American girls were intimidating physically, with their big-knuckled hands, big feet, and round eyes that revealed all they thought. Janet was reading from her book, taking notes. Good, Kung-chiao thought. She wouldn't be asking to borrow his notes, wouldn't be asking him to help her. He pushed open the library door and walked rapidly down toward Broadway.

Bao was sitting at one of the front tables, smoking a cigarette, when Kung-chiao stopped to poke his head in the open doorway. People were beginning to come out into the streets again, anticipating the dinner hour and the second wave of business.

"You're getting lazy in your old age, Bao," Kung-chiao teased.

Bao shrugged wearily. "You want to earn an honest living, Kung-chiao? Take the place of one of my waiters tonight. He has to run off to attend his sick father. Last week it was also his sick father. You'd think he'd have a little more imagination, mix it up a little, have a sick mother once in a while. What do you say?"

For once Kung-chiao was glad Roger and Diana were coming over after supper.

"Sorry, Bao. My cousin is coming tonight."

Bao snorted out a lungful of smoke. "Relatives! Why is it everyone's relatives are so accommodating all of a sudden?"

Wo-fu, one of the waiters, came out from the back of the restaurant. "Hey, old man," he said, taking off his waiter's jacket, "lend me some money for a token, will you?"

Bao turned away, looking far off into the distance through his ring of smoke.

"So I can get to my sick father." Wo-fu turned, appealing to Kung-chiao, standing in the doorway. Kung-chiao gave him a nickel.

"Thank you. I'll pay you back." He took off down the street.

Bao got up from his chair and beckoned to Kung-chiao. "Wait here. I have something for Mei-yu."

Kung-chiao watched as the older man made his way back to the kitchen. Bao walked as if one leg were shorter than the other. The strings of his apron trailed behind him. He came back carrying a paper sack. Kung-chiao accepted it, politely tucking it into his satchel without looking inside.

"Oxtail," Bao said. "The child must have meat."

"Thank you, Bao. If Wo-fu is not back tomorrow, I'll be your waiter."

Bao shrugged.

Mei-yu smoothed cornstarch onto Fernadina's body. The child was fragrant after her bath. Standing in Mei-yu's lap, she looked in the direction of her father, who sat on the bed, watching them. Mei-yu had seemed uneasy at dinner, he was thinking. Perhaps because of Roger and Diana coming tonight. Yet now she seemed as soothed as Fernadina with the stroking on of the cornstarch. He jingled the change, his lunch money, in his pocket. Mei-yu's hair had begun to come down over her face. Her arms in her sleeveless cotton dress seemed thin. He came over to take Fernadina from Mei-yu and, bending low, caught the delicately acrid smell of the sweat at the nape of her neck. He kissed the bone below her nape. She looked up, startled.

Diana couldn't come tonight, Roger said.

Diana had never wanted to come, Mei-yu thought. The last time she came she had worn a silk blouse and a white linen skirt, dressed to go out to dinner on the East Side after they made their charity call. Mei-yu knew Diana needed the compensation of dinner out whenever she and Roger, Kung-chiao's second cousin, visited them. Mei-yu was glad that by not coming tonight Diana had at least dropped the pretense. Perhaps she had been bothered by the fact that they had only two chairs and the bed. It was too awkward; the other times they had come, Kung-chiao had stood the entire time. Perhaps she disliked the cheap cardboard wardrobe, the tiny stove. Perhaps she disliked everything about them.

Roger was dressed in a gray American suit. "How's your study coming?" he asked. "Exams this week, eh?"

Roger, five years in this country and sounding like an American already. Mei-yu winced at the casual heartiness in his voice.

"How about that interview I lined up for you?"

He sat on their bed. They sat in the chairs at his feet.

"Next Monday," Kung-chiao said. Mei-yu was glad he did not thank Roger again for calling a friend of his in the city engineering department.

"Well, I hope things work out. It'd be good for you to work for the city. You wouldn't be making all that much, of course, but you could move out of Chinatown at least. Maybe into the Bronx." Roger wrinkled his nose. He could smell what they had had for dinner. Stinking dried fish. Didn't they eat anything else? he thought. It was either that or something with terrible amounts of garlic. Diana said she could smell it on her clothes afterward.

"Would you like tea?" Mei-yu offered politely.

"No, thanks. Too hot." Roger took a handkerchief from his pocket and wiped his face. He had a narrow face with a long nose, unusual in a Chinese. When he smiled, he showed gold-capped teeth. He had taken the name Roger when he had moved to Hong Kong. The name served him well when he moved his import business on to New York. It helped him win his wife, Diana, born of Chinese parents in New York State. He took the envelope of money from his pocket and extended it to Kung-chiao, who took it and placed it on the table in back of him.

"Thank you, Roger," Kung-chiao said simply.

Roger tried not to frown. He understood why they did not like him. They envied his success, his clothes, the style his wife had. They would pay him back like they said they would, he was certain, but meanwhile he knew they resented having to depend on him now. It was his luck to have refugees for relatives, and proud ones, at that. Proud ones were better than leeches, clinging onto him for years, though, he thought. Still, didn't he deserve a little more respect? What if he chose not to behave honorably, like a good Chinese, helping out his relatives, even distant ones, second cousins? After all, where would they be without him? He stood up. "I'd better be going. Diana's waiting. We're having guests for dinner tonight." He had been speaking Mandarin in their place; it would be a relief to go back uptown and speak English again.

Kung-chiao opened the door for his second cousin and walked down the stairs with him. Mei-yu was grateful for her husband's silence, his dignity. She tucked the envelope under the teapot. When he came back, sometime later, he handed her a cold chunk of watermelon. Another extravagance, she thought. But it was so hot. He cut her a piece. She mashed the sweet red pulp in her mouth with her tongue and felt the cold juice trickle down her throat. Kung-chiao bit into a wedge and gave some to Fernadina, who pressed her face into it, letting out strange little cries. Mei-yu then watched Kung-chiao as he put their daughter to bed. It was getting dark out. A breeze began to waft in under the shade. He turned out the light and pulled up the shade; the breeze grew bolder. They sat on their bed, watching the neon dragons and Chinese characters flashing on the signs all along their street. People strolled along the sidewalk, looking in at the diners chewing on chicken bones and clacking chopsticks against their bowls. Mei-yu looked at Kung-chiao's hand on the sill; long, bony fingers, sensitive, strong. The blue veins were prominent, pulsing under the brown skin. She knew how he had had the money for the watermelon. The change he had in his pocket when he got back from the university was gone. They stared at each other in the darkening room, watching the reflection of the flickering neon lights in each other's eyes.

"Mei-yu," her husband said softly, his hand reaching out to touch her. They kissed, tasting the sweetness of each other's tongues, and Kung-chiao, pulling Mei-yu to him, marveled at how his wife's face softened, and broke.

○   ○   ○

Kung-chiao woke not to the sound of Bao's chopping but because of the sensation he had of being watched. When he opened his eyes, he saw that Mei-yu lay next to him, looking into his face. He felt shy, as if the previous night had been their first night together. It had been their first night like that in a long time. Now, as then, he felt the warmth of her body close to him. He reached over and gently pulled on the luxuriant mass of his wife's hair, bringing her face closer to his. She playfully buried her face under his chin.

"Shh, Kung-chiao, not now, Fernadina is awake . . . I hear her singing to herself."

"So, let her sing, what better accompaniment could we have?"

"But she may come in! Shame on you, to think of yourself first, always!"

But her voice thrilled even as she scolded, and Kung-chiao heard the real meaning of her words, saw the promise in her eyes. Later. Tonight.

Fernadina's voice came clearly from the foyer. "I'm getting up now!"

Fernadina announced her intentions before she did anything, as if she were telling her own story to herself out loud, as lonely children often do. Or perhaps it was her child's way of warning her parents of what she was about to do next, for in spite of both their teaching, she never asked for permission but assumed that whatever she chose to do would meet their approval.

It seemed odd to Mei-yu that Fernadina, though curious and bold, always sensed the limits of what she was permitted to do. She would approach the stove but never reach up to touch it while her mother was cooking. She would pick up whatever garment Mei-yu was working on and look at it closely, seeming to count the stitches in the seams, as if she were planning to add her own details to it. But just as Mei-yu began to feel uneasy, to wonder what her daughter had in mind to do with her work, Fernadina would replace it back in its box, carefully patting down the tissue paper on top. She would also try to comb her hair herself, grabbing a handful of hair on top of her head and rubbing her mother's comb against her head. Every day she found the comb too big for her hands. She would bring the comb and place it on the table in front of Mei-yu. Her mother would guide her hands through the motions, show-ing her how to gather a little tuft of hair on top of her head and wind a rubber band around it, and then tie a ribbon around that. All little Chinese girls wore their hair like that, gathered into little black foun-tains on top of their heads until their hair was long enough to braid. Fernadina would often sit on her parents' bed looking out the window, watching the street down below. She would have the thumb of her right hand tucked securely into her mouth, the left hand up on her head, holding on to her beribboned tuft. She seemed to be contained and complete then, and Mei-yu saw that she was content.

The only time Mei-yu grew concerned was when they went walking, when Fernadina would let go her grip of Mei-yu's little finger to inspect the crates lying in the street, the fish swimming in their tanks in the fishmonger's shop, or to greet the neighborhood dogs that lay in the doorways and who reciprocated her greeting with solemn licks to her face. Mei-yu might be picking over cucumbers to buy from a street vendor, releasing Fernadina for a second while she searched her purse for change, and Fernadina would vanish. More than once Mei-yu had frantically searched the crowds for her small daughter. Her ears strained to hear Fernadina's voice calling for her, but always she found her, or rather, Fernadina would let herself be found, several shops down the street, performing her quiet inspections.

Now she came into the big room, carrying her one toy, a stuffed rabbit. "Let me out, please," she said in perfect Mandarin, pointing to the door. Her face was earnest. Mei-yu quickly put on her robe, flinging her hair away from her face as she tied the sash. They were late; already Bao could be heard chopping and screaming at Shen down below. Kung-chiao lay back on his pillow. Today was so different from yester-day. Perhaps he would stay home today, take a rest from studying. That he entertained the thought, even for a moment, astounded him, alarmed him. Then his daydream overtook him again. He could help Mei-yu with the shopping, watch Fernadina while she went to pick up her next assignment. Or maybe he would go with her, stare down the pug-nosed, squat women who dared jeer at her. He was still in bed when his wife returned with Fernadina.

"Ai yah, lazy one, are you spending the day in bed?" Mei-yu said to him as she pulled a cotton shirt over Fernadina's head.

"No. I'm spending it with you."

She stood there, heedless of Fernadina's head stuck in the armhole of the shirt. The child waited patiently. Then her mother shrieked.

"Kung-chiao! How can you be so casual about your exams? Have you gone crazy? Do you know how long we've waited for this, for you to graduate from school? How can you graduate unless you pass your exams? How can you get a job unless you graduate?"

"I am touched by your faith in me," Kung-chiao said, rising out of bed, laughing. "Please help Fernadina, she's stuck in the armhole."

Mei-yu yanked the shirt off. Fernadina took it from her and poked her head determinedly toward the largest opening. Which was a good thing, Mei-yu thought, since the child's father was coming toward them completely naked; it wasn't good for children to see their parents so undignified. Kung-chiao took Mei-yu by the shoulders. Such fine bones! he thought.

"Don't worry, Mei. If it frightens you so much for me to be at home, I will leave to study after lunch. Do I get lunch today, by the way?"

She stepped on his foot. "Devil!"

Fernadina held on to her father's little finger as the family strolled down Mott Street. The Union Center, where Mei-yu went to see Madame Peng's assistant, was only blocks away. Mei-yu didn't know if it was merely her imagination, or whether it was true that the women standing in the doorways were silent today. Kung-chiao even nodded to Mrs. Liu. The noodlemaker's wife's voice was the one that brayed above the others in her disapproval of Mei-yu. Today she leaned against the doorjamb of her husband's shop, her broad face impassive. She wore her short hair permed in the American style, looking like a poor imitation of the wealthy merchants' wives. Kung-chiao carried it a step further.

"Good morning, Mrs. Liu," he called, bowing his head politely. "Please give my family's regards to your husband, whose noodles are the finest in Chinatown."

Mrs. Liu smiled, her eyes disappearing into her fat cheeks as she giggled and waved her acknowledgment of his greeting. Mei-yu pinched his arm after they had passed. "Flatterer! Why do you ingratiate yourself with these people?"

Kung-chiao stared straight ahead. "It never hurts to pave the path to our neighbors," he said. "You never know when you may need their kindness."

Mei-yu shook her head with annoyance, remembering Mrs. Liu's voice when she had spoken loudly behind her fan to her friend tending the shop next door. Who did Mei-yu think she was, wearing her hair in that manner? she had said. Mei-yu imagined the day when she would have different neighbors. But what kind of neighbors? White, American people? As far as she knew, from the way they behaved in Chinatown restaurants, they would despise her as well.

They reached the Union. Built of red brick, it was one of the largest nonresidential buildings in Chinatown. The City of New York had proposed the establishment of a place that would function to help the Chinese assimilate into American society. When the city officials met the Council of Chinatown Elders, they were uncertain how their ideas would be received, for it was always a delicate matter with minorities. The two groups met in back of one of the finer restaurants and were served savories and green tea. The Elders listened quietly. When the officials finished their presentation, Madame Peng slapped the table and shouted, "Excellent! We shall start straightaway!" and then proceeded to explain that she and the other Elders would of course be running the proposed Union entirely on their own. It was a matter of trust, she said. The people of Chinatown trusted only in the judgment of their Elders; therefore, the Union could succeed only if the Elders administered it. The Elders would ensure, with monthly reports, that the activities and classes within the Union were functioning according to the guidelines set by the city officials. "What about inspection?" the officials asked. "Does the concept of inspection inspire good faith?" demanded Madame Peng. "We would be glad to invite visitors from the City Council from time to time," she said, "but there will be no inspections."

The City Council retreated back uptown to consider the Elders' proposal. The Chinese were a proud, clannish people, loyal to their leaders, it concluded. How else would the city establish communication, but through the Elders? Previous overtures had been politely rebuffed. Ignored, actually. But now that dragon lady, Madame Peng, offered them something.

Two months later the officials returned for the signatures of the Elders. Three years later, the redbrick building was completed.

The Wong family passed the reception desk in the front hall and started up the stairs to the right toward the craft and design section. The Union was like an ant nest. Bodies pressed in the hallways on the way to and from the many rooms. The ground floor was reserved for the Chinese and Western music, opera, and dance sections. Kung-chiao had not been there in months; the pounding drums, the wail of gut-stringed Chinese instruments, and the meowing of beginners' violins drowned out all sensibility. The nursery was also on the ground floor, where working parents could drop off their children on the way to work. The children were attended by older women who patiently and lovingly extracted them from the hands of their playmates, fed them lunch, and watched to make sure they napped.

The rooms were larger on the second floor, with long tables arranged in the center. Women from many families sat around these tables, bent over their fine silk needlework. On Saturdays the rooms were filled with children who chanted their English lessons with their teacher, a young Chinese studying at Columbia University uptown who journeyed down to make pocket money.

The administrative offices were located on the sixth floor, along with the Chinese Christian Association office and the Family Counseling Service. Neither Mei-yu nor Kung-chiao nor any of their neighbors had ever found sufficient reason to visit this floor, whose offices had originally been intended by the New York City Council to be installed on the ground floor. When the officials came for their first "visit" and discovered what they considered the most vital offices of the center in the remotest vicinity of the sixth floor, they protested vigorously. They knew the Chinese preferred their Buddhist shrines and the advice of their sages and soothsayers, but the money had been set aside for the purposes of assimilation, and the Chinese Elders had promised cooperation. Madame Peng, when approached with this problem, smiled, and said the Elders would consider moving the offices. That was two years ago. The one lone Christian representative and the young Chinese woman therapist continued to sit in their offices on the sixth floor, segregated from the hubbub of life and activity below.

Mei-yu recognized the wife of the President of the Union. No one knew how the President had come into his money, but all knew his wife came to the Union not to find work but to visit her friends and sit at the long tables, chatting and sewing. Her husband was something of a benign presence, like fungus on a tree. He was an old gold-toothed man who was rumored to spend his days playing cards and mah-jongg with cronies upstairs in his office. Today he was wandering throughout the second floor, looking for his wife. She had packed his lunch and now he had forgotten where he had left it. He embodied the convivial and haphazard spirit of the Union. Administrative matters were taken care of in the simplest manner: he simply roamed the halls and told people what to do. Gossip and rumors from the usual reliable sources helped him form policy and administer the delicate hierarchy of influence within the Union. Whoever had his ear, slipped the bill or two into his hand, was assured of favor for the moment. The President carried memos of his policies on bits of paper and stuck them into his pockets, where he also kept his dried sour plum suckers.

Mei-yu approached Madame Peng's assistant while Kung-chiao stood holding Fernadina's hand just outside in the hallway. The women seated at the table continued to talk but allowed intervals of silence in their conversation to keep track of what went on between Mei-yu and Mei-ling.

"You were supposed to turn it in today," Mei-ling said.

"No one told me that. I had no idea it was needed for today."

"Well, it is. And Colonel Chang's niece said she saw your last design on a friend of hers. She wants to look elegant, not outlandish."

"My designs are not outlandish," Mei-yu said, feeling something rise up in her throat.

"Just keep it simple. Madame Peng may find a certain charm to your work, but I have difficulty finding buyers for it."

Mei-yu knew this was not true. She knew that her designs, her jackets and skirts, were much-desired items, especially among the younger women who ventured out of Chinatown.

Mei-ling had hair that had been chopped off below her ears and straight across her brow. She looked out as if from beneath a shiny steel helmet.

"Just bring in the jacket tomorrow."

"I cannot possibly bring it in tomorrow. I'll need until Thursday at the very earliest."

Mei-ling shrugged and turned away. The other women resumed their normal rate and pitch of conversation, satisfied.

Mei-yu almost collided with Kung-chiao in the hall.

"What's the matter?" he asked.

Mei-yu shook her head, speechless. Kung-chiao felt her anger, knew the force of it, the power it gave her. He followed her down the stairs. Someone brushed against him.

"Wo-fu?"

Wo-fu barely glanced back and continued taking the stairs up two at a time.

Strange, to see Wo-fu here, and at this hour, Kung-chiao thought.

Not wanting to return to their apartment directly, especially with Mei-yu in such a state, Kung-chiao took her arm and steered her to one of the quieter side streets. He bought his wife and daughter a sweetened rice cake to share. Mei-yu smiled, although her misery was plain.

"Oh, Kung-chiao," she said, tears of frustration squeezing from her eyes in spite of herself, "it's no use, I must get back home to make that jacket. I have so little time. Our day is ruined."

He took her back to the apartment. He boiled noodles for lunch and chopped peanuts to sprinkle on top. When Fernadina sleepily allowed herself to be taken in for her nap, Mei-yu took out her scissors and the silk fabric she had been given at the Union. Kung-chiao took up his satchel.

"I'll be home by six," he said. His wife was leaning on the table, frowning in concentration at the piece of fabric. He closed the door quietly.

The next morning Kung-chiao awoke to see his wife sitting at the table, fitting lining into the sleeves. She looked as she had when he had gone to bed.

"Did you sleep at all?" he asked.

"A little," she said, her head bent low to see the inside of the sleeve.

When he left, he took Fernadina with him to the Union, where she would stay until the afternoon. Mei-yu watched them leave, her dark eyes full of fatigue and regret.

In the afternoon Mei-yu was startled by a knock on the door. Thinking it was Yung-shan, she sat quietly, listening to the blood pounding in her ears.

"Mei-yu! It's me, Ah-chin!"

Mei-yu opened the door. The friend she had met at the children's nursery stood in the hallway, carrying a basket of small ripe peaches.

"Here. Aren't they fragrant? Kung-chiao stopped by the shop early this morning and told me to come rescue you. Can I look?" Ah-chin pointed to the half-finished jacket lying on the table. She handed the basket to Mei-yu.

The jacket was simple, made of dark blue silk, lined with silver-colored silk. Silver piping ran the length of the front opening and neck edges. The sleeves were set low with wide armhole openings.

"Oh," Ah-chin said, her eyes shining. "May I?"

Mei-yu smiled, bringing the peaches over to the sink to rinse off as her friend tried on the jacket.

"Mei-yu, you are an artist, a wonder with fabric. This is perfect. I love it! I wish I could afford it."

"I'll make you one, Ah-chin."

Ah-chin carefully removed the jacket.

"It's not finished," Mei-yu said, picking up the raw edges of the bottom and inspecting them critically. "I have to finish it by tomorrow." She placed the jacket carefully in a box and put a clean cloth over it. She looked at her friend. Ah-chin was thin, bent, concave-looking. She was about Mei-yu's age, although her stoop made her look years older. Her lanky hair fell into her face, like a damaged wing, covering one eye. Her son, called Wen-wen, was Fernadina's age.

"Where's Sing-hua?" Ah-chin asked.

"Kung-chiao took her to the Union. It seems to be the only way. . . . I have been trying to finish this jacket, and Kung-chiao has to study for his exams on Friday."

"You're not usually having to hurry like this on projects, are you?"

"No. I have had . . . difficulty with Mei-ling before, but this is the first time she has deliberately misinformed me of my deadline. I was sure I had plenty of time."

"That's strange," Ah-chin said. She shifted in her chair. She picked up one of the peaches and ran her finger lightly, thoughtfully over the silver fuzz. "But I'm not surprised, either. Strange things are happening everywhere, Mei-yu."

"What do you mean?" Mei-yu looked up, interested.

"Have you noticed anything different in the streets? Like people watching people, whispering behind each others' backs . . ."

"Oh, that." Mei-yu shrugged. "That's nothing new."

Ah-chin saw the curl of Mei-yu's mouth. "I'm not talking about the women, Mei-yu. They're harmless, really. Pay no attention to them. No, I mean something else. There are rumors—" She stopped.

Mei-yu took a peach and bit into it, releasing juice, which ran partway down her arm. She knew Ah-chin was waiting for her to urge her to divulge the latest gossip. She said nothing but continued to eat her peach, watching, amused, as her friend slid into a little sulk. Ah-chin was her good friend, her only woman friend in Chinatown. Honest, intelligent, hardworking, but naive, with a child's curiosity. She went to the soothsayers to find out if her husband remained faithful to her. How could he have time to be unfaithful? Mei-yu thought. Ah-chin and her husband worked side by side in the bakery on Canal Street and went to the Union together to pick up their son, Wen-wen, late in the afternoon. Seeing the two of them walking down the street to the Union, Mei-yu thought of a pair of tired animals yoked together. She knew, from what Ah-chin told her, that Ling neither drank nor played cards, and most often fell asleep, exhausted, after dinner. For Ah-chin to suspect Ling of unfaithfulness was silly but somehow touching, Mei-yu thought.

But Ah-chin's chief fault, Mei-yu thought (and often chided her friend for her preoccupation of it), was her love of gossip, something she had in common with the other women of Chinatown. She seemed always to be tuned into the channels of talk that circulated throughout Chinatown, and kept abreast of the latest scandal, the most recent intrigue between the powerful families. She was Mei-yu's contact with the Cantonese circle of society, having befriended the outsider in spite of what her other friends had told her about the Mandarins.

Finally Ah-chin could stand Mei-yu's silence no longer. She shook herself of her sulk in the way a bird shakes its feathers of rain.

"There are rumors," she declared, ignoring Mei-yu's smile, "that the police are investigating certain powerful parties here in Chinatown." She leaned forward. "Parties like Lo, the importer, and Colonel Chang."

Mei-yu licked the peach juice from her arm. People like Lo and Colonel Chang were always being watched by the police. She had noticed the two patrolmen walking down Mulberry Street at the beginning of the week. So what if Yung-shan's father had been careless? What did she care? The politics and power struggles of Chinatown did not interest or concern her. What was it that Colonel Chang was reputed to be? A drug dealer, a gambler? And Lo supposedly had control of a prostitution ring. No doubt he had other illegal interests as well. This kind of activity was not strange to her; she had known of it in Peking, in Shanghai, in Canton, as well. Why not here?

"They questioned Liu, the noodlemaker, the other day," Ah-chin went on. "Chang's men were hanging around to make sure he had nothing to say."

Mei-yu chuckled. Liu, as pasty-faced and limp as the noodles he made, an accessory to Colonel Chang's dealings? She watched her friend grab a peach and take a quick bite out of it.

"I don't know why you laugh," Ah-chin said. "It is a serious matter for all of us. It gives me a strange feeling, I tell you, seeing the police prowling around, and Colonel Chang's men on every doorstep. No one is doing anything about it, either; no one is brave enough. We are all tending our little shops, going our way, everything about us shut tight, like clams in the mud. And you! You who pride yourself on being different. You're no different . . . all you think of is yourself and your family." She pulled the stem from her peach, and then, seeing no reaction from Mei-yu, sighed. "How is Kung-chiao, anyway? He looked tired and bothered about something this morning."

"He is. Both tired and bothered. We've waited for him to take these exams for three years. I will be glad when it is Friday evening, when they'll be over." Mei-yu suddenly took hold of her friend's arm. "Ah-chin, can you keep quiet about what I am about to tell you? Especially to Kung-chiao; I want it to be a surprise."

Ah-chin nodded, sweeping her hair away from her face with her hand so that she could see Mei-yu clearly and make certain of every word.

"Promise me you won't tell."

Ah-chin nodded again, vigorously, seeing how Mei-yu's face radiated excitement.

"I'm hoping, with the money I earned last week from those extra shirts I made and this jacket, that we'll be able to afford a celebration, a feast. A surprise for Kung-chiao. Bao said he would help me. Can you and Ling come?"

Ah-chin laughed, pinching Mei-yu's arm. "Of course! That is a wonderful idea, Mei-yu! When did you say? Friday? Ling and I will come. We'll bring Wen-wen with us."

"He and Fernadina could play."

"Fernadina makes him cry. She's such a bully, Mei-yu."

"She's just spirited and bold, that's all." Mei-yu did not want to tell her friend her son was a limp little newt. "Please come Friday. It will be great fun."

They finished the peaches. When Ah-chin stood up to go to the Union to fetch Wen-wen, Mei-yu decided to go with her. The jacket could wait until tomorrow. She missed her Sing-hua, Fernadina.

Mei-yu was still out when Kung-chiao returned. It was early yet, around four thirty. He was surprised to find the apartment empty, but then, he had never been back this early. Perhaps Mei-yu had gone shopping, or to the Union to get Fernadina.

He remembered the nursery that morning. The women who cared for the children smiled, trading glances when they saw him. Few, if any, fathers took their children to the nursery, for that was the mother's duty. Fernadina saw Wen-wen sitting in a corner and rushed to him, shouting in her peculiar, hoarse little voice. When Wen-wen saw Fernadina running toward him, he hid his face in his hands. The matron waddled over to console him as Fernadina picked up his plastic toy car to examine. Kung-chiao did not wish to remain long, but he did not want to give the women the impression that he was in a hurry to leave, either. He deliberately looked at everything in the room. Besides the dozen or so children, there was the scarred upright piano against the wall, the boxes overflowing with toys, scattered bits of clothing, books lying splayed on their faces. Perhaps because they sensed in Kung-chiao a new and more responsive audience, the children set about making a spectacle for him, screaming with new energy and leaping at each other fearlessly. How could the women stand being with the children all day long? Kung-chiao thought, as he nodded to the matron and left the room. He looked back inside through the window in the door. Fernadina was busy playing with Wen-wen's toy car. Kung-chiao smiled ruefully. Although his daughter always seemed so glad to see him, he wondered if she ever really felt his absence when they parted, if she ever missed him as he missed her.

Now, back in the apartment, he wandered between the foyer and their bedroom. He could not read another text, open another notebook. The unfinished jacket lay in its box on the table. He lifted the cloth and admired Mei-yu's work. Even with his inexperienced eye he appreciated the neatness of the stitches, the clean lines of the garment. He had not been fully aware of his wife's talent. Indeed, she had not been aware of it herself until she had been forced to find a way of augmenting their allowance. Now, when she began a project, she became totally committed, working with intense concentration, a wholeheartedness that Kung-chiao envied. He himself did not feel passion for his work. He had written "engineer" as his declared field of study at the university, but the numbers, figures, and diagrams did nothing to inspire passion. He knew, however, that engineering was an honorable profession, and more importantly, a well-paying one. He knew it would get his family out of Chinatown. He knew it had to get better.

He remembered waking the night before and finding himself alone in their bed. The lamp threw a soft yellow light onto the table surface. Mei-yu's face had looked hollow, waxy with fatigue, as she sat pinning the pieces of the jacket together. She had use of a machine, although then, at night, it sat quiet in its case on the floor by her feet. Roger had lent them Diana's old sewing machine, a black skeletal thing that rattled like bones. She used the machine only in the daytime when Kung-chiao was away at the library. Because of Roger, Mei-yu did not work in a sweatshop any longer. In the beginning she had, crammed in a room with thirty other women. It was on the top floor of an old warehouse. At the end of each day, when she came home after working there for ten hours, Mei-yu would tell Kung-chiao the number of women who had fainted. "Four today," she would say, wiping the sweat from her face. It was sometimes ninety-eight degrees inside and not a breeze stirring except for the tiny, furious whirring made by the sewing machine needles. There were women who cut thread, who made pieces of garments at three cents apiece, who pressed over steaming cloth-covered presses. These were the ones who fainted, dropping like heavy sacks of flour onto the wooden planked floor. Mei-yu came back with thread cuts on her fingers. She lost weight. She began to see things. One evening as she made soup she screamed there were live spools with spinneret legs swimming in the pot. In her sleep at night she mumbled, "Twenty pieces not enough, thirty pieces before lunch."

Kung-chiao remembered those nights. He shared dinner with Mei-yu at five o'clock, before he left for work, staring at her as she sat in an exhausted stupor across from him, Fernadina at her breast. He worked as a waiter from six until midnight. From six until nine he was a magician, balancing stacks of trays and dishes on his shoulders and arms as he whisked from kitchen to dining room, making dishes appear and disappear in a flash, bowing, smiling, acknowledging the nickel tips. After nine, when business slowed, he would study in the back of the restaurant, in the alcove behind the kitchen. When he got home afterward, Mei-yu would awake to rub ointment onto his aching arms and shoulders and fall asleep again before he turned off the lamp. They lived in a different room with another family then, an older Cantonese couple and their grown daughter. The daughter and mother worked in a sweatshop; the father peddled candy and newspapers on the corner down the street. The Cantonese man and woman muttered and rolled their eyes, huddling together as if in defense of Kung-chiao and his family. "Are we rats to them?" Kung-chiao once asked Mei-yu when he entered the room and heard the hissing intake of breath. The daughter slammed doors and crashed plates together in the kitchen they shared. Both families cursed the Community Housing Council for putting them together, like caging lions and bears in the same pen. But housing was desperately short. At night, separated by a frayed curtain strung the length of the room, Mei-yu could hear the daughter complaining loudly in Cantonese to the mother about the stench of Fernadina's diapers and how she had caught Mei-yu stealing from their store of food. "Lies, lies," Mei-yu would whisper hoarsely into Kung-chiao's ear. She had washed the diapers immediately after each changing; she had measured rice from the bag under their bed. She would look at Fernadina sleeping in her box next to their bed. "Cry, scream, little daughter, roar your outrage at these people whose sensibilities are like those of howling monkeys that spit and bare their teeth at their own kind," she had whispered. Even then, Kung-chiao was astonished at the energy Mei-yu gained from her anger. Too enraged to sleep, she would get up to cut, pin, and sew garments by hand, and take them around to the shops on Mulberry Street to sell in the daytime, during the lunch hour. Kung-chiao wondered if she slept at all that first year in Chinatown.

Then, a year later, things began to happen for them. Because of his outstanding record, the university awarded Kung-chiao a complete scholarship. He was then able to reduce his shift waiting tables to the weekends only. Scarcely a month after that, Mei-yu was admitted to an interview with Madame Peng. There, in the dark parlor, she struck her bargain, agreeing to work for the old woman. She would earn more and, better yet, be able to work at home. She could keep Fernadina with her. And then finally, miraculously, an opening appeared on the Community Housing Council list, and with Mei-yu's increased salary, they were able to move into quarters of their own.

The Cantonese couple arranged to be out the night Kung-chiao and Mei-yu moved. They preferred not to witness the Mandarins gaining a better situation in life. The daughter glared out the window. Another family of Cantonese was moving in. They were from the same region, spoke the same dialect, but they had two small children.

This room had been an improvement, Kung-chiao thought, looking around. At least they had privacy. But he knew it was still shabby and noisy, situated as it was, facing Mott Street. At first it had seemed like a haven; it seemed enormous, and Mei-yu shrieked and ran to turn on the tap at the sink next to the two-burner stove. A cooking area to themselves! Mei-yu objected at first to placing Fernadina's crate in the foyer, but Kung-chiao needed to study at night, and she needed to run the sewing machine in the daytime, during Fernadina's nap. Their daughter grew accustomed to the sight of her mother at work at the metal table, and slept peacefully through the sound of the clacking and whirring of the machine.

Kung-chiao touched the sewing machine now at his feet. Mei-yu had left Fernadina with Ah-chin the night they had ventured uptown to fetch the machine. It was too cold a night, she said, and the subways screeched to shatter babies' ears. They sat on the cold metal benches and felt their bodies sway with the rocking motion of the subway car. Each time the train screeched into a station, Mei-yu pressed her hands against her ears. She read the advertisements on the upper parts of the cars: ads for aspirin, radio stations, life insurance. At least the car they were riding in was warm. She stared at the old black man whose legs were wrapped in newspaper, the shabby woman who crouched low over her bag of rags. They seemed to be enjoying their respite from the cold, sitting with their eyes closed, dozing like hens. When Kung-chiao and Mei-yu finally stepped out onto Eighty-sixth Street and Broadway, it had begun to snow, and when they reached Riverside Drive, the wind all but knocked them down, sucking the air out of their lungs. They walked two blocks. Roger's building seemed to have been carved out of stone. It stood, solid and square, between two large redbrick buildings of the same height. It was nothing like the tenements in Chinatown.

Inside the warm, softly lit foyer a man in a dark maroon uniform asked their names and the name of the person they wanted to see. He looked at them from beneath the bill of his guard cap, noticing the snow-flecked yellow faces, the worn padded coats—certainly not made in the U.S., he thought—her flimsy silk scarf, which had slipped down around her neck, his bare, chapped hands. Roger's voice, metallic, crackled over the intercom. "I'll see them, Thomas," he said, in the same tone of voice he used when he admitted the housekeeper, the exterminator.

"So nice to see you," he said, his sharp features crinkling unnaturally as he opened the door, extending his arm for them to come inside. They stood in the foyer of the apartment and tried not to marvel at the tile on the floors, the high ceilings, the polished antique pieces against the wall. Fresh chrysanthemums and tiger lilies stood in a vase underneath the mirror. Mei-yu caught sight of herself and hastily pulled off her scarf and wiped her damp face.

"I'm sorry I couldn't bring you the sewing machine myself," Roger began, taking their coats and hanging them on the coatrack in the foyer. "I suppose I could have brought it on my next visit to your place, but that is three weeks away, and I knew you wanted the machine before then, isn't that right, Mei-yu?"

Mei-yu forced a smile. She knew what he meant.

"I see you are looking at my new acquisition," he said proudly, walking over deliberately to the elegant rosewood table, which stood on legs as long and slim as a crane's. The head of the bird was carved on the front of the piece with the bill and crest flowing in a single fluid line. Roger looked at Mei-yu, who seemed, to Kung-chiao's intense displeasure, mesmerized by the exquisite piece.

"Would you care to guess the value of such a table?" Roger asked. Kung-chiao and Mei-yu looked at each other. After several moments, Kung-chiao found himself muttering that he was not an expert on furniture.

"Hello," Diana said, appearing suddenly in the doorway. She wore a circular plaid skirt and a soft fuzzy sweater with a collar that lay on her collarbone like two petals. Her black hair was short and wavy, permed American style. She wore rose-colored lipstick and rouge, and had lined her eyes with black crayon to make them appear larger, rounder. Mei-yu stared, fingering the thin fabric of her own faded jacket and fearing that Diana would see the shine of her worn trousers. Kung-chiao turned away, not understanding his own embarrassment.

"Will you have coffee?" Diana asked, heading back into the living room. They followed. She was as bold and outspoken as an American woman, Kung-chiao thought, at the same time wondering what it would be like to be kissed by lips smeared like that. She certainly was not modest or demure like a proper Chinese hostess.

"Oh, I'm sorry." Diana laughed, her voice sounding high-pitched. "Or would you prefer tea? I think I have some tea on hand." She spoke in English, English being the language she had been raised in. She never addressed Kung-chiao or Mei-yu by their names, directly. Kung-chiao knew it was mostly because she felt awkward with them, uncomfortable with their poverty. She was young, newly wealthy, and resented feeling awkward with anyone, especially poor relations. But he also knew she did not say their names because she was unsure of her pronunciation. She had not spoken Chinese since she had been a small child.

They sat and drank some overly strong tea and ate the sweet cookies Diana passed around. Roger talked about his business. It was getting more difficult to import things from Hong Kong cheaply these days, he said, but he was managing. Kung-chiao could not tell if his cousin was complaining or boasting. In either case he felt himself growing more and more irritated. The steam radiator against the wall hissed and clanked like a balky locomotive, sounding very much like their own wretched unit at home. Its noise seemed to compete with Roger's monologue. Diana started with each hissing burst and turned to glare at it. Kung-chiao glanced over at Mei-yu and saw how her eyes remained fixed on the radiator, as if acknowledging its success in commanding all the attention in the room.

Finally Diana stood up impatiently, her plaid skirt swirling prettily around her slim ankles. Mei-yu saw that Kung-chiao had seen that as well. She also saw that Diana wore stockings and leather pumps.

"Well," their hostess said, "I suppose, Roger, you should bring the machine in so I can show her how to use it."

"I've seen one before," Mei-yu said quickly. Kung-chiao was an engineer, wasn't he? He could figure it out if she couldn't.

It was black and shiny as a beetle, with brass trim and a carrying case besides. She saw with relief that it worked much the same way as the factory machines in the sweatshop.

"Here. I've wrapped up some butter cookies for your baby," Diana said, giving Mei-yu a napkin filled with the goodies. Mei-yu found herself bowing in thanks. Diana was spoiled, but not a bad person, she thought. It was apparent that even Diana got annoyed with her husband.

"Good-bye," Roger said at the door, smiling so that his eyes shut, like a cat's. "I will see you in three weeks. Have fun with the machine, Mei-yu."

"What did he mean, 'have fun'?" Mei-yu asked Kung-chiao as they got into the elevator going down.

"It's just an expression. He has no idea how we work."

By the tone of his voice Mei-yu knew to drop the matter. She touched the sewing machine, which rested at her feet. She knew its power, the freedom it could give her. She looked at Kung-chiao and then laughed aloud with happiness. When the guard saw them emerge from the elevator, he frowned. It wasn't likely they were laughing because they had stolen that heavy-looking box, but then, why were they laughing like that, and on a night as miserable as this? he wondered.

Kung-chiao was brought abruptly back into the present when the door to their apartment opened and Mei-yu and Fernadina came into the room. When she saw her father sitting at the table, Fernadina pushed in front of her mother's legs and ran to him.

"Ba ba!" She laughed, climbing onto his lap. Her fountain of hair tickled his nose. He saw her scalp in the part of her hair, pink, fragile-looking. He held her close, marveling at how heavy and dense her little body was. She swung her legs as she sat in his lap. Mei-yu came over and put her shopping basket on the table. Kung-chiao could see the three fresh eggs, the bunch of bok choy, the long, thick white radish. Things were better. They had plenty to eat for supper for tonight. He looked up at his wife and smiled.

Friday finally arrived. Mei-yu put a piece of dried fish in Kung-chiao's porridge that morning, for energy, for clearness of thought. He seemed calm. He had slept well. She had awakened several times during the night, turning over to look at his face, to see if he slept. Fernadina seemed to sense her mother's unease in the apartment and sat chewing on a dried fig, watching quietly.

"Don't worry," Kung-chiao said as he opened the door to leave. "I will not bring disgrace to our family, Mei-yu." Then, seriously, "I won't be late."

Mei-yu scrubbed the floor furiously when he had gone. She took all her plates and teacups and teapot off the hinged board, wiped that carefully with a damp cloth, and replaced everything just as they had been. She had done the wash yesterday. She took old newspaper and wiped the window until the greasy smudges disappeared, then smoothed out the bedspread again. It was nine o'clock. At ten o'clock she was to go back to the Union to pick up her pay from Mei-ling. Yesterday, Madame Peng's assistant had seemed satisfied with the new jacket but had not said how much Mei-yu would be paid. "Come back tomorrow," she had said. That seemed to be the song in Chinatown. "Come back tomorrow."

She took the house wallet and slipped it inside her blouse. Fernadina recognized the gesture and ran to open the door. The halls and stairway were pungent with the smell of anise; someone was making red-stewed pork. Perhaps her neighbors were planning a birthday, an anniversary, a celebration that called for meat. A building filled with people knowing good fortune, the rich smells of celebration, could mean only good things, Mei-yu thought.

Next door, in the kitchen of the Sun Wah Restaurant, she found Bao stripping the small leaves from bunches of broccoli. Fernadina placed herself in the chair next to him and put her little hands on the table, as if she were waiting for work to do, too. Mei-yu found another knife for herself. Shen was sweeping the floor of onion and garlic peel.

"Hai, little monkey," Bao said to Fernadina, wagging his paring knife at her. "I have something for you." He got up stiffly from his chair and went over to the refrigerator. He brought back a bowl filled with fresh pearly lichee nuts. Fernadina stuck her finger into the bowl, impaling one of the hollow fruits on her finger. She slipped the fruit into her mouth and sucked happily, tasting the sweetness, inserting her tongue into the hollow where the pit had been. The lichee nut was smooth, fleshy. She could suck on it for a long time.

Mei-yu took up a stalk of broccoli and quickly stripped the peel from the stem. She and Bao worked together silently for a few minutes. The slow, rhythmical sweep of Shen's broom helped soothe Mei-yu's spirit.

"Ai," Bao said, leaning back with exaggerated nonchalance. "Kung-chiao should be describing the building of bridges and canals now, eh, Mei-yu?"

Mei-yu shook her head, laughing nervously. "I suppose so, if that is what his professors require on their exams."

Bao watched the broccoli flowers tremble in her hands. She and Kung-chiao were young, tender, like bamboo shoots, he thought. "Don't worry," he said loudly, returning to his work. "Kung-chiao is intelligent, and quick, too. Perhaps he is already through, and is only sitting there, waiting for the others to finish. Hah! Yes, he is taking a nap now, I can see it."

He laughed with his mouth wide open; Mei-yu could count his teeth. Bao grinned at her and winked. She laughed. She felt affection for him as a niece does for an uncle who spoils her. Bao was one of the few people besides Ah-chin who had befriended her in Chinatown. At first, Mei-yu had avoided the restaurant. The thump of the cook's feet on the floor above them in the morning, his coughing and spitting, his foul language, and his treatment of Shen frightened and repulsed her. He was coarse, brutish, like all the rest of the Cantonese, she thought. She would hurry by the restaurant on her way back from the Union with Fernadina, and would see him sitting at one of the front tables when business was slow, smoking a cigarette. She knew Bao watched them each afternoon, perhaps even arranged to smoke his cigarette at four thirty, when she usually hurried by. She walked with her head bowed, and Fernadina would often look up at her mother, as if to ask why they always went faster when they got near the Sun Wah Restaurant. Sometimes, when Kung-chiao walked with them, Mei-yu would look in the window directly, as if to defy his stares. Kung-chiao told her Bao was harmless, merely a man who carried his restaurant on his back. That was why he often brayed and kicked. As if to prove it to her, he would stop to speak to Bao, and Mei-yu would be forced out of politeness to at least greet the cook. She spoke Cantonese fluently, though reluctantly. Hsiao Pei, her nursemaid, had come from the south and had spoken the dialect with her. Here, in Chinatown, it took on a more boisterous, desperate character. But Bao spoke politely to her, and seemed smitten by Fernadina, who stood regarding him from behind her father's leg. At first Bao gave her dried sour plum suckers. Then rice candy. Fernadina began to pull her mother along when they drew nearer to Sun Wah. Bao would pull out a pork bun, or a tangerine from underneath his apron, to give to her. Fernadina would eat the tangerine right there, resisting her mother's efforts to hurry her along. She would answer Bao's questions in between sections of her tangerine. Tangerines took time to eat. Mei-yu saw the affection grow between the two, and found herself yielding as well. Then one day Bao shoved a package at her, and turned and went back into his kitchen before she could protest and give it back. Later, in their room, she opened it to discover a pair of fresh pork kidneys. She rushed out to buy a small piece of ginger to sauté the kidneys with, but as she cooked them she began to feel misgivings; she resented the sly tactics of the cook, knew he was using bribery to soften her heart. At dinner that evening Kung-chiao scooped up the tender bits of kidney with his rice and said, "See, Bao is a good person. You need not be so haughty and judgmental. There are kind people in Chinatown."

Now, as they sat working together in his kitchen, she finished stripping a stalk of broccoli and looked at him. He worked quickly, unerringly, his knife whisking peel off in long strips. His eyes were small, almost hidden between the puffy lids and the pouches of fatigue underneath. Bloodshot, they looked like the eyes of a man perpetually drunk, but everyone knew Bao drank only beer, after the Sun Wah closed, and on Sundays, when he returned from his visits to his second aunt. His nose was short with round nostrils, and his face always seemed to shine with the oil that spattered from his heated woks. His hair was thin, combed in shiny strands across his freckled scalp. He seemed to sense Mei-yu's eyes on him and shifted in his seat, tossing the last broccoli stalk into a bowl.

"What do you want this evening for your celebration feast?" he said, not looking at Mei-yu. "I saw some very large she-crabs at Kwong's. Or how about a fine steamed sea bass?"

Mei-yu laid down her knife. "I've been thinking, Bao. I have seven dollars here, and will have more in a little while. I want to have a wonderful feast. I want Kung-chiao and our guests to eat as if they lived in the Summer Palace in Peking, and I want green, not black tea. I want roast duck, quail's eggs, the newest, most crisp snow peas, and, yes, she-crabs with black beans and garlic sounds wonderful."

Bao's eyes widened. "How many people, to eat all this food?"

"Kung-chiao and myself, Fernadina, Ah-chin and Ling, her husband, their son, Wen-wen, who is afraid to eat crabs, and then, I would be honored if you would join us too, Bao."

Bao sighed. "Friday is one of my busiest nights. I will be cooking, but perhaps Shen will take care of the other orders and I'll sit at your table for a while. Hai, with all this food, how many days do you plan to sit here in Sun Wah?"

Mei-yu pulled the house wallet out of her blouse and laid the seven dollars on the table. "We've waited three years for this feast, Bao, and we will sit here until we are full." She smiled as she stood up to leave. Both she and Bao knew that even a feast with twenty different dishes would not satisfy them, could not wipe away the memory of those nights past when there had been no food, nights when they had drunk black tea and sung songs, instead.

Kung-chiao had finished the first of his three exams. He sat in the cafeteria, drinking tea, preparing his mind for the next exam in an hour. It had been difficult, more difficult than he had anticipated, but he had done well, he thought, unless the professor had intended to trick everyone with the endless rows of questions that seemed to have no real answers. But Kung-chiao had found answers among the material he had stuffed into his brain. He hoped he had been clear. Suddenly he had a horrible thought, a thought that went through him like a shock. Had he written his answers in English? Had he lapsed into Chinese during those long hours of intense concentration, filling his blue exam books with characters that looked like leaning trees and chicken wire, as his American friend and fellow student John had once described them? He thought he remembered writing in Chinese, and was about to jump out of his seat to run back to the professor to explain that he really was able to write in English, to tell him that it was just a lapse, a mistake. Then he stopped, remembering the horizontal lines in the exam book, and knew that he had to have written in English, because he wrote Chinese in vertical lines. Gradually the images of the pages he wrote came clear to him, and certain words, English words, stretched out horizontally, such as _angles, degrees, support,_ and _pressure._ Goblins were only teasing him, playing tricks on his brain. He laughed to himself with relief. He closed his eyes, knowing he needed to relax, regain his concentration for the next exam.

It was a little before ten o'clock, and Mott Street was quiet when Mei-yu left the Sun Wah Restaurant with Fernadina to walk to the Union. Mrs. Liu was inside her husband's shop behind the counter, measuring out packages of noodles. All the other storekeepers were also inside their shops. The pennants and strings of cheap little dolls and kites fluttered unattended in the stalls lining the street. Because no one hawked them, waved them in her face, Mei-yu stopped to look at a little wooden toy horse with movable legs. Fernadina reached up for it with love on her face. Mei-yu saw the look on her daughter's face. It was a day of celebration, was it not? She took the wooden horse and went inside to pay for it.

When she came out again, she saw two policemen talking to Liu. The policemen were white men, dressed in the New York City Police uniform. Liu's wife had gone to the back of the store, or had gone home. Liu looked at the ground and shook his head slowly, insistently. When the policemen asked him another question, he shrugged his shoulders. He didn't speak English, he was telling them with his averted eyes, his posture of retreat. "Leave me alone," he was saying, "I know nothing." The policemen turned from him and walked in the direction of the Union. Mei-yu slowed her walk on the opposite side of the street, watching them as they paused at the next shop and went inside. Through the window she saw Pan, the greengrocer, throw up his hands as if to hide his face, as if he expected a blow from the police, but the two officers stopped four feet from him, a respectful distance. Mei-yu turned away and hurried on to the Union.

Mei-ling put five wrinkled bills on the table in front of her.

"You can thank Madame Peng for this money," the assistant said. "Colonel Chang's niece was prepared to pay ten, but Madame Peng insisted on fifteen. This is your share."

Mei-yu knew the jacket must have gone for twenty, even twenty-five dollars. Still, this was much more than she had ever gotten before. Two, two dollars fifty was what she had always been paid. She took the bills and put them into her wallet. Mei-ling was busying herself with papers at her desk. The assistant had forgotten about her, or did not want to be thanked or share in her good fortune. Mei-yu turned and left the room.

Outside, she looked up and down the street but did not see the two policemen. She took Fernadina's hand and walked quickly toward Pell Street. She must thank Madame Peng, she thought. The old woman was a benevolent spirit, a kindly aunt, another who spoiled her. Mei-yu walked along quickly, and every now and then would look down at Fernadina, who clutched her little wooden horse to her chest. "If Kung-chiao is as lucky as we are today," she said to her daughter, "we will be singing and crying with happiness tonight, all of us."

Mei-yu paused outside the red door of Madame Peng's apartment. She heard low voices inside. Min-di, the pug, was yapping, from the sound of it, from inside the kitchen. Mei-yu could not make out the words but heard that one voice was a man's, and the other a woman's. She was not certain it was Madame Peng's voice, however. She had never seen or heard Madame Peng angry. The female voice inside was shrill, speaking rapidly and sharply. Mei-yu did not know if Madame Peng lived with anyone else. The old woman had always been alone when Mei-yu came to visit before. Ashamed that she had stopped as long as she had, Mei-yu turned quickly and went back through the cool hallway. She would send a message to Madame Peng to thank her, or ask to see her tomorrow. She should have known, she thought, that no one visited Madame Peng on impulse, unannounced.

Bao's gift to them that evening was to close the Sun Wah Restaurant and push all the tables except the large round one to the side, against the walls. The strips of paper from the string fluttered gaily as he set up a revolving fan near the table. The linoleum floor shone from a recent washing. While during normal business hours Sun Wah seemed dimly lit and people would have to try the door to make sure it was open, tonight Bao had put in a new bright light bulb above the table in the center of the room. Those passing by Sun Wah saw that the two families sitting around the table were celebrating a very special occasion indeed.

Bao had covered the table with a thick white cloth and laid it with his heavy white red-trimmed china. He had carefully picked out the best plates, the ones without chips in the rims. Green tea in squat pots stood steeping. The chopsticks were laid neatly beside each plate; napkins, teacups, and small wineglasses were set at each place. In the kitchen, the she-crabs lay quietly in their crate as the oil in the wok began to sizzle and spit.

Ah-chin's husband, Ling, called to Bao, "Hurry up, old man, bring out the wine so that we may toast Kung-chiao." Ling was short, square, good-natured. Ah-chin sat next to Kung-chiao, who looked wan, but happy. He held Fernadina in his lap. "How does it feel, Kung-chiao?" Ah-chin said, sounding strangely happy and relieved herself. "Do you feel twenty pounds lighter?"

"A hundred pounds lighter," Kung-chiao exclaimed, smiling, shifting

Fernadina to his other knee. She had brought her toy horse. Wen-wen sat opposite them at a safe distance. He sat on a telephone book placed on a chair, his chest barely touching the table's edge. He grasped a chopstick in each hand and watched anxiously for Bao, who he knew usually brought in the food.

Bao came in with the rice wine and filled the glasses of the adults. They raised their glasses to Kung-chiao.

"*Gan bei,* to our scholar," Ling said.

They drank. Mei-yu had been alarmed at how drained Kung-chiao had looked when he had come home. He had held her close and kissed her and told her he thought he had done well, but the exams had been very difficult. Then he took off his glasses, removed his shoes, and lay down on their bed. He fell asleep instantly.

When he woke up an hour later, Mei-yu told him Bao wanted to congratulate him on the completion of his exams and was waiting for him downstairs. Kung-chiao splashed water on his face and changed his shirt. He had sensed his wife's excitement, noticed that there was no pot of rice cooking on the stove, a bright new red ribbon in Fernadina's hair. He knew then what had been planned. Still, he cried out loudly and clapped his hands when he walked into the Sun Wah and found his friends waiting, assembled around the white-covered table. He had known they would be there, but seeing them, nodding and smiling with the happiness that was quick in his own heart, he looked up quickly at the ceiling, afraid that his tears would fall.

Now, Mei-yu thought, he seemed quiet but relaxed, smiling as he leaned back in his chair with Fernadina in his lap. Mei-yu drank a second tumblerful of wine and felt herself growing excited at the dinner to come.

Bao sat down and drank his wine, then jumped up again and ran to the kitchen. They heard him berate Shen, then heard the sizzling and popping noise as things went into the hot fat. It was seven thirty and they were all very hungry.

Finally the first course came, fried dumplings. The dumplings were made with ground pork, seasoned with ginger and scallions, sherry and soy sauce, and were pleated and folded in rolled-out dough rounds. Now they looked like plump, golden-brown little bonnets arranged in a ring on the large platter. Mei-yu passed the vinegar and helped her guests to the tasty appetizers. Wen-wen dissected his dumpling, leaving the meat on the side of the plate and chewing happily on the dough. Fernadina bit a hole in the corner of her dumpling and carefully sucked out the juices before she ate the dumpling in tidy bites. The adults popped the entire dumplings into their mouths, and biting down, felt the hot juices squirt all over inside. Kung-chiao raised his glass.

"To Bao, master of dumplings!"

Bao had just arrived with the platter of crabs glistening in black bean and garlic sauce. For long moments no one talked but concentrated on cracking the crab shells and sucking out the sweet flesh. Mei-yu helped Fernadina poke her fingers through the chambers of the crab body, searching for the parcels of meat and showing her how to suck out the meat from the legs.

Ling raised his glass. "To Bao, master of crabs!"

Bao and Shen arrived with large trays. Now the eating began in earnest. Mei-yu felt her heart swell as Bao put down platters of roast pork spareribs, quail eggs, shrimp with snow peas, spicy chicken with peanuts, roast duck, sautéed new broccoli with delicate yellow buds, beef with oyster sauce, and last and most magnificent, a whole sea bass, a king of a fish resting in a sinuous curve on the plate, dressed with delicate strips of scallion and ginger, steamed just so, the flesh pearly white. The entire company rose and held their glasses high.

"To Bao, master of all cooks!" They clapped their hands and laughed approval as Kung-chiao pulled out a chair for Bao. Mei-yu beckoned for Shen to come to the table. He looked to Bao for permission, but Bao was already deep into his explanation to Ah-chin about how he happened to get the fish from Kwong that morning, how he had bid against and triumphed over two other cooks. Shyly Shen took a seat next to Wen-wen and nodded his head in thanks as Mei-yu poured him a cup of tea.

For an hour there was little talk but exclamations of delight at the food in front of them. The rice bowls were held in hands and raised to their lips, and chopsticks rapidly tapped the food into their mouths. Mei-yu picked out choice morsels from the platters and presented them to her guests. Finally all that remained were some peas and the spine of the fish. Fernadina was the first to sigh and drop her chopsticks with a clatter onto her plate. She picked up her horse and pretended to let him graze on the tablecloth, walking him carefully between the drops of grease around her plate. Wen-wen dropped a shrimp on the floor and burst into tears. Ah-chin put her chopsticks on her plate and picked him up to rest in her lap, his head under her chin. His shiny black hair was damp. His mother put her face against it, all the while humming to soothe him.

Bao leaned back and reached for the toothpicks on the table behind him. Ling took a toothpick and sucked on the tidbits poked from the cracks between his teeth. Mei-yu looked around the table. Her guests looked happy, satisfied.

Ling drank the last of the wine from his glass. He looked at Kung-chiao across the table from him, the picture of a contented man, he thought. Then he felt shame as he knew suddenly that he envied Kung-chiao, envied him bitterly. Kung-chiao was not his friend at first, but the husband of his wife's friend. Ah-chin had told him about the serious, white-faced young woman from Peking she had met at the nursery; how she spoke Cantonese as well as Mandarin, how lonely she seemed. One day Mei-yu stopped in at their bakery and bought a moon cake for Fernadina, and he spoke to her and sensed the vulnerability behind the mask she assumed. Then one evening the two couples and their children met in the park, and talked, and grew friendly. They began to share meals, and the women left their children with each other when either had errands to do.

Ling had known all along that Kung-chiao was a scholar, that soon he would finish school and go beyond Chinatown. Ling himself was from Canton, like his wife. He knew the Wongs were from Peking and suppressed the thoughts he had on certain evenings after their visits at how strange their friendship was, like four fish swimming against the currents of the other fish in their school. He never thought beyond the time of their visits, but enjoyed Kung-chiao's wit, his ease with his neighbors, his recognition and acceptance of his place in Chinatown. Perhaps, Ling thought bitterly, Kung-chiao could be relaxed and easy because he knew he would be leaving Chinatown soon. It was the confidence the Mandarins had that grated on him and other Cantonese so. It was that air of superiority, of prior knowledge, of culturedness. But Kung-chiao was not arrogant, or like any of the other Mandarins. Ling realized that. He also finally realized, to his sorrow, that even with their feelings of affection and kinship toward each other, there would always be this insurmountable barrier between them, the scholar and the simple workman, the one from the north, the one from the south.

Ling felt the sadness overcome him. Kung-chiao and his family would be departing soon, leaving him behind to toil endless hours in his stifling-hot little shop, peddling black bean buns and rice cakes and moon cakes. Perhaps he would go to school himself. But the idea was preposterous, and he chided himself as a foolish man for even thinking it; he knew hardly enough English to greet the Americans who came into his shop. He looked over at Ah-chin. She was hugging and rocking Wen-wen, rocking herself as well; he knew she was as tired as he. Life was endless toil, endless fatigue. He was exhausted even as he lay in sleep. Wen-wen had stopped whimpering. Wen-wen, his frightened, round-faced son. Ling wondered if he would feel envy, or even greater sorrow, when his son grew old enough to fly away.

Overcome by these thoughts, and made even more bold by the wine, Ling stood up.

"I want to congratulate Kung-chiao again," he said, "for the successful completion of his schooling, and for what will surely be a bright future."

Ah-chin looked at her husband proudly. He caught her glance, and raised his glass, feeling suddenly like a truly generous man. "And I want to say, Bao," he continued, turning to the cook, who was wiping his shiny face with his apron, "that never, never have I eaten a more wonderful meal, and that I shall be a lucky man if I ever have one again half as delectable, half as tasty, half as wonderful . . ." He saw Ah-chin begin to frown. Too much wine, her eyebrows said. He looked around, seeing the nodding and beaming faces that agreed with him, and sat down, satisfied. Later, Ah-chin saw how he stared at the tablecloth, and her heart sank within her because she knew the reason behind his change of mood. She looked at her friend, Mei-yu, who sat looking radiant. A baker had an honorable profession; she and Ling lived a life of dignity in hard work, she thought fiercely to herself, hugging Wen-wen and forcing herself to smile.

Kung-chiao stood up. "I give thanks to you all, my friends, for gathering here tonight. I have been extremely fortunate in having friends such as you, and Mei-yu, my wife, thanks you. . . ." From somewhere behind him he heard a door open and saw Bao's eyes turn in that direction. "We have lived in Chinatown for four years now," he continued, and then stopped. Ling had shifted his chair so abruptly that it scraped the floor loudly. Kung-chiao saw Mei-yu's face turn suddenly pale, and the tears that had been shining in them tumbled down her cheeks not as tears of joy but as tears of fear. He turned to face the two policemen in their dark blue uniforms. Their metal buttons and badges shone bright under the center light.

The policemen stood blocking the way to the front door. One looked at the platters of what had been their feast on the table. Later, Ah-chin said she could hear him sniffing at the lingering aromas, as if he hadn't had his supper yet.

"Which one of you is Wong?" one policeman, the taller one, said.

There was silence. The policeman looked directly at Ling. "Are you Wong?"

Wen-wen began to whimper. Fernadina stared at the buttons on the officers' uniforms, which were as bright as the scales on a fish.

"Are you Kung-chiao Wong?" the other officer asked Bao. The cook sat silent, sucking on his toothpick.

Kung-chiao stood up. "I am Kung-chiao Wong. What do you want? I have done nothing wrong."

"We have a warrant to search your apartment."

Kung-chiao's throat tightened so he could barely speak. "What do you seek? I have nothing of value, nothing to hide."

The taller officer pulled out the warrant. "We have a man who says you gave him money to keep him quiet because he found out about your gambling deals. We believe you may have accounts of your dealing in your apartment."

Kung-chiao turned to the figure who stood in the shadow just outside the doorway. "Who is this man?" Kung-chiao said, scarcely noticing that Mei-yu had stood and was now gripping his arm.

The officer beckoned to the figure. "We have witnesses who say they saw you give money to this man three days ago in front of this restaurant."

The figure came forward slowly. Bao stood up, knocking his chair over. "Dog!" he cried. "Curse the day your mother bore you!"

The man stepped just inside the entrance, his face tinted green from the flashing neon sign above the Sun Wah Restaurant. It was Wo-fu.

○ ○ ○

"So, Wo-fu," Kung-chiao said, his voice cold. "A nickel brought you far more than a token, did it not?"

Wo-fu's face was impassive. He stepped aside as the officers directed Kung-chiao past him toward the entrance, then followed, pressing himself alongside the shorter officer. Like a slinking dog, Mei-yu thought. Ah-chin tried to hold her back, but Mei-yu turned with such anguish on her face that her friend took hold of Fernadina's hand instead. Fernadina allowed Ah-chin to hold on to her hand, but her eyes followed her parents as they were escorted out of the Sun Wah Restaurant by the police. "Ba ba!" she called, but her father did not hear her.

Mei-yu knew better than to speak now, to ask Kung-chiao the many questions that pushed their way to the tip of her tongue. They walked up the stairs to the apartment, the taller officer ahead of Kung-chiao, the shorter one behind Wo-fu, and she, last. The hallway still smelled of stewed pork and anise. Their apartment door swung open easily, although Mei-yu knew they had locked it before they had left to go to Sun Wah, hours ago. She turned to tell this to the officers, but something inside her warned her to be careful, to avoid the risk of a gesture or a word, anything that might be interpreted by the policemen as guilt. She felt herself shrinking, sucking back inside herself.

The policemen first surveyed the shabby room, then quickly walked around and began their search, looking under the bed, around the metal table. Wo-fu stood in the foyer behind Kung-chiao and Mei-yu, who watched the officers with stunned faces. Wo-fu coughed, and Mei-yu, suddenly remembering him, turned and was about to speak to him when Kung-chiao gripped her arm and shook his head. Wo-fu was worthy of nothing but contempt, his eyes said. She turned and watched again as the officers continued to go through their few belongings. She saw the pages of the calendar flutter as one officer opened the wardrobe and searched among their clothes. The other policeman came over and demanded to see their identification papers. Kung-chiao went to the wardrobe and pulled out the shoebox that held all their valuable things; their wedding certificate, the photographs of their families in China, his student visa. Mei-yu closed her eyes when the officers, satisfied with their search of the bedroom, approached her, standing in the foyer. She took a step backward, then realized they were not coming for her, but were pulling down the padded coats that she and Kung-chiao had hung on the pegs, lifting the mattress of Fernadina's bed. It was as if they were assaulting her child, pulling her bed apart like that. She began to cry out, then stopped abruptly as the officer straightened and held up a notebook. He showed it to the other officer, paging through it quickly. Both Kung-chiao and Mei-yu could see the columns of figures.

"Is this yours?" the taller officer asked Kung-chiao.

"No."

"Is this the notebook you were talking about?" the officer said to Wo-fu.

"Yes," Wo-fu said.

"He lies," Kung-chiao said, turning to Wo-fu.

"The notebook speaks for itself," Wo-fu said, not looking at Kung-chiao.

"But our door was open, and I knew we locked it when we left tonight," Mei-yu said, hearing her voice rise out of herself in spite of Kung-chiao's look of warning. "Someone put the notebook there while we were gone!"

She looked into the faces of the officers. "If Kung-chiao were dealing, as you say, why would he give this man money in full view of witnesses? Isn't it clear what is happening here?" Terror crept into her voice, for although she knew with absolute certainty that Kung-chiao was innocent, she also knew that the evidence was there for all to see.

"Why did you scream when I pulled up the mattress?" the tall officer asked her.

Mei-yu looked at him quickly, seeing nothing behind his eyes. "Fernadina . . . my daughter, sleeps there . . . that is her bed." She stopped, unable to explain. The forces affecting her and Kung-chiao were too large, too shadowy for her to understand, much less make clear to the officers. Doubt was beginning to show on their faces, convincing her that any further attempt at explanation would be futile.

The policemen looked at Wo-fu, then at Kung-chiao.

"We'll have to ask you to come to the station for questioning," the taller officer said.

Kung-chiao nodded, then looked at Mei-yu. Her hair, which had been pulled back smooth from her face for the dinner, had escaped from its clip and now hung in wild wisps around her face. Her eyes were swollen with fear.

"How long will I be detained? Will I be able to come home tonight?" he asked the tall officer.

"I can't say," the policeman said, looking at his watch. His partner was already at the door, waiting.

Kung-chiao turned to his wife but, because of the strangers, did not touch her. "Stay with Ah-chin and Ling, Mei-yu. They have a phone at the bakery. I will call you there."

"C'mon, let's go." The officer at the door reached over and grasped Kung-chiao by the arm. Kung-chiao tried to pull his arm away. The officer's partner came over and took his other arm. Kung-chiao became still, but Mei-yu could see the anger in his face. What right did they have to take Kung-chiao away? What was the law in this land, that men in uniform could come and take innocent people away from their homes? Mei-yu stared at the officers, seeing their grip on her husband. Suddenly she felt certain that if Kung-chiao left now, she would never see him again.

"Don't go, Kung-chiao," she cried, taking hold of his hand, as if to pull him away from the officers.

"Please, Mei-yu," Kung-chiao said, his voice shaking, "there is nothing to worry about." He looked at the policemen. "I have done nothing wrong. They will release me as soon as they realize that. Right now, I have no choice but to go with them."

She turned her head from his face. She could see the pistols in the officers' holsters for herself.

The policemen escorted Kung-chiao from the apartment. Wo-fu followed close at their heels. Mei-yu stood frozen in the middle of the room, listening to the footsteps growing faint. Then suddenly she remembered her daughter. She slammed the door after her, hearing the lock click, then ran down the stairs.

Later, an officer from the Fifth Precinct called Ling's Bakery to say they would not be releasing Kung-chiao that night; they needed more time to question him, as well as other witnesses. In spite of her friends' urging, Mei-yu decided to return home. Ling and Ah-chin shared a room with another Cantonese couple, two blocks away from the bakery, and Mei-yu knew her presence would mean that her friends would insist on giving her their bed for the night, and that they would have to sleep on the floor. Ah-chin, seeing how her friend would not be persuaded otherwise, pressed a bag of black bean cakes into her hand and watched as she carried Fernadina, who had fallen asleep long ago in her arms, out of the bakery.

"Try not to worry, Mei-yu," Ling said as he walked with her back to Mott Street. Sightseers jammed against them on the sidewalk. The restaurants on either side of the street were busy, filled with the Friday night crowd of Manhattanites on their after-theater jaunt to Chinatown. The streetlights and the lights from within the restaurants illuminated the night. It was as if the night had been transformed; not into a day of sunlight, but into a day of phosphorescence, where people jostled into one another, grinning, green-skinned. Ling worried about Mei-yu, who walked along as if in a trance. She seemed not to notice the people who bumped against her, holding on to Fernadina only more tightly, hugging her close.

"It is Colonel Chang's work," he said in Cantonese, his voice low, his mouth close to Mei-yu's ear. His eyes looked to either side of the street for figures in the shadows of the doorways, in the alleys. He pulled Mei-yu aside, out of the stream of people. He had wanted to warn her in the bakery, but had not wanted to mention the name in front of his wife, who was frightened enough.

"I'm sure it is Colonel Chang," he repeated. "He has put the scent on Kung-chiao so that the police will let go of his leg and sniff elsewhere. They were getting too close."

Mei-yu looked at Ling. "What am I to do? How can I prove Kung-chiao's innocence?"

"I don't know much about the law," Ling said, "but I don't think Kung-chiao has been charged with anything yet. From what you tell me, the entire scheme was carried out clumsily. Perhaps the police have already seen through Wo-fu and are merely holding Kung-chiao, playing along with Colonel Chang, waiting to see what he will do next."

"But what if they do suspect Kung-chiao? They looked as if they believed the notebook was his," Mei-yu said, feeling the panic rising within her again. "We have no lawyer. Who will help us?"

"I will, Ah-chin will," Ling whispered fiercely. "Bao will. If you need a lawyer, we will find one. Don't give up hope, Mei-yu. Right now, I think we simply must wait and be patient." Ling shrugged his shoulders helplessly. He could see that Mei-yu's thoughts preoccupied her, and he gave up his attempts to reassure her. They continued down Mott Street. He was relieved when they reached the Sun Wah Restaurant and saw Bao standing out in front, smoking. The interior of the restaurant was dark. The cook flicked his cigarette away and reached out to take Fernadina from Mei-yu. Realizing there was nothing further to say, Ling turned to go home. Mei-yu put her hand on his arm.

"I am sorry, Ling. You have helped me very much. Thank you, and thank Ah-chin for me also."

Ling waved and walked away.

"Bao," Mei-yu said, the sight of the kindly cook bringing tears to her eyes again.

"Shh, shh, you'll wake the little plum," he said.

"Thank you, Bao, for tonight. It was a splendid dinner. Kung-chiao was honored and pleased—" she stopped, fearing the trembling in her voice.

"We'll have much time later to remember the evening," Bao said. "Now you must rest." It was late. He had sensed Kung-chiao would not be coming home that night. He did not mention Kung-chiao but carried Fernadina, still asleep, up the stairs behind Mei-yu. He looked around the apartment when Mei-yu turned on the lamp and, seeing the disarray of the child's bed, laid her gently down on her parents' bed. He put his hand briefly on Mei-yu's shoulder, then went back down to help Shen lock up.

Mei-yu sat on the bed and smoothed a strand of hair from Fernadina's face. The child's fountain of hair had come loose; her new red ribbon lost. At least she had not seen the policemen walking through their room, picking up, dropping their things, pushing aside the photographs in the shoebox, Mei-yu thought. She looked over at Fernadina's bed, at the pulled-up mattress, the sheets that spilled over the sides of the crate. She shivered, feeling cold in spite of the hot night. She had known that cold feeling before. She had felt it as a girl in China, when the Japanese had pushed their way into her family's home. The first time they had come, in the summer, Mei-yu had merely been startled, as if she had been overtaken suddenly by a thunderstorm. Thunderstorms, she knew, were violent but were over quickly, leaving the air clear. The Japanese, however, kept coming back. "Why are they here? Why do they keep coming?" she asked her mother. Her mother had no answer.

Mei-yu remembered one day when she, her two brothers, her mother, and the two nursemaids were sitting down to breakfast. They heard the tinkling of the front gate bell. Mei-yu remembered seeing her mother, Ai-lien, stiffen. The gate bell had sounded every morning for a week now, and at the same time, while they were having breakfast. Moments after the bell sounded they heard the sound of boots crunching in the courtyard outside. After that came the pounding on the door. On this day, Hsiao Pei rose and opened the door. The Japanese officials swept in. In the beginning they had been polite. Now, on the eighth day, they were familiar with this kitchen and dropped all formalities. They passed Ai-lien without acknowledgment, kicked up the rug, poked under the stove. Mei-yu saw her mother holding her hands down before her, saw her eyes stare at the floor.

"How many people in this household?" the Japanese official asked. He took out the familiar notepad.

"Seven," Ai-lien said. "Seven, as always."

The Japanese walked over to where Mei-yu and her brothers sat and stared at them. Ai-lien moved to stand between him and her children.

The official turned to her abruptly. "Where is your husband?"

"In his study, preparing for his classes."

"We want to speak to him."

Ai-lien bowed, her eyes continuing to stare at the floor.

Mei-yu quietly followed the Japanese officials to her father's study and stopped, unseen, outside in the hallway. Pressing herself against the wall opposite the room, she could just see the figures of her father and the officials. The senior Japanese official leaned across the desk, thrusting his face close to Chen Yuan-ming.

"We know you have been holding meetings in your house," the official said.

Yuan-ming remained seated. "They are university matters," he said, finally. "You need not be concerned."

"We will decide what we will be concerned about, Chen," the official snapped. "These meetings will cease."

Yuan-ming's eyes remained on the papers in front of him. "As you wish," he said.

The official noted the direction of Yuan-ming's glance.

"What are those?"

"Notes for my lecture today."

"Give them to me."

Yuan-ming leaned back in his chair, moving his hands away from his papers in a gesture of release.

"I want you to hand them to me," the official said, leaning further forward.

Yuan-ming took the papers and extended them. He remained seated.

The Japanese official stood still. "I can't reach them," he said.

Mei-yu saw her father rise halfway from his straight-backed chair and hand the sheaf of paper to the official. He sat back down, quietly.

The official glanced through the papers. Then, walking around behind Mei-yu's father, he began to inspect the bookcase against the wall. Mei-yu knew her father's favorite books were there, books written in English; the novels of Dickens, the poetry of Donne, Shakespeare's plays. The official selected one book, riffled through it casually, snapped it shut with a clap. Then he dropped it on the floor. Mei-yu saw her father start, then hold himself very still. The official continued to select books from the case, sometimes leafing through one slowly, as if browsing, sometimes opening another one not at all. One by one they fell onto the floor. Mei-yu heard the backs of the books break as they landed, saw the pages crumple underneath the heavy bindings. Finally the Japanese official seemed satisfied. He signaled to his companion. Mei-yu ran noiselessly down the hall to her bedroom next door. She heard the officials' boots as they left her father's study and proceeded out into the courtyard. Then she heard her father's voice, sounding clear.

"Ai-lien!"

Mei-yu heard the soft shuffle of her mother's footsteps as she came to the entrance of the study.

"Please ask Tsu-lu to prepare some savories for this evening, after supper. I am expecting guests."

"Please, Yuan-ming, it is too dangerous, especially now."

"Ai-lien!"

Mei-yu knew the will behind the voice.

"As you wish," she heard her mother say, softly.

Did uniforms give men everywhere leave to enter people's homes? Mei-yu wondered, laying her head down next to her sleeping daughter. Kung-chiao had been mistaken. It was no different here. She closed her eyes, thinking that if she slept, the memory of the Japanese, the more recent memory of the police, would vanish. Still, later, in her dreams, she thought she heard the sounds of book backs cracking.

On Sunday, two days later, Kung-chiao came home. His shirt was damp, oily; a stubble grew above his mouth and on his chin. He sighed when Mei-yu put a bowl of porridge and a cup of tea in front of him. His right eye twitched with fatigue. Fernadina sat on his lap, listening as he slurped his tea wearily, smelling the unfamiliar odors of stale smoke and sweat on his clothes.

"They weren't unkind," Kung-chiao said. "But they kept asking me things I knew nothing about. At first I was angry, and I was ashamed to be so weak in showing my anger. But then I realized that by being angry I might actually make them believe me. I think they were surprised, perhaps because of my English, and then because no Chinese had ever spoken to them openly before, even through a translator. I think they knew I was being as cooperative as I could. I don't know why they let me go. Perhaps just so they could watch me. I think we must be careful, Mei-yu."

"Careful of what, Kung-chiao?" Mei-yu said. "Who are we to watch out for? The police? Colonel Chang? How can we see through shadows? Are we to look over our shoulders everywhere we go?"

Kung-chiao sighed. "I don't know. While I was at the station I kept thinking I should find a way to fight Colonel Chang, to expose his scheme. But how can a man like me fight forces like his? Then, I thought, it would be safer just to lie low, and try to leave Chinatown as soon as possible. I don't know. Perhaps we should just stay here in the room for a few days. Perhaps Ah-chin could bring us food. I'm too tired. I can't think straight. Just let me rest awhile. I'll be able to think more clearly in the morning. Go now, Fernadina. Please, Mei-yu."

Mei-yu led Fernadina away, then ran hot water for Kung-chiao to wash his face and torso. Afterward, he lay on their bed. His body seemed shrunken, like that of a young boy, Mei-yu thought. He fell asleep quickly, his breathing coming in long and deep. He had not spoken like the Kung-chiao she knew. Perhaps it was as he said, fatigue was clouding his mind. But surely he would find a way to confront whoever it was who was doing this to him. He had always found ways before. She covered him with the bedspread, then sat at the metal table and poured herself a cup of tea. Fernadina came to her and put her toy horse in her mother's hand. Mei-yu took the toy and fingered the smooth wood, then the grooves where the mane and tail had been carved. Her eyes returned again to the door. Would the police come back? Would Colonel Chang send men to threaten them? Threaten them for what reason? She looked over at Kung-chiao, asleep on the bed. His breathing was barely perceptible under the light spread.

"Kung-chiao," she said softly. "What is happening to us?" He slept on soundly. She felt Fernadina's hand on her arm. Mei-yu picked up her daughter and buried her face against the child's chest. She heard the rapid, light heartbeat. She drew her head back and gazed into her daughter's face. It was then that she saw the resemblance, in the curve of the brow, in the set of her dark, wide-set eyes. For the first time Mei-yu saw her father, Yuan-ming, reflected in Fernadina's face. Now she needed his counsel, longed to hear the voice that was measured and calm. "Stay quiet," he had always said whenever she ran to him with her childhood fears. "Summon your strength, daughter." He had placed his hand on her head, and she had felt the spreading warmth of his fingers. Her fears had fled then. *Stay quiet*, Mei-yu said silently to herself, pressing her forehead against her child's chest, listening to the heartbeat, listening to her own voice, which repeated only, *What is happening to us now?*

"The police released Wong this afternoon. They must not have believed Wo-fu's story."

The man speaking was tall, thin, dressed in a dark gray American business suit. He sat on the silk-covered sofa. In his hand he held a cigarette from which curled thick, sweetly pungent smoke. A man sat opposite him in a bamboo chair. A third man stood at the window in front of the drawn curtains, his back to the other two.

"The police are hoping he will lead them to us," said the man sitting in the bamboo chair.

The two men looked at each other, waiting for a response from the third one at the window.

"We think he knows who set him up," said Tam, the man on the sofa. "We think he knows about Wo-fu and us." He traded glances again with his partner. Several seconds went by. Tam noticed that his tea in the delicate porcelain cup no longer steamed; they had been sitting there for over fifteen minutes.

"We do seem to find ourselves in a rather precarious situation, do we not?" Colonel Chang said finally, stepping from the window and advancing to join the others in the circle of light glowing from the lamp next to the sofa. He was of medium height, compact, his hair growing thin and clipped at the sides so that it bristled on end. His face was round, heavy, developing the jowls of old age. His eyes were small, full-lidded, seeming to sleep. But his men knew better. They pulled their knees together and drew themselves up when he joined them.

"It is such a precarious situation," he continued, looking slowly from one man to the other, "that it could only have been engineered by imbeciles!" He spat the last word. He was angry with his men, but angrier with himself for not having had his son, Yung-shan, take care of the matter. Yung-shan! Ah, what to do with his son! He had been distant these days, tending the books and taking care of the office, quietly finding excuses for not tending to certain matters, personal matters that were essential to the continued success of their business. He had been too lenient with his son, Colonel Chang thought. He had become soft, like an American, lacking authority. It would never have been like this in China. He gingerly touched the sore that had mysteriously appeared on his neck weeks ago. He looked at the man sitting on the sofa.

"Your tea is cold, Tam," he said, ringing a brass bell. He looked down at the man sitting in the bamboo chair. "So, Lee, what do you propose now?"

Lee shifted in his chair. "I think it is obvious," he began.

Colonel Chang fixed his eyes on him. "Obvious? What is obvious, Lee?"

Lee looked up at the Colonel quickly, then lowered his eyes to stare at the rug at his feet. "That we should kill him," he said at last, expelling his breath with the words.

Colonel Chang was motionless for several moments. Then he showed all his teeth as he smiled at Lee.

"That is an interesting idea, Lee. I am afraid it was not obvious to me at all, I must say."

The hot tea arrived. Colonel Chang sipped his carefully. When the servant had left, Colonel Chang looked around for a place to set his cup down. Then, smiling, as if in apology, set it on the flat arm of Lee's bamboo chair. Lee held his right arm away from the cup with his left hand, close to his side.

"But I have a question for you, Lee," Colonel Chang said. "If it is true that the police are watching Wong, and I agree with you that they are, for why else would they have let him go? If this is true, Lee, then who do you think they would suspect if Wong were killed?"

Lee was prepared for this. "Wong could have an accident. No one would be able to link his death to us."

"Ah!" Colonel Chang smiled and clasped his hands behind his back. "So you believe this Wong really capable of doing us harm? You think he knows we were using him as our pigeon and that he would turn the police on us?" He turned to the other man. "What do you think, Tam? Do you agree?"

Tam crushed his cigarette, using the time to choose his words carefully. He knew the Colonel's game. "Although I have respect for Lee's suggestion," he said finally, "I myself look at it differently. I don't think Wong is that kind of man. He is a student, a scholar. Only a small man. To kill him would draw attention to ourselves. I think we should wait. We don't know what the police are thinking."

"So." Colonel Chang unclasped his hands and walked back to the window. For the first time he was uncertain. In spite of what Tam had said, he knew Wong could be dangerous to them. Lee may have come up with the correct solution, after all. He sighed. It was a curse to grow old. He needed Yung-shan's counsel. He parted the heavy fabric of the curtain and looked out into the morning light, onto the street.

"We have some very good ideas here, don't you think?" He let the curtain drop again, turning to smile at his men. "I will consult Yung-shan, perhaps. He is so clever in these kinds of situations."

The two men exchanged glances. They knew how things were between father and son. They stood up, however, recognizing that they had been dismissed. They bowed and, not looking at the face that scrutinized them from the shadows of the curtains, left the room.

That night, Mei-yu had a dream. She had not had a demon dream since childhood, but this one strangled and clawed at her so that she screamed as she had as a child, only no sound came out of her throat. The demon was part dragon, part snake, writhing along its looped underbelly. It grabbed Mei-yu in its jaws and she struggled to escape, only the demon had seized her so that she stared down its gullet, which was black, and her screams disappeared into its maw as if swallowed by the monster. Sometimes the demon released her, played with her, displaying its claws like scythes and its shining teeth of steel.

Then, in this, her adult dream, she saw Kung-chiao. The demon saw that she saw him and turned its scaly head to regard Kung-chiao as well. Then it caught him and began to play with him. It placed its enormous claws over his head, forming a trap, and laughed as Kung-chiao struggled to free himself. Mei-yu tried to run to Kung-chiao but could not move. Her limbs were heavy and would not obey her will. Kung-chiao opened his mouth but no sound came out. She watched as the demon released Kung-chiao and then caught him again, only this time she heard the noise, the rumbling coming from the beast's belly, and she knew what was to come. She struggled to move her legs, to run to Kung-chiao, but could not. Then she watched in horror as the demon grasped Kung-chiao in its jaws and sank its teeth into him, and then swallowed him. Then, grinning, the demon curled up, its scales rasping as its body coiled into a smaller, tighter ball. It began to spin, and flatten out, and throw off many different colors: red, yellow, purple, green. It spun faster, still faster, grew flat, like a disk, and then disappeared. It turned into another dream. But Mei-yu woke up remembering only the demon and what it had done to Kung-chiao. "Listen and heed your dreams," she remembered her nursemaid, Hsiao Pei, saying, "for they are the only truth." Knowing the meaning of this, her most terrible dream, Mei-yu knew at last what she must do.

○ ○ ○

Kung-chiao awoke Monday morning and shaved carefully. He stood in front of the mirror over the sink and put on the blue American jacket and striped tie Roger had given him. They were the only pieces of clothing Kung-chiao had accepted from his cousin, and he had accepted them only because Roger insisted that now that he was in America, he would be looked upon favorably only if he dressed like the Americans, and assumed their manner as much as possible. His cousin had also been vague about the interview he had helped arrange, saying his friend at the city bureau could promise Kung-chiao nothing beyond a place on the interview roster. It had taken a great deal of persuasion just to get his name on the list, Roger had said. Kung-chiao had thanked his cousin adequately for the favor, he thought. Now his slender fingers probed nervously at the knot in the tie he had tied around his neck.

Mei-yu watched him from her place at the table where she was giving

Fernadina her congee. Earlier, before her husband had risen, she had stood in front of the same mirror and had seen how pale she looked. Still, she tried to act as if she were calm. She had decided not to tell him about her dream.

She saw that the blue American jacket was far too large for Kung-chiao; the shoulders too wide, the lapels flapping on either side of his chest. It was as if the jacket mocked him, his serious expression, she thought. She recognized that look in his face, the unblinking eyes and set mouth. He had dressed that morning, seemingly without awareness of her or Fernadina. Mei-yu knew the stillness of his attitude stemmed from a deep concentration. She had first seen that look in China, before they had left. She saw it again afterward, whenever Kung-chiao studied, when he left to take his exams. She realized it existed in herself as well, and she saw it mirrored in Fernadina, too, even at this early age. Her daughter played with her horse with purpose, making it behave according to a plan she had in her child's mind.

Still, as much as she felt Kung-chiao's strength this morning, he seemed strange to her in these borrowed clothes, and her fear returned. The demon dream was still too real to her.

"Kung-chiao," she began, hearing her voice break into the stillness between them, "remember what you said about not going out for a few days, to watch and wait, here . . ."

Kung-chiao turned to her, his fingers still at the knot in his tie.

"I was not myself yesterday," he said, seeing the uncertainty in her face. "We cannot be afraid, living like animals in their burrows."

Mei-yu thought of what Ah-chin and Ling had said, of Colonel Chang's men being everywhere, watching everything and everyone. "Please, Kung-chiao," she said, helplessly.

He sighed impatiently. "I will not embarrass Roger, who has arranged this interview for me. There is the chance I may get the position. It would be a very important step. I would be a fool not to go."

Mei-yu hated the sound of dismissal in his voice. He would not even acknowledge that he was in danger. She watched him wipe the lenses of his steel-framed spectacles and hook the endpieces over his ears. He looked stern, old. She looked away when he turned in her direction.

"Will you be going out today?" he asked, his voice gentle again.

"Yes. I have errands to do."

"Mei-yu." He came over and put his hands on her shoulders. "There is nothing to be afraid of, really, believe me. We simply must be a little more careful, that is all. If you think someone is following you, or watching you, go sit with Bao in the restaurant, or stay with Ah-chin at the bakery. You will be safe there."

Mei-yu pulled away. "I can take care of myself! I do not want to involve our friends in this matter!"

Kung-chiao stepped back, surprised. He saw his wife's lips trembling. She avoided his eyes.

"You are right, of course," he said finally. "I am certain you will be all right. Will you wish me luck, though, today?"

Mei-yu embraced her husband but was still reluctant to look him in the eyes. She wanted to hold on to his arm in the American jacket, but he pulled away gently.

"Good-bye," he said.

"Good-bye, Kung-chiao," she said.

Kung-chiao brushed Fernadina's face with his fingers and left.

The Union was not busy that morning and Mei-yu was relieved to see that Ah-chin had already left Wen-wen there. She did not want to meet any person who might be interested in where she went. She kissed Fernadina good-bye, and waited until her daughter turned her attention to one of the many books lying on the floor. The child grasped a book by the binding and opened it out on her lap. As soon as she was absorbed in its pages, Mei-yu quietly left the nursery.

She hurried down Mott Street, then headed east, where she knew the business offices of Chinatown were located. She stopped abruptly in front of one of the redbrick buildings, as if she had changed her mind, then walked quickly beyond the building toward a tiny tea shop in the middle of the block. She had been careful; no one had followed her.

Mei-yu entered the tea shop and was glad the owner was busy talking to his customers. She slipped, unnoticed, to the back of the shop, where she knew there was a telephone. She, like most of the people of Chinatown who had no telephones in their homes, knew where the public phones were in cases of emergency. She sat in the dark booth and gathered her thoughts together. There was no other way. All she could remember were the words he had left her with when she had last seen him. Only she could prevent him from going further, from carrying out his threat.

She had to look up his number in the tattered telephone book. There were at least twenty listings under his family name. She found his. Her fingers poked numbly at the rings in the dial. She dialed once and then hung up, unable to imagine what she would say, how she would say it.

Finally she dialed the number again and listened to the ringing at her ear, hoping he would not be there, that she had gotten one of the wrong names.

"Hello," he said.

She knew his voice. "Yung-shan," she said, her voice not her own. "It is I, Mei-yu."

Later that afternoon, Kung-chiao left the city office building and pulled at the knot in his tie, loosening it. He inhaled deeply and removed his jacket. He stood on the stone steps, recalling the words of the personnel supervisor with the disbelief that had finally displaced his initial anger.

"You seem well qualified, Mr. Wong," the supervisor had said from behind his large cluttered desk. "But we are looking for someone with more experience. I can refer you, though, to the janitorial services department. Perhaps there will be a place for you there."

Before Kung-chiao could speak, the supervisor reached for his phone, dialed, and spoke briefly, swiveling in his chair so that his back was turned to Kung-chiao. After a few moments, during which Kung-chiao heard his name being spelled, Wong, W-O-N-G, the supervisor hung up and turned around to face him.

"Room 011, in the basement," he said, standing, his hands in his pockets. "You can apply there."

Kung-chiao turned to leave. "Thank you for your time and effort," he said. "But I am not interested in viewing your basement."

Outside the supervisor's office he passed the others as they sat waiting their turn to be interviewed. He noticed they were dressed in jackets that fit, in trousers with sharp creases. They were all white men.

He had seen his résumé on the supervisor's desk; he knew the man had been aware of his qualifications, his record at the university. He saw no need to beg for a position. He stepped into the elevator and pressed the button for the ground floor.

On the steps of the building outside he stopped to think of the words of his advisor at the university, who had warned him about the hiring practices of certain companies. He had appreciated Sol's gentleness, his tact, but gentleness and tact had not prepared him for the rudeness of the supervisor.

Kung-chiao decided to walk back home, even though it was more than fifty blocks. He did not feel like hurrying back to answer Mei-yu's questions, to share his burden of humiliation with her. He needed to walk, to stretch his legs, to free his limbs and body from the tension of the past weeks. He looked up into the sky of the city. He began to feel a strange exhilaration, a sense of freedom, freedom from having to study, to adhere to a schedule or a restricted area. Perhaps it was being so far from Chinatown, he thought, as he entered Times Square, that gave him the sensation of freedom. Here, no one knew him. The Chinese of Chinatown seldom ventured out of their bounds. Unless Colonel Chang's men had followed him since morning, and he had been careful, was certain none had, he was the only one of his kind on the busy walks around Forty-second Street. Still, he was not anonymous. People, white people, stared as he passed. He was an oddity, clearly out of his territory, like a migratory bird blown off course.

The shop windows filled with radios, cameras, clothes, and cheap souvenir items fascinated him. Neon lights blinked here, too, flashing above marquees that advertised films of nearly nude women. Kung-chiao stopped to look closely at a picture of a woman that was featured in a glass case outside the theater front. She had wavy silver-blond hair that swept forward over her shoulders. Her enormous breasts seemed to be nestled in little feather cups. Girded around her waist was a belt studded with shiny stones, and streaming from the belt was a diaphanous skirt that stopped just above her silver-slippered feet. Her toenails were painted a deep red. Kung-chiao stood mesmerized in front of this vision, stunned by its excesses. Everything, from her coloring to the abundance of her flesh to the expression on her face, shocked him. He moved ahead hurriedly.

The streets were wide, filled with taxis that rushed and jammed forward into pockets of space like giant angry insects. Inside the taxis Kung-chiao caught sight of elegant-looking men and women wearing dove-colored clothes, hats, even in the heat, and expressions that appeared to armor them against the noise and turmoil and soot of the streets outside. *What do these people do?* Kung-chiao thought as he stared at a man sitting inside a taxi that waited at a red light. The man wore a dark pinstripe suit and held a newspaper up to his face, but he gazed distractedly beyond it, out the window. *Why isn't he at work?* Kung-chiao thought. The light changed, and the taxi roared off.

Farther downtown the buildings reached higher and higher into the sky. Kung-chiao stood at the base of the Empire State Building and looked up, wondering if the people inside it could feel it sway. It was a marvelous structure, an extraordinary feat of engineering, he thought. Most of the buildings in Peking were flat, because an emperor of long ago had decreed that no one could be situated higher than himself; that he must, as a supreme being, look down at everyone from the vantage of his palace, which was built up high. Still, there was nothing in China as high as this building, Kung-chiao thought. He stood for several moments looking up at the skyscraper before he was jostled and forced to move along with the crowd.

Everything was huge, shiny, spectacular. Kung-chiao could feel the strange electricity of the city, as if he had contacted it at the source and pulsed with the current of Manhattan himself. He could feel himself drawn to it, feel its powerful attraction like any other forbidden thing, and suddenly he was overwhelmed with the desire to live in it, to work in it, breathe it. He stopped, shaking his head to clear his thoughts. What was happening to him? Was it the heat, the glare of the sun reflecting from the melting asphalt? He knew Mei-yu wanted to escape Chinatown, but would she want to come to this? Thoughts tumbled in his head like dried peas in the lacquered Chinese rattles. When he finally reached Mott Street, he had forgotten about his interview. There would be other opportunities, at other places. He would talk to Sol again on Tuesday. Perhaps Sol would know of someone who needed his skill, his knowledge.

When Mei-yu set his dinner in front of him, she saw that he had been stricken, enchanted. She was grateful, for then he would not notice the trembling of her hands as she set his bowl down, or ask her about her day and in doing so prompt her to blurt out her confession that she had called Yung-shan and struck her bargain with him, that she would get word to him as soon as she knew when she could get free, and go to him.

She looked over at her husband as he gave Fernadina tidbits from his bowlful of vegetables and rice.

"Kung-chiao," she began.

He looked up, his gaze as usual engaging something deep within her. Only, this time it was as if a lid had slid over a hole inside her, and she said, "Never mind, it's nothing."

For what could she say?

On Tuesday, Mei-yu sat with Bao outside the Sun Wah Restaurant. She embroidered a chrysanthemum on a blouse Mei-ling had ordered for a customer. Mei-yu made three or four of these every week. Her needle pricked the fabric steadily, accurately, burrowing into the design she had drawn as if it had a life of its own. It was good that it did, for Mei-yu's mind was elsewhere. Bao was showing Fernadina a puzzle of interlocking wooden pieces. Fernadina wanted to put them together herself.

"No, no, little plum, you must allow your uncle Bao to reveal his wisdom and show you how to solve the puzzle. Here."

He proceeded to lock two pieces together when Fernadina pointed to the bulge in his apron pocket.

"Hai! You must concentrate, Sing-hua, or you will never learn. This is a complicated puzzle. Mei-yu . . . do you know how it works?"

Fernadina tugged on the cook's apron.

Bao sighed and gave the little girl the puzzle. "Too difficult for me," he said, and pulled out the almond cookie from his pocket. Fernadina took the puzzle and cookie and sat down to ponder one and eat the other.

Bao wanted to ask Mei-yu about the days Kung-chiao had spent at the police precinct but refrained. "Where did Kung-chiao go so soon after lunch today?" he asked her instead.

"To the university, to speak to his advisor. He should be back very soon now." She wound the thread around her needle, making a knot, and bit off the thread.

"Look," said Bao. "Those officers are here again."

Mei-yu looked up. She recognized the officers from Friday evening. Then, from the side of her eye, she saw Kung-chiao coming down the street. The sidewalks were almost empty due to the heat and the hour of the afternoon. Most of the shopkeepers were sitting just inside their shops, fanning themselves. Kung-chiao was about thirty paces away. The police officers walked up to him and he stopped, putting his hands on his hips. They placed themselves on either side of him. Mei-yu stood up, letting the shirt she was working on fall to the ground. Fernadina looked up over her almond cookie. The shopkeepers came out of their shops. Mei-yu could hear Kung-chiao's voice, and the voices of the policemen, but could not tell what they were saying.

"Fools," Bao hissed. "Don't they know it is dangerous for Kung-chiao to be seen in public with them? Look, everyone can see."

Indeed, the shopkeepers had stopped their fanning in order to hear better. Kung-chiao was shaking his head vigorously, angry. The police said something. He shook his head. He made a chopping motion with his hand, as if to sever any more talk with the police, and walked away from them. They did not follow.

"What did they want?" Mei-yu asked when he drew close.

"They wanted to know why I went uptown yesterday. I told them why. I don't think they believed me." He turned to look at them. The officers were still looking at the three of them, but then they turned slowly and walked away up the street.

"Pah!" Bao said. "Why do they persist in coming here? They'll only make more trouble."

Kung-chiao had picked up Fernadina. She gave him a piece of cookie. Her father took it but did not eat it. He was still staring at the backs of the officers, and was aware of the shopkeepers along the street staring at him.

On Wednesday morning, Kung-chiao awoke with the feeling of fish flopping in his stomach. He would find out the results of his exams that day. For a brief moment, even before he opened his eyes, the thought flashed to him of seeking out one of the Chinatown soothsayers to see what he would say. But Kung-chiao knew he would find out soon enough. Besides, he thought, he was a modern man in a modern country, and such men no longer put store in the words of soothsayers.

He told Mei-yu at breakfast that he planned to meet John, his American friend, in a tavern near the school to celebrate later that evening. John had suggested the celebration when they had run into each other at the administrative offices the day before, after Kung-chiao's meeting with his advisor. Kung-chiao had hesitated to accept the invitation at first, saying he had never been in a tavern before, but when John insisted, saying it was time he was initiated into an American ritual, Kung-chiao gave in. Later, walking home, he began even to look forward to it.

"This is the first time I've been invited to a social activity outside of Chinatown, outside of school," he told Mei-yu, trying to keep the eagerness from his voice. "I think I should go, don't you?"

Mei-yu was still. Kung-chiao knew his wife despised the men in Chinatown who spent their evenings drinking wine, playing cards. And who knew what went on in American taverns? But she turned to him suddenly, her face opening with an almost startled look.

"Yes," she said. "You must go out tonight to celebrate with your friends. It will be good for you."

Her reply surprised him at first. Then he felt relief. Perhaps she knew his going out tonight would help him forget the entire matter of Colonel Chang, the police, if even for a few hours. He returned to his porridge, feeling that the day had already begun auspiciously.

After breakfast, Mei-yu asked him to stay home with Fernadina, saying she had to go to the Union to select new material for her next project.

"But today is Wednesday," he said, tying Fernadina's ribbon in her hair. "Don't you usually go to the Union on Thursdays?"

Mei-yu looked at him quickly but saw that he was intent on the ribbon. "Yes," she said. "But Mei-ling said the new shipment of silk arrived yesterday, and I want to select my pieces. We're also out of rice."

"All right. Fernadina and I will find plenty to do, won't we?"

"Yes, Ba ba."

Kung-chiao smiled at Mei-yu. She was standing in the middle of the room, her hands fidgeting with the folds of her skirt.

"Don't forget the wallet," he said.

Mei-yu ran to the wardrobe where the wallet was hidden and slipped it inside her blouse.

"Are you all right?" Kung-chiao asked his wife, pausing to look at her as he got out Fernadina's wooden puzzle.

"Yes, yes. I'll be back soon. Don't worry."

She closed the door behind her.

Kung-chiao spread the puzzle out on the table and watched his daughter push the pieces together. There were twelve pieces and he saw that she would have it mastered in a matter of seconds. He thought about Mei-yu, wondering if this matter with Colonel Chang was the cause of her nervousness, or if she, too, felt anxiety over the matter of his exam grades. It was good that she continued to immerse herself in her work, he thought. It was not good to dwell on matters over which they had no control.

Fernadina solved the puzzle, shouting happily as she clicked the last piece in place.

"More, Ba ba!" she cried and, spreading out both hands, jumbled up the pieces again. "You start!" she commanded.

He put two pieces together and clucked his tongue when she pushed his hands away and continued to assemble the puzzle on her own. She looked up occasionally to see if he watched. He saw that he would have to get another, more complicated puzzle for her very soon.

Later, just as Kung-chiao was beginning to worry about her, Mei-yu returned. She carried several cuts of silk fabric under her arm. He wondered why she had taken so long. She had also forgotten the rice. She lay the pieces of silk, still rolled up, on the table. Kung-chiao knew that whenever she came back with new bolts of fine silk, she usually had them unfurled and laid out neatly on the table immediately, the pupils in her eyes narrowed to pinpoints as she made her plans for them. Now she seemed hardly to look at them.

"Are you upset that I have made plans to go out tonight?" Kung-chiao asked.

She looked up quickly. "No!" she cried. Then, composing herself, "I am not upset, Kung-chiao. Please go. You should meet your friends as you planned."

"Are you certain?"

She began to unroll the rose-colored fabric.

"Of course."

She was looking intently at the silk. He could not read her face. But because he wanted to go, he did not pursue the matter with her further. His thoughts returned to his exam grades.

At two o'clock Kung-chiao and ten other students gathered around the exam results sheet tacked up on the bulletin board in the administration building. Kung-chiao saw his name at the top. John's scores were four places below. Elated, they shook each other's hands and invited two other classmates to meet at the tavern later that evening at nine o'clock.

At eight thirty Kung-chiao washed his hands in the sink and, glancing into the mirror, saw the reflection of Mei-yu sitting at the table with Fernadina, in back of him. He could see how she toyed nervously with the lacquered stick in her hair. He turned to look at her. She saw him and turned away, picking up Fernadina's comb and running it through the child's hair. His wife looked as if she had been weeping. Had something happened while he had been gone? he thought. Had the police returned? She had evaded his glances all evening, had said nothing at dinner. When he was ready to go, she held on to his hand and looked at him with large, unblinking eyes. Her forehead was covered with a fine sweat. He saw nothing unusual in that; his own skin was moist from the humid evening. He kissed her and left.

Wednesdays were usually quiet at the tavern Kung-chiao entered, but on that particular Wednesday evening, his three American friends filled the place with their laughter and whoops of relief. The other, regular customers sat in their dark booths and drank their beer, hardly noticing the party at the bar.

"Is he with you?" the bartender asked John, jerking his thumb at Kung-chiao.

"Sure. He's the guest of honor," John said, pushing Kung-chiao toward the bar. Then he ordered a round of beer for all.

Kung-chiao watched as his friends mimicked their professors; one who walked like a duck, another whose delivery was so slow and mannered as to lull them all to sleep. They constructed models of their future buildings out of matchbooks and toothpicks and knocked them down by flicking wadded paper balls at them. Their voices grew louder with their second round of beer. They behaved like unruly children, Kung-chiao thought, feeling like an indulgent parent, feeling pleasantly warm, benevolent from the beer.

He listened as Howard, one of the other friends in his class, described his interview with a power company executive in New Jersey. He was confident he had the job, he said, although he knew, as they all knew, that those men at the top of the class usually got the best jobs. He gestured at Kung-chiao. John pushed another bottle of beer in front of Kung-chiao. His face was flushed pink, sweating, his wet blond hair dark against his forehead. Kung-chiao saw the empty beer bottles clustered at his elbow.

"What's the matter, Kungy boy?" John said, leaning back, squinting, as if assessing Kung-chiao from afar. "You're awfully quiet tonight."

"Nothing is the matter," Kung-chiao said, smiling. "I'm having a very good time."

"He says he's having a very good time," John said, nudging Howard, who nodded. John turned back to Kung-chiao. "Well, you don't look like you're having a good time. You look too serious. You're always serious. Always the perfect scholar, aren't you, Kungy?"

Kung-chiao looked away, stunned at the tone of his friend's voice.

"Hey, Steve!" John called to their other classmate, who was stacking empty beer bottles into a pyramid on the wet bar counter. "Kungy says he's having a very good time!" John thrust his face close to Kung-chiao. Kung-chiao smelled his yeast-sour breath, tasted the bile rising in his own throat. "Kungy the Chinaman can get high on one beer! Tell me the secret, Kungy, tell me how you do it . . . how you ace the exams and then get drunk on one beer . . . yellow magic, isn't it? Hey, Howie! Kungy knows yellow magic!"

Kung-chiao saw the bartender wiping the glasses, grinning at him. His own friends were laughing, their red faces split with drunkenness, spittle spilling from the edges of their lips. He saw in the bar mirror how his own face had turned red, his eyes bloodshot. He looked at the empty beer glass, warm in his hand; even half a glass of wine had that effect on him. He shoved the glass away from him in disgust. The alcohol had bedeviled them all, he thought. His head felt swollen. He could feel his pulse pounding in his ears. He saw that the others had turned away, engrossed now in the building of the pyramid of bottles. Kung-chiao counted out the change for his beer and quietly slid off his stool. As he closed the door to the tavern he heard the sound of glass clinking and splintering as Steve's pyramid collapsed and bottles rolled and fell onto the floor. It was almost eleven o'clock. He stood in front of the tavern, thinking the walk home would help clear his head. The night air was hot, humid. Inside, he could hear the bartender shouting angrily at his friends.

Kung-chiao walked down Houston Street toward Mercer. He blinked rapidly, trying to clear his head. His mind seemed packed in cotton, stunned by the alcohol in his blood, weighted by the humidity. His shirt was sweat-soaked. Everything seemed too bright; the pavement glittering under the streetlights, the fragments of mica shining in the stones of the buildings on either side of him. He walked slowly on the sidewalk, breathing deeply, gradually feeling the pounding in his head growing less. He reached Mercer Street. He had not seen another person. Here, turning the corner, the street was soothingly dark, lit only at the intersections at the end of each block. He walked, hearing the evenness of his own footsteps. He thought of Mei-yu, at home.

Suddenly a man stepped out of the darkness and crouched in front of him. Kung-chiao instinctively stepped back, clenching his hands into fists. He stared at the man before him, seeing only the slashes where the eyes were staring at him from behind the black mask. Then he saw the knife. In a crazed instant he thought of the many films he had seen where the heroes defended themselves from knives and whirling maces with their bare hands. But now, seeing the knife in front of him, he knew all he could do was run. He looked away, down the street, hoping to see someone, thinking that if he could run to the corner under the streetlight, he might be able to get help.

The man with the knife moved forward, and Kung-chiao jumped backward, hearing himself shout. Someone grabbed him from behind, pinning his arms. Kung-chiao kicked, bucked wildly, trying to free himself, but the grip was too strong. Then he felt a terrible blow to the back of his knees, and he pitched forward, losing the sense of his legs. He saw the flash of the knife. He flung up his arms, but he knew his flesh would yield to the metal, and gasped as the silver slid into him, ripping its way through his abdomen. He stared at the knife, marveling at how it seemed to stem from his body, sending its blood roots over his skin. The men in black ran. The knife turned black. Kung-chiao fell, hearing his bones strike the pavement. The blood pounded in his ears, louder, louder, coming from a burning source in his belly. He saw brightness shining all around him; metal, skyscrapers, the blinding light reflecting from the glass, the steel, the stone. It was all too bright. He shut his eyes.

* * *

Sometime after eleven o'clock, Mei-yu, in Yung-shan's embrace, felt something detach itself violently from her body. She moaned. _Something is wrong,_ she thought, _even more wrong than what is happening here._ Yung-shan, thinking she writhed in passion, rose above her again and kissed her fiercely below her throat.

Later, she pulled away and struggled into her clothes. Yung-shan called her name, his voice hoarse with love. She turned away from him, hurrying, twisting her hair on top of her head. It was almost midnight. In the hallway outside his apartment she watched and listened for sounds from the other apartments, but all was quiet. All the doors were shut, all the ears deaf with sleep. Outside, in the night, she wrapped her arms around herself, hurrying, feeling her perspiration turn cold on her skin even as she saw the street surface sweat from the heat. The streets near Yung-shan's place were dark, and Mei-yu ran from streetlight to streetlight, reaching each bright stem with relief. All of Chinatown seemed strangely hushed to her. Even when she reached Mott Street at last, the night there, though lit up as always, was silent.

Only two customers remained in the Sun Wah Restaurant. They were drinking tea, sitting with their backs to the windows. Bao was probably in the rear, rubbing his great woks with oil, sweeping up. Good. No one had seen her.

She ran up the stairs of her apartment building and, with her heart pounding, approached the door of their apartment. The door was still locked . . . Kung-chiao was still away, still at the tavern, she thought. Relieved, she quickly went inside and knelt beside Fernadina's bed.

Forgive me for leaving you while you slept, she begged, looking at her still-sleeping daughter. _I did not want to leave you with Ah-chin or Bao, for they would have wanted to know why I needed to go out at this late hour. I did not want to leave you, Sing-hua, believe me. I will not leave you ever again._ She placed her hand lightly on Fernadina's forehead and, seeing that she slept soundly, went into the bedroom. She looked out the window for Kung-chiao, and saw again how empty Mott Street was. Strange, how still everything was, she thought. The restaurant across the street from Sun Wah had closed early. Mei-yu saw the cook lock his door, slip the key into his pocket. She looked down the street again; Kung-chiao was not there.

She splashed water into the sink, washed herself quickly. Then, catching sight of her face in the mirror, she shuddered. How would she be able to face Kung-chiao now? Even if she had had no choice, how would she be able to live with her shame, keep her shame from him? She forced herself to look at her image in the mirror, stared hard at her face. She would look out from now on as from behind a mask, a screen. A screen that would shield her shame. A screen that would be impenetrable from now on, a silken, shimmering screen that no one, even Kung-chiao, would be able to see through.

She lay down on their bed. It was well past midnight, closer to one o'clock. The feeling she had had before came back to her, gripped her. Her heart began to pound. Kung-chiao was not one to stay up late. He had always fallen asleep before one. Surely he was late only because his American friends had coaxed him into some drunken foolishness. Surely he was only now dull with drink, unable to find his way home. Then she remembered the deed she had done, felt the shame flailing again within her. She was suddenly glad that Kung-chiao had not come home. She felt unable to face him this night. She sat up in bed, lifted the shade, and looked again down Mott Street. Bao had turned off the green sign of Sun Wah. One by one, all the other signs along the street flickered off. Now she heard Bao's slow steps on the stairs, going past her landing, up to the floor above. Mei-yu pulled the sheet up to her neck, closed her eyes. Surely if she slept, she thought, she would not have to face Kung-chiao when he came home.

Later, there were three knocks on the door. Then they called her name. "Mrs. Wong," she thought she heard, "Mrs. Wong," again, louder. Mei-yu woke up and stared wildly around her. The bed beside her was empty. The lamp at the table was still bright; now Fernadina was calling for her. Then she heard it clearly, the knocking on the door. She quickly wrapped her robe around herself. In the foyer Fernadina was standing at the head of her bed, her arms outstretched. Mei-yu picked her up. The pounding began again within her. Her mind struggled to become clear. Where was Kung-chiao?

"Who is it?" she said from behind the door.

"Police, Mrs. Wong."

Ai, ai, Mei-yu thought, *are they bringing him home drunk?* She opened the door. The two officers who had searched their apartment stood before her.

"Mrs. Wong, we are sorry to disturb you."

Mei-yu looked into their faces. They were not here to search the room again, she could see that. They had not brought Kung-chiao. They kept their eyes down. What did it mean, what did it mean?

"Your husband has been stabbed, Mrs. Wong. He's dead."

Sometime afterward, she could not remember when, Mei-yu felt cold. She could not tell if she dreamt, but she remembered the cold. It was also dark. She knew Ah-chin was nearby, watching her with swollen eyes. She could not breathe; the smell of incense thick in the room, the scented paper flowers crowding the casket, the perfume they had sprinkled over Kung-chiao's body all suffocated her. The hands reached to her, the hands of her friends who touched her softly as they tried to comfort her, and then of Yung-shan, whose face emerged from the shadows and whose lips said, "I was not responsible, Mei-yu." His was a sorrowful face, but she did not believe it, or the lips. She had not been able to weep until she had seen Yung-shan's face. When it and all the other faces had retreated, leaving her alone again in the darkness, she finally gave herself over to her grief and wept.

○ ○ ○

"It is the nature of grief," the old man said.

Ah-chin listened to his voice as if charmed. Everything about him radiated wisdom. His face, as smooth and clear as a monk's, his long, sparse beard, his shaved pate, suggested a life of asceticism, prayer. Yet, Madame Peng had introduced him as her physician, not a monk. Ah-chin found herself trembling in the presence of these two eminent people.

She had never been in Madame Peng's parlor before. She took quick sideways glances at the sumptuous furnishings around her as she listened to them discuss Mei-yu's condition. Then she realized the physician was addressing her.

"How long do you say she has been like this?" he asked.

Ah-chin sat, thinking, counting, losing track of the days. "I think it's been close to three weeks," she said finally. "Ever since her husband's funeral she's been in a kind of trance, a shock. She doesn't seem to recognize anyone, not even her own little daughter. I've been looking after her every day, bringing her food, making sure that she eats, but it's frightening to see her so. She has lost weight and I don't know if she sleeps, like normal people do. She just lies there and looks out the window. She doesn't seem to see or hear me when I come in. I brought her child in once, thinking that seeing her might make her come out of herself, but even Sing-hua could see that her mother did not know her."

The physician sat with his hands tucked in his wide sleeves. "Yes," he said. "She has suffered a terrible trauma. I have seen cases similar to this on battlefields in China. Such cases are very difficult, but not impossible. I must see her. Perhaps I will give her something, something that will force her from where she is inside now. She is clinging to something in order to avoid the terrible pain of the present. Perhaps she is in a fantasy world or a ghost world, or perhaps she is in the past. I will try to bring her forth again."

"I am glad you are able to help, Ah-chin," Madame Peng said, smiling at the humble woman before her. "Mei-yu is fortunate in having you for a friend." She shook her head. "The poor child has had a terrible shock indeed. It is appalling, what Chinatown has come to these days. At least I hear the police have arrested one of Colonel Chang's men. It is only a matter of time now before the old man himself will be caught and punished, as he deserves. This time he has gone too far." The old lady paused. "Yes, poor Mei-yu. I had heard that she was not well. I had fruit and a soothing tea sent to her. I would have gone to see her myself, but my legs!" She laughed, slapping her short, plump thighs. "Quite worthless, as you can see. I am lucky enough to turn around in my apartment before becoming dizzy and leg-weary. Now, let's see, what was I saying? Cursed old age!" She shook her finger at Ah-chin. "Pray to die before you lose your mind, young woman, for that is the worst fate of all. My head is that of a cabbage now. There is nothing worse, nothing, unless one leaves no heirs. But to continue . . . have patience with the old woman . . . ah, yes, do not worry about Mei-yu, Ah-chin. My physician has worked miracles with people suffering from all kinds of ailments, from tumors to liver disease to simple sleeplessness. I am confident he will have Mei-yu back to herself again. Meanwhile, I will say it again, you have been a great friend, a great sister to Mei-yu in her trouble. Has it been a strain for you?"

Ah-chin hesitated. "I am not complaining, Madame Peng. I will gladly continue to do what I can for Mei-yu, but you must understand, I have my own family, my husband and son, and we live with another family in a single room. While we love Sing-hua, Mei-yu's daughter, our neighbors do not think . . ." She shrugged wearily. "It is a matter of space, Madame Peng."

"And she is another mouth to feed, I am sure," Madame Peng said, matter-of-factly.

"Also," Ah-chin continued, pushing a strand of her hair back behind her ear, "the Community Housing Council said that Mei-yu and her daughter could no longer stay in that apartment by themselves, because they no longer made up a family unit without Kung-chiao." She bowed her head. "They said they must move to a smaller place or another family must move in with them."

"Pah!" Madame Peng shifted in her chair. "And this second cousin of theirs, has he come forward at all?"

"Yes, Madame Peng. Roger called the bakery and has sent money, but he has not come to see her. Oh, but I told him Mei-yu would not recognize him," she continued hurriedly, seeing Madame Peng's frown. "I am sure he will do his duty by her when she is well. He seemed worried about an official matter, I think something about her immigration papers?"

"Yes, yes." Madame Peng waved her hand impatiently. "She cannot legally rely on him any longer. She is, after all, not a student, is she? Well, one cannot really blame him. After all, a second cousin is only a second cousin."

Ah-chin looked at her blankly.

"Never mind." Madame Peng seemed to think for a moment. "Well, it is all very clear to me what needs to be done."

Ah-chin waited respectfully.

Madame Peng laughed suddenly. "Don't worry, Ah-chin. I will take care of everything. You have done more than your share. Go now, take Dr. Toy to see Mei-yu. And come tell me how she is tomorrow."

Ah-chin and the physician left Madame Peng's apartment and walked down Pell Street. His shop was just a block away. Ah-chin entered the shop with him and waited while he went into the back room to prepare the medicine for Mei-yu. She stood at the front of the shop and stared at the rows of glass compartments built into the display case. There were rows and rows of compartments, each containing articles or powders or vials of some sort. Some contained pale dried roots, tubers whose ends tapered off into threadlike strands. Others contained gnarled branches wound into tightly twisted fists. The powders were of all different colors: black, ash gray, bright blue, red. Some were flaky, iridescent, others dull. Some seemed to contain only a slight layer of dust, but Ah-chin could not be sure. She could hear Dr. Toy grinding something with his mortar and pestle. He reappeared once, took a pinch of powder from one of the glass cases, and returned to the back room again. She could hear him talking to himself as he ground the powders. Minutes later he came out, tucking a small yellow envelope into his front pocket.

"Let us go see this young woman now," he said, making sure the door was locked after them.

○ ○ ○

Mei-yu had retreated to where time did not matter. She slept, she woke, she became aware of light and darkness but remained outside the cycle, disengaged and floating. Faces appeared and withdrew; only the sound of their voices lingered, like smoke. Occasionally, upon waking, her eyes would focus. She recognized the calendar on the wardrobe across the bed where she lay; she saw something familiar in Ah-chin's face. She remembered eating a nectarine. But more often, she dwelt behind a screen, not looking out, not allowing herself to be seen. Sing-hua, her daughter, seemed always on the periphery of this screen, disappearing behind it whenever Mei-yu turned her head to look at her directly. But somehow this did not worry Mei-yu, somehow she knew Sing-hua was safe.

Then another face appeared, came close to hers. Someone pulled up the shade at the window. Mei-yu closed her eyes against the bright noon light. The face, a man's, drew close as fingers gently pulled her eyelids up, then down.

"She is very weak," she heard him say. "Prepare the water for the powder."

Mei-yu felt fingers probe under her jaw, around her neck. They pressed gently into her side and abdomen. She turned her head and saw Ah-chin coming across the room, holding a steaming cup between both hands, taking small steps, her shoulder hunched with care. The man, tall, with a shaved pate, took an envelope and stirred its contents into the cup. Ah-chin held the cup in front of Mei-yu's lips.

"Mei-yu," Ah-chin said, stroking her friend's arm, holding the steaming cup close to her lips, "you must try to get well. We are all worried about you. Don't you remember your daughter, Sing-hua? Here. You must drink this. The doctor says it will help you. You must drink all of it."

Mei-yu saw the cup, wondered what was in the reddish liquid. She saw fragments of what looked like bark and other dried vegetable matter. The smell was faint, not unpleasant, like dry earth. She sipped. Particles in the liquid clung to her upper lip. Ah-chin wiped her mouth with her handkerchief and held the cup until Mei-yu had drunk it all.

"You may leave now," the physician said to Ah-chin. "I will sit with her today. Today is the most important day of the treatment."

Ah-chin brought over a bowl of apples. She looked at Mei-yu, who had closed her eyes once again. There was no movement underneath the papery eyelids.

As she slept Mei-yu began to feel the weight of her body sink deep into the bed. She no longer floated aimlessly, drifting like a dry rice husk on stagnant water, but felt herself carried on a powerful course, upstream. She began to see distinct shapes and forms, to hear voices and other sounds: laughter, the chirping of crickets, running feet. She felt she had traveled a long distance and was now arriving in another place that was at once familiar, yet altered. She heard someone running. She had heard that sound many times before. "Hsiao Pei?" she called.

The physician gently pressed her outstretched arms back to her sides and rearranged the pillows as she lay back. Hsiao Pei. He had heard her say the name quite distinctly. The name of someone, something small, *hsiao*, meaning "small." A childhood friend? A pet? He examined Mei-yu's face, saw that she was perspiring lightly now, flushed. A good sign. The drug was taking effect. She was focused within now, no longer wandering.

"Hsiao Pei!" she called again.

A name from the past, the physician thought, more certain, now. He sponged her face. Good. She would work her way back.

It was 1938, in Peking. Mei-yu was ten years old. She heard the footsteps coming closer, hurrying. Hsiao Pei was always in a hurry. She had always forgotten that as a member of the household of an important scholar, it was more fitting to pass through the hallways and rooms with dignity, with a certain measured grace. Mei-yu's mother, Ai-lien, moved slowly on her bound feet, her tiny shoes making uneven shuffling sounds as they dragged on the floor. Mei-yu recognized the rhythm of her mother's gait as she passed from room to room . . . short-long, short-long, like labored breathing. Mei-yu seldom heard her father's footsteps, but they were unmistakable; even, purposeful. His Western-made leather shoes made soft clapping sounds on the hard floor. Mei-yu's brothers, Hung-bao and Hung-chien, two and three years younger than she, churned through the house, their exasperated nurse in pursuit; there was no mistaking their approach. In the early morning, though, as now, even before her father rose to commence his study, Mei-yu woke to the sound that made her glad the day had begun—the sound of her amah's hard cotton shoes pattering as rapidly as paws on the concrete floor.

The door to her room flung open. "Wake, wake, little monkey, it is time you got up for school!"

Mei-yu lay encased in her stiff cotton sheets, her ears acute but her eyes still sealed, as if lacquered shut. The birds were trilling, but she knew it was dark yet. She felt Hsiao Pei's nimble fingers pulling the sheet down, tickling her neck, pulling the string from her sleep shift. Hsiao Pei, not herself, she thought, was the monkey, the monkey whose arms were always poking, probing, pressing gently. She allowed herself to be propped up against her amah's knees as Hsiao Pei slipped the shift over her head.

"Ai yah, sit up, jellyfish, lazy one!" She bumped down the small knobs of Mei-yu's spine one by one with her knuckle. She had Mei-yu's school uniform ready, clean, freshly starched, and ironed. Mei-yu opened her eyes. It was no surprise to see the uniform, for she wore it every day, but the thought of school made her eye the rumpled sheets. Hsiao Pei saw this, and quickly, before Mei-yu could dodge, grabbed one arm and pushed it through the armhole of the blue blouse and then pulled the other through the sleeve. Mei-yu watched as Hsiao Pei buttoned her blouse. Although Hsiao Pei was her amah, a servant in the household, Mei-yu was Hsiao Pei's willing slave. Hsiao Pei scolded and flapped her apron at her, but Hsiao Pei never told her to go away, Hsiao Pei always had something delicious for her to eat.

Mei-yu's amah was small, which was why they called her "hsiao." Pei was her family name. Her face was round except for her pointed chin, her black eyes tiny like watermelon seeds. Mei-yu asked Hsiao Pei once if she was indeed Chinese, because she looked so different from her mother, Ai-lien. Hsiao Pei laughed for a long time. She and Ai-lien were indeed different. Ai-lien was six inches taller, her bones long and elegant, her hands slender with tapered fingers. Her face was oval-shaped with large, tilted eyes.

"We look different because we come from different families of people. Your mother is from the north and I am from the south. Your mother was born into a wealthy family and I was the third daughter of eleven sons and daughters of a poor peasant farmer."

"Do you miss your brothers and sisters and your parents, Hsiao Pei?"

"I think of them sometimes, little monkey. But life was very hard then. We never had enough to eat . . . there were always so many of us! And we never had enough room. I slept on a mat on the floor with my four sisters. No, I am glad I came north."

"Were you always in my father's house?"

"I was a house servant for your grandparents, your father's parents. I worked in the kitchen from when I was twelve or thirteen. They were not wealthy, but I did not need much money. Only a roof and some food."

"Did you ever think you would marry my father?"

Hsiao Pei laughed until she couldn't see through her tears.

"Such questions! No, no, I, marry your father?" She burst into giggles again. "I will tell you the story of your parents' marriage one day. But I did marry, sometime after your father did, and I left your grandparents' house to live with my husband for a year."

"Did you ever go back to visit my grandparents?"

"Yes." Hsiao Pei seemed to think back to that time. "When my husband died, I went back as their cook." She paused. "I worked there until you were born."

"When I was born?"

"Yes, that was a great day, when you were born. Your parents were not like other parents, Mei-yu. They did not curse you that you were not born a son, an heir. They were educated people. To them you were beautiful and they loved you at first sight. It was after your birth that I left your grandparents to become your amah, your nursemaid. And that is my story."

Hsiao Pei did not have bound feet like Mei-yu's mother. Peasant women imitated that custom of the gentry less often now, for peasant women were expected to work, while women from fine families preferred to remain demure. Mei-yu could not imagine Hsiao Pei with bound feet, for Hsiao Pei did everything quickly, like a bird. Even if Hsiao Pei had had bound feet, Mei-yu was certain she would have hobbled on them quickly, regardless, beating them to a pulp on the hard concrete.

Concrete and bricks surrounded Mei-yu and her family, as they were the building material of theirs and almost every other modern house in Peking. To others, concrete was solid, cheap, durable. To Mei-yu, it was something alive, a substance with different natures. In the summer it was as bright as stone, warm and white. In the winter it was dark, like the walls of a cave.

Four walls, or wings, surrounded the courtyard, the focal point of the house. All windows and doors of the rooms in these wings faced out into the courtyard. There were no openings from any of the rooms out into the alleyway on either side of the house, or facing the neighboring houses. Visitors who came to the Chen house passed through the main gate, continued across the courtyard, and were received in the main waiting room. This room was sparsely furnished with a table, a few chairs, a simple altar at which Ai-lien burned her incense sticks and spent her time in meditation. Mei-yu seldom went into this room, for it was austere, formal. Her family was not known for its stand on formality, however. Most visitors were immediately ushered into the dining room or kitchen, where tea and savories were served and where many could gather close together.

Hung-bao's and Hung-chien's bedrooms adjoined each other to the left of the main reception room. The walls between their rooms were so thick that their tapping codes to each other at night could hardly be heard on the other side. For this reason they preferred to go out of their rooms to confer in the courtyard, to plan their schemes for the following day. Sometimes, when Li Ma, their nursemaid, snored through the night, they remained free in the courtyard, and their whispers, like the chirp of crickets, would lull Mei-yu to sleep. At other times Li Ma would wake up and chase them back into their rooms. Then their boyish shrieks, echoing throughout the house, would wake all.

Directly across from this section of the house, about thirty paces across the courtyard, was their parents' room, and next to that, their father's study. In the middle of this room was the prized desk carved out of blackwood, and in back, the shelves filled with books written in English, Chinese, and Japanese. Mei-yu's room was in the northwest corner, adjacent to her father's study. On summer evenings when it was too hot to sleep, she would slip outside and watch her father from beneath his window. He usually worked in his study after the children went to bed, on those evenings when he did not have meetings. Mei-yu watched the movement of his pen, the curl of smoke from his pipe. She thought her father extremely handsome. Hsiao Pei told her she had gotten her thick black hair and pale skin from her father. Mei-yu began to look in the mirror every day to make certain Hsiao Pei was not teasing.

The kitchen, with its simple charcoal stove, washbasin, and faucet, was down the hall from Mei-yu's room, and next to that was the dining room. Hsiao Pei's and Li Ma's rooms were at the very end. Tsu-lu, the cook, who did not live with them, came very early each morning, swinging the main gate open, knocking the rooster from his perch. Each day began in that way, with the tinkling of the front gate bell, the squawk of the rooster, the scrape of the coal buckets as Tsu-lu lit the fire, and then the rapid pattering of Hsiao Pei's shoes.

In school Mei-yu studied English, Chinese classics, and now Japanese. Her teachers did not explain why they were suddenly given Japanese primers, but Mei-yu knew that day by day Peking bowed lower and lower to the Japanese.

They had entered Peking one year earlier, and had now taken over the food stores of the city. Hsiao Pei told her they had taken the trains bringing in food from the countryside to transport their troops through China, and now the markets in town had barely enough food. Mei-yu's father had planted winter cabbage in what had once been their chrysanthemum garden, and it was only because of his salary as a professor at the university that they were still able to buy whatever food was available.

She walked to school in the morning, seeing Japanese soldiers strolling in the streets in pairs. They stopped the citizens of Peking to search them for food, shoving them away roughly when they were through. They grinned with arrogance, she thought.

Mei-yu's teachers told the students about the two Chinese parties. Mei-yu still did not understand who the Kuomintang were, or where the Communists had come from. To her, they were like two ribbons of color that clashed on the big wall map at her school, ribbons that twisted and knotted together so tightly as to break each other apart. The Japanese she understood better, had seen up close. They came into their house more often now and continued to speak rudely to her father. And despite the shortage of food and the presence of the Japanese soldiers on the street, this was what truly frightened Mei-yu most. For not only had the Japanese increased their visits to her house, but her father had begun to go away, more and more frequently and for longer lengths of time. One day, in school, a classmate sidled up to her and whispered, "My father says your father is a fool. Soon you will have no father."

Mei-yu stared at her uncomprehendingly.

"Soon you will lose everything, including your haughty airs," her schoolmate continued. "Families like yours have the most to lose."

Mei-yu jumped on her and pulled her pigtail, delighting in her cries, until their teacher hurried over and dragged her off.

At home Mei-yu told Hsiao Pei what her schoolmate had said.

"Pay no attention," her amah said, combing Mei-yu's hair before she was to go to sleep. "Your father is a very brave man. A very patriotic man. China needs more men like him, especially now."

Mei-yu knew her father was important, judging from the number of men who came to see him at night and from the way the Japanese came to disturb him day after day. But fear remained with her. That night, she woke up trembling and got up to creep down the corridor and into Hsiao Pei's room. She caught sight of her father pacing in the study. Dressed in his gray padded robe, he looked pale in the light of his reading lamp. She stopped at the window and, although chilled through her bones from the cold concrete floor, watched him as he paced, his hands clasped behind him. Occasionally he would sigh, mutter something, light his pipe. Mei-yu could see the crease deep between his eyes, his eyelids heavy from lack of sleep. Then, unable to stand the cold any longer, she hurried, her chilled toes cracking, to Hsiao Pei's room. She climbed under the blanket of her amah's narrow cot and watched while Hsiao Pei took out her embroidery and threaded her needle.

"I'm afraid, Hsiao Pei."

"Is it about your father again?" her amah said, squinting at the tiny stitches she was making. "Don't worry. You father is a very clever man."

She felt Mei-yu's eyes looking at her from the dark corner of the room.

"I see that tonight I must tell you the story of the Great Lie," she said, and chuckled. She heard Mei-yu settle down, her elbow leaning on the pillow at the head of the bed.

"Your father was seventeen at the time," Hsiao Pei began. "I was fourteen, employed as a kitchen maid at his parents' house. His father was a blacksmith, a very hardworking man, always covered with soot from the fire, and sweat. He used to come into the kitchen at the end of the day and pour water over himself and glisten like a great black slippery eel! I remember how the kitchen floor got muddy from all the water he spilled, for we had a dirt floor then. Your father's mother scolded him every time, but it didn't matter. Anyway, at seventeen, your father had just finished school. He was brilliant, the first in his class. He could recite the classics by memory, could argue against the most learned scholars in the village, on every subject. He shamed his father, I tell you, for his father was a simple man. I don't intend to sound disrespectful, Mei-yu, but it was as if a donkey had begotten a great young stallion. No, really, don't laugh, little monkey, it's true! Your grandfather would come home from pounding pieces of metal, and finding his son with his head buried in books angered him. He would grab the books and toss them against the stove, causing great clouds of charcoal dust to fill the kitchen. It was as if someone prodded a hot poker into his side every time he saw his son so. It didn't make sense for him to have a son like that and not be bursting with joy and pride, a sense of honor! Well, at least that is how it was with your father's father. But your grandmother, now, she was rightfully proud of her Number One Son. She wept with happiness when he came home with his scholar's prizes. She was an unusual woman, for even as poor as she was, she had learned to read. She had a great respect and admiration for men of learning. Anyway, the parents fought frightfully over their son's future. The father wanted to apprentice him in his trade, while the mother begged her husband to send their son to the university so he could become a distinguished scholar and bring honor to their house. "What, my profession is not good enough?" your grandfather the blacksmith would yowl, and would begin to throw things so that we in the kitchen had to jump to find places to hide. There were many weeks of this sorrow, and still much fighting. Everyone in the household, including your father's three sisters, was affected. The sisters lost weight, became ugly. Your grandfather worried that no men would marry them. "What good is a household with three unmarried daughters?" he thought, wringing his hands. Then the devils began to act. The chickens began to hatch chicks with three legs, and horns. The dogs would hide behind the trees in the yard and laugh. Spirits in the house stole my bucket and mop and I had to buy new ones with my own money. You would not believe the trouble! Your father was especially sad to be the cause of the trouble between his parents, who truly loved each other and lived in perfect harmony except for this one thing. He would sigh and look so unhappy. I had to coax him to eat his congee.

"One day, though, I had a lightning storm in my head. For it was I, Mei-yu, and don't let anyone tell you otherwise, who brought this idea to your grandmother. 'Consult a soothsayer,' I said, 'and let the soothsayer, one who knows about such things, determine Yuan-ming's future.' Your grandmother was so grateful, she gave me a shawl and four hen's eggs. I didn't crack them open right away, of course.

"So your father went to the soothsayer, who lived in the neighboring village. He was an old yellow-toothed man who sat in his dirty blue robe and scribbled on paper bits all day long. He was sitting cross-legged in front of his low stone table, his little tube of sticks at his knee. I know this because Yuan-ming told me this himself, later, when he returned. When the soothsayer heard Yuan-ming's question, whether or not he should apprentice himself to his father or apply to the university, he stroked his beard for a long time. It was a difficult question for him. Usually soothsayers set wedding dates, picked funeral sites, told people when to cut their hair. We don't use them often now, Mei-yu, but then, at that time, especially in the smaller villages, their word was carefully listened to. Anyway, this soothsayer picked up his handful of sticks, thin as straws, and threw them down on the ground. Yuan-ming looked at the old man's face fearfully. After much muttering and shaking of the head, the old man told Yuan-ming what he feared most to hear . . . that he was to remain with his father and become an apprentice! Well, I tell you. Your father was stricken. His heart was smashed, as if trod upon by a great water buffalo. He paid the old man, who went back to his scribbling, and started on his way back home."

Hsiao Pei bit the green silk thread and laid her work down. Her eyes shone brightly.

"It was fortunate also that Yuan-ming was walking that day, and that it was thirteen miles from his village to the village of the soothsayer, for during those thirteen miles he began to use his brilliant mind, and in those thirteen miles he came of age, for he made the decision of his life. When he reached home, his mother, white of face and trembling, asked him what the soothsayer had said. Your father replied without hesitation, "He said I am to go on to the university." His mother fainted and lay as if dead. I had to revive her with a splash of vinegar to her face. I, too, was happy for him, for I had known all along what he had wanted. When his father came home, all black and sooty, he asked his wife what the soothsayer had said. He trembled, too, for they had agreed beforehand that they would abide by whatever the soothsayer said. When she told him, he roared so that all the goats in the village stopping chewing, and the milk they were to give the next morning went sour, right there in their udder bags. Your grandfather did not believe your grandmother. He wanted his son to tell him to his face what the soothsayer had said. Yuan-ming came and told his father to his face what the old man had said. At the time I believed he was telling the truth, you see, and was almost saddened to see the old man so unhappy. His knees shook and then he sat down in the tub of water, as dazed as if the ceiling beam had fallen on his head. Later, much later, when Yuan-ming had come home for a visit after almost two years at the university and was already considered the most brilliant scholar they had ever had, he told me his secret, the secret of the Great Lie. I hit him with my thimble. I told him he had done a terrible, dishonorable thing, lying, especially to his parents. But his secret was safe with me. I have never told anyone but you, Mei-yu. And I believe I have done rightly so, keeping this secret, because everyone seems to have done well by this Great Lie. For aren't you here, alive and well, and your mother and brothers alive and well, and myself, aren't I well, in spite of all the evil that is going on in this country? That is proof, isn't it, that the fates can be outwitted? Yes! And Yuan-ming's father eventually shed his pride, and sent the soothsayer a great sow with seven piglets dangling from her teats. He is now the proudest father in the entire province, and Yuan-ming remains his loyal and respectful son. Now, Mei-yu, have you ever heard a happier story? Do you see that your father is a great and clever man, and that you need not worry about him?"

Mei-yu, who had known all along how the story would end, of course, had allowed herself to fall asleep on her amah's bed.

Now Mei-yu stirred within herself, slipping out of sleep and feeling as if she were traveling again, pulled back by an invisible force to another place. She opened her eyes and saw the moon hovering above her. The moon smiled, and she saw that it was the face of a man, round and clean, bending low over her.

"I am Dr. Toy," the man said. He beckoned to someone in back of him. "She is back now," he said.

Mei-yu looked about her and saw that she lay in a large bed, not her amah's cot. The bed felt familiar, though, as if she had lain in it many times before, and the face coming toward her was not Hsiao Pei's.

"Ah-chin?" she said, hearing her voice come as if from afar.

"Mei-yu!" Her friend knelt by the bed and held her hand. "You do know me, don't you?"

Mei-yu looked at the gaunt face of her friend. *Ah-chin is beginning to get gray hairs,* she thought. *She is looking old and tired these days. What has been happening?* Ah-chin was saying something.

"What?" Mei-yu said.

"We have been worried about you. You have been far away."

Mei-yu began to remember. Her chin sunk down to her chest. Ah-chin looked at Dr. Toy in alarm, but he shook his head in warning. Then Mei-yu sighed deeply. "Yes," she said. "I remember now. Kung-chiao is dead."

Ah-chin fought not to look away from Mei-yu's face, for her friend was hardly recognizable. Her skin was sallow, drawn, her cheeks sunken, so that her teeth seemed to protrude, like those in the jaw of a naked skull. Her hair hung against the sides of her face in coarse strands. Her hands, lying limp on the bedspread, appeared to be translucent and twitched with weakness.

"Sing-hua," Mei-yu said. "Where is she?"

"With Ling, at the bakery. She is well, Mei-yu. She has become like one of our own family. But she asks for you every day, and cries for you at night."

Ah-chin immediately regretted her words, for Mei-yu threw back the covers and struggled to get up from the bed. Dry sobs came from her throat. Ah-chin saw that her legs, bare under her nightgown, had grown thin, her knees grotesquely large in contrast to her thighs and calves. Dr. Toy took Mei-yu by the shoulders and gently pressed her back onto the bed.

"You must not tire yourself, Mrs. Wong," he said.

Mei-yu felt her strength fade against the pressure of his hands on her shoulders. She lay back against the pillow, breathing heavily.

"Bring Sing-hua to me, please," she said.

Ah-chin looked helplessly at the physician, who was taking Mei-yu's pulse. He released her wrist gently and began probing her neck below her ears.

"I think your daughter can wait until tomorrow morning," he said. "First you must eat, then you must sleep, really sleep. Then perhaps Ah-chin will help you prepare yourself to see your daughter."

Mei-yu put her hands to her face, felt the sharp bones above her cheeks. Tears welled through her fingers. "Am I such a fright?" she cried. She wept quietly for several moments. Then she accepted the handkerchief Ah-chin offered her and wiped her eyes. "I am sorry. I will do as you say. I know I must get well." She leaned back. "Ah-chin, please tell Sing-hua to wait for me." Her breathing became regular. Ah-chin saw that she had fallen asleep.

"Dr. Toy?"

"Do not be alarmed. This is to be expected. She is still very weak. She may lapse back to where she was previously, but she has too strong a hold here, and I believe she will be fully recovered within a few weeks. I will prepare more medication for her, to be taken every day. Meanwhile, she must eat. She must have food high in protein, but very mild. Could you make her a broth with tofu and egg noodles? Very good. Come by tomorrow morning and I will have more medicine for you to give her."

"Thank you, Dr. Toy. Shall I stay with her tonight?"

"It is not necessary. She will sleep very soundly. Do not be alarmed if she sleeps for another full day. She has not really slept, in the restorative sense, in a long time. I will stop by tomorrow afternoon to see how she is. But don't worry. She is basically strong, and the fact that she has come back this quickly after taking the medicine is a good sign."

He walked to the door, shaking his head. "Actually, her recovery has been remarkable. I've seen patients who struggled for weeks to come back. Then there were those who simply remained where they were. They were the ones who went mad."

Ah-chin waited until he left the room, then bent over to look in Mei-yu's face. There was a flickering movement under the eyelids; dreams. She pressed a clean cloth to Mei-yu's forehead, saw her friend smile in her sleep.

"Come back, Mei-yu," Ah-chin said softly. "Come back."

○ ○ ○

Several weeks later Mei-yu sat on the bed, holding on her lap the calendar that had been tacked on the door of the wardrobe. On the top page September's face smiled out at her, the face of an actress portraying a young peasant girl. Rosy cheeked, eyes shining, she promised a bountiful harvest for the season. Mei-yu smoothed the page and placed the calendar in the cardboard box on the floor. Next would come the photographs from China, her papers, her clothes.

She had already wrapped the teapot and teacups in newspaper, then packed them carefully among the padded coats and bedding in another box. Three boxes were all she needed. Sing-hua could carry her own toys to the new place. She looked at her daughter, playing quietly at the table with a new wooden puzzle Bao had given her. The little girl seemed content. Mei-yu, upon awakening from her long sleep, had not known at first how to tell her daughter that Kung-chiao was dead. At five years of age, Sing-hua had asked about death only once before. It had been during one of their walks down Mott Street. She had found a dead pigeon in the gutter, and had wanted to pick it up.

"No, Sing-hua, no," Mei-yu had said, grabbing her daughter's arm. "It is dead, probably from disease."

"What does that mean?" She still peered at the bird. "Where are its eyes?"

"Its spirit has gone, Sing-hua. Only its body is left, and because it has no spirit, it will soon go, too."

"What is a spirit?"

"Life, Sing-hua." Mei-yu pulled her daughter along. "Our spirit is our life. When we lose our spirit, then we are dead."

"Like those ducks?" Sing-hua had said, pointing to the roasted ducks hanging in the shop windows.

"Yes. The ducks' spirits have left them now."

"So they won't know it if we eat them?"

"No."

"Good!" Sing-hua said.

When Mei-yu was sick, Ah-chin had told Sing-hua that her father had taken a journey far away, and would not be home for a long time. Sing-hua had been very quiet at first, but as the weeks passed she began to ask more often as to when they expected her father to return. When Mei-yu became stronger, she saw that she would have to tell her daughter the truth. Finally, one evening, she held Sing-hua in her lap, stroking her hair, and told her gently that Kung-chiao would never be coming back.

"Is he like the ducks, then, Mama?"

Mei-yu could not answer her.

"Will somebody eat him, then, Mama?"

"No, Sing-hua!" Mei-yu held her daughter close to her. "Your father will not be eaten by anybody. He is safe, close by. We will never see him again, but we will always feel his spirit close. Kung-chiao will never leave us, Sing-hua!"

But she was not certain that Sing-hua had understood her. The little girl had remained solemn, puzzled looking, until one evening Mei-yu found her huddled under the sheet in the large bed, crying, clutching something to her chest. Mei-yu kissed her tears away, pried the glinting treasure away from her hands; it was Kung-chiao's spectacles. "How did you find these, my little girl?" Mei-yu wept. "Ba ba! Ba ba!" her daughter cried, and Mei-yu knew then that she had come to understand.

Mei-yu folded her clothes into the box and went into the foyer. Sing-hua's things were few. They would leave the crate bed here; Sing-hua was getting too big for it now. Mei-yu stared at it, remembering how Kung-chiao had gotten it from behind the Sun Wah Restaurant. They had not known Bao then. Bao had thought Kung-chiao intended to steal it, to sell, as others had done, and the two had argued. Then Kung-chiao told the cook what he wanted to do with it, and Bao had let go his grip of the crate, shaking his head. Kung-chiao then scrubbed the crate with lye soap, sanded it until the surface was as smooth as the top of their metal table, and fitted a wooden platform in the bottom on which they put a foam rubber pad. Sing-hua had slept in it for four years. Now she would sleep in her mother's bed.

Mei-yu was folding the blanket from the crate when Ah-chin tapped on the door and walked in.

"I see you don't need my help. . . . Hello, Sing-hua, your auntie Ah-chin has brought you something nice."

Sing-hua put her wooden puzzle aside and came forward to accept a turnip cake from Ah-chin.

"She is doing fine," Ah-chin whispered to Mei-yu when the girl went back to work on the puzzle.

"She seems to be," Mei-yu said, putting the blanket into the box. "There. I think it is all done."

She turned and looked back into the main room. "Ai, Ah-chin," she said, "I didn't think it would be so difficult to leave here."

Ah-chin looked at the room, seeing the stripped mattress of the large bed, the bare shelf. "Just think of where you are moving to, though, Mei-yu. The place is perfect for you and Sing-hua. And imagine, living in the same building as Madame Peng!"

Mei-yu nodded. The apartment, one floor up from Madame Peng's, seemed ideal. It was only one room, but it faced a quiet, sunny alley, was clean, and had a balcony with a jasmine plant. Madame Peng said she kept the apartment for visitors; her son, Richard, stayed there whenever he came to see her from Washington, D.C. It barely cost her anything to keep, she said. But Mei-yu asked her what the rent was, insisting she wanted to pay; Madame Peng had already been too kind. The old woman had sighed. "Why can't you allow an old woman satisfaction?" she had asked. "We ancient ones like to show that we are still capable of worthy deeds." But she saw that Mei-yu would not be persuaded. "All right, stubborn girl, here is a bargain for you. Perhaps you will come to my apartment to fit the clients who come to my door . . . fit them personally. They are my best clients, the most demanding, and you will have more than enough to do. Such services, in addition to your regular work assigned by my assistant, will pay for the apartment. Does that satisfy you, then?" Mei-yu knew the old woman's ways, knew that the bargain was still too much in her own favor, but she would work hard, she would find a way to fulfill her part of the bargain. "Yes, Madame Peng," she said finally, and the crone had rocked back on her heels and nodded, satisfied.

"I owe much to Madame Peng," Mei-yu said out loud.

"Then be grateful to her, Mei-yu," Ah-chin said. "It isn't often someone like that takes such an interest."

Mei-yu smiled at her friend. Ah-chin showed no sign of envy.

"Oh!" Ah-chin started. "I almost forgot to tell you. Roger called the bakery this morning. He wants to see you. Would you call him back, Mei-yu?"

Mei-yu leaned against the wall of the foyer. "I wonder what he is thinking now. Have you told him anything, Ah-chin?"

"Nothing, only that you have been feeling stronger and are moving today to another place. He sounded surprised."

"No doubt," Mei-yu said.

"He did call and ask about you when you were ill, Mei-yu. He doesn't seem like that bad a person."

"Oh, he isn't a bad person, Ah-chin. But our relationship is not simple. I am sure we will have much to talk about. I will call him this afternoon."

Ah-chin leaned close to Mei-yu, keeping her eye on Sing-hua in the next room.

"I also heard some very interesting news today, Mei-yu. You asked me to tell you if I had heard anything, remember?"

Mei-yu glanced quickly in her daughter's direction, seeing that she was still busy with the puzzle.

"Yes. Only, please whisper. I don't want Sing-hua to hear anything . . . too much, I mean, about what happened to Kung-chiao."

"Well, I hear that Lo, the importer, has left Chinatown, supposedly on vacation, but everyone knows better. Also, there was something in the Chinatown newspaper yesterday. Colonel Chang apparently has vowed to stay in Chinatown, to prove that he has nothing to hide. Everything is stirred up now, Mei-yu. It seems like Kung-chiao's murder—" Ah-chin stopped abruptly. "I'm sorry. I don't mean to gossip about something like that, Mei-yu."

Mei-yu put out her hand and touched her friend. "Never mind, Ah-chin. News is news. Please, go on, tell me all of it."

"There's not much more. Only that the police have questioned both Colonel Chang and Yung-shan. They are still the prime suspects. Also, they picked up Colonel Chang's man, Lee, and have him in jail on a minor charge. They'll get him to talk. There'll be an arrest for the murder soon, I'm sure of it."

"An arrest," Mei-yu repeated, shifting her weight as she leaned wearily against the wall. Everyone in Chinatown watched for an arrest, even though they pretended not to know anything about it. She was too tired, too grieved to find any joy in the prospect. An arrest would not bring Kung-chiao back. She could find no more cause to rage at whatever person, whatever force had killed him. It was as senseless as raging at the pounding waves of the ocean, or a mountain.

"Don't you want them to arrest the people who killed Kung-chiao?" Ah-chin asked.

"Shh!" Mei-yu said. She looked at her daughter, who had turned to regard them, her hand still clutching a piece of puzzle.

"Yes, of course," she said, taking hold of Ah-chin's arm and pushing her gently toward the door. "Of course I do. That is good news, Ah-chin. Thank you for telling me. Please tell Ling he need not come by, Sing-hua and I can manage very well. You can see we do not have much. Bao said he would carry my teapot and teacups. Thank you, Ah-chin, I will stop at the bakery tomorrow to see you."

"Don't forget to call Roger!"

"Yes, yes, good-bye."

Mei-yu closed the door behind Ah-chin. When she turned, she met Sing-hua's eyes. She saw then that her daughter had heard all, and knew all now.

The next evening, Mei-yu helped her daughter cut a piece of news-paper to put in the bottom of her new canary's cage. The bird had been in the apartment, waiting for them, a gift from Madame Peng on their moving day. It was a male, for it had sung and trilled all afternoon, and Mei-yu had seen her daughter smile for the first time in weeks. She had swept the floor and the bird had cocked its eye at the dust and flicked its tail. Her daughter had taken the seed cup to the edge of the open balcony and blown the chaff away. Madame Peng scolded loudly from the balcony below, complaining that the chaff had blown into her rooms. The day had seemed almost bright, Mei-yu thought, as she stood on the balcony and felt the warmth of the sun. But after they had swept the floor, wiped the dust from the furniture, and unpacked their things, she saw that the sun had sunk low. The air on the balcony had grown chilly, and she closed the doors, drawing the curtains.

Now, despite the bird, despite the presence of the old woman so near, Mei-yu sat with her daughter as they ate their supper and fought to keep from weeping. The room they lived in now was small, com-pressed, and intense in its strangeness. The single wooden bed, table, two chairs, and dresser and mirror were finer than any of the things they had had in their old place, but their polished surfaces reflected her own still, unsmiling face, nothing more. The kitchen area included a modern sink and little stove, a small cabinet for storage. Mei-yu's dragon teapot and teacups were hidden away there. She had not real-ized how, in the other room, her eyes had often rested on the teapot sitting on its hinged shelf, and how she had found a strange comfort there. It was something of her own that she had brought with her, something that had completed the journey with her. Now she found herself staring around this room, looking for something to look at that would afford her such comfort. She could find none. _I am just tired,_ Mei-yu thought, trying to eat, trying to feign appetite for her daughter's sake. But her efforts were not noticed, for Sing-hua had stopped eating as well, and was now watching the canary in its cage. It sat very still on its perch, regarding them, tilting its head from side to side, silent. *I have affected the poor bird with my gloom as well,* Mei-yu thought. *I must stop this, I must be strong!* Then her eyes rested on her daughter, and she saw how Sing-hua had grown, her arms and legs lengthening, her face gaining definition. *Ai,* Mei-yu thought, her heart aching faintly, *Sing-hua will never be a beauty, she looks too much like Kung-chiao, solemn and dark.* Then Sing-hua looked up at her mother, and Mei-yu looked away, struck by the look of life intense in the small face. *There is something else of Kung-chiao in you,* she thought as her daughter came and pressed her face against her knees. *Small as you are, you are stronger than I, Sing-hua. And you will emerge from this sorrow even stronger, I can see it.* Mei-yu knew then she need not fear for her daughter and, in knowing that, began to feel her own fear slip away.

Mei-yu cleared the small wooden table and washed their supper dishes. She smoothed the bedcover and poured fresh water into the pot for tea. Roger said he would arrive at eight o'clock.

He was prompt, as usual. Mei-yu invited him to sit at the table, then excused herself while she walked with her daughter down to Madame Peng's, where the old lady had promised the girl a visit with her pop-eyed little dog. "I won't be long," Mei-yu reassured her daughter. "I will come back to get you very soon. Be polite to Madame Peng! Be respectful!"

Roger was standing out on the balcony when she returned.

"You have a beautiful little place here, Mei-yu," he said, coming back into the room, rubbing his arms. "It's getting cooler these days, isn't it?"

Mei-yu brushed past him to close the balcony doors.

He looked thinner, his nose longer. She could smell his unease; he was grimacing with cordiality.

"Mei-yu . . ." He came over close to her but sensed the wrongness of his approach and stopped short of touching her. "Both Diana and I are very sorry . . . I know we have not always understood each other very well, but you must know that we always wished the best for Kung-chiao and you, and now, with his death . . . his murder, it's awful . . . we feel terrible. We'd like to help you somehow, if you will let us."

His voice shook. Mei-yu gestured for him to sit down at the table. "Thank you, Roger," she said. "You and Diana are very kind."

Roger continued to look around the room, directing occasional glances at Mei-yu. "I'm glad to see that you are feeling better. You're looking thinner, but well. I'm sorry I didn't come to see you earlier, but Ah-chin said—"

"Please, Roger, there is no need to apologize. I am very glad that you have come tonight."

Mei-yu put the water on to boil.

"This is a very nice place. Very nice."

"Thank you. It suits us very well."

"Mei-yu . . ."

Mei-yu waited.

"I was wondering, we were wondering, if you don't mind our asking, what your plans are from now on. We're only asking so we can do what we can to help, you see. Have you looked into the matter of your visa, for instance? Will you still be working for Madame Peng, and will that be enough to support you and Fernadina?"

Mei-yu looked at her husband's cousin. He was chewing his lip, a habit she had never noticed before. Was he afraid she was going to ask him for money? Was he afraid she was going to ask him to intervene on her behalf, to become entangled in some bureaucratic mess in order to settle the matter of her visa papers? Or was he afraid that she would bring his name into the Chinatown murder case, link him with the entire dark affair, besmirch his name? She looked at him again. He seemed changed, no longer the arrogant benefactor of before.

"Roger, please don't worry about Sing-hua and me. My friends in Chinatown have been more than kind. I will take care of the visa matter myself, somehow. I am still working for Madame Peng, and am doing better work, better-paying work. This room costs less than the other one. I am managing for now, as you can see."

"Yes, yes, I can see that, certainly, you are managing quite well," Roger said, weighing his words carefully. "I was thinking more in terms of the future, though. . . . You have thought of the future, haven't you, Mei-yu?"

"Every day I wake up is another day in the future, Roger. What do you mean? A year from now, two years from now?"

"Yes, something like that!" Roger seemed to rush forward, as if he had found encouragement in Mei-yu's words. "Mei-yu, many people, many Chinese, are thinking that their future lies in China, the People's Republic of China, now that Mao is Chairman. He has called on Chinese everywhere to lend their talents to the new government, to help implement his new policies. It is a great, patriotic movement! Have you heard of that, have you ever thought of going back?"

Mei-yu looked up. "What do you mean?"

"I mean, go back to China to live, you and your daughter."

"Go back to China?" Mei-yu could not believe what Roger was saying. "Your family is there, Mei-yu. Don't you want to see them again?" *Go back? Go back to my father, who has pronounced me dead?* "In China, you could begin anew . . ."

Mei-yu watched the steam rising from the steeping tea. She could not deny that she had wanted to go back, to return to her home and say to her parents, "I have wronged, I have nothing left now, take me back!" But now that Roger said it out loud, she saw how impossible it was. She had severed herself from her family, she had promised herself to Kung-chiao. She had borne his daughter. She and Sing-hua, Fernadina, were here now.

"It would be much easier for you there, Mei-yu," Roger said.

Mei-yu suddenly understood Roger. Of course, she was a widow now, raising a child alone. As a widow, she did not fit in here, in Chinatown. Most of the other unmarried people here were very old, or were men looking for wives from their own region, speaking their own language, who would share their burdens. She had felt alone in Chinatown before, while Kung-chiao was alive, but at least when he walked with her, people had looked upon her with respect. Now she was alone. Even her few friends would not be able to ease her aloneness, for it was more clear to her than ever that she did not belong.

And what of her present situation with her benefactress, Madame Peng? Would not the people resent her even more, thinking that she had curried favor with the old woman? Would not that situation isolate her even more? Or would they accept her as the newest member of Madame Peng's coterie? One could never predict the reaction of those in Chinatown. Kung-chiao had always scorned what other people thought, what other people said. It had been easy for Kung-chiao to go his own way. Mei-yu was not as certain of hers.

"Forgive me for saying this, Mei-yu," she heard Roger say, "but I am sure you have thought of Sing-hua's future. Do you wish for her to remain without a father?"

Mei-yu stared hard at Roger. Yet, she knew he spoke the truth. Here, in Chinatown, where the old traditions remained strong, widows were not expected to remarry. Yet, even if she were to take the chance of remarrying, was there anyone here in Chinatown she would consider taking as her husband? In China there had been those men who had lined up at her father's door, intent on asking for her hand. Now any one of them would be more suitable than the men here, even if she were to return to them as a widow, with a child. Perhaps, in the new

People's Republic of China, people had changed. Women were equal there now, were they not? They were entitled to the same things as men, the same opportunities, were they not?

"Mei-yu." Roger's voice startled her. "Please. We know you have important decisions to make. We want to help you, believe me. Here." He held out a white envelope. "This is not charity. There is enough there for passage for you and Sing-hua to go back to China. Please take it."

Mei-yu remained still. Roger laid the envelope on the table.

"There is no hurry. Make your decision in your own time. But I think it will be easier for you if you went back. That is why I came, to try and help."

Mei-yu smiled wearily. She did not doubt that Roger meant to help. But knowing Roger, she was aware he had his own interests at heart as well. She knew that if she and Sing-hua returned to China, Roger would be freed from his obligation to them, his poor relations, forever. Poor Roger, willing to pay such a price to free himself from an obligation that Mei-yu had never intended asking him to fulfill.

"I have looked into it for you," Roger said. "It is difficult to find passage, but I found a boat leaving next month on the fifteenth. If you book passage, you must book now."

Mei-yu looked at the envelope on the table. Now she was certain of his intent. She imagined picking up the envelope and flinging it in her cousin's face. Instead, she hesitated, allowing herself to imagine Sing-hua and herself on the boat back, leaving this land that had remained strange to her, leaving behind loneliness. Then she realized that she would be leaving Kung-chiao behind, too, as well as his vision. She could not forsake what he had left with her. Sing-hua, Fernadina, was to grow up here, in this country. Mei-yu knew that very clearly now. When she looked up at Roger again, she laughed, half with relief because she felt so sure of her decision, half in amusement. Roger looked as if he had not breathed in several minutes.

"Roger, I have so much to thank you for," she said, pushing the envelope back across the table toward him. "You have helped me come to a decision. You have convinced me my place is not in China, but here."

She saw that Roger was unable to think of anything to say. She picked up the envelope and put it in his hand.

"And, Roger, I have always known you as a patriot. Why don't you go back to China?"

She stood up, turning her back to him. She heard his chair scrape as he stood up.

"Good-bye, Mei-yu," he said.

She walked with him partway down the stairs, to Madame Peng's apartment, where Sing-hua was waiting. The old woman herself shoved the girl gently into the hallway. "I can no longer tolerate youth in my house," she said. "It depresses me too much. Ah! Who do we have here?" She eyed Roger, standing on the landing.

"My second cousin, Roger, Madame Peng."

Roger came forward awkwardly, took the old woman's hand, and bowed.

"Second cousin, so you are the second cousin!" Madame Peng held on to his hand as if she had forgotten it belonged to him. Roger had to turn his eyes away as Madame Peng scrutinized him closely. He finally pulled his hand from her grasp.

"Tell me, second cousin, how do you find Mei-yu?"

Roger looked at Mei-yu, confused. "I think . . . I think she looks well, considering what has happened to her recently, Madame Peng."

"Yes, doesn't she?" Madame Peng smiled at Mei-yu. "She is a strong young woman, with a strong spirit. She is making herself a new life here. I'm sure she will make us all very proud of her."

Both Mei-yu and Roger stared at the floor. Then Roger mumbled that he had to go.

"Good-bye, second cousin," Madame Peng called as Roger continued on his way down the stairs. "Do visit Chinatown again!"

Mei-yu gathered Sing-hua to her and bid Madame Peng good night. The old woman looked tired. She had muttered something, Mei-yu could not tell what, and closed the door. Back upstairs, in their own room, she watched Sing-hua as she scrubbed her face with a cloth in preparation for bed. Clearly, uncannily, Madame Peng had suspected Roger's offer, had rebuked him, imposing her way there as she did everywhere else. Clearly she expected Mei-yu to stay in Chinatown. Mei-yu looked around the little room. The radiator had begun its first sputtering of the season two nights ago, when the frost had appeared on the windowpane. She and Sing-hua would be warm this winter. They would have enough to eat. All this thanks to Madame Peng. But Mei-yu thought again of Roger's words. She knew she would have to venture forth from this room, and she knew outside, below, was Chinatown. Chinatown, which had always looked upon her with suspicion, all the while keeping her within its tight embrace.

Where was her own voice in the midst of all this, what way should she seek for Sing-hua and herself? she asked herself as she covered the cage of the canary, turned off the light. She slipped into the bed next to her daughter. Their room, unlike the room they had had on Mott Street, faced an inside alley. No lights flickered in from the street. All she really knew of this country was Chinatown, Mei-yu thought. Kung-chiao had spoken of leaving Chinatown, but even he had not known where they would have gone. Now he was gone. Dare she take Sing-hua beyond the only place she had known? What was it like, what were the people like, out there? Were there more white people, more Chinese people like Roger, pretending to be white? Mei-yu looked at her sleeping daughter. *What shall I do now, where are we to go now?* she thought, her eyes searching the darkness.

o o o

Lee felt his eyes roll back under his upper lids, his head loll to the right. Officer Pino stepped forward and shoved him upright again. Lee felt the hard wooden chair against his spine. *I am becoming part of this chair, wooden, dead,* he thought. What time was it now? He fixed his eyes on the desk in front of him. He knew it very well; he had sat in front of it how many times? He had lost count. Very little had changed. Every time he had come, he noticed the shape of the stack of papers on top of the desk had shifted somewhat, but the stapler remained in the same position, the box of paper clips, the dish of rubber bands, had remained undisturbed. The black typewriter had sat, silent, a sheet of white paper scrolled halfway through the carriage. Had the police nothing to do but work on his case?

The only thing that had helped him keep track of the times he had faced the desk was the ashtray. The first time he arrived it had been empty, but it had gradually filled with cigarette butts during the three hours of questioning. The second time he came it had been full, and was emptied out twice before the three hours were over. The third time he was brought in from his cell there had been a single cigarette smoldering in the ashtray, and when he left, he saw that it had become full again. Then it had remained full, and he had lost count of the times after that. The police were wasteful, too, he remembered thinking. They never smoked their cigarettes to the end. They had not offered him one, either.

It had helped him, keeping his eyes fixed on the ashtray. It had helped him not look into the face behind the desk. It had been the voice behind the desk that had changed, he could tell that now. Sergeant Kravitz had lost patience. Good. Impatient people were better to bargain with; better deals could be gotten from them, he knew. Now they had called the Bureau of Immigration and were waiting for the representative. Very good. He would wait until the bargain was right, and then he would hand them what they wanted.

Lee looked to his left. Fong was still there, lackey, police dog, spy. The police had brought him here to translate for them, but he would not speak to him. Let him lap the milk from the pan they put for him on the floor. Then let him run to wag his tail elsewhere. Lee closed his eyes, waiting.

"Mr. Lee," someone said, close to him.

Lee opened his eyes.

"My name is Thomas. I'm from Immigration. I would like to ask you some questions."

Lee fixed his eyes on the ashtray.

"We have reason to believe that you are in this country illegally. You have not been able to prove to us that you had a legal sponsor when you came. What year did you arrive here, Mr. Lee?"

Thomas motioned to Fong. Fong came forward slowly.

"Ask him, Fong," Kravitz said.

"Get away from me, dog!" Lee snapped at Fong in Cantonese.

Fong looked at Kravitz, then at Thomas. He shrugged.

"Mr. Lee," Thomas went on, his voice even, "we don't have any record of your arrival here in the United States. Not under the name you claim to have, anyway. We have reason to believe that your real name is Gow. You don't have an uncle Lee, do you, you never have. Your so-called Uncle Lee was only a paper uncle, wasn't he, someone who vouched for you, gave you the name Lee for a price!"

Thomas waited. "If you do not cooperate now, we will begin proceedings to have you deported."

Lee saw how Kravitz's cigarette had burned in the ashtray, waited for the inch-long ash to fall in a puff onto the glass bottom.

Someone grabbed him. Kravitz's face pushed close to his. Lee saw the tobacco stains on his teeth.

"Okay, Lee," Kravitz said. "Four months of your crap is enough. This is the deal. We now have enough evidence here to have you deported.

You know what that means? It means you get kicked out. You want to go back to the PRC, get shipped out to chop rocks like the rest of them? Or do you want to get sent to Hong Kong, where your buddies there will find out about your little operations here? How long do you think they'd take to find you, how long do you think you'd last?"

Kravitz released him. "Tell him, Fong!" he shouted.

Lee pretended to listen to Fong's muttering. They were getting closer, he thought. Still, the Americans had much to learn in the way of bargaining. He noticed the ash from Kravitz's cigarette had fallen.

"Just tell us what you know about the Wong murder. In exchange, we could arrange for your uncle Lee to appear. You know what that means, don't you?"

Fong muttered again in his ear. Fong, fishbreath, Lee thought, turning his head in disgust. But they were getting very close now. He waited.

Kravitz looked at Thomas, who shrugged.

"If you cooperate, perhaps we could even arrange to misplace your Chinatown file, Lee."

Lee saw that Kravitz's cigarette had gone out. He stared at it to the slow count of ten. Then he nodded.

"Bring the paper, Pino," Kravitz said.

Pino held a typewritten page in front of Lee.

"This is all you have to do, Lee," Kravitz was saying. "Just sign this. Tell him what it says, Fong."

Fong came forward slowly. Lee waited until he got close, then kicked at him, the force of his kick almost throwing him off his chair. He had missed, but Fong stumbled backward, grabbing on to Officer Pino. Kravitz grabbed Lee and pinned his arms behind him. Lee struggled, lowering his head, trying to pull his arms free.

"Pino!" Kravitz bellowed.

Pino had already rushed forward, grasping Lee's shirtfront, his police stick held in front of the Chinese's face. Then he saw that Lee was gesturing with his head. He was indicating the paper, which had fluttered to the floor.

"Paper," he was saying, his voice hoarse from his struggles. "Sign paper!"

Kravitz released him. Pino picked up the sheet from the floor and placed it on the desk in front of Lee. Thomas held out a pen.

"Sign here. It says you knew that Chang had planned the murder of Kung-chiao Wong."

Lee was well aware of what the paper said. He took the pen.

Kravitz grabbed the paper as soon as Lee had scribbled his name. "We got the old man," he said.

Lee slumped back in his chair. He had seen Fong slip out the door. Fong was not his problem. Let everything take its course now, he thought.

○　○　○

Mei-yu walked down Mott Street quickly, pulling her coat closer about herself. At four thirty the sky was already darkening. The sun was so much more impatient, so much less indulgent than just a few weeks ago, she thought. The wind whipped the pennants and kites attached to the stalls, tugging at them until the thin strings that held them were pulled taut. Plastic pinwheels, tied in bunches, caught the wind and whirled crazily, jerking as if to escape their colorful bouquets. Shop-keepers came out to look up at the sky, and began to gather up their wares to bring into the shelter of the stores. In the park yesterday Sing-hua had stood in the pile of brown leaves and shivered. She would need a new coat this winter, Mei-yu thought. She hurried, lowering her head against the wind, hoping she would be able to fetch Sing-hua at the Union and return home before the rain began.

She pushed open the glass door of the Union and entered the swarm of children in the main hall.

The Chinese children, just released from their American primary schools, had entered the Union to begin their Chinese language classes scheduled for five o'clock. They moved around her, chattering in Cantonese and English, entering their classrooms like bees returning to the hive. Sing-hua was old enough to begin speaking English, Mei-yu thought. She resolved to talk to her in English more often. She saw the President, Mr. Leong, outside one of the classrooms. He was cracking open a pistachio nut. She watched as he pondered the nut. It seemed it had not been cracked, or cracked open enough, because he was unable to pry the two halves of the nut apart with his fingers. She watched as he put the nut in his mouth and worked it busily with his tongue, maneuvering it until it lay between his teeth at the right angle. His lips were raised, showing teeth yellow and sharp as a squirrel's. Finally Mei-

yu heard the sharp crack, and pretended not to see as the President spat
the shells onto the floor and munched the meat of the nut. Then he
turned and saw her.

"Ah, Wong Mei-yu," he said, coming toward her. "I've not seen you
in a long time. How have you been?"

Mei-yu could not avoid speaking to him. "I have been well, thank
you, President Leong." She looked past him down the hallway. "I've
come to fetch my daughter, who must be waiting."

"Little ones learn patience by waiting," he said. "Tell me, are you
well, have you been managing? You look much better, I can see."

"Yes, President Leong, thank you for asking. I have been busy."

"We in the community wish you well, Mei-yu. You know that you
will always find help within the community. We always help our own.
If you ever need anything, please call on me."

Mei-yu nodded. "Yes, I'll remember that. Thank you, President
Leong."

She watched as he looked distractedly about him, then appeared to
have made up his mind to go up the stairs.

"I have things to tend to now," he said. "Good-bye. But don't forget,
if you ever have any need, come to us."

Mei-yu watched as the old man reached for the railing with a brown
speckled hand and slowly raised one foot after another up the stairs. It
was true, she thought, continuing on her way down the hallway past
the stairs, the Union had provided emergency care for many people in
Chinatown. Perhaps there were more than a few concerned and kind
people in Chinatown, as Kung-chiao had always said.

But was it out of kindness that people looked at her differently now
when she walked down the street? she wondered. In the beginning,
when she had first begun to go out after she had recovered from her
illness, there had been looks of pity. She had found parcels of food
lying outside her door. Then she discovered that people did not care
that she had moved into Madame Peng's building. Or at least, no one
had said anything. The women no longer even whispered about her as
she passed them on the sidewalk. Was it out of kindness that they
allowed her peace, or was it because she was husbandless now, a woman
without status, no longer someone to envy? When she went into the
shops, people nodded politely to her, did business with her as they did
with anyone else. That was how it seemed; she was anyone else now.
She told herself she was glad to fade into the fabric of Chinatown, to
disappear; it was better than the whispers. Besides, winter was coming,

and people were busy, getting ready. Everyone pulled their collars up over their necks, minded their own business. The young widow was not their concern. Besides, she appeared to be doing well enough.

Only Madame Peng had said to her, "You look terrible, Mei-yu."

They had been in her parlor. A client, who was being fitted with a new pattern by Mei-yu, had just left. Mei-yu had put her pins back into her sewing box, rolled up the tape measure, and was carefully folding the plain tissue paper that she used for her patterns when she felt Madame Peng's eyes on her.

"You have been working very hard, Mei-yu," the old woman said. "Mei-ling tells me you are at the Union every day for more fabric." She paused. "Come here. Let me see your hands."

Flustered, Mei-yu remained standing, holding her sewing box, wondering where to put it. She had not had her hands looked at since she was fourteen, when her mother had her show them to her. "A woman of good family should have hands that are white and soft-skinned," Ai-lien had said. Mei-yu had been as embarrassed then as she was now.

"Come, come," Madame Peng demanded impatiently. "Put the box on the sofa, show me your hands!"

Mei-yu obeyed. She held out her hands, knowing too well what they looked like.

"Ai yah," Madame Peng cried, taking Mei-yu's hands between her own. "They look as if you work in a restaurant! See the cuts, the calluses! Your nails, my girl, they are shameful!"

Mei-yu pulled her hands away. She did not like being inspected; after all, was she a piece of fruit to be bought, a dainty to be eaten?

Madame Peng clucked her tongue.

"Working to the point of ruining your hands will not lessen the loneliness, Mei-yu. For that is why you are working, driving yourself, isn't it?"

Madame Peng could see that what she said was true.

"Well, you are young. What is youth without loneliness? The old now are never lonely, for we have our memories. Either memories, or decrepitude, in which case we haven't the brains to be lonely, ha ha!" She waited, then shrugged. "Yes, I apologize. That was a poor joke. For what do I know of youth . . . it has been much too long ago."

Mei-yu picked up her sewing box.

"Mei-yu, my dear . . ."

Mei-yu looked at the old woman.

"I knew widowhood myself."

Mei-yu sighed. "Forgive me, Madame Peng. I do not mean to be rude. I seem to be unable to find words these days."

"Ah."

Mei-yu stared at the old woman, who seemed to wait, still.

"It is difficult to explain," she began. "In spite of all that you have done for us, in spite of the comfort that we have in our lives now"—she hesitated, looking at her benefactress, who encouraged her to continue with a nod of her head—"I feel that what my cousin said was true; Sing-hua and I do not belong here in Chinatown."

Mei-yu paused. Madame Peng gave no sign.

"I thought that, in order to prepare myself, to gather courage, I would work hard, save money." Mei-yu stopped, confused. It was not until now that she realized how much she had been thinking about leaving Chinatown. She had not even told Ah-chin or Bao what her thoughts had been.

"I see," Madame Peng said. She sat very still on the sofa. She seemed to be thinking. Mei-yu picked at the corners of the sewing box she held in her lap.

"Well," the old woman said finally, sighing. "I was an old fool, thinking that you might stay here in Chinatown. I was being selfish, I suppose, thinking that if I made the conditions good enough, you'd stay. You cannot blame a businesswoman for recognizing her best opportunities, can you? For you are the best, Mei-yu. But you must know I always meant well . . ."

"Please, Madame Peng," Mei-yu protested, twisting the tassels of her sewing box into little knots. "You know I owe all I have to you."

". . . and I certainly will not try to convince you to stay here against your will. But to leave Chinatown! When? Certainly you are not thinking of leaving this winter!"

"Oh, no! That would be much too soon!"

"Have you thought of where you would go?"

Mei-yu shook her head.

"Have you any other relatives, friends elsewhere in this country?"

"No."

"I see. That makes it more difficult, doesn't it? I myself have only visited a few other cities. Boston, and Washington, D.C. Nice cities, although not as interesting as New York. Still, opportunities are possible. . . . Have you ever been to Washington, for instance?"

"No, Madame Peng."

"It is the capital of this country, as Peking is to China. But of course you knew that. It is a lovely city, especially in the spring. The weather there is very much like Peking's, too. It is practically on the same latitude, you know."

Mei-yu tried to envision Washington, D.C. She had seen a picture of it, a postcard that showed the tall monument shaped like a thick upright spear, the white official-looking buildings. Then she thought of Peking, with the winding alleyways, the Forbidden City, the Summer Palace. How was it that two cities so far apart could share the same weather? She thought of the swallows that returned to Peking in the spring, the fragrance of the plum blossoms. Were there plum blossoms in Washington, D.C?

"You were born in Peking, weren't you?" Madame Peng asked.

"Yes."

"My son, Richard, finds Washington, D.C., very much to his liking. But he, of course, lived in other places in this country much longer than you before he moved there. He feels at home in Washington. There is hardly a Chinatown there, but there is a growing community of Chinese working in the State Department as well as elsewhere in the government. More and more are settling in the outskirts of the city. Suburbs they're called, I believe. Anyway, my son seems to like Washington. He is a lawyer, you know."

"Yes, I remember you told me."

"Well, then, that is a place to think about, to begin with, anyway. I have thought of starting a small business there, but Richard has cautioned me to wait. He thinks Boston may be a better place. But there are enough Chinese people in Washington. If you like, I could contact some of them for you, possibly arrange—"

Mei-yu shook her head. "Please, thank you, Madame Peng, but you go too fast. I still have much to consider. I still have my visa status to worry about—"

"My dear girl!" Madame Peng interrupted, laughing. "I forgot to tell you! That has all been taken care of! Pff! Such an important thing, but old woman that I am, I completely forgot!"

"Taken care of, what do you mean?"

"While you were still ill, Ah-chin told me how worried you were about losing your status. So I asked my lawyer to take care of that. That was months ago. You should receive your papers soon . . . any day, in fact."

"But I don't understand, Madame Peng. What is my status now?"

"Don't worry, Mei-yu! My lawyer has seen to it that you are as legal as I am! When you get your papers, you will see."

"Well, then." Mei-yu hesitated. "Thank you, Madame Peng, you have helped me once again. I am so much in your debt! How am I to repay you for all your kindness?"

"You repay me by being happy and well, Mei-yu." The old woman seemed to think for a moment. "I think back to what it was like for me when I came to this country, having no family, knowing very few people, having no one really to trust or ask for advice. The community was helpful in a way; at least I did not starve. But I managed somehow, and I remember thinking then that if I ever had the chance to help another like myself overcome the hardships I had endured, I would take it."

"Madame Peng . . ."

"Say nothing, Mei-yu. We of the Chinese community must help one another as best we can. We are aliens in this country. You will know that soon enough, if you have not experienced it already." Madame Peng sat for a moment, silent. "But let us not end this talk with such gloom! I am glad, Mei-yu, that you have told me this. We will talk further about Washington, D.C., shall we? Now, I will tell Mei-ling not to give you more than three pieces of silk a week, and one piece of flannel, one piece of wool. That should prevent you from ruining your hands further. Also, I want to see you fatten up a bit. You are much too thin. Will you heed this last bit of advice?"

"Yes, Madame Peng."

"Ah! A smile!" Madame Peng clapped her hands. "I have succeeded in bringing a smile to your face. That's much better! I have done my good deed for today. My conscience is clear now. You may go whenever you like."

Mei-yu bowed, and was about to thank Madame Peng again when the old woman waved her hand, dismissing her.

When Mei-yu left, she found herself thinking for the first time since Kung-chiao's death that there looked to be light in the life ahead of her. Before, it had been as if she were sealed up inside a lacquered box, unable to find the crack of the lid, unable to see her way out. Now it was as if the lid had been lifted for her, and she could stand up out of the box and look around her.

She saw the children of Chinatown as if for the first time. They hurried about her in the hallway of the Union, carrying their English and Chinese books, chattering in both languages. Some wore American clothes—corduroy pants and flannel shirts—others the padded jackets their mothers had made from the old patterns. Where would these children go when they grew up? Mei-yu thought. Would they remain in Chinatown, taking over their parents' businesses, struggling as their parents struggled, or would they venture outside of Chinatown in order to find better situations? "Fernadina shall have the best in education," Kung-chiao had said. In China, education had always been the most important thing: scholarship, the examination of thought, the study of science, literature. What would Sing-hua learn here in Chinatown, besides the minimal amount of English; how to sew buttons on a shirt, chop chicken, press a collar? Make correct change? It was not enough. She would not see Sing-hua hunched over a sewing machine, squinting. Yes, she thought, she was certain now. A better life was possible. She herself had known a better life; she would see that her daughter would know a better life, as well.

She looked at Sing-hua now, watching her through the window in the door of the nursery. Sing-hua had been building a tall structure out of wooden blocks with great patience and care. Another child had wandered too close, and Sing-hua had firmly steered her away. Willful, Mei-yu thought. She knew her daughter would not be happy in the lacquered box, either; she would also struggle to look out, to see. Mei-yu was certain of that. She pushed open the door and clapped her hands.

"Sing-hua!" she called. "Come! Time to go home!"

Sing-hua looked at her mother, startled at the clear sound of her voice. She began to go to her reluctantly, turning to look back at her building. The other children stayed a respectful distance away from it now, but she knew it would be a jumble of blocks again when she came back in the morning. Still, she was glad to see her mother. She reached up to take her hand, and allowed herself to be taken from the nursery.

They came upon President Leong in the main hall, looking out beyond the heavy glass doors.

"Terrible weather!" he said to no one in particular. "Icy rain, strong wind!"

Mei-yu looked beyond the glass and saw what the President was saying was true. People were hurrying along the sidewalks, newspapers and satchels held over their heads against the rain, their eyes half closed against the wind. She looked up. The sky was a low ceiling of black clouds.

"Come, Sing-hua," she said, opening her coat and pulling her daughter close to her. "Hold this side over you. Run with me. We'll stay close to the shops. We don't have far to go."

She pushed open the door, feeling instantly the icy rain on her face, stinging her skin like thousands of tiny glass needles. She turned to her left and began to move against the flow of people. She soon realized they would have to cross the street in order to go with the flow of people who were going in her direction.

"Come, Sing-hua!" she called to her daughter and pulled her firmly to her as she crossed the street.

Then she saw the uniforms, the badges shining on the police great-coats. Four policemen were walking rapidly down the sidewalk opposite her, in the direction of the Fifth Precinct. They held someone between them. She, like everyone else, strained to see. She saw the balding head, the cropped fringe of hair on the sides of the head, now flat with rain, the great age blotches on the scalp. People were pressing against her, raising their heads to see. It was like this when a patron in a restaurant became ill; people surged forward to see, blocking the arrival of the ambulance, creating trouble upon trouble. Mei-yu slipped on the icy curb, reached up to fling her soaked hair from her eyes. She looked for a space in the crowd through which to steer herself and Sing-hua. She pushed forward to her left. The policemen were directly ahead. Then she heard the chanting begin.

"Colonel Chang! Colonel Chang!"

She found herself moving forward, drawn by curiosity as well as dread, pushed by those in back of her. She felt her daughter's body next to hers, her small legs bumping against her own as she tried to keep up. She gripped her close.

"Colonel Chang! Colonel Chang!"

She was near now, saw the old man being pushed along by the officers on either side. Two officers in back of them held their police sticks up, warning the people on the sidewalk to stand back. Mei-yu saw the bandage on the Colonel's neck, the splotch of infection underneath. Then she saw him begin to turn to look back at the mob behind him, saw his yellowed rheumed eyes roll, his mouth twist as he strained to turn his head. He raised a fist over his head, shouting something that was carried away by the wind. A raincoat flapped around his shoulders, looking as if it had been flung over him in haste. In his other hand he held a white cloth napkin. He was also wearing Chinese slippers, the black rubber-soled kind, now soaked with rain. His feet slapped unevenly on the wet sidewalk as he walked, slipping as he struggled against the grip of the officers on either side of him. He continued to turn, opening his mouth to shout in defiance of the crowd, his head jerking as the officers pushed him forward. Mei-yu suddenly pulled back, pressing herself under the awning of a dry goods store. She held Sing-hua close to her, shutting her eyes against the crowd of people that continued to surge by, chanting, cursing the old man's name. *Go away,* she thought, *go away, it is too horrible to see, this awful old man!* She had envisioned him, her husband's murderer, a sleek, healthy, oily man, a grinning man, a powerful man. This man she could throttle with her own hands, his neck as thin as a chicken's! Yet the yellow of his eyes revealed the poison within him, poison that had become distilled, more deadly with disease and age. She waited, listening to her own breathing, listening for the dying sounds of the crowd. Her daughter stirred under her coat.

"I saw him, Mama," she said.

Mei-yu looked down at the wet white face staring up at her. "Shh, shh," she said. She looked out into the rain. Were Chang's men watching? What more could they want from her? She felt Sing-hua shivering under the coat. "Two more blocks," she said, more to herself than to her daughter. "Come, Sing-hua, there is nothing to be afraid of, we will be home soon." She held the coat over her daughter again and stepped out onto the sidewalk. She peered through the rain in every direction. The crowd had gone on its way to Elizabeth Street now, leaving the street in front of them clear. She could see no one. "Now, Sing-hua!" she cried, and the two of them ran to Pell Street.

○   ○   ○

Mei-yu rubbed her daughter's hair vigorously with a towel, but whenever Sing-hua's face appeared from the folds of the towel, Mei-yu saw that her eyes remained fixed upon her face. *The child has seen too much,* Mei-yu thought, bending her daughter's head down so that her eyes looked upon the floor. They had reached their room at last, moments ago, and she had turned on the light, her hand trembling. She knew she had also felt the hunger of the crowd as it had gathered behind Colonel Chang, she knew she had hoped that he would fall before her, and grovel, and beg for forgiveness for what he had done. But the sight of him had made her shrink back. She found herself unable to face the bitterness bright in his eye, unable to withstand the sight of his disease. She wanted to forget, instantly, the vision of the old man in the slippers in the rain. She looked again at Sing-hua. Had her daughter seen what she had seen and felt? The little girl was quiet, but her eyes told all, her eyes burned bright. How would she ease her daughter's fears? Mei-yu asked herself. She hung the damp towel up to dry.

"Sing-hua, what you saw this afternoon . . . you are too young to understand."

Her daughter sat quietly on the bed, pulling off her wet socks.

"Colonel Chang will be taken care of by the police, by the law. He will be punished by them. That is what justice means, Sing-hua. Are you listening?"

Her daughter pulled off her shirt.

"You have nothing to fear now. You and I will never see him again. Here." Mei-yu took a clean shirt out of the dresser and gave it to her daughter. She could not tell what the child was thinking, or if she had listened.

Sing-hua pulled her playbox from underneath the bed and took out paper and crayons. Good. She would amuse herself. Besides, there was nothing more to explain, Mei-yu thought. She measured out a cup of raw rice in a pot and poured in water. She put the pot on the stove and turned on the heat, watching the electric coils underneath begin to glow red with the current. She turned around to look at her daughter, but the child seemed preoccupied, sitting now at the table with her paper and crayons. She had selected a crayon and was busy drawing, frowning slightly with concentration.

How did parents explain to their children about the troubles of grown-ups? Mei-yu wondered. Was it fair, telling them things that darkened their childhood, frightening them with things they could not understand? Yet she knew parents could not shield their children from everything; larger forces overshadowed all, adults as well as small ones. She had seen things as a child she had wanted to forget. Things that even as an adult she had not been able to forget. The recent memory of the sight of Colonel Chang and the police stirred those terrible memories of her childhood, memories that then seemed to spring suddenly alive, like embers fanned by wind.

Her younger brothers had also been witnesses. She remembered how, after the war, she and her brothers had talked far into the night, recreating and sharing those memories between them. The memories had seemed less painful, divided that way. But she had left her brothers behind when she left China. Where were they, Hung-bao and Hung-chien? Was she alone with those memories now?

It had been Hung-bao who had first told her of her father's activities against the Japanese. It had been on a winter afternoon in 1943 that her brothers had come home from school, shouting, searching for her throughout their house. Their father had taken short trips away from home before, but this time he had been gone for two weeks and had not written, or left word of his whereabouts. His colleagues at the university had come by to ask their mother if she had heard from him, but they always left after only one cup of tea, sighing heavily. Their mother had been silent even with them, the children, refusing to answer their questions as to where their father was, what he was doing.

But on this one afternoon, Hung-bao had run into her room and grabbed her by her long braid, shouting, "Sister! Sister! Our father is a revolutionary! We found out today he is up north helping students organize guerrilla forces against the Japanese! Isn't that exciting? Isn't Father brave?"

Her other brother, Hung-chien, had joined them and was bouncing up and down on her bed like a grasshopper.

"Who told you this?" she asked Hung-bao.

"One of our classmates, who overheard his father talking about Father to some of their university friends."

"Are you sure this is true?" Mei-yu grabbed Hung-chien to make him still. Her younger brother pushed her hand away roughly.

"Yes. It is all they talk about in school. Father is not alone. Other professors from the university are with him."

"Where are they now?"

"Up north, up north!" her brothers chanted, bounding out into the courtyard, punching at each other. Mei-yu watched them disdainfully.

Now that Li Ma, their nursemaid, had gone, saying she felt safer with her brother's family in the west, the boys had become even more unruly. Fighting, fighting all the time. Little oafs. Even their games were about fighting. She heard Hsiao Pei's rapid footfalls down the hall.

"Hsiao Pei!" she called, running to join her amah.

"What is it, Mei-yu?" Hsiao Pei laid a cloth-wrapped bundle of dried beans on the table. All household duties had fallen to her now, since Tsu-lu, the cook, had fled weeks ago as well, gone to her son's farm in the south.

"Hung-bao says Father is organizing students to fight the Japanese!" Mei-yu said.

"Shh!" Hsiao Pei hissed. "Keep your voice low! What did those scamps say? Why are they spreading news like that around, eh? Hung-bao! Hung-chien! Come here!"

The boys came into the kitchen, looking at each other, grinning. Hsiao Pei snared Hung-chien by the ear.

"Listen now, this is serious. You must not say anything about where your father is, or what he is doing."

Hung-chien burst into a fit of giggles.

"Hah!" Hsiao Pei pulled his face close to hers. Her face was red. Mei-yu had never seen her so angry. "Laugh, laugh, foolish boy, while your father risks his life! Do you realize you endanger him further with your boasting and noise?"

Hung-chien turned white. Hsiao Pei released his ear. The spot where she had pinched it looked as bloodless as the rest of his face. He bowed his head. Seeing his distress, Hsiao Pei gave him a quick, gentle pat on the side of his face.

"Now, Hung-chien, I was angry, and said a foolish thing. I do not mean that you have endangered his life. But to speak about his activities, as proud of him as you are, is not wise. There are enemies everywhere. You must keep your father's work a secret for safety's sake. Do you understand?"

Hung-chien nodded, his head still lowered to his chest.

"Do you understand?" Hsiao Pei asked Hung-bao.

Hung-bao nodded.

"Good." Hsiao Pei glanced at Mei-yu, who was still staring at Hung-chien. "I am glad we all understand. We must be patient. I am sure your father will be coming back soon." She reached out her hand again to pat Hung-chien reassuringly on the shoulder, but he ducked and ran away. She sighed and turned to put the beans on to soak for supper.

Yuan-ming returned to his family three days later. He appeared at the back gate just as Hsiao Pei was stirring the millet cooking on the stove. When she saw him, she dropped her spoon and cursed for having left the cleaver on the table across the room, for he looked like a bandit.

"It is I, Hsiao Pei," he said, bending down to pick up the spoon for her. When she looked at him closely, she saw that he was indeed the master of the house returned.

"Welcome home, Master Chen," she said. I will tell the mistress you are home."

"I will need to bathe, Hsiao Pei. Please bring my towel and razor, and my clothes."

An hour later Hsiao Pei carried his dirty clothes away. He had told her to burn them. She had never seen clothes such as these; dark green, of coarse cotton, soiled as if dragged through mud and grease. At the supper table the three children greeted their father, who looked as if old, dressed in his pale gray padded robe. It was only when Mei-yu came forward for her father to touch her cheek with his hand that she saw the deep lines around his eyes and mouth, the look in his eye that seemed to perceive not only her but through her, into worlds she knew nothing of. Hung-chien, the younger son, threw his arms around his father and sobbed loudly. Yuan-ming gently pried his Number Two Son's arms from him, looking questioningly at his wife. Hung-bao, who had greeted his father first, as befitting the Number One Son, stood by awkwardly, embarrassed for his brother. He stared at the new scars on his father's hands, his forearms. As Ai-lien gazed at her husband, Mei-yu was shocked to see for the first time how much her mother had also changed. Her hair, though still black, had lost its famous luster, and her face was drawn with worry.

Her father's friends from the university arrived soon after supper. After the obligatory cups of tea, they withdrew to her father's study. Mei-yu watched as Hsiao Pei finished washing up in the kitchen. Ai-lien had retired to her bedroom as soon as supper had ended.

"Amah," Mei-yu said, watching the shadows change shape in her father's study as the men walked about the room. She watched them through the window from across the courtyard. There were five other men besides her father. "What are they talking about?"

Hsiao Pei wiped the wok clean. "If your father wanted you to know, he would tell you himself."

Mei-yu threw the chopsticks she had been drying onto the floor. "Why am I not told anything?"

Hsiao Pei looked at her in astonishment.

"We live like ghosts here, always whispering secrets and waiting, waiting. Why doesn't my mother make my father stop these dangerous meetings?" She glared at the shadows of the men in her father's study.

"You misunderstand your mother, Mei-yu. Shame on you for speaking disrespectfully of your parents!"

Mei-yu was three inches taller than her amah but smarted under the heat of Hsiao Pei's gaze.

"Your mother has tried, but even she cannot stop your father once he has made up his mind. And your father has decided that in order to protect you, all of you, none of his activities can be known to you. So stop troubling yourself about things you cannot understand."

Mei-yu left the kitchen. She walked down the hallway to her father's study, pausing to listen to the voices within. Two men were arguing, their voices rising angrily. Mei-yu heard her father's voice break in, then continue on its own in a softer tone. She hurried past the room and into the courtyard. She was fifteen years old, she thought, and still it was as if she knew nothing, and would never know more than nothing. Her mother was firmly aligned with her father, and both seemed to float in lives separate from her, viewing her with gentle, distant concern. And Hsiao Pei, amah that she was, still treated her like a child. Mei-yu hurried down the hallway toward her brothers' rooms. Perhaps they knew more about their father's activities and could tell her. Through Hung-bao's window she saw that he was absorbed in his studies. Next door, Hung-chien was playing the flute. She stopped to listen. He had only begun the study of the flute one year ago but was already able to play simple folk songs with flair and feeling. He played a melancholy song now, the low, slow tones warbling a little when he ran out of breath. Still, Mei-yu heard the sadness. She began to feel the cold of the courtyard but did not want to leave. _That is how I feel,_ she thought, listening to the song. She wanted to go in to speak to Hung-chien, but she did not want him to stop playing. She wanted to hear all of the song. She also knew that if he stopped playing, he would probably break into his oafish ways, pulling her pigtail, joking. Then suddenly the playing stopped. She looked in the window. Hung-chien stood in the middle of his room, his head bowed, his flute held loosely in hand. How troubled he looked, Mei-yu thought. Her twelve-year-old brother suddenly looked much older to her, not silly at all. She shivered. She turned away from the window and went back down the hallway to her own room. She passed Hsiao Pei's room, saw the light within. No, she would not visit her amah tonight, she decided. She was old enough now not to be afraid.

In her own room she undressed quickly and burrowed under the quilt on her bed. She was old enough not to be afraid, she repeated to herself, and closed her eyes so tightly, she saw blue flames licking behind her eyelids.

Many hours passed. Then Mei-yu began to hear noise coming to her from far away. It got closer and closer; she could hear men shouting. Where was she? She thought she heard sounds of people running barefoot, of furniture being pushed around on the hard floor. She struggled to lift her head, heavy with sleep. She heard Hsiao Pei's voice, shrill, outside her door. She swung her legs over the edge of her bed and crossed the cold floor of her room. She opened the door.

The Japanese soldiers stood inside and around the entrance of her father's study. There were many of them, at least a dozen or so. They held their rifles at shoulder height, poised. The commanding officer barked out orders for the Chinese men inside to come out into the courtyard. Mei-yu could see the hands of the Chinese bound behind their backs with rope. Her father was among them. The Japanese must have come upon them suddenly, silently, for she could see her father's pipe still in its dish on the blackwood desk behind him, smoke rising up in little tendrils. Then she felt Hsiao Pei's hands grab her and pull her into the shadows against the wall. Across the courtyard Mei-yu saw Hung-bao and Hung-chien, shivering in their night robes. The court-yard was brightly lit by the lanterns held by the Japanese, the shadows cast by the bobbing lights dancing like devils on the walls. Down the hallway Mei-yu saw the figure of her mother, dressed in her long white robe, her hair loose to her waist. In the distance her white face was featureless. She stood as if frozen.

The Japanese commanding officer barked again and the soldiers in-side prodded the Chinese men with the butts of their rifles. The six Chinese began to move slowly into the courtyard.

"Ba ba!" cried Hung-chien. He broke from the doorway of his room and ran halfway across the courtyard before a Japanese soldier grabbed him. Hung-chien kicked at him with his bare feet and tried to pull away, but the Japanese held him as easily as if he were a puppy.

"Hung-bao!" Their father's voice was clear. "Bring your brother back to his room!"

Hung-bao's shadow came forward. He took hold of his younger brother, who was still struggling, and pulled him backward, back into the dark.

"Ai-lien—" Mei-yu's father called, but his voice broke off when the soldier closest to him struck him with the butt end of his rifle. Mei-yu heard the sound of the wood striking her father's body.

"Ba ba!" she cried, then fell silent as the soldiers began to push the Chinese men toward the main gate. Mei-yu's mother remained frozen.

The Japanese followed the Chinese men out of the courtyard, their lanterns flickering, leaving the area dark as they withdrew. Gradually the sound of their boots clopping on the hard dirt of the alleyway out-side became faint, then disappeared. The courtyard was quiet again. Hsiao Pei rushed across the courtyard and knelt next to Ai-lien, who had fallen onto her knees. Mei-yu followed her and took her mother's hand. Ai-lien's eyes were staring, unseeing. Hsiao Pei and Mei-yu helped her onto her feet. Supporting her on either side, they began walking with her back to her room. Bent down, her mother's weight on her shoulder, Mei-yu saw Ai-lien's tiny bare feet, each toe crumpled, folded under the sole of each foot like the petals of a lotus bud. Slowly, matching their rhythm to her hobbling steps, she and Hsiao Pei es-corted her to her room.

The next morning, Mei-yu woke to the deadly stillness of the house.

She had not heard Hsiao Pei's footfalls, or the scrape of the coal bucket in the kitchen. She dressed and went to the kitchen, then, finding no one there, went to the main entrance room, where she found her mother lighting the incense burners.

"Mama." Mei-yu stood close to her mother, anxious, yet fearing to intrude upon her thoughts.

"Mei-yu, daughter." Ai-lien looked into Mei-yu's face and Mei-yu was startled to see the tears. "Hsiao Pei and Hung-bao have gone to search for Hung-chien. He has run away."

Mei-yu set the bowl of rice in front of her daughter. She had not told her about her uncle Hung-chien, how he had, at the age of twelve, gone after his father. Hung-chien had followed the company of Japanese soldiers that were bringing his father and a hundred other Chinese prisoners up north, to Fushun, and was only three days behind them, traveling on foot, catching rides with villagers, when he was caught. The Japanese sent him back to his mother four weeks after he disappeared from the Chen house.

During those four weeks Mei-yu remembered many things. One was the day her father's colleagues from the university came to console her mother, only to be turned away. "Tell them to leave," Ai-lien had told Hsiao Pei, "they are responsible for his arrest. If they had not pressed him into leadership, he would not have exposed himself to such danger." Hsiao Pei did as she was told, but even she knew that Ai-lien had spoken out of grief, not reason. Even though it was true that his colleagues had come to him for help, she knew, and she knew Ai-lien realized, that Yuan-ming had freely undertaken the responsibility himself.

Then there were the dreams that began to trouble Mei-yu every night, the dreams of her father dead at the hands of the Japanese, of her brother's flute lying broken in the dust. After two weeks of such dreams, Mei-yu finally went to Hsiao Pei.

"Hsiao Pei," she said softly, tapping on her amah's door.

Hsiao Pei had been sitting in the dark. She jumped up and turned on the light when Mei-yu opened the door.

"Hai, Mei-yu, you have not been to see me these many nights. I was beginning to get very sad, thinking that you have grown too old for your amah."

For the first time Mei-yu thought her amah looked tired, old. True evil had befallen their household, for Hsiao Pei, strong, quick Hsiao Pei, had never looked so beaten. Mei-yu looked away from her. She saw the unfinished embroidery on the table. "Will you show me, Hsiao Pei?" she asked, pointing.

Hsiao Pei picked up the work. It was a silk shawl, ivory-colored. Rose-colored silk threads had been sewn into the border. "See what I do now," Hsiao Pei said.

Mei-yu watched as the small fingers expertly guided the needle into the silk.

"Let me try!"

"All right. Use the blue thread now. See how it begins at the bottom of that edge and works into this other pattern. Do that much and then show me. Be sure to stitch closely, and try to catch the silk thread by thread. No gaps between stitches, now."

They sat in silence for a few moments. Mei-yu strained to see the threads of silk in the dull light. After a few stitches, she let the shawl drop into her lap.

"Finished already?" her amah said.

"No, Amah."

"What? Are those tears?"

"No, Amah."

"Was supper so bad? I did the best I could, eh?"

"No, it was not supper, Amah." Mei-yu laughed and wiped her tears with the back of her hand. "I have been having dreams, Amah. I am frightened for Father. And Hung-chien."

Hsiao Pei sighed heavily.

"I'm afraid I'll never see them again."

Hsiao Pei reached over and took the embroidery from Mei-yu. "There is nothing to do but wait, Mei-yu. But I am certain your father will return. Hung-chien, too. Your father's great strength is his devotion to his family. Hung-chien is like his father. They will return."

She waited, watching Mei-yu closely. Mei-yu said nothing.

"I see that it is time for me to tell the story of your father's great journey overseas, when he was a student in England."

Mei-yu looked up. Hsiao Pei sat in her chair, her back straight. Her eyes shone by the light of the lamp.

"It is a wonderful story. It is the greatest of all my stories."

"Oh, Hsiao Pei!"

"Have I never told you?" her amah teased.

Mei-yu arranged herself cross-legged on her amah's hard bed.

"Very well. Let this story replace your bad dreams, then."

Hsiao Pei measured out a long length of blue thread, for she intended to embroider while she told the story. She made certain the thread was long enough, as she did not want to interrupt the story with thread changes. She cleared her throat.

"After your father graduated from the university, the same one where he teaches now, he won a full scholarship to study in Oxford, England. You have heard of England, haven't you?"

"Of course, Hsiao Pei! Stop teasing me. Tell the story!"

"Very well. Many Chinese students were going abroad at that time; to America, to England, to France. Your father was very honored to have been chosen to go to Oxford, which was and remains one of the most famous universities in the world. He went there to study English literature and philosophy. His mother wept when he left, for the farthest he had ever been from his village was Peking, one hundred miles away, and now he was leaving China!

"He went on a steamer boat. It took him two months to get to England, and when he arrived, he was sick. I believe it was a combination of the wallowing of the ship and the ocean vapors. The English weather did not help any. I hear the English heating system is even more backward than ours. Anyway, your grandmother was very grieved when she received a letter from an old friend of hers who was traveling in England on business at the time. This friend saw your father and wrote to your grandmother, saying that her son was white with illness and very thin. But he said there were Chinese restaurants in London and that he would take her son there to help him overcome his sickness and gain his strength back. Apparently that helped, because a month later Yuan-ming himself wrote a letter to his mother and said that he was well and studying very hard. The professors at Oxford were very demanding, but he felt he would do well. I remember your grandmother reading Yuan-ming's letter out loud to your grandfather in their kitchen. I was pressing the bean curds for supper in the kitchen, so of course I heard, too.

"Yuan-ming wrote beautiful letters, and so many of them! He described the buildings in his school, how they were also built of brick and stone but rose up high, high into the sky with towers on every corner. You know that here in Peking, all the houses are built low because the emperor wished to be able to look down on everyone. Yuan-ming did not say so, but I think the English built their towers for the same reason, so they could look down on everybody else. Does not that make sense to you? But to continue . . . In other letters Yuan-ming described the beautiful English gardens, with roses, chrysanthemums, and other wonderful flowers not found in China. He also wrote that the English were very happy to eat huge quantities of meat, and described one dinner at his professor's house where they gave him a piece of cow as big as a shoe! Imagine that! Oh, yes, and their tea was very dark red, Indian tea, and they heaped great amounts of sugar into it. What a barbaric custom! I remember that letter especially well, for in reading it aloud your grandmother said she quite lost her appetite, and I didn't have to cook supper that evening.

"We looked forward to Yuan-ming's letters so much! Every time one arrived there was a celebration. Once there was a letter that also contained a photograph. This came after Yuan-ming had been at Oxford for nearly a year, and the photograph was of him in English clothes! Well, the whole village saw this photograph, and everyone thought it was quite marvelous, Yuan-ming in a shirt with a stiff collar and a tie around his neck, trousers (which I thought were too tight, but of course I kept my opinions to myself), and leather shoes. And then we noticed that he had grown a mustache! I had to pretend to choke on a bone and leave the kitchen because I was afraid to laugh in front of your grandmother.

"Now, let me see, what was his last letter about, before he stopped writing? Oh, yes, in this letter he described the English people, and in this we were sad to read that he was not well received by the people outside of the university. He said he was sometimes refused service in shops and turned away quite rudely at the very entrance of others. The natives were shocked that he could speak their language, and seemed insulted when it turned out he spoke it as well as they did. In this letter he asked your grandmother to thank the missionary Father Joseph for the English lessons he had taught him in secondary school, for although there were some unhappy situations that came about between him and the natives, he was generally well received at the university because of the way he could speak English, and that was what was most important. He said he could understand why the natives had difficulty with him because he did look so different, after all. He closed the letter saying that in spite of these unhappy situations, he had met English people who had been nice to him, as well as some who were even charming, intelligent, and fairly good-looking.

"And then, Mei-yu, your grandparents did not hear from your father for three months! Your grandmother's hair turned gray from worry. Your grandfather began to come home from his shop early to wait for the post. Finally your grandmother, who had become quite frantic, sent a letter to her friend in London, and asked him to see if Yuan-ming was still alive. We all waited with great anxiety for her friend's reply. Your father's sisters ran out to read the stars every night to see what had befallen their brother. And they saw the message written there in the sky even before the family got the reply from your grandmother's friend in London. They already knew that Yuan-ming had fallen in love. But what a shock to find out, from this friend's letter, that Yuan-ming's lady love was a young Englishwoman, fair, blond, with blue eyes! When your grandmother read this, she fainted dead away, and I was so upset I splashed soy sauce on her face instead of vinegar! I burst into tears when I saw how I had blackened her face! Your grandfather reacted in typical fashion by dropping his hammer right there on the kitchen floor, digging a hole next to the stove, and cursing his son for bringing dishonor to the family name. His sisters began to run about like chickens in the rain, for they knew their name was tainted and that no men would want to marry them.

"After two days of this sorrow, I stepped forward again with an idea that I had thought of immediately but which I had kept to myself until I thought the family had calmed down enough to listen to me. This was the idea that they hire a matchmaker without delay and arrange for Yuan-ming to marry a girl in the village or from a nearby village. I proposed this in the hope that Yuan-ming still had honorable feelings left in him and would return to obey his parents' wishes. Your grandmother fell onto her knees to thank me, and I was very embarrassed, but I accepted the eight hens' eggs she gave me and this necklace. You've seen it before, I wear it all the time. Aren't the beads lovely?

"Your grandfather rushed out the next day and found the matchmaker in the village. Four girls were chosen as likely candidates, but one by one your grandparents decided they were all unsuitable save one. This was Ai-lien, the daughter of a wealthy merchant in the village. Yuan-ming's father knew this man, and had done business with him before. The matchmaker assured your grandparents that all the omens were favorable, and that Ai-lien was gentle, obedient, very beautiful, and kind. She could embroider, knew how to manage money, and was healthy, ready to bear children. She could not read, but everyone knew that was a small matter, since Yuan-ming was a brilliant scholar and to have another in the family was not necessary. Ai-lien's father was approached, and the match made. Grandfather was particularly pleased, for Ai-lien's dowry was no mean sum. He had also worried at first that Ai-lien's father would not permit his daughter to marry the son of a blacksmith, but Yuan-ming's reputation as a scholar was now widespread, and the father considered it an honor to be joined to his family.

"Your grandparents went to the village scribe to have their letter written properly, for this was the most important letter they needed to write to their son. They wrote to tell him formally of the betrothal, and to inform him of the date of the wedding. The soothsayer had been consulted, and May tenth had been selected as the most auspicious day. They sent the letter and waited.

"A month later they still had received no reply. Again, your grandmother wrote to her friend in London, and a month later the friend wrote to say that Yuan-ming's friends at Oxford said he was suffering from heartbreak and conflict and had gone to France to think things over. Other than that, no one knew where he was. By now it was January. In February the friend wrote again and said he had heard Yuan-ming was back at Oxford but had changed his address. The friend said he was sorry, but he was returning to China himself and did not have the time to trace Yuan-ming's whereabouts. He wished the family good fortune.

"The family continued to wait in agony. So much was at stake! They wondered if Yuan-ming would go on to blacken the family name by continuing to carry on, or even worse, by marrying the English girl. But finally, in March, a letter from Yuan-ming arrived at the Chen home. Your grandmother sat for many minutes with the letter in her hand, not daring to open it. I remember the day well, for I was trying out a new recipe for supper, a dish of chicken braised with pine nuts and tree ears. Finally she opened the letter, and after reading the first few lines, shrieked with joy. For Yuan-ming had written that he had decided to honor his parents' wishes, and that he was coming home. There was such a celebration that evening; I was even given a sip of wine! Your grandmother hugged me and beamed with happiness, and your aunts braided their hair to look pretty again. How I remember that evening! The chicken dish turned out well, too.

"And so, before two months' time, Yuan-ming was home again. He was taller, thinner, very serious. He had shaved off his mustache. He seemed dazed at first, following me around the kitchen, asking this and that, the most foolish, simple questions. At first he wouldn't even eat anything, but it wasn't long before I couldn't give him enough. The preparations for the wedding drove us all into a frenzy, but the wedding day itself was magnificent; such a warm, clear day! I have already told you all about your parents' wedding, but this part is so wonderful I must repeat it. Yuan-ming and Ai-lien met only once before the wedding. When Yuan-ming came back from this visit, he was very serious, very quiet. I could tell he was already in love. And on the day of the wedding, Ai-lien was so radiant, dressed in red and gold, her skin like a pearl, her face shining with goodness, that everyone fell in love with her. Your grandmother wept with happiness."

Mei-yu remembered how Hsiao Pei had finished the story, her face tilted toward the light. She had stopped embroidering long ago. When she finished describing the bridal chamber and how Ai-lien's nephews had stayed and stayed, making things unbearable for the young newly married couple, Mei-yu remembered how they had both burst out into laughter. Her amah then made shooing motions with her hand.

"You must go to bed now, Mei-yu, while you are still laughing. Bring this story with you to dream about. It will make the bad dreams go away, I promise."

What would her childhood have been like had it not been for Hsiao Pei's stories? Mei-yu thought as she washed Sing-hua's rice bowl after supper. At first, when she was very young, but old enough to listen to stories, there had been the stories of the magic monkey king. Whenever they had suffered from a childhood sorrow, like a skinned knee, or a stomachache, Hsiao Pei would hold them and tell them about the magic monkey king. She had spun the stories of the monkey king as tirelessly as the silkworm spun its cocoon. Mei-yu had lost count of the number of stories of the legendary monkey king, who could transform himself into a huge white bird so he could fly, or change himself into a great red carp so that he could swim through the rushing waters of the Yellow River. The monkey king saved children from the grasp of all monsters, covering miles through tangled forests with every step in order to rescue them. The stories of his exploits were balm for all childhood hurts. Later, as they grew older and knew different hurts, Hsiao Pei told them other stories, stories about the leaders of China, or about their parents.

The story of Yuan-ming and Ai-lien's wedding, for instance, had served its purpose, at least at first. No longer did her dreams of her father's arrest and Hung-chien's disappearance come upon her in the night and suffocate her. She dreamt instead of her father's and brother's return, and indeed, in two weeks' time, following the telling of the story, Hung-chien was back. Following this good omen, Mei-yu was certain that her father would come home next. But two years passed and he still did not appear.

It was at that time that Mei-yu stopped asking Hsiao Pei for stories. She decided she had become a grown-up, past the point of stories. For what could the magic monkey king do against the Japanese soldiers?

And had Hsiao Pei's story of the wedding brought her father back? She stopped dreaming. Mei-yu began to wonder what grown-ups had to ease the pain of adulthood.

Mei-yu pulled her daughter's sleep shift over her head and untied the ribbon in her hair. All through supper and afterward she had been thinking, *Sing-hua has seen too much today, she is still afraid. I have told her all I know, and I have told her there is nothing to fear, but still, she does not understand, she is too young.*

"Come, Sing-hua." Mei-yu held her hand out to her daughter.

Sing-hua came to her and sat on her lap.

Mei-yu thought for a moment, trying to recapture herself in childhood, how Hsiao Pei had been with her when she was afraid.

"Have I ever told you the story of the magic monkey king, who was stronger, faster, and more wise than anything in this world, and whose duty it was to protect and rescue all children?"

Sing-hua shook her head.

"Well, then, let me tell you. This one is about the time he heard about a little girl who lived in a village that had been attacked by a very bad tiger."

Mei-yu continued, remembering bit by bit the story as it had been told to her by Hsiao Pei. When she forgot a detail, she supplied one from her imagination. Her monkey king wore a gold cape now, and carried a magic rope. He was able to make himself invisible. She began to spin the story, watching as her daughter's face began to open up, her eyes softening as she surrendered herself and her fear to the tale. *Work your miracles, monkey king,* Mei-yu thought. *Soothe this child's spirit; soothe mine, as well.*

The next morning Mei-yu woke up and pulled the balcony curtains aside. Sunlight streamed in through the frosted panes. She looked up; the sky above the rooftops of the tenements was bright, cloudless. It was a good omen, she thought. No longer would Colonel Chang shadow her life. She smiled to herself, wondering how long it would take Ah-chin to come to her with the news of the arrest. She would be able to surprise her friend this time, though; she would be able to tell

Ah-chin all that happened as she herself had witnessed it. "I saw this with my own eyes, Ah-chin," she would say, "this is not gossip."

Mei-yu watched her daughter as she tied her shoes. Sing-hua had become adept at the task, forming the loop and the knot of the shoe-strings with sure fingers. As Mei-yu watched, the feeling grew within her that today was an auspicious day, a day to celebrate, to act. Perhaps today was also the day she would tell her friends of her decision to go to Washington, D.C. She had saved up over one hundred dollars; she would have more in the spring. Now, with Colonel Chang safely away, she felt keen, free, like a falcon released from her hood. She looked out past the balcony again, measuring the height of the sun. It was still early. She decided she would not wait for Ah-chin to come to her this time.

"Sing-hua, put on your jacket, we are going to visit Uncle Bao and Auntie Ah-chin this morning," she said, reaching for her coat.

Sing-hua ran to the closet and pulled down her jacket.

"Uncle Bao!" she said, laughing. She had not seen Bao in a long time.

As they went down the stairs and reached Madame Peng's floor, Mei-yu considered stopping. She stood in front of the red door, her hand poised to knock, but then changed her mind. It was early yet; Ya-mei, the maid, had probably not even arrived. Mei-yu did not want to disturb Madame Peng. There was the whole day ahead to share the good news, to talk. She also wanted the time to think of the proper way to ask Madame Peng about finding work in Washington. She would stop by later. She continued down the stairs with Sing-hua clattering close after her.

The man must have been waiting for her, for as soon as Mei-yu stepped out of the building, he was there, talking, showing her a card of identification. She started back, grabbing instinctively for her daughter, putting herself between the man and Sing-hua.

"Frank Collins, _Daily News_," the man said. Mei-yu stared at the card he held out to her in the palm of his hand. The card confirmed what he had said. The photograph on the card matched; there was the same pale face with the flat-planed cheeks. Even so, Mei-yu shook her head and pushed Sing-hua ahead of her along the sidewalk. The man followed them.

"You're Mrs. Wong, aren't you, the wife of the guy who was murdered on Mercer Street this past spring?"

Mei-yu walked faster. He began to trot heavily alongside her.

"Look, I'm not going to hurt you. We just want to know how you feel now that the police have arrested Chang. It's not often we get a story like this from Chinatown. Police headquarters uptown has been pushing for a break like this for years."

Mei-yu reached Mott Street and turned right. The man kept up with her, his breath uneven as he jogged and talked at the same time.

"Look, will you stop running away? Just stop for a moment." He reached out and held on to Mei-yu's arm. She jerked her arm loose but faced him now. The few Chinese people on the sidewalk stopped to stare.

"Leave me alone," Mei-yu said.

The man was breathing hard; clouds of vapor puffed from his nose and mouth in the cold morning air. To Mei-yu, he was huge, like a bear, standing a foot taller than she, wearing a wool outer coat that increased his bulk. He breathed down on her, his eyes and nose watery from the cold.

"Look, it won't hurt you to tell us a little about yourself, your family," he said. "People uptown want to know." The man looked around him, down the street. "Have you had breakfast yet? Can I buy you some coffee? Is that your little girl there?"

Mei-yu pushed Sing-hua behind her. They stood in front of a jewelry shop that had not opened yet. As she pushed Sing-hua back her hand touched the cold glass door, its surface still wet from the melting frost.

"Leave us alone," she said, her voice breaking. She and her daughter were free now. She did not want to say or do anything that would draw attention to them or get them into trouble again. She did not like the looks of this white man, the tone of his voice, the way he had grabbed her. He was from uptown. Those from uptown came always to Chinatown to gawk, to point. She looked to the other faces staring at her from the sidewalk. They turned away.

The man seemed to sense his advantage as the people, her own kind of people, began to drift from them.

"C'mon, let's talk," he said. He reached into his coat breast pocket. "Could your daughter use a winter coat? Here."

Mei-yu saw the twenty-dollar bill he held in front of her. She spat in his face. He cursed, fumbling for his handkerchief. Mei-yu grabbed Sing-hua's hand and ran.

"Damn you, yellow Chink!" she heard him bellow, but she was already a block away and knew he would not follow.

The Sun Wah Restaurant was not open for business, but Bao saw them at the front window and unlocked the door for them.

"Mei-yu!" He saw the wild look on her face and ushered her back to the kitchen. Shen took her coat and Sing-hua's jacket and poured tea for them. Mei-yu sat down at the round table in the kitchen, feeling comforted at once by the rich smells coming from the pots cooking on the stove. Her heart slowed, its pounding gradually diminishing in her ears.

"What happened?" Bao asked.

Mei-yu breathed deeply. "Someone from a newspaper was waiting for us when we came out this morning. He wanted to know how we felt about Colonel Chang's arrest yesterday."

"Pah!" Bao slapped his hand against the table.

"He wouldn't leave us alone. I spat on him."

Bao put his hand on Mei-yu's shoulder, feeling the trembling.

"Never mind, now. He won't bother you here. Have you had breakfast?" Bao turned to Sing-hua. "Eh, little monkey, have you had anything to eat this morning? No? Uncle Bao will see to that."

He pulled out cold steamed bread rolls from the refrigerator and put them in the bamboo steamer. Shen ladled juice from the pot where they had been stewing pork and hard-boiled eggs in soy sauce and anise.

While the bread was steaming Mei-yu sipped tea. She saw the morning Chinatown newspaper that was spread out on the kitchen table. The picture of Colonel Chang looked out at her from the front page. It was an earlier picture, taken when he had been perhaps fifty years of age. His face had been round then with jowls, as she had imagined him. The face of a prosperous man. She recalled again the man she had seen dragged away by the police yesterday, the dried skin of his throat hanging like the dewlaps of a lizard.

She read the article printed underneath the picture:

"Yesterday, police from the Fifth Precinct in Chinatown arrested C.K. Chang, reputed Chinatown boss and head of large-scale gambling operations, in connection with the Mercer Street murder. Police claim they also have in custody Y.C. Lee, reported to have been one of Chang's hitmen. Police say Lee will serve as the key witness in testimony against Chang.

"The case of the Mercer Street murder has baffled police since June 23, when Kung-chiao Wong, a student at the City University of New York, was fatally stabbed while walking home following a meeting with friends at the Gough Tavern. . . ."

Mei-yu looked away from the article. Bao, who had been watching her read, motioned to Shen.

"Take Sing-hua to the front of the restaurant, will you? Bring this food, and this puzzle, with you. I found it yesterday in Kwong's shop and was going to give it to her today. Perhaps she will have better luck with it than I did."

Mei-yu smiled gratefully at Bao as Shen took her daughter by the hand and went out of the kitchen with her.

Bao picked up the paper and studied the picture of Colonel Chang. Then he dropped it back onto the table.

"When the lead wolf falters, all the others turn on him," he said. "Not only has Lee turned against Chang; I hear Tam has left town as well. Or at least the police have been unable to find him. It will be strange to go down the streets of Chinatown and not see those two about. And Wo-fu . . . did you know Wo-fu has disappeared? To think that Wo-fu once worked for me, here, in my restaurant!"

Mei-yu stared at the picture of Colonel Chang. "Is it true, Bao, that even if Colonel Chang ordered Lee or Tam or both to kill Kung-chiao, he will be the only one punished? Will Lee and Tam get away altogether?"

Bao shook his head. "I don't know. The police must have made some kind of bargain with Lee in order to make him talk. Tam could be as far away as San Francisco by now. Who knows if the police will ever be able to track him down. Or if they will even take the trouble to. They have who they wanted to get in the first place. Chang is the only one they really care about. It doesn't seem fair, does it? Even so, Mei-yu"— Bao hesitated—"I'm afraid this is far from the end of the matter. There is still the trial."

"The trial!" Mei-yu thought of the sentence that would be given Colonel Chang. Certainly the law would see that he would be punished for Kung-chiao's death, even if he had not held the knife himself.

"I have lived in Chinatown long enough to be wary of such business," Bao said. "There is hardly ever an end to it. There is still Yung-shan, for instance."

"What do you mean?" Mei-yu asked.

"He's the only one left. Despite the differences between them, Yung-shan remains his father's only son and heir. He is very clever, very stubborn. I would wager a week's earnings that he is the reason the police have Lee under such tight guard."

Yung-shan. Mei-yu had tried to forget the name, yet it remained with her. What was a man like Yung-shan capable of? What did she know of a man with whom she had been for only a few hours, with whom she had lain, her eyes shut tight the entire time? Mei-yu shuddered, feeling suddenly filled with bitterness. What did she know of a man she had seen only on shadowed staircases, spoken to hurriedly from dark phone booths? She knew only that he was Colonel Chang's son, the son of a criminal, someone who had lied to her and betrayed her, conspired with his father to kill her husband. This man was still free. What was he yet capable of? Mei-yu looked at Bao. Did Bao know? What had he seen, all these years in Chinatown?

The cook turned, hearing the front door open. He craned his neck to see beyond the partition separating the kitchen from the front of the restaurant.

"Ah-chin!"

Ah-chin gave Sing-hua a hug, then hurried through the restaurant toward the kitchen, rubbing her hands.

"Hello, Bao. Mei-yu! I've been looking for you. Have you heard the news?"

Mei-yu moved her chair to make room for Ah-chin.

Ah-chin saw the newspaper on the table. "Oh, I see the newspaper has been improving, getting the news the day after instead of two weeks later. Isn't that good news, Mei-yu? They've finally got the old man!"

"Yes." Mei-yu looked down at the tea leaves in her cup. "I saw the police taking Colonel Chang to the Fifth Precinct late yesterday afternoon."

"You saw them?" Ah-chin exclaimed.

"Yes." Suddenly Mei-yu did not care that she had known something before Ah-chin had told her.

Ah-chin sat down, accepting a cup of tea from Bao. She looked at Mei-yu, then at the cook, trying to see what they were thinking. "It must have been a terrible sight. I heard they took him away right as he was about to have his dinner, in the Quon Luck Restaurant. They dragged him through the wind and rain. What an end! Still, he was an evil man, and deserved no better."

Ah-chin talks too much, Bao thought, putting a steamed roll on the plate in front of her. *Can't she see Mei-yu is upset?*

"Well, then," Ah-chin said, leaning back, playing with her steamed roll as if it were a bird that she, a cat, had caught, "have you heard about Yung-shan?"

Mei-yu looked at her friend.

"This is not just gossip," Ah-chin said. "I know the woman who cleaned Yung-shan's apartment once a week. She comes to our shop for cakes. She says Yung-shan disappeared two days ago. She says someone came to warn him that the police were about to move in on his father, and he slipped away, just like that, right from under their noses. Can you imagine, the son deserting his father in that way?"

Mei-yu wondered with pounding heart what else the cleaning woman knew. But she saw that Ah-chin's face betrayed no other secret.

"I doubt if Yung-shan deserted his father," Bao said. "More likely he has gone to a safer place in order to think things over, to make plans. No, he is not one to give up."

"Well, I think he has fled, just like Lo, just like all the others," Ah-chin said, her voice pinched with pique. Bao had a way of throwing water on the little fires she liked to light. Suddenly she brightened. "Then that leaves only the Old Heads!"

"Old Heads? What are you talking about, Ah-chin?" Mei-yu asked.

"She means the original group of Elders who tried to oppose Colonel Chang in the old days," Bao said. "They were the same ones who founded the Union later on. Madame Peng and President Leong are the only ones left of that group now."

"Yes," Ah-chin continued, "now we are left with the Peng-Leong guard of old women with their thimbles, old men with their flyswatters, new symbols of Chinatown, hoo hoo hoo!" Ah-chin howled at her own joke. "Oh, Mei-yu," she gasped, trying to speak between her spasms of laughter, "I didn't mean to insult your benefactress. Only, don't you see what has happened now? Madame Peng and President Leong were the old guard, the symbols of China back home, traditionalists. They had always opposed Chang and men like him, criminals who brought trouble to Chinatown and gave it a bad name, yet they could not control or stop them. The most they could do was to try to preserve whatever was good in Chinatown, to preserve the community. That's why they started the Union. We were grateful for that. At least we could take care of our own. We didn't want any more trouble, especially from outsiders. All we wanted to do was live, in the ways we were used to living. All we needed was business. The Old China image of the Old Heads helped bring tourists, business. And even though the reputation of Colonel Chang frightened some tourists away, we managed. Now that he is gone, it is as if Chinatown were purged. Tourists will come in even greater numbers, and business will be better than ever!"

"Stop it, Ah-chin," Bao said, pushing her more than a little roughly. "All you young people think about is business. Our Elders deserve more respect. They believed in what was right for our people. They believed in dignity, integrity. They believed in justice! So rather than talk of business, selling your silly pastries and moon cakes, we should talk of what is really happening here in Chinatown. There're still serious matters to be taken care of, the trial, for instance."

"Well, then," Ah-chin said, stung only slightly by Bao's reproof, "I hope they proceed quickly with the trial, if there is even to be one, for people say Colonel Chang will not live long."

She saw Bao and Mei-yu look at her with startled interest.

"If he dies, sick as a dog in jail, that will still be too good an end for him!" she said.

"Ah-chin!"

"It's true, Mei-yu! And you should be glad, for what he has done to you!"

"Ah-chin," Bao said, "where did you hear of this, that he is dying?"

Ah-chin dipped her steamed roll into the bowl of gravy, then took a bite. She saw she had reestablished her credibility. *Let them wait for the news*, she thought, seeing how both Bao and Mei-yu watched her with growing impatience.

"Ah-chin, tell us!" Mei-yu said.

"Everyone knows," Ah-chin said finally, her mouth still full. "Doctors have been seen going up to Chang's apartment for months now. They say Yung-shan even had a doctor from uptown come to examine his father. Chang has a tumor, a cancer. He will not live long."

Bao and Mei-yu listened to Ah-chin chew. She took a noisy sip of tea.

"You mean, then, there may not be a trial?" Mei-yu said.

"That's right," Ah-chin said.

"Pah!" Bao snorted. "The old man is tough. He will live to see his own trial just to spite everyone."

But Mei-yu had seen the old man, and she knew, in spite of what Bao said, that the Colonel did not have long to live. What difference did it make what people did to him now? She felt even more that things had come to an end for her here in Chinatown. Yung-shan was the only important link yet remaining. He could reappear any day, although it was not likely to be soon, with the police looking for him. By the time things settled enough for him to return, though, Mei-yu knew she would be gone.

Mei-yu looked at her friends. Bao had begun paging idly through the newspaper. Ah-chin was eating her second steamed roll.

"Friends," Mei-yu said, touching them lightly.

They looked up expectantly.

"I have been meaning to tell you this sooner, but I have only just recently decided."

They waited patiently.

"I am taking Sing-hua with me to live in Washington, D.C."

"Mei-yu!" Ah-chin cried.

"What for, what for?" Bao said, getting up abruptly. He went to stand by his stove.

Mei-yu immediately regretted her words, for the look on the faces of her friends was of shock. Now she felt shame at her own selfishness. She was telling them she was leaving them, those who had been her closest advisors and friends. She tried to explain her hopes for her daughter's education, and how, in spite of the friendship she had known with them, she felt she was an outcast, still, in Chinatown.

"But Washington is so far away!" Ah-chin exclaimed. "Why must you go there? Why can't you go to the Bronx, or to Brooklyn, or to somewhere uptown, even? Who put that notion of Washington into your head, Mei-yu? Was it Madame Peng?"

Mei-yu shook her head, but then realized that Ah-chin was right. "It is true Madame Peng told me about Washington," she admitted, "but only after I had asked her about other places to live. I did read about Washington on my own, and I came to see that it is a good place to live." She heard herself speaking rapidly, as if afraid Ah-chin would interrupt her with more pricking questions. "It is the capital, like Peking."

Ah-chin nodded triumphantly. "You may think you leave China-town, but you will see how Chinatown remains with you, Mei-yu. Madame Peng may be a harmless old lady, but she has her ways." Ah-chin wagged her finger at Mei-yu. "Watch out, she has designs for you. I can smell it!"

Mei-yu shook her head with exasperation. "You are wrong! She has only encouraged me, helped me; never has she forced me to do anything against my will. True, she has offered to help me find work in Washington, but what of it? What kind of designs are you talking about, Ah-chin? Are you afraid she will have me working for her? I have worked for her nearly the whole time I have lived here in Chinatown, and have been grateful for the work! And going to Washington is my decision, mine alone!" Mei-yu became aware that her voice had risen.

Bao returned to the table and stood opposite Mei-yu with his hands in his apron pockets. He heaved a heavy sigh.

"Well, I see you are bound to leave, Mei-yu." Then he turned to Ah-chin with a warning look. "What kind of friends are we to stand in your way? If this is what you have decided, then we are happy for you, aren't we, Ah-chin?"

"But Washington!" Ah-chin threw up her hands. "I hear it is a city of officials who rush from building to building, meeting in secret behind closed doors. It does not sound like a place for honest folk, Mei-yu. How will you find friends there?"

"I also hear there are no good Chinese restaurants in Washington," Bao said, shaking his head sadly. "And only two Chinese groceries, which receive few shipments." Then he added generously, "But I will send you food, if you need it, Mei-yu. Once a week."

"Ai, Mei-yu!" Ah-chin threw her arms around her. Mei-yu embraced her. Bao went back to his stove and began to lift lids and stir things. As Mei-yu hugged Ah-chin she thought, *I could hardly bear leaving my father's house, even knowing that he cursed me. What will it be like, leaving these two?*

An hour later, she and Sing-hua were walking back to their place. They had stopped by Liu's for a package of noodles after they had left the Sun Wah Restaurant, and now they went into a shop for special heavyweight thread. She planned to measure Sing-hua for a new winter coat when they got back. She had saved enough leftover wool and cotton wadding from the Union to make her a coat that would keep her warm through even a Peking winter. Mei-yu gave the shopkeeper's wife the quarter for the thread. The woman accepted the money from her without looking up.

Back on the sidewalk, Mei-yu saw for the first time that day that nothing had changed. People bustled along as usual, tending business, aware that the noon hour was approaching. Had she expected things to be different today, in Chinatown, the day after Colonel Chang's arrest? she asked herself. Certainly she had not expected a celebration in the street, or for shopkeepers to tell her they were glad her husband's murderer had been apprehended, but neither had she been prepared for this oppressive feeling that nothing, not even the feeling of the air as she walked on the crowded sidewalks, had changed.

She passed the jewelry store where she had confronted the newspaperman earlier in the morning. It was open now, the proprietor inside, standing behind the counter, polishing silver spoons. Kwak the dry goods grocer stepped out of his shop and rolled out a barrel of refuse onto the sidewalk. No one looked her way. It was as if nothing had happened.

She felt Sing-hua tug on her hand. Looking up, standing at the corner of Pell and Mott, Mei-yu saw President Leong coming out of their apartment building. He paused to light a cigarette. She had never seen President Leong outside of the Union before. She had presumed he lived very near to the Union, as he did not appear to be able to walk very well. She hesitated, not knowing whether to continue to the entrance of their building and greet him politely, as if it were the most natural occurrence for them to meet, or to wait for him to leave. She knew he also might decide to come down the street in their direction, in which case there was no way of avoiding him. She drew back against the wall of the building in back of them and pulled her daughter to her. She watched as President Leong puffed on his cigarette, then proceeded to walk, in a surprisingly fluid gait, away from them, up Pell Street. What had he been doing in their building? It was not likely he had come to see her, Mei-yu thought. He must have come to see Madame Peng. That was not so strange, for the two still served on the Union Council. Doubtless they had much to discuss, for the operation of the Union demanded that attention be paid to countless details. His presence probably only meant that Madame Peng was receiving visitors now. Mei-yu took Sing-hua's hand, continued up the sidewalk, and entered the building.

Ya-mei, Madame Peng's aging maid, opened the door.

"Come in, come in," she said, standing aside. "Madame has been expecting you. She has saved some special candies for you, Sing-hua."

Mei-yu watched as the maid ushered her daughter into the kitchen, then entered the parlor, where she knew Madame Peng was waiting.

The old woman was sitting, as usual, on the sofa. She nodded when she saw Mei-yu and gestured for her to sit in the chair opposite her. Although she had seen it many times before, today Mei-yu looked closely at the heavy wooden screen that stood in back of her chair. It was of the old traditional design with ornately carved edges, inlaid with intricate mother-of-pearl depicting different scenes on each panel. There were five panels, each unfolding stiffly from its neighbor on brass hinges. She sat in front of it, seeing peripherally the outer panels as they enfolded her, casting shadows that extended to the far end of the room. As she looked out from the vantage of her chair she was impressed again by the careful arrangement of the furniture in the room, the darkness. She experienced the same queer, conflicting sensation:

that the darkness and the panel-wings of the screen were at once protective, but oppressive, as well. She smelled the familiar scent of camphor, cedar, sandalwood, smells that filled the room as if emanating from an ancient sealed chest recently reopened. Mei-yu looked at Madame Peng, opposite her, dressed in her blue satin jacket. The Chinese frog fasteners closed the stiff upright collar tightly around her throat.

Ah-chin was right, Mei-yu thought, _how old-fashioned Madame is, like the antiques she surrounds herself with._ How odd she looked in today's Chinatown, for Chinese people in the street had taken to wearing American clothes; Chinese children could be seen licking American ice-cream cones. She imagined the old lady making her way slowly down Mott Street, past the whirling plastic doodads from Hong Kong. Then she realized Madame Peng was speaking.

"There has been good news today, Mei-yu," she said. "It is a day for celebration, don't you think?"

Mei-yu hesitated. "I feel I should be glad they have arrested Colonel Chang, Madame Peng, and I am glad, yet, I feel a strange emptiness, as if that meant very little now."

"Yes, I can understand that," Madame Peng said. Mei-yu was struck by how tired Madame looked. It was as if she had not slept well, or suffered from indigestion, or some other old person's malady. Even the high arch of her eyebrows failed to lift her face, to counteract the downward pull of the flesh of her cheeks. Her eyes rested within puffy lids and seemed to regard Mei-yu wearily. Again Mei-yu remembered Ah-chin's words. Certainly the old lady had her ways, was eccentric in her blunt manner of speech, but she seemed too old, too tired to have designs, as Ah-chin said. Madame Peng was speaking again.

"I am glad, Mei-yu, even though Chang's arrest will not bring back your husband. His arrest is the beginning of justice. I am glad for Chinatown, for he has been an evil influence here, giving our community a bad name to those uptown, to Americans everywhere in the country. We have waited long for him to become careless, too bold, to make one mistake too many. It is only sad for you that Chang's final mistake was the murder of your husband."

Madame Peng studied Mei-yu's face.

"It will take you many more months to feel real gladness again, Mei-yu, but remember, Kung-chiao's death was not for nothing. Kung-chiao made the greatest sacrifice, his life, so that the bad elements here may be extinguished."

"You make him sound like a martyr, Madame Peng," Mei-yu said, her voice trembling in spite of herself. "He did not choose to be murdered!"

Madame Peng nodded. "That is true. I see that I have misspoken. I apologize. I am only trying to make you see, Mei-yu, that Kung-chiao did not die altogether in vain. We in Chinatown are grateful." She paused. "That is why I wanted to ask you if you would allow us to conduct a memorial service in his honor at the Union in two weeks' time."

Mei-yu looked up, surprised.

"It would not be a religious service. It would be a community service, where we would honor Kung-chiao and remember him. It would be very simple. We would announce the establishment of a special college scholarship fund for gifted students in the Union School in his name. That is all. What are your feelings on that?"

Mei-yu was not certain what her feelings were. She had never attended a community gathering before. She was not certain she wanted Kung-chiao's life remembered in that manner. But if it was for a scholarship fund . . . she could see it was what Madame Peng wanted. What harm could there be in allowing the community this gesture? she thought.

"I . . . I am very moved, Madame Peng," she said.

"Then I have your permission?"

"Yes."

"Thank you." Madame Peng sighed. "I am glad that matter has been concluded satisfactorily. I will tell President Leong to go ahead with the preparations, then. Even though you make plans to leave us, Mei-yu, you will see how Chinatown can show its gratitude."

Mei-yu bowed her head in acknowledgment. Then she remembered her other business.

"Madame Peng," she began.

The old woman looked up.

"Since you make mention of my plans to leave . . . do you recall our talk about Washington, D. C.—how you said you could perhaps contact people you know there. . . ?"

"What is it, Mei-yu, have you made your decision to go there, then?"

"Yes, Madame Peng."

"Very good. Yes, that is very good." She thought for a while. "I believe I shall have good news for you soon. I am expecting word from my son, Richard, in Washington; I am hoping he will approve the final plans for the opening of my new shop there. If he gives his approval, then we shall move forward. I shall need a new head seamstress there. Would that interest you?"

"Yes! Yes, that would interest me very much, Madame Peng."

"Very well. Consider it a bargain struck between us, then." She rang her little brass bell. "Now, let us have some refreshment."

While they waited for Ya-mei to come with the tea and cakes, Madame Peng told Mei-yu what her ideas were for the memorial service planned in two weeks. Mei-yu listened with half an ear, for she thought more of Washington, of her departure from Chinatown in the spring. But she looked up when she heard the old woman mention Kung-chiao's name. *Let them claim him,* she thought, *let them go ahead with their service. For what did it mean, really; Kung-chiao belonged to no one now. Let his name at least be honored,* she thought.

President Leong was still directing the rearrangement of the large sewing room when the more than one hundred people crowded onto the second floor of the Union two Sundays later to attend Kung-chiao's memorial service. He had told two men to push the large tables against the side walls, and began to line up the chairs to face the front of the room himself. People who had stopped at the doorway to watch the transformation of the room came forward when they saw him moving chairs and began to move chairs for themselves. Mei-yu stood at the side of the room, watching as the men and women and children, some of whom she had never seen before, selected their chairs and dragged them to a place where they thought they would have the best view, or to a spot next to someone they knew. Screeching filled the room as the metal folding chairs were dragged across the linoleum floor. Some chairs became snagged on the legs of others, and metal crashed noisily on metal as the people tugged their way to their places. This activity was accompanied by idle chatter, little exclamations of greeting as people recognized each other, and grumbling as people put chairs square in front of others. Mei-yu wondered if she were indeed in the right place, for the noise and confusion were more like that of a village bazaar. It hardly befitted what should have been the solemn air of a memorial service.

As people settled in their places she began to see familiar faces. There was Ah-chin and Ling with their son, Wen-wen; Bao; Kuo, the old toothless man who spent most of his day at the Sun Wah Restaurant; Mr. and Mrs. Liu; Kwak, the dry grocer, and his tiny wife; and several women whom Mei-yu recognized from the Union sewing room. Madame Peng and President Leong were conferring with each other at

the front of the room. President Leong had even found a lectern somewhere in the building and leaned his elbow on it while he talked with
Madame Peng. He held in his hand a small slip of paper on which he
had scribbled notes for the service.

He had never presided over a memorial service before. The Union
was a place of work, of community service, not of worship or commem-
oration. Chinatown had its one small funeral home, church, and Buddhist temples in which the people held services or prayed for the dead.
But Madame Peng had said this case was different; that it was for the
good of the whole community. For that reason, and because no one
denied the will of Madame Peng, President Leong had agreed to call
the gathering. As he looked over the faces in front of him, he saw his
neighbors and friends. Some chatted, some dozed, sleepy from eating
too much dim sum, and some waited expectantly, even somewhat impatiently, for time on this only day of rest was precious. It seemed like a
good number of people, he thought. These were good citizens. He stood
at the lectern, wondering what to do or say next. He was relieved when
Madame Peng pushed him aside and said she would preside over the
service. He walked over to the side of the room, found himself an
empty chair, and dragged it over to the doorway, where he settled himself.

Mei-yu sat in the back of the room, holding Sing-hua in her lap, not
hearing Madame Peng's words exactly, even though the old lady spoke
with a clear, ringing voice. She was thinking rather of the people in the
room with her, how they had given up an hour of their Sunday to come
to this service. Was it respect for her husband that had brought them
here on this day to honor his name, or was it merely obedience to the
community call? True, the population of Chinatown was thousands of
people; this number was small in comparison. But still, they had come.
They were sitting with their backs to her now, facing the front. She
looked at their backs with gratitude. Then she heard Madame Peng say
her name, and they all turned to face her. Mei-yu saw the smiling,
nodding faces. She nodded in return, feeling her face grow hot. She
saw Kwak, the grocer, one of the more prominent merchants on Mott
Street, stand to present a check to Madame Peng. Madame Peng held
the check up for all to see. The beginning of the Wong Scholarship
Fund, she announced, five hundred dollars collected from the community to be awarded to the outstanding student in Chinatown whose
ambition it was to go to college. Everyone applauded. It was an enormous sum. People turned around to smile at her again, and Mei-yu felt
herself yielding to the warmth of the gathering. She looked at the indi-

vidual faces: Mrs. Liu, who had never smiled at her before; Kwak, who had always seemed to stare down into his wooden barrels whenever she came into his store. They were all applauding her now, and she stood up to give her thanks, all the while keeping her eyes on her closest friends, Ah-chin, Ling, Bao. They nodded their encouragement. Finally, after more speeches, one of which was made by President Leong about the arrest of Colonel Chang, and after which there were loud shouts of approval and more applause, it appeared that the service was over. With a loud scrape people got up from their chairs and began to move toward the door. Mei-yu saw Madame Peng making her way to her.

"That wasn't so bad, was it, Mei-yu?" She patted Sing-hua on the cheek. "Thank you for permitting the community to pay its respects to the memory of your husband. I think the service has celebrated the beginning of a new era in Chinatown, one which will show everyone, both inside and outside the community, that hardworking, honest people live here."

"It was a fine idea," President Leong said, joining them. "We are very grateful, Mei-yu."

"Please, President Leong," Mei-yu said, inclining her head politely, "it is I who am grateful."

"There is more good news yet, Mei-yu," Madame Peng said, taking hold of her arm and pulling her away to a far corner. She waved to President Leong, who turned obligingly to chat with some people who had lingered behind.

"I have heard from my son, Richard, in Washington," Madame Peng said in a hushed voice. "He has given his approval for me to set up my new business there. He says he has found a suitable building and that we can move right away to begin operations. He has found an assistant to manage things. Are we still agreed, then—shall I tell him you will be going there in the spring as the head seamstress?"

Mei-yu was stunned. Things had happened so quickly. Yet, she found herself nodding to Madame Peng.

"Excellent! I will send three girls down to work for you, after you and the manager set up the shop." Madame Peng continued excitedly, "Richard says he thinks we could do very well in Washington. Your pay would be double, more than double, what it is here. What do you think, eh, Mei-yu?"

"I am overwhelmed, Madame Peng!" Mei-yu said, shaking her head. "I had not thought things could be arranged so quickly, so easily."

The old lady gave Mei-yu's arm a quick pinch. "Well, there are still minor details to work out, but those are not for you to worry about. You will leave in the spring, eh? Good! Come to me later. We shall talk more. Now I must leave."

Mei-yu watched as Madame left the room, walking in her stiff, uneven gait. She noticed that the room was empty now except for Ah-chin and Bao, who waited for her. Ling had already gone, probably to take Wen-wen, who had squirmed throughout the service, home. She knew her friends had seen her talking to Madame Peng, and when she approached, they kept their eyes to the floor. She embraced them. "Don't worry, I will come back often to see you," she promised. But the looks on their faces crushed her heart. She was suddenly seized with the terrible thought that she had struck her bargain with Madame Peng too quickly. She remembered the feeling she had had when the people in the room had turned to her, only minutes before. She had felt a part of the community then.

Bao saw the confusion within her. "Come, let us go have something to eat, Mei-yu. Come, Sing-hua. Ah-chin, send for Ling and Wen-wen. Today is Kung-chiao's day. We will honor him with a special meal. I have some fresh winter melon soup with smoked ham, soft homemade noodles with scallops and squid, and vegetables. Doesn't that sound good?"

Mei-yu nodded. She saw that Ah-chin's face had become blank. She could not tell what her friend was thinking. She was grateful for Bao's suggestion. But as they all left the room Mei-yu could not help thinking about Washington, D.C., about her new life. A new life in a new place seemed suddenly terrifying to her now, especially since her life here in Chinatown assumed a new face, a community of new faces.

Throughout the remaining days of winter Mei-yu continued to see faces of Chinatown that she had not seen before. She wondered if the memorial service had opened eyes, both hers and those around her, for now the people on Mott Street greeted her with smiles, jokes, and even scolded and complained in front of her in the same singsong whine they used with their own kind. "What has happened, Ah-chin?" she asked one day as they marketed together. Ah-chin brushed her hair from her eyes as she considered Mei-yu's question. Then she replied, "I think it's because people don't look upon you as strange anymore, like the white people, or someone who thinks she's better than they are. They've seen how you've suffered, too. You're like anyone else; they can look at you now. Here in Chinatown, because we all have known so much trouble from strangers, and even from our own kind, like Colonel Chang, who dealt with strangers, we are careful who we look at. With strangers, it's as if we think, if we don't look, then maybe they won't see us. They won't bother us. For that's the main thing, that no one bother us anymore."

Mei-yu thought such was the reason why birds thrust their heads in the sand. She looked at Ah-chin in disbelief. But as she walked through Chinatown that winter, she began to see the truth in what her friend had said. She saw how the Chinese never looked white people in the face. She saw how white persons came into the Sun Wah Restaurant to order their dinner, how the waiters scribbled their orders without looking at them. She saw how the white people stared at the waiters, then glanced sideways at each other, sniggering, even mimicking the singsong voices. Always the waiters looked away, staring over their heads at the tablecloth, at the grease spots, at anything but the white faces. This seemed to encourage more of the white people's ridicule. _Look them in the face!_ she thought as she watched from the kitchen.

Bao snorted when she told him her observation. "Look them in the face and you get no tip, Mei-yu! Hah! And you, if you look them in the face on the street, they think you're China doll!"

Mei-yu turned away from Bao.

"Best way is blank face, Mei-yu. No look, no see. No trouble. We do business with white people to live, that is all."

Bao's words remained with her. The more she watched the people of Chinatown and the white people, the more she thought, _Perhaps Bao is right; blank face is best._ But then she remembered what Madame Peng had said about the Chinese in Washington, D.C., who had found places to work in the government and homes in the suburbs. Surely they had found ways of living peaceably with the white people, Mei-yu thought. Ways of living openly, without the mask of the blank face. Surely they had found other ways of living outside the box.

"I am leaving, and I am taking my daughter with me," she sang to herself as she sewed and pinned patterns. She had told Sing-hua they were leaving. She could see, though, that like death, Sing-hua did not understand at first what it was to leave. _She will understand when we are gone,_ Mei-yu thought. There remained scenes in Chinatown that she did not want her daughter to forget. That Chinese New Year, which began in the second week of February, she buttoned Sing-hua in her new winter coat and brought her to stand on the sidewalks along with the hundreds of other Chinese and white curiosity seekers to watch the

New Year dragon dance down the street. "Remember this, Sing-hua," she said, positioning her daughter in front of the crowd so she could see. "This is part of your heritage. This is what is good." Drums beat. The dragon made its way down Mott Street, the five men underneath the dragon costume coordinating their movements expertly. The head man manipulated the huge papier-mâché head, working the jaws as the dragon twisted and turned in its pursuit of a cabbage strung from the end of a pole held by another man running in front. When the drums beat slowly, the dragon moved deliberately, eyeing the cabbage, seeming to plot its capture. Mei-yu pointed out the legs of the men to her daughter. The men were dressed identically, in black trousers with white socks and black shoes. They curled their feet, walking on their heels, imitating the stalk of the dragon. When the drums beat fast, faster, the men ran, twisting the back of the dragon in S-shaped curves down the street, their legs running in quick small steps like those of a centipede. Sing-hua shrieked. The head of the monster gaped before her, the huge glass eyes glaring from their sockets, the nostrils, painted red and gold, flaring, looking aflame. "It is a good dragon," her mother told her. "It is proud, fierce, and strong, a symbol of good luck for the New Year!" Finally, with a ferocious thrust of its head, the dragon seized the cabbage. Sing-hua turned to her mother, her eyes shining. Then the firecrackers began. All along the sidewalks the rows and rows of firecrackers exploded, popping in a terrifying din. Mei-yu covered Sing-hua's ears and, squinting through the smoke released by the fireworks, hurried her to the Sun Wah Restaurant, where they had planned to have their New Year's supper. "Don't forget this day, Sing-hua," Mei-yu shouted to her daughter as they ran down the street. Sing-hua answered her mother with a scream of excitement, skipping over the red paper of the firecrackers still sputtering in the street.

Mei-yu spread a clean sheet of paper in front of her daughter and printed F-E-R-N-A-D-I-N-A.

"This is your American name, Sing-hua," she told her daughter, giving her the pencil. "You must learn to write your American name now, because soon you will go to school, and that is what they will call you."

She watched her daughter grasp the pencil, holding it down close to the lead, scrawling the letters. Her fingers were pressed white against the wood of the pencil, her tongue curled out of her mouth with concentration. *This is for you, Kung-chiao,* Mei-yu thought. *Your daughter will become Fernadina in school, as you wished. But at home she will remain Sing-hua. At home she remains Chinese.*

Mei-yu turned to her own books. She had gone uptown to the main public library and borrowed volumes on American Government, American History. Now she opened another book on Washington, D.C., written for tourists. _This is where the President lives,_ she thought. _It must be a wealthy city._ The book also said there were many black people living in Washington. She had seen them before, uptown. They wore blank faces, too. She had often wondered what their hair felt like. Was it as soft as it looked? The color of the palms of their hands was pink, unlike the dark skin on the top. They had wide nostrils, too, like many of the Cantonese. She had never heard one speak. They never came to Chinatown. Were they like white people, except for their color? Mei-yu thought. Best to be careful with them, also, best to be blank.

"Count from one to one hundred," she told her daughter. Sing-hua had covered the sheet of paper with writing her American name, and now, on the other side, she began to write numbers. _You are different enough, daughter,_ Mei-yu thought. _The white children will think your beautiful eyes, your skin, your strong shiny hair strange. But they will see how you write your name, how you count to one hundred. They will see how strong you are._

Mei-yu put a new sheet of paper in front of her daughter.

"Just a little more, Sing-hua, and then we will go to visit Ah-chin and Wen-wen. It is lovely outside today, already warmer!"

Sing-hua sighed.

"Here. Write this. This is your family name. Wong. W-O-N-G. You will use this at school, as well as at home. This will always be your name. A name of honor. Write it now."

Mei-yu watched as her daughter wrote. _Learn your name, daughter,_ she thought. _It is the name of your father, who left it to you. Learn your name and write it clearly, so that others may remember it with respect._

○　○　○

Bao had been to Port Authority before. Years ago he had taken his wife there to board a bus to Oklahoma City, where she had a sister. He did not hear from her for two months. His regular customers at the Sun Wah Restaurant asked him about her, asked when she was coming back. After another month had passed, they teased him, saying she must have found a nice Chinaman in Oklahoma City who owned his own laundry. Finally he received a letter from his wife, saying there was more air out there on the prairie and that life was not so hard; her sister said she could work in the dress shop, making alterations with her. She said she was sorry, but she was not coming back. She said she would understand if he divorced her, and even added she hoped he would marry again. When his customers saw Shen working in the kitchen, coming out to sweep the floor or arrange the settings on the tables, doing things Bao's wife used to do, they fell silent.

Bao carried a large cardboard box tied with string, and a brown paper bag. Inside the box were Mei-yu's teapot, teacups, and plates. Ah-chin carried another box that contained Mei-yu's portfolio of designs and other miscellaneous items. Mei-yu had two new cheap suitcases filled with her and Sing-hua's clothes. Also packed inside were photographs, jewelry given to her by her mother, and the four books of poetry she had brought with her from China. The three adults stood in the ticket line. Sing-hua perched on the larger suitcase and watched the people rushing by in the station.

Ah-chin shifted her weight from foot to foot. These Americans rushed everywhere they went, but their lines remained as slow as the ones in China, she thought. She looked at the big clock at the end of the station lobby. She was anxious to get back to the shop before noon so that Ling could take enough time to eat his lunch. Wen-wen was at the Union. She looked at Mei-yu, who was studying a bus schedule. Her friend was still thin, her skin sallow. Ah-chin, who had envied her friend the pearly luster of her skin, now mourned the fading of it as if it had been her own. Mei-yu had at least regained most of her strength and the quick look in her eye. She would regain her beauty, too, in time, Ah-chin thought.

Bao craned his neck to see what was happening at the front of the line. There were eight people before them, all sitting on their suitcases. They glared at the person first in line. The clerk behind the ticket window took a sip out of a paper cup and stared at the large lobby clock as the man in front of her searched his pockets. Bao looked around, remembering the station well; the floor that was littered with ticket stubs, candy wrappers, cigarette butts, the air filled with the smells of disinfectant and stale smoke. Occasionally women dressed in scarlet or purple rapped by in their high heels, leaving the scent of cheap perfume in the air. But most of the people looked to Bao to be honest common folk, studying the schedules posted on the walls with furrowed brows, or dragging their suitcases along behind them through the lobby. Others, like the ones waiting in front of them, sat among their bags in dispirited heaps.

Mei-yu had begged him not to come, knowing how painful the memory of the place must remain for him. She insisted she could have her teapot and teacups shipped to her in Washington, saying they had survived longer and more dangerous journeys. But Bao told her he would not allow her to go to the bus station alone. Even if she were accompanied by Ah-chin, he had said, they were still only two frightened-looking women vulnerable to the assault of bandits who lurked in the station. Besides, he had said, Americans had no respect for a person's property. He had seen them unload boxes and crates of vegetables in front of the restaurants in Little Italy, which bordered Chinatown. The white men stood in the cavernous bodies of the trucks with big cigars in their mouths, wearing grimy undershirts and stained green pants, hefting crates of lettuce and dropping them with loud crashes onto the sidewalks. Bao envisioned Mei-yu opening her box of precious teaware and finding them in shards. No, he had said, swallowing his memory of the bus station, he would carry the box for her.

Mei-yu looked up from the bus schedule. Buses to and from Washington appeared to be frequent; if they missed this one, they could get on one an hour later. She looked again at Sing-hua. The little girl was standing, chatting with Bao, swinging her stuffed rabbit from side to side. Her toy horse and wooden puzzles were packed safely inside her suitcase. Mei-yu had told her once again what leaving meant, that they would not see Uncle Bao tomorrow, or the next day, and probably not for many days. They would come back to see Uncle Bao again, though, sometime in the future. Sing-hua had nodded. Mei-yu had looked into her daughter's eyes, had seen no fear. Still, she was glad that Bao had come with them.

She saw from the bus schedule that the trip to Washington took only four and a half hours. The train she and Kung-chiao and the baby Sing-hua had taken from California to New York had traveled four, five, how many days? She had forgotten. She had slept during the day and through the night, rocked by the swaying of the car on the rails. Kung-chiao had walked up and down the car with Sing-hua, giving her to Mei-yu at intervals to nurse. As with all the other times in this country, the white people on the train had stared, pointing to their tunics and trousers and flat shoes. Kung-chiao had kept his eyes lowered, or focused on the flat prairie land through which they rocked. When Mei-yu woke up during the day, she saw the bright color of the sky and land reflected in her husband's eyes, and when she turned her head to look herself, she saw that all was flat, broad, featureless. Whenever she felt the white people's eyes upon her, she closed her eyes. It was best to sleep, she remembered thinking.

She knew she and Sing-hua would not be going through prairie land on the way to Washington, for she had seen the map in her books. This part of the country had a spine of gentle mountains, as well as valleys, and green land that edged toward the ocean to the east.

She finally reached the ticket window. Madame Peng had given her money for the trip, and she carefully counted out the bills, and counted the change given her. She held the tickets in her teeth and picked up the suitcases.

Bao hovered near the driver of the bus to make sure the suitcases were placed in the luggage area underneath the coach. He insisted on putting Mei-yu's boxes there himself, despite the protests of the driver.

"No speak English," he said to the driver, shrugging, pushing past him and ducking his head as he placed the boxes on the floor of the luggage area and pushed them in firmly.

"Watch that they are careful unloading it," he admonished Mei-yu in Cantonese. The driver muttered something, but Bao gave him his radiant idiot's smile. The driver grunted and turned to collect tickets from the other passengers.

"Ah-chin!" Mei-yu embraced her friend. They both wiped tears from their faces, laughing from embarrassment and sadness.

"Write to me," Ah-chin said. "Send me pictures of Sing-hua and I will send you some of Wen-wen; he will catch up with her yet!" She reached inside her blouse. "From Ling and me," she said, pressing something wrapped in tissue into Mei-yu's hand. Mei-yu hesitated, then unfolded the tissue. It was a bracelet made of little ivory balls the size of peas, intricately carved and strung with waxed string.

"Oh, Ah-chin!"

"We carried it from China. Please take it. To remember us."

Mei-yu refolded the tissue around the bracelet and put it in her purse. She smiled again at Ah-chin, who hid her face in her handkerchief, blowing her nose. Mei-yu turned to Bao. He shoved the brown paper bag into her hand. She smelled the fragrance of the freshly made pork buns. "Your lunch," he said, stepping back.

"Thank you, Bao."

They stood there for several moments, allowing the other passengers to push past them and give their tickets to the bus driver.

"Say good-bye to Uncle Bao and Auntie Ah-chin," Mei-yu said, giving Sing-hua a little push. Her daughter stared, frowning, at Bao and Ah-chin. Ah-chin came forward and hugged her.

"Go on, Sing-hua!" Mei-yu said, pushing the girl toward Bao, seeing the line dwindling behind them. It was time to go.

"Uncle Bao?" her daughter said, looking up at the cook. She had dropped her stuffed rabbit. When he bent down to pick it up, she threw her arms around his neck.

"Uncle Bao!"

"Shh! Shh, little plum," Bao said, patting her back gently as she sobbed into his shirt collar. He pulled out his handkerchief and passed it quickly over his face, then held it in front of Sing-hua for her to wipe her nose.

"Shh, little monkey, are you crying because you think I forgot you? Look what I have here!"

He reached into his pocket. Sing-hua saw the necklace swinging from his hand. It was a little jade pendant, carved in the shape of a flower.

"For you," Bao said, slipping the necklace over her head.

"No! No! No!" Sing-hua cried, shaking her head back and forth vehemently, biting her lip. "I don't want to go!"

The bus driver asked Mei-yu for her tickets. She gave them to him, then held out her arms to her daughter. Sing-hua turned away from her mother, burying her head into the cook's shoulder. Bao patted her again.

"See what else Uncle Bao has," he whispered into her ear.

Sing-hua lifted her head. Her face was red, her eyelashes tangled with tears. She had forgotten about the bulge in his jacket pocket. Bao reached in the pocket and pulled out a new wooden puzzle. It was a grown-up's puzzle, a ball made of many interlocking pieces of multi-colored wood. She stared at it intently, snuffling.

"Will you promise to come back to see Uncle Bao if I give you this?" the cook asked, holding the puzzle in front of her.

Sing-hua studied it. She reached out for it, hiccuping.

"No!" Bao pulled it away from her. "You must promise to be good, to obey your mother, and come back to see me very soon. Only when you promise will I give this to you."

"Come on, we're late already," the bus driver was saying.

Sing-hua looked at her mother, who smiled encouragingly. Then she nodded, dipping her head quickly, and reached out for the puzzle. Bao gave it to her and carried her onto the bus.

Mei-yu waved to her friends from behind the tinted window of the bus. Ah-chin waved back. Bao stood on the curb with his hands in his pockets, staring in her direction, seeming to be deep in thought. It had been the same when someone else had left him, he was thinking. He wondered if Mei-yu would ever come back.

Mei-yu looked out at the city as the big bus roared through the streets. It was now mid-morning and the sky was still gray, like the dawn. She saw the people on the streets, thinking how similar they were to the people in Chinatown, even though they were white. They stood by their fruit stands, their shoe-shine platforms, their candy stores, and waited for business in the same way, calling out for people to look or buy. She saw how their eyes were constantly shifting, not looking directly at customers or passersby but looking through, looking around, looking for something not there.

The bus entered a long black tunnel. When it emerged and climbed up onto the highway, Mei-yu turned in her seat and watched the skyscrapers recede, like mountains sinking into sand. Sing-hua had lain with her face buried in her mother's skirt until the bus entered the tunnel; then she grasped the pendant around her neck and stared at the endless yellow tiles of the tunnel wall that flashed by as the bus rushed through. The rocking of the coach lulled her. By the time the bus emerged from the darkness, she was asleep.

Mei-yu looked out and saw the endless rows of telephone poles, electrical stations, and fuel tanks. The air was noxious, as if the bus were emptying its fumes into itself. She leaned her head back against her seat, weary.

"Everything has been taken care of," Madame Peng had told her. "There will be someone to meet you and Sing-hua. Her name is Kuei-lan Woo. She will take you to your new place. On Monday, she will take you to your new job."

Madame Peng had made everything sound so simple. She herself had seemed as excited as Mei-yu when they met in her parlor for the last time. She gave her the envelope of money for the bus tickets and for their first few weeks in Washington.

"Watch out for the white people in the banks and the offices, Mei-yu. Count all your change. Watch out for the black people on the streets, also. Walk very quickly and make certain they don't follow. Mrs. Woo will help you. Richard says she is very kind, very efficient. She will take care of you. And, oh!" The old lady had smacked her forehead with her hand. "I almost forgot! Stay here, I shall be right back!"

Madame Peng walked as quickly as her legs would permit her, disappearing into her bedroom, which adjoined the parlor. Mei-yu waited, standing in the middle of the thick blue rug, her feet next to the woven motif of the blue bat. She looked down at the bat. It seemed to hover at the center of the rug, its wings outstretched. White people looked at them with loathing, she knew. But in China they were more like birds than rats; they were animals that brought good luck, always. Madame Peng returned, holding out in front of her a wooden box slightly larger than a cigar box. It was handsome, made of polished cedar, plain but perfectly fitted.

"Do me this favor, Mei-yu. I have been meaning to give this to Richard for many years now, but have never managed to remember it in all my journeys to Washington. Will you give this to him? Do his old mother this favor, will you?"

Mei-yu took the box. It was light. There was no lock on it. "Certainly, Madame Peng," she said.

"So, Mei-yu." Madame Peng ushered her to the door. "Have you any more questions to ask? I think I may have remembered all that I wanted to say to you. Write to me often. Perhaps, after things have settled down a bit, you will come back to visit us, eh? Meanwhile, remember that Mrs. Woo will look after you, and Richard, too, although he is a very busy man. Don't forget the box, eh?"

"Good-bye, good-bye." Mei-yu had never seen Madame Peng looking so well. Her eyes looked clear, her face freshly powdered. She smiled, waving from the crack of the red door as Mei-yu went upstairs to finish her packing.

Good-bye, good-bye, Mei-yu said to herself, watching the landscape change outside the window as the bus rocked down the highway. The skyscrapers and electrical stations had disappeared, and now they passed rows and rows of houses, all looking exactly alike. She suddenly felt very tired. She did not know what lay ahead of her. She tried not to think of the future, in the same way she tried not to imagine her dreams when she lay her head down to sleep at night. Her immediate past, Kung-chiao's death, lay like a fresh clot next to her heart. Why had he been so trusting, Kung-chiao, he who had always been so wise? she thought.

She looked down at her sleeping daughter. "Where are we going?" Sing-hua had asked, days ago, when she saw her mother packing the boxes. "To Washington, D.C., to a new life, Sing-hua," Mei-yu had said. Mei-yu was relieved that her daughter had seemed satisfied with her answer. She watched the rows of houses outside the bus window. The sun was brighter here, outside the city. Women were hanging wash outside in the yards behind the little houses. *Is this right, Kung-chiao?* Mei-yu thought. *Was this what you were thinking of?*

PART
TWO

WASHINGTON, D.C.
1955

Kuei-lan Woo slid under the steering wheel of the Ford and turned the key in the ignition. To her amazement, as always, the engine rumbled to life, surrounding her with its growling. She stretched her neck to look through the curved windshield and down the length of the shiny black hood, sighting the ornament at the end. *Follow the nose,* she told herself. As a girl she had held on to the string that had been fastened to the ring in the nose of her father's water buffalo. By tugging on it gently, she could make the beast rumble, and by prodding it behind the ears with a stick, she could make its nose point straight ahead, down the rows of the rice paddy, or to the left, to the right. She sat behind the stonelike skull, in between the horns that swept to either side of her body like scimitars. From this parapet she was able to see the entire watery field before her; the grassy stalks of rice waving like seaweed in the shallow ripples, and closer, the snails clinging to them, the tiny fish darting among the roots. Balanced in the crook of the buffalo's neck, between his skull and his knobbed shoulders, she could see the long lashes of his eyes underneath, feel the slow plodding of his heart against the small of her back. She would kick the mud-covered hide with her heels and shout, "Ai yup!" prodding the tender spot behind his ears with her stick, delighting in the power she held over the immense body. The buffalo would low in protest, preferring to stay in its wallow through the hot afternoon, but Kuei-lan would rap on his skull and pull on the ring piercing the tender flesh of his nose to make him move. She heard the little squawks made by his hooves as they pulled out of the ooze. The hindquarters would rise first, pitching her forward so that she balanced herself by spreading her palms against the headbone, feeling the bristles that grew there three inches long. Then, with a heave, the forequarters would shove up into her chest, and suddenly they were standing, dripping, surveying the field from an even higher vantage. Kuei-lan leaned with the slow round sway of the buffalo as it made its way through the paddy. Sometimes its tail, flicking for flies, would swipe her back. Their progress was leisurely, rolling, accompanied by the soft splash of water and the sucking sound of mud. The fish underneath darted frantically, fanning to other rows. The sun would heat her straw hat as she sat, rocking, nearly dozing, atop the buffalo. She watched the broad wet muzzle swing side to side as they went. Her father waited at the far end of the field, ready with the yoke. Though she knew he waited, she knew there was no hurry; there was no hurrying the buffalo.

Now, surrounded by the sound of the mechanical beast, Kuei-lan shifted the gears and pressed the accelerator pedal slightly. This machine raced impatiently, its innards throbbing with energy. Kuei-lan still expected the day when it would yank from her grip and run away with her, hurtling its mindless, shiny black body against a wall, into a ditch. Her foot shifted nervously from the accelerator pedal to the brake. She looked to her left and then to her right, then steered the car from the apartment parking lot onto the street. In previous weeks, when she had just been learning to drive, she had kept her eyes fixed to the road, fixed to the painted lines on the pavement that pointed the way. "Just follow the nose of the car," the instructor had said. She gladly obeyed him, daring neither to look to the side of the road nor to use her mirrors. The mirrors confused her, reflecting images of cars that appeared out of nowhere to bear directly upon her. She always felt she would be trampled. But now, after weeks of driving, she had courage enough to take her eyes off the painted lines long enough to cast quick glances at the side of the road. She saw people walking on the sidewalk, peeling off jackets in the warm air; she saw budding dogwood trees. Some of the buds were pink, some white. All were pale in contrast to the bark of the trees, which remained black from the early morning rainshower. While she waited at a stoplight she looked about her and noticed that now, in the early part of April, even the sootiest clumps of snow next to the road had melted, leaving only gravelly crumbs at the curb. The light changed and Kuei-lan put the car back into gear. It lurched forward, startling her again. She knew the machine she rode was a product of modern American technology, but still, she could not altogether put her faith in it. The very feel of it, the roar of it, the lack of the heartbeat, made her wary.

A policeman on a motorcycle rode up next to her and watched her as she drove, like a fly that suddenly buzzes up and begins to accompany in a parallel path. He had thought she had been a child driving, for she sat low in the seat, peering through the steering wheel. It was impossible to tell the age of Orientals, he thought, checking her flat profile. Twenty-five-year-old Orientals looked like twelve-year-olds. The newer ones, especially. She had turned her head swiftly to look at him once but kept driving. This one did not look quite new; her hair was pulled back into a short ponytail, clipped to the sides with barrettes. She had on a red cotton jacket, the kind his daughters wore. And in spite of her tenseness, she seemed to be in control. He pulled back. He saw her eyes flicker to her rearview mirror, then back to the road in front of her. He let her go.

The bus Kuei-lan was to meet would be arriving at the downtown Greyhound station in less than an hour. Mr. Peng had told her that his mother was sending a woman, a widow, and her child from New York. He said they were not fresh off the boat, as they had lived in Chinatown for four years. But Kuei-lan knew they would be almost as green, almost as uncertain as the most recent refugees, for what did those from Chinatown know of America? She pressed the accelerator pedal with new determination, feeling a kind of fearful exhilaration as the car leapt forward. She herself had arrived right after the Second World War; she had been one of those fresh off the boat. She and her husband, Ting, had worked in her uncle's laundry in San Francisco. From there they had moved east, to Chicago, then finally to Washington, D.C. She had sorted jujubes and measured rice into brown paper bags, while her husband loaded vegetables for the Wing Fat Trading Company on H Street. They lived in a tiny room above the trading company, sharing the downstairs kitchen with Mr. Lom, the proprietor, an old man from Canton with no teeth. In the winter Mr. Lom hung his fatty, pungent Chinese sausages up in their room to cure. They were strung on every middle rafter, dangling down from the ceiling like succulent vines. Newspapers were spread on the center of the floor to catch the drippings. Kuei-lan and Ting pushed all their belongings to the sides of the room to avoid the drippings and walked, clinging close to the walls, like rats in the night.

After two years at the Wing Fat Company, Ting heard of a Cantonese couple in Arlington who had made enough money from their laundry business to move out to Bethesda, in Maryland, where the husband intended to set up his own electrician's shop. Kuei-lan borrowed money from her uncle in San Francisco and, with that money, plus what they had saved, took over the lease of the tiny laundry shop on Washington Boulevard. They packed their things and moved to Arlington, into the room in back of the laundry.

Ting took his place at the front counter, taking in the shirts and sheets and underwear. Kuei-lan could hear him greet their customers in his cheery way, shouting, "Hoy, hoy, hoy," at everyone. He took the dirty clothes and stuffed them into large gray canvas bags. Then he would carefully twist wire around the necks of the bags and label them. Every day a van would come by to collect the bags and take them to the washing factory in nearby Fairfax. In twenty-four hours the clothes would come back clean, but damp and wrinkled. Then it was Kuei-lan's turn. She starched the shirts and pressed them with her iron. Then she folded the shirts, pinning the sleeves back, wrapping them in clean brown paper. She had long lost count of the brown paper bundles she had made.

On her bad days, when she had spent nine or ten hours at the iron, she thought that her women customers were too lazy to wash their own clothes. And American men probably did not even know how to wash clothes. Only Chinese men washed clothes. Americans seemed to be glad to let Chinese men wash their clothes. Ting even helped her with the ironing when the canvas bags began to crowd them out of their room. Then, late at night, tying strips of cloth around their foreheads to keep the sweat from running into their eyes, they would make up stories about the owners of the garments they ironed. Clothes gave clues as to what their customers ate. One shirt was still dyed blue on the front from some kind of fruit—grapes or berries. Another shirt bore the stubborn rusty stain of blood. They concluded the Carters must have only one set of sheets. They always brought in the same set. What did they sleep on while their sheets were being laundered—didn't Mr. Carter earn enough for another pair? The Guilfords' children were rough on their clothes. Holes, tears, everywhere. Maybe the Guilfords beat their children!

On other days, when the pile of bags remained manageable and Kuei-lan could sort the clothes almost at leisure, she began to recognize the same things, as if they were the well-worn clothes belonging to her own family. Even rags that must have been used for dusting and cleaning tumbled out of the canvas bags, so she knew her customers must be thrifty, honest. She decided they were not lazy, but simply not wealthy enough to own their own washing machines. This surprised and saddened her, for she had believed that all American families owned their own refrigerators and washing machines.

But Kuei-lan knew some of their customers were well-off. Occasionally she would find a stray lace pillowcase, a silk slip. These must have made it into the Chinese laundry pile by mistake. These she carefully set aside and wrapped up separately.

The pickup tickets were yellow cardboard with red numbers, given to customers when they brought in their laundry. On the day when their laundry was ready, the customers would give their ticket to Ting, who would then match the number on the ticket with the customer's package of clean laundry. The shop and their living area in back were littered with the tickets. No matter how often Kuei-lan complained, her husband would not find a place to store them. The tickets turned up in their own sheets, or under the card table, where they had their meals. She found one in her shoe. "*Ai yah!*" she scolded her husband, until finally he swept the tickets into a shoebox. Soon, shoeboxes began to stack up underneath the counter. They were knocked over. One day they disappeared. "Where are the tickets, our records?" Kuei-lan cried at her husband. "What if the Immigration people come to ask us about them? We have to be more careful, we could be thrown out of the country!" Her husband shrugged but set out another shoebox. Now she kept the shoeboxes under the bed, in neat rows.

Business appeared to be steady, but Kuei-lan was lonely. There were no other Chinese people in the area. In Washington, D.C., at least, there were other Chinese families, and a place, a Community Center, where they could all gather. Here, in the little shopping area where they had their laundry, all the other stores were run by white people. Kuei-lan noticed, whenever she went into the dime store across the street, that people called the cashiers and even the owner of the store by their first names. It was more than business there, it was friendliness. People chatted, stayed to talk. She missed that. Whenever she came to the front of the laundry to greet customers, they were always polite, calling her Mrs. Woo, but after they handed their laundry to Ting and collected their tickets, they would turn around and leave. Perhaps it was because Ting's English was bad, and hers no better. They practiced their English with each other, but neither knew enough to correct the

other. Kuei-lan began to feel a great jumble of words building up behind her tongue, piling up in a lump that swelled into her throat.

She went to the bakery down the street and listened carefully to the
baker chatting with the customers as she stared at the glass case full of
doughnuts. She heard how people began their chats by calling one another by their first names. Then she heard the phrases *How are you?*
Fine day, isn't it? How're the kids? She bought two doughnuts and walked
home, practicing the phrases.

She waited for Mrs. Weaver to come in. Of all their customers, Mrs.
Weaver seemed to be the friendliest, a middle-aged lady with three
daughters who sometimes brought in a copy of *Life* magazine for Kuei-
lan and Ting to look at. "This is America, if you want to learn about
it," she said, always with a pleasant smile. Kuei-lan could feel the
promise in the smile. When Mrs. Weaver did come, on a Tuesday,
Kuei-lan left her ironing and joined Ting at the counter, smiling shyly
as she watched her husband stuff the pink, yellow, and light blue girls'
clothes into the canvas bags. There were full, frilly crinolines, as well.
She began to sense the lump moving behind her tongue as she saw Ting
tear off the ticket to give to Mrs. Weaver. Then she reached out and
took the ticket from Ting's hand.

"Mrs. Weaver," she began.

"Yes?"

The woman had kind eyes. She was smiling.

"My name is Kuei-lan." Suddenly Kuei-lan felt lost. She grabbed her
husband's arm. "His name is Ting."

Mrs. Weaver looked at the couple in front of her. The husband was
muttering something to the wife.

"Kway long, and Ting, did you say?"

"No, no." Kuei-lan began to laugh, even though she knew it was not
good to laugh at customers. She especially did not want to insult Mrs.
Weaver. "You say Ting, Ting is good. My name is Kuei-lan. Kuei-lan.
Not Kway long."

"Kway lang?" Mrs. Weaver tried again.

"No, no!" Kuei-lan shook her head, laughing with confusion.
Couldn't the lady hear the difference?

"Kay lang . . . oh, dear, that's not right either." Mrs. Weaver made a
face. "I don't seem to be able to say your name, Mrs. Woo."

Kuei-lan's heart begin to sink. But she held on to Mrs. Weaver's
ticket. "Is better. Kuei-lan, try again, okay?"

"This could take all day, I'm afraid." Mrs. Weaver sighed. Then she
said, "Kay Lynn? Is that right? Is that your name, Kay Lynn?"

It wasn't. But Kuei-lan nodded her head and smiled. It was close enough. The woman could at least say it. "Kay Lynn, that's me," she said. "That's my American name."

Mrs. Weaver made an exaggerated face of relief. "You're very kind, Mrs. Woo. I know it's still not right, but it's the best I can do. At least I can say your husband's name. Ting. Is that right?"

Ting nodded.

"Mrs. Weaver," Kuei-lan said, giving her her laundry ticket. "Ting . . . is not American name. . . ."

"No . . ."

"Then what is American name for Ting?"

Mrs. Weaver thought for a moment. Ting was muttering something again to his wife.

"Tim, I guess," Mrs. Weaver said. "Tim is the closest I can think of."

"Tim!" Kuei-lan laughed. "That very good! I like it, Tim very close!"

"Tim," Ting said, trying it out.

"Well, Kay Lynn . . . Tim," Mrs. Weaver said. "I'll be back tomorrow for my things. Remember, now, no starch." She paused, as if she were about to say something further, but changed her mind. She waved in a friendly way as she left the shop.

"She no say her name to us," Ting said to his wife, who was heading back to her ironing board.

"Never mind," Kuei-lan said, pointing her finger at her husband. "We must practice our own names," she said. "I am Kay Lynn from now on!"

Ting shrugged. "Tim. Tim," he repeated to himself. It lacked the ring of his own name. Still, he could see how it would help in their business. Tim it would be, then.

"Kay Lynn, Kay Lynn, I have been Kay Lynn for two years now, why can't I get used to it?" she whispered to herself as she drove the car across the 14th Street Bridge. The Potomac River rushed underneath, swollen and yellow with mud. The dried sticks and clumps of weed that had been encrusted with ice during the winter were now submerged by the swirling currents. Traffic on the bridge moved rapidly, as it was nearly two o'clock, well past the noon rush, and hours before the end of the day, when everyone working in Washington would be heading home. Kay Lynn was grateful for that. She was still afraid to drive in heavy traffic, afraid of being bumped in the herd.

As she got off the bridge she saw the rounded dome of the Jefferson Memorial to her left, and farther on, the tall spear of the Washington

Monument. She passed a row of massive stone buildings, each fronted by tall columns. Coming into Washington, D.C., was like entering another country, a country of gray stone fortresses, she thought. She had seen other American cities—San Francisco, Chicago—but none had the temples built for the heroes, none had these massive stone places of worship. She thought of the mountainsides of China where towering Buddhas had been carved into the stone. Relatives and friends had told her some of the Buddhas were thirty feet high. Her cousin Yung had stood on a Buddha's toe the size of a boulder.

She gripped the steering wheel tightly, making sure she remained on 14th Street. She had made this journey before but still dreaded the confusion of the streets. She knew if she made a wrong turn, she would be lost forever. She knew Washington was a city of one-way streets, all planned to lead one away from one's destination. Mr. Peng had told her not to worry, that getting to the bus terminal was a simple task. Everything seemed simple to Mr. Peng, she thought. He had lived in the area for many years now. It was easy for him to say.

Finally she came to New York Avenue and the sign of the lunging dog. She thought it peculiar that Americans considered dogs fleet, that they traveled in vehicles marked with these dogs. She parked her car and went into the terminal, watching the people around her carefully. The bus arriving from New York was due in at gate six.

She knew who her charges were as soon as they got off the bus. She saw the thin young Chinese woman in the cotton shirt and blouse, the cheap new sweater. Stepping down from the bus, she looked this way and that, as if questing the air, like a shy forest animal. A rumpled child held on to her hand. She clutched her straw bag close as she peered at the crowd of people surrounding the bus, and then underneath, at the luggage area, as the driver began to unload suitcases and boxes. Kay Lynn stepped in front of the young woman.

"Wong Mei-yu?"

The woman nodded, her eyes shining with relief. "Are you Mrs. Woo?"

"Yes. Welcome, Mrs. Wong."

Both women spoke English. Kay Lynn extended her hand. The new woman's hands were slender, callused. Kay Lynn caught a faint whiff of camphor. The new people smelled alike, as if they had come from the same box. She knelt down and touched Fernadina's cheek. "Your daughter?"

"Yes. This is Fernadina," the woman said. "Be polite, say hello to Mrs. Woo, Fernadina."

The girl ducked behind her mother. She had an unusual name, Kay Lynn thought. She stood there on the platform, feeling the awkwardness increase between them. She had met other new people here at the station before, but they had all burst out with questions as to where they would be taken, what they would be doing next. This woman stood before her, silent, almost grave. Kay Lynn could not tell what she was thinking. She did not seem unfriendly, but her self-containment seemed foreign to Kay Lynn. Kay Lynn was used to people speaking their minds. She also saw that the new woman was a good foot taller than herself; probably from the north of China. Mr. Peng had said nothing except that she was a widow and that she would be working at the new store. His instructions had been to show her her new home and to explain to her what was to be expected of her at work. Then she noticed that the woman was looking anxiously in the direction of the driver, who had picked up a large cardboard box and placed it on the curb.

"Your luggage?" Kay Lynn asked.

"Yes, my teacups!"

Kay Lynn tried to heft the box but shook her head. _These new people, with all their mementos and gewgaws from home!_ she thought.

"Stay here, Mrs. Wong. I bring car here."

Kay Lynn walked away with a brisk step. She had seen how the new woman had been impressed by the mention of the car. She hoped that she would also notice the quality of her red jacket, her shoes with the smart heels and the leather uppers. She enjoyed the thought that she could impress someone. The new woman was quiet, but she could not hide her newness at this life in America. Kay Lynn jingled the keys in her pocket as she went to get the car from the parking lot across the street.

Minutes later they were in the black Ford. Mei-yu sat next to Kay Lynn in the front. Fernadina sat in the back, next to the box of teacups. Kay Lynn ignored the sweat underneath her hands on the steering wheel and turned the key in the ignition. The car roared and the girl in back shrieked excitedly, sitting up on the seat, patting her mother on the head.

"Have you been in car before?" Kay Lynn asked Mei-yu.

Mei-yu shook her head. Her right hand gripped the armrest of the car door. "I rode in a truck, in China, a long time ago, but not in a car like this."

"Don't worry." Kay Lynn laughed, stepping on the gas pedal, making the car pitch forward.

Mei-yu did not watch her as she backed the car out of the bus terminal and joined the traffic heading out of the city. She watched for the cars around them, flinching as one drew within inches of her side of the car. Fernadina flung herself from one side of the car to the other, craning her head to look out the windows at the massive buildings lining the avenue. The teacups clinked faintly in the box as they hit a bump in the road. Mei-yu saw the Washington Monument, then the Jefferson Memorial, and pointed them out to Fernadina, telling her briefly what she had read about the presidents. Kay Lynn threw her a swift look.

As soon as they crossed the river into Virginia and found themselves out of the heavier traffic, Kay Lynn seemed to sigh with relief. She rolled down the window and leaned her left arm on the window ledge, driving with one hand on the wheel. She turned to Mei-yu and asked how the bus ride had been, how old Fernadina was. Mei-yu answered her questions easily. She was rubbing her neck, enjoying the warmth of the sun on her side of the car. Then Kay Lynn asked, "Where you from, Mrs. Wong?"

Mei-yu looked over at Kay Lynn. "Do you mean, in China?" she asked. She had hoped that issue would not come up between them.

"Yes."

"I was born in Peking."

"I see!"

Kay Lynn was quiet for a moment. She was thinking to herself, *Yes, I could tell from the way she talked. She is high-born, educated. But still, she's green, fresh like cabbage. She still has much to learn here, as much to learn as the rest of us.*

"Do you know what kind trees they are?" she asked suddenly, pointing out her window to the left.

"No," Mei-yu said, craning her neck to see. "They're very beautiful." She glanced back at Kay Lynn.

"Dogwood. State tree of Virginia!" Kay Lynn answered proudly.

Mei-yu saw that Kay Lynn could not be much older than herself. She was small, slightly pug-nosed, her face made even rounder by the severe pull of her ponytail. Her English was inflected with the Cantonese dialect, her *b*'s and *p*'s bitten off, her vowels swallowed. Her grammar was also strange. She, like Bao, had not grasped the tenses of speech, and she left out articles of speech as well. She appeared not to be ashamed of the way she talked, though, as she spoke loudly and made emphatic gestures with her hands. Mei-yu listened to her chatter on about the pink and white varieties of dogwood trees, watching with a mixture of fear and admiration as she drove, rounding the curve of the boulevard so fast that the car tires squealed. She knew Mrs. Woo was showing her her place. She accepted it; it was always like that, coming to new places. In China, though, at least among people of her class, adults sought to establish stature in the eyes of others by showing that no one was more humble and deferential than any other. She had witnessed countless scenes involving her parents' friends in which they had bowed and blocked the doorways of home by insisting that others go through first. Finally it seemed to her they had always shuffled their way in backward, like ponderous crabs. She had never experienced vying for place in Kay Lynn's aggressive and straightforward manner. She found it disturbing but also refreshing, lacking pretense.

"Hey, here we are!"

Kay Lynn pulled the car off the boulevard into a compact parking area. She parked in a square lot bordered by four identical brick buildings.

"This is where you live," she said, pointing ahead. "Yours is building second from right. My husband and I live in next building, on end."

She hopped out of the car and reclipped one of her red barrettes. Then she thrust her head back into the cab of the car. Mei-yu had not yet moved. She was staring at the brick buildings.

"You like car?"

"Yes!" Fernadina said. She opened her door and jumped out of the automobile.

Mei-yu sensed that Kay Lynn had addressed her. She turned her head then and nodded vigorously. "Yes, yes, it is a wonderful car."

Kay Lynn beamed, then shrugged. "Not my car. But Mr. Peng said I am driver from now on. He said our business needs car so we can deliver samples to our customers. We are only ones to do that around here."

She went to the rear of the car to open the trunk. Mei-yu opened her door and watched as Fernadina ran off to explore the area to the side of the buildings. She saw her examine the swing set, a sandbox, and further on, a clothesline strung between two metal poles. The brick buildings themselves looked solid enough, Mei-yu thought, but they also looked strangely stark, standing square apart from one another. The buildings of Chinatown in New York were set right next to one another, so close that they shared common walls between them. Also shared were heat in the winter, protection from the sun and rain at all other times. Here, the buildings were spaced about twenty feet apart, sharing nothing but the black paved parking lot in front.

Still, what Mei-yu noticed most was the faces of the buildings. In

Chinatown there were neon signs, awnings, or shutters, carved stone above the doorways, wood trim. Here, the doors and windows were unadorned, rectangular and square, made of brick mortared in perfect angles. It was as if she stared at faces with no eyebrows, faces completely blank of expression.

"We move here one year ago," Kay Lynn was saying, lifting the suitcases from the trunk of the car. Mei-yu hurried to help her. "Our laundry shop is there, in shopping center. I used to work there with Tim, my husband, every day, but since I work for Mr. Peng, we hire boy for help."

Mei-yu saw the small group of shops set on both sides of the boulevard, about three blocks down from the apartment buildings. She could see the signs of the drugstore, the grocery store, a beauty parlor, the post office, a bakery, a small family restaurant.

"And happy for you, elementary school is just there," Kay Lynn said, pointing to a large brick building beyond the post office. "Arlington has very fine public school system, I hear."

"I'm sure my daughter and I will like it here very much," Mei-yu said, hoisting the larger suitcase and following Kay Lynn toward the brick apartment building. She saw that Fernadina was still out by the swing.

"See?" Kay Lynn said, running her hands along the edge of the kitchen sink. "Modern kitchen. American kitchen. Brand-new. Mr. Peng is part owner. He said he very lucky to find apartments."

Mei-yu turned around in the center of the room. It was an extravagant kitchen, with appliances larger, shinier even than the ones at her cousin Roger's in Manhattan. She looked at the four-burner electric stove and the icebox as large as a bed standing upright, wondering about the electricity bill. Then she saw the sink.

"See, hot water, cold water, magic!" Kay Lynn said, turning on one tap, then the other, gushing water, obviously delighting in Mei-yu's look of disbelief.

Suddenly Mei-yu understood. "When are the others coming?" she asked.

"Who?"

"The others who will be living here. The seamstresses I was told about. When will they be coming?"

"Eh, what are you talking about, who told you that?" Then Kay Lynn understood. This one was a cautious one, she could see that now. "Oh! I see, no, you are wrong, no one living here except you and daughter. Different families do not live together here."

At first Mei-yu felt relief. Perhaps it was because she was tired; she looked forward to having space just for herself and Sing-hua. But as she walked through the apartment she began to feel that the place was too large. Something within told her it was a shameful waste of space; another voice told her that it looked large only because it was bare, empty except for strange objects placed here and there, a few simple furnishings. Plastic orange flowers poked stiffly from a green pot on the windowsill of the kitchen. A stuffed chair and a plain brown sofa flanked by two end tables were arranged in the living room. Off to the side of the living room was a small square dining room. Mei-yu tried to imagine Sing-hua and herself eating their rice while seated on the chrome-and-plastic padded chairs.

Down the hallway was the bathroom and two bedrooms situated opposite each other. Mei-yu looked out the window of the smaller bedroom, catching sight of Fernadina still outside, now soaring high on the swing.

"I hope you like how I decorate your place," Kay Lynn said, joining her in the small room. "This is daughter's bedroom."

The square room contained a small bed and a cheap chest of drawers. The walls were white, made of some hard, smooth material, neither plaster nor stone. Mei-yu heard the faint echo of their voices as they talked.

"Mr. Peng gave me money and told me to fix up like my own house," Kay Lynn was saying. "Did you see, in living and dining rooms, everything is modern!" She looked around the small room, sighing softly. "No more money for this room. It's okay for now, for your daughter? My husband and I don't have children yet. Sometime you come over to see our place. We have TV, too."

Mei-yu had seen a TV once. She had seen men and women running around inside the TV, throwing pies at each other. The TV had made a laughing sound. She did not need to have one here, she thought.

"Does Mr. Peng live in these apartments?" she asked.

"Oh, no. Mr. Peng lives in Washington."

Mei-yu imagined him in an old-fashioned apartment similar to his mother's. "It was very kind of him to arrange everything for me," she said.

"Oh, he is very important man, very, very busy. He ask me to take care of things here," Kay Lynn said, patting out a wrinkle in the bedspread. "Modern apartment okay, eh?"

"I am very grateful," Mei-yu said politely. She was already making plans in her mind for the changes she would make, thinking of designs for the slipcovers and bedspreads she would sew after she was settled. "Will I meet Mr. Peng soon?"

"I don't know. He is very busy man. He told me to take you to shop on Monday, where you meet manager, Nancy Gow. We will show you what to do at work. Maybe you meet Mr. Peng later, next week."

"Oh." Mei-yu felt strangely disappointed, then embarrassed for having assumed that because Madame Peng had taken a personal interest in her, her son might, as well. She felt suddenly lonely for Madame Peng.

She looked out the window, watching as Fernadina swung higher and higher, seeing with alarm how the back legs of the metal swing set rocked out of the ground with each kick. She opened the window, then discovered that she could not lean out; a metal screen was built into the windowframe. "Come inside, Sing-hua!" she shouted through the screen. She closed the window, then turned to see that Kay Lynn had been watching her.

"There's much to learn, eh?" Kay Lynn said.

"Yes."

"It's very strange now, but you find it easy, soon." She gestured around her. "You get used to everything. I did." Then she laughed. "Perhaps you even learn to drive!"

Mei-yu shook her head, shrugging, as if to show driving was completely beyond her.

"Well, okay," Kay Lynn said, beckoning to Mei-yu. "We start with easy things. First, I show you how oven works. Then we go down to basement, where washing machines are. Good thing all places around here don't have machines, or my husband and I be out of business!"

Mei-yu followed Kay Lynn back into the kitchen. She was glad to feel the easing of the tension between them. Between two, there is always a teacher, she thought, remembering an old Chinese saying. She gladly accorded Kay Lynn the role of teacher, gladly accepted the role of student, for now. She knew she needed friendship, even if it were the teacher-student kind. Fernadina rushed through the apartment door. "Mama!" she cried. "A girl downstairs told me the swings were hers!"

"Ah, she probably Simpson girl," Kay Lynn said, nodding knowingly, touching Mei-yu on the arm. "Watch out for Mr. and Mrs. Simpson. They live downstairs. They no like Chinese. They think all Chinese are bad, all Chinese Communist." She shook her head. "But don't worry, other nice people live here. I bring you to see Mrs. Johanssen. She has daughter and son her age." She reached to tweak Fernadina's cheek, but Fernadina drew away. Kay Lynn shook her finger at her.

"You go ahead and ride swings. Don't let Simpson girl scare you. Swings are for all children here."

"Don't worry, Sing-hua," Mei-yu said, patting her daughter gently, all the while trying to imagine what the Simpsons looked like. She saw them as tall people, looking down at her. She could already feel their hatred, their fear of her. She thought of ways to avoid meeting them, of taking Sing-hua to find other swings. Then she felt a tug on her sleeve and turned her attention to Kay Lynn, who was now turning the knobs of the miraculous stove and explaining the levels of heat.

O   O   O

Richard Peng fingered the pages of the brief in front of him but could not focus on the words. In a half hour, at three o'clock, the senior partners would be summoning him to tell him of their decision regarding his promotion. He was in his tenth year at the firm of Christensen, Adler, Booth, and Johns. Given the way things were now structured at the firm, given his contributions, he knew it was his turn. But still, he could not be certain. They had given him a generous increase in salary before, when his name came before them, but had denied him the title of associate. He had not needed the money. It was the title, the mandate, he wanted.

He knew the matter of his promotion had been a sensitive issue in the firm, increasingly so in the past few months. He had been careful, thorough, discreet in his negotiations and conduct in order to assure himself this rise in the firm. Perhaps he had undertaken too much in the past, he realized now. He had not recognized his priorities; he had promised too much to too many people. The people at the Chinese Community Center in Washington had expected his legal counsel every time a new Chinese person or family arrived in town. He found himself accompanying people to the Immigration Bureau, to the Employment Office. He translated official documents for them. He performed these services during his lunch hour and after work at the firm, but soon found that the people from the Community Center began to call him regularly, not only at his office, but at home, with questions, pleas, saying that only he knew the law, only he knew how to help. He found himself locating doctors for the new families, mediating intercommunity quarrels, as well.

At first he thought his services were welcomed, accepted in the same spirit as they were given. He knew the people would not have accepted his services without pay, so he kept his fees modest, and often ate meals in their homes instead. The people at the Center thanked him profusely for his help. Then he began to hear that certain people in the community were complaining that he remained more interested in making money as a "hotshot American lawyer" than as a full-time counselor for his own people. It was as if they bowed and smiled and plucked at his sleeves when they most needed him, then spat at his name when he turned his back. It was a strange game they played with him, a game he soon realized there was no way for him to win.

Finally, when the pressures at the firm began to build as the day of the meeting of the Review Committee approached, he made up several pamphlets of instructions for the people at the Community Center to hand out to all the newcomers, and told his secretary to hold all calls from there. He called the Center every two weeks to check on certain families. At home he left his phone off the hook, except in the evening, when Lillian might call.

He rearranged the items on his desk. He noted in his datebook that today was the day the woman and child his mother had written about were arriving in town. He had given Kay Lynn the proper instructions. Kay Lynn would see to the new people for now; he would check on them himself later.

His mother's request to set up her shop in Washington had come not only at an inopportune time, but was a distracting proposal in itself. He had hardly the time or interest to oversee such a venture. Still, he knew his duty by her, felt it keenly, for his mother had no other children to see to her affairs. Because of this additional project, he had had to hire Kay Lynn as a kind of assistant. With money sent by his mother combined with his own investment, he paid her salary and arranged for her driving lessons. She took over tasks that he had previously undertaken—escorting people to their appointments at the Immigration Bureau, meeting new arrivals at the bus terminal. He also knew her experience with storefront operations at the laundry would prove to be valuable at the new shop. He was relieved to see that she worked well with Nancy Gow, whom his mother had sent down years ago. Nancy had gained experience working in a small store on H Street and, throughout her interview with Richard, revealed herself to be an intelligent, business-minded person. Richard had been impressed by his mother's choice.

The two women had worked together with the contractors as the new store took shape. They had fussed excitedly over the placement of the front counter, the layout of the working area in back, the light fixtures. They insisted on setting up comfortable padded chairs in the front room for customers who might wish to wait as their clothes were being pressed or altered. With the arrival of this new woman his mother was sending from New York, the shop would be ready for opening soon. Hopefully, after making sure everything was running smoothly, he would be able to leave the entire operation to the women and direct his attention to his job at the firm. And more to Lillian, whom he had not seen enough of lately, as well.

Richard jotted down the names of the men in the conference room. He penciled checks next to the names of the men he knew would vote for him. He knew he could count on Peter Booth's vote. Eric Johns would vote no. Had always voted no. Lawrence Christensen maybe. Gerry Adler quite possibly yes, and Frank Lewisohn, the only junior partner on the committee, only maybe, though he had invited Richard to dinner last month. Lewisohn's children had stared at Richard throughout the carving of the roast. Mrs. Lewisohn had been overly generous, heaping his plate with potatoes, which he did not normally eat. He ate them that night.

Richard crumpled up the paper and tossed it into the wastebasket. He pressed his intercom. "Linda?" he said. "They're still talking, Mr. Peng," his secretary said. "They said they would call you as soon as they're through." Richard turned his attention to the brief in front of him, forcing himself to read.

"What's the solution, then?" Chairman Lawrence Christensen said, leaning back in his leather swivel chair. He was sixty-two years of age, his rust-colored hair expertly barbered. "Are we going to give him the same thing as last time?"

Peter Booth finished his doodle on his notepad. "I think it would be a real mistake to deny him the associate title this time. I think he deserves it, as I said before. His handling of the Corcoran brief was exemplary; meticulous, brilliant. His work with us has always been at the very highest level. If we don't give him the title, then we deserve to lose him." He looked at his four colleagues, who were seated around the oval conference table. "What is it, gentlemen? Can't we see it for ourselves to be represented at higher, more visible levels by a Chinaman?"

"Come on, Peter, that's not it!" Eric Johns dropped his pen onto the table with impatience. "We've been over this before. It's not our perception, but the perception of our clients that we have to take into consideration."

"That's bullshit, Eric," Peter Booth said, tearing off the doodle page of his pad. At forty-eight, Peter was the youngest of the senior partners.

"For the past thirty minutes we've all been saying that Richard's work has been excellent, and that he is definitely an asset to the firm," Christensen said. "At least we're all agreed on that. But Eric does have a point. These are crazy times. People are suspicious of all Orientals now. If they're not afraid of them being Japanese, then they're afraid that they're Koreans, or Chinese Communists fighting on the side of the Koreans. Did you ever see McCarthy on TV? He's got everyone spooked. If Richard were promoted to associate, he would be in the position of handling matters in person with some of our most important clients. Some of these clients come from the most prestigious families in the District and Virginia, clients we can't risk alienating."

"And what about his family?" Eric Johns said. "He's divorced, isn't he? Isn't that unusual for a Chinese?" No one answered. "Didn't he marry an American woman?" he asked, leaning forward on the table. "Were there any children?"

"He doesn't talk about it, the divorce," Booth muttered. "I don't think he has any children."

"He's seeing someone here in town now, a Chinese woman from Taiwan," Frank Lewisohn said. "She's with the Chinese Embassy, a cultural attaché or something."

"What does this have to do with anything?" Booth said, exasperation in his voice.

"Basically, I think Eric is making the point that Richard does not fall into the prescribed category of character to which our clients are accustomed." This was spoken softly by Gerald Adler. "Our clients demand not only that their lawyers be of unredoubtable character, but that they reflect the highest moral and social standards in this community. That preferably they be white, married, church-going. That's the image that Christensen, Adler, Booth, and Johns has always prided itself on, right?" He had been quiet for most of the meeting, up to now.

"I don't appreciate the sarcasm, Gerry," Eric Johns said, frowning, leaning forward in his chair. "There's nothing wrong with that kind of character. It's character that inspires trust, a real community spirit. It's character we all strived to develop, growing up, isn't it?"

There was silence for a moment. Then Frank Lewisohn said softly, as if he weren't sure he wanted to be heard, "There is the matter of precedence, too."

Peter Booth looked down the table at his colleague. "Could you tell us what you mean by that, Frank?" he said.

"I mean," Frank said, shifting uneasily in his chair, "that if other people like Richard see that he can attain associate status in the firm, then what's to stop them from demanding equal consideration at these Review Committee meetings?"

"What do you mean by 'other people like Richard,' Frank?" Gerry Adler said. "As I recall, Richard is the only Chinese in the firm. By 'other people,' could you be referring to Eugenia Powell, perhaps, who happens to be a clerk-typist, and a Negro?"

"Gentlemen." Lawrence Christensen placed both hands on the table. "I'd hoped we wouldn't allow this meeting to dissolve into an argument about sociological issues. I will note Frank's comment, but I personally do not think we need be concerned about setting precedence here. We must still, however, come to a decision. Does anyone have anything more to say before we take a vote?"

There was silence in the room except for Peter Booth's pencil tapping on the table. Then Eric Johns said, "My main concern is still the reputation of the firm. I think that must remain our first responsibility. Yet, I believe Richard is valuable, and I would like to see him stay. What if we give him the title, but keep his assignments more or less the same?"

Peter exploded. "You don't think he'd catch on? He'd resign within a month!"

"Peter!" Christensen held up his hand.

"I don't like the sound of it," Gerry Adler said from the far end of the table. "It's patronizing and cheap."

"It stinks," Peter Booth said.

"All right. I didn't mean it that way," Eric Johns said. He brushed the sides of his head with his hands. He and Christensen were the founding partners. He knew they had the power of veto on the vote, but he did not want to antagonize the other partners unnecessarily. "What I meant was, I think Richard deserves the title. I do. I also think he can handle any assignment we give him. But I know that some of our clients would simply refuse him as counsel. That's a plain fact. All I'm suggesting is that we exercise discretionary judgment as to what cases we assign to him. That's all."

"You mean, keep him behind the front," Gerald Adler said.

"Yes," Christensen said. He leaned back in his chair, folding his arms across his chest. He seemed satisfied.

Peter Booth tossed his pencil onto the table. It rattled across the grain of the wood and fell off the other side.

"Well, gentlemen," Christensen, the chairman, said. "Shall we take a vote?"

Moments later Richard Peng came into the room. All the partners stood. Peter Booth tried to smile as Christensen congratulated the new associate. Richard was smiling. An elegant man, Peter thought. A Mandarin. Not an effete man, not one of those who sat around on silk cushions, drinking tea, languidly citing odes to orchids, but someone with discipline, a deep introspection, ambition, and the capacity to do many different things. Peter knew of Richard's involvement with the Chinese community in Washington. He thought wryly to himself that for all his partners' talk of community commitment, none of them was involved in community affairs as deeply as Richard.

He watched as Richard moved down the line of partners, chatting, shaking hands with the other senior members of the firm. Like a diplomat, Peter thought. He had often wondered what Richard's political stance was in light of the current China issue. Washington had yet to recover from the shock of Mao's Communist victory in mainland China, and members of the China lobby were vigorously campaigning and raising funds to support Chiang Kai-shek in Taiwan. Yet, except for his relationship with this woman at the Chinese Embassy, Richard seemed uncommitted on the issue; no one knew how he was aligned, or if he aligned himself at all with either faction. Peter realized that he actually knew very little about Richard, except that he showed ambition and promise in the firm. It had been no mean feat for him to rise to the position of associate at age thirty-seven, but Peter knew Richard had the desire and talent for the mandate of a full partner. He also knew that he would never attain it. Not here, at any rate. Then it was his turn to shake Richard's hand.

"Congratulations, Richard," he said.

"Thank you. Thank you very much, Peter."

"Are you doing anything later on? Care to have a drink?"

"Thanks, Peter, but I had planned to meet Lillian."

"I see." Peter smiled. "Well, some other time. Congratulations again."

Richard nodded and moved along the line to shake Eric John's hand. Peter watched as Eric grasped Richard's hand with his crushing hand-shake. Eric had always measured sincerity by the strength of a hand-shake, Peter thought. He excused himself from the group.

Henry Campbell had often driven past the chancery of the Chinese Embassy on Massachusetts Avenue, but he had never entered the drive-way bordered by magnolia trees and laurel bushes until today. He walked past the gray stone columns of the portico and entered the high-ceilinged foyer. The guard at the reception desk was speaking on the telephone. When he saw Henry, he held up his hand for him to wait. Henry nodded and, looking around, saw a long hallway beyond the foyer lined with rows of glass display cases. At the end of the hallway was a massive wooden staircase. When he turned around to the desk again, he saw that the guard had hung up the telephone and was re-garding him impassively. Henry had noticed no other official in sight.

"Hello," he said. "I'm afraid I'm a bit early, but my name is Henry Campbell, from the Committee for a Free China. I have an appoint-ment to see Miss Lillian Chin at three thirty."

The guard looked down at the appointment book in front of him and told Henry that Miss Chin was still in a meeting. He indicated for Henry to wait in the small anteroom located just off the foyer.

Henry nodded and went into the room, hearing the creak of the wooden floors underneath the thick rugs as he walked. The anteroom was furnished with dark antique Chinese furniture. Against the wall to his right were two ornate chairs of blackwood, and next to them, two smaller matching tables. Henry bent to look closely at the two vases the color of milky jade placed on the side table against the wall. An ama-teur collector, he prided himself on his knowledge of Chinese artifacts. The vases appeared to be authentically old, the surface of the glaze looking like lacquered eggshell that seemed to have suffered thousands of tiny, delicate fractures.

Photographs of Sun Yat-sen, Chiang Kai-shek, and Madame Chiang, taken during successive years, were hung on every wall of the ante-room. From his most recent photograph, the eyes of Chiang looked out beneath withered eyelids. Madame Chiang's mouth and eyebrows looked dark, heavily stained. Both looked as if they had been dried, prepared by an embalmer's ancient art, set forever behind the protec-tive glass of the photograph frames. It was difficult for Henry to imagine that at that moment, both Chiang and Madame Chiang were alive in Taiwan.

Henry passed through the anteroom and entered a much larger room. On the right was a fireplace with a mantelpiece the height of his head, and above that, an enormous oil painting of Chiang. The wall at the far end of the room was covered with a traditional landscape painting executed on silk. Henry realized this was the room where the guests of honor stood to receive the company of the Embassy. Off to the right of this room was a short hallway that led to a still larger room. It was in this larger room, Henry knew, that the celebrated buffets of the Chinese Embassy were laid out.

Washington newspapers covered the receptions at the Chinese Embassy with the hyperbole normally reserved for centennial celebrations, the birthdays of kings. Henry and his colleagues had often complained about the drabness of social life in Washington, D.C. President and Mrs. Eisenhower were hardly known as social luminaries. But here, at the Chinese Embassy, evenings were legendary. Henry had heard about the musky perfumes, the shine of the silk worn by the porcelain-faced ladies, the scintillating talk. He had read about the extraordinary buffet of circular and oval dishes of food arranged in elegant symmetry on the large round table. One columnist had raved about the buffet, calling it "an irresistible culinary kaleidoscope." He looked at the large, still room, trying to imagine its transformation into the exotic fantasy he had heard about.

Someone touched his arm. "Miss Chin will see you now," the guard told him, pointing to the stairway at the end of the foyer.

Henry passed the rows of glass exhibit cases on his way to the stairway. Inside them he saw snuffboxes of all shapes and sizes. Some were carved out of cinnabar, the size of pear apples. Others were ceramic, or carved out of jade, the shapes of locusts with folded wings, or laughing, squat Buddhas that could fit in the hand. Another case displayed cricket cages, tiny houses made of split bamboo the size of a box of playing cards. Next to them were tiny cricket drinking cups the dimension of acorn caps, and cricket ticklers that looked like stalks of wheat. A strange people, the Chinese, Henry thought as he went up the staircase. They were a people capable of producing some of the world's most exquisite, sophisticated artwork, yet were also a people who indulged, passionately, in a seemingly senseless activity—tickling crickets. He decided, as he reached the top of the staircase, that he would have to examine the Embassy collection more carefully on his way out.

"Hello, Mr. Campbell, please come in," Lillian Chin said, rising to shake his hand. Her hand was cool. She indicated a chair for him opposite her desk. Her office was small but scrupulously organized. Books filled the shelves built into the walls on either side of the room. On her desk were neat piles of paper in file folders, a metal box of index cards, a black enamel pen. She was striking in her paleness, Henry thought, the skin of her neck so thin that he could see the faint blue veins there. She also had large eyes for an Oriental, black and soft-looking, accentuated with black pencil makeup. She wore a ring, a solitary pearl set in gold, on her right hand.

"I understand you are here to discuss the reception scheduled here at the Embassy on June tenth, Mr. Campbell," she said. Her voice was high, soft, her English inflected with the British school.

"Yes," he said, taking out his notes from a folder he carried under his arm. He handed her a list of names. "Members of our board are honored to have been invited to this reception. We look forward to meeting the Minister of Finance from Taiwan very much, and are especially pleased that you have encouraged us to introduce you to other persons who might be of interest to your important guest."

She scanned the list. She recognized names belonging to the Committee for a Free China, one of the most powerful pro-Nationalist China, anti-Communist lobbies in Washington. Included were the names of millionaires, men who had made their fortune in trade with Taiwan, seat of Chiang Kai-shek's regime. "Yes, I am familiar with most of these names," she said, continuing to read down the list. "Ah, but here is one I do not recognize. Who is Edward Wolfert?"

"He is a businessman who has shown interest in the committee, but who has yet declined to join. He is interested in maintaining commercial ties with Taiwan, but he is hesitating because of what he is hearing in Washington about Red China. He is one of those doubtful about the continuing status of Taiwan here in America. He's very powerful in New York, and there is no question we could use him in the lobby. I'm hoping that meeting the minister and seeing all of those who support the Taiwan issue might help him decide to come to our side."

Lillian Chin inclined her head in assent. "Certainly, we here at the Embassy are most receptive to making new friends."

"Thank you, Miss Chin." Henry thought for a moment. "There is another, related matter, that perhaps you, as attaché, might be able to help us with."

"If I can oblige, Mr. Campbell."

"We at the committee wonder if you would have a list of Chinese here in Washington, besides those in connection with the Embassy, who you could invite to attend the reception."

"I'm not sure I understand, Mr. Campbell," Lillian said.

"Well"—Henry searched for the proper words—"we need new faces to show to potential members like Mr. Wolfert. Because of his business, he is already well acquainted with most of the influential Chinese in the area. We of the committee would like him to see that other Chinese, besides those with commercial interests, are sympathetic to the Taiwan side of the issue, as well. Do you know of any Chinese involved in other professions, such as doctors or lawyers, perhaps, small-business people, teachers, who might be interested in attending? People who would represent a cross section of the Chinese population here?"

Lillian immediately thought of Richard, although she knew he preferred to remain clear of the issue. Perhaps she could ask him for a list of names, in any case. She was certain there were people in the Washington Chinese community who would be delighted to receive invitations to the Embassy. Even if they came solely to enjoy the social aspects of the evening, their mere presence would imply support of the Embassy and the lobby. She uncapped her enamel pen and wrote in her notebook to ask Richard for a list. Then she nodded again at Henry.

"I will do my best, Mr. Campbell. I think I may be able to come up with a list for you."

"Excellent!" Henry beamed at Lillian. He had feared trouble in that quarter. But looking at the calm, helpful face before him, he felt certain of the evening's success. The attaché was an enchanting person, and the Chinese people were an enchanting race, he thought to himself.

A half hour later Lillian Chin rose to escort Henry Campbell to the door.

"Thank you again for your time, Miss Chin," Henry said, shaking the soft cool hand once again. "I think we've covered everything."

"I believe the evening will be a great success, Mr. Campbell. I look forward to it."

Lillian watched, smiling, as he walked down the hallway past the other offices and began his descent of the staircase. Then she closed her door and returned to her desk. She was relieved Henry Campbell had been her last appointment. Things had gone smoothly; nothing untoward had arisen. She glanced at her watch. It was nearly four thirty. Richard had told her the Review Committee had planned to convene at two o'clock. Surely he knew what they had decided by now, she thought. He would be calling her soon. She turned her attention to the notes lying on her desk and decided to make a timetable for the evening of the tenth of June: when to call the florist, when to set the menu with the chefs, when to arrange for the limousine service to call for the Minister of Finance at his hotel. She glanced at her phone. Why wouldn't they give him the promotion this time? she thought, recapping her pen and shuffling her note cards together. Two years had gone by since the first Review Committee meeting, when they had voted to deny Richard the title. At that time she had known him barely six months. Still, even then, news of his future in the firm had been important to her, to them both, although they had not spoken about their own future together.

Neither of them had dared speak of their future. Richard had known at the outset, when they had met, that because of the nature of her job in foreign service, and in particular because of the current political situation involving her Embassy, Lillian might be called back to Taiwan. Even so, they had proceeded to see each other, cautiously at first, then more seriously.

Lillian had been discreet; no one at the Embassy was aware of her liaison with Richard. They moved invisibly in the mute, gray social arena of Washington, dining out in quiet restaurants, attending concerts at the Library of Congress. When Richard became aware that the Review Committee planned to meet to discuss his position at the firm, he told Lillian, and was shocked, as was she, to realize for the first time the implications that affected them both. They suddenly realized their own relationship had grown to the point of asking the question.

Lillian was thirty-two years old. She had lived in the United States for over two years now. Because of Richard, she wished to stay. She found herself searching her feelings, her sense of allegiance to her Embassy, to her country, Taiwan. She did not seek citizenship of the United States, yet knew she would accept citizenship if it were offered to her in the form of a wedding gift.

Richard had remained cautious, quiet. One could never tell how things were decided at the firm, he told her. He had not told her to wait, but she waited, in spite of herself, and felt that he waited, also. They both waited for the promotion, the catalyst.

But then the promotion had been denied. The question was not asked. They continued to move together like shadows, drifting, unresolved. Now tension grew between them, for they knew that the question still existed between them. Tensions at the Embassy also increased. The tone of communications between Washington and Taiwan fluctuated between warm and assuring to accusatory and hostile. Lillian began to feel as if she dangled, anchored securely neither here nor there. Worried, Richard would ask her about the Embassy, about her position. She often felt he approached the question between them out of desperation, but knew, when he backed away, that he could not ask it when he was not certain himself. Now it was two years later, and the Review Committee was meeting again. The waiting had begun anew.

The phone rang. "Richard?"

"Hello, Lillian."

"How are you, how was it?"

"They gave me the promotion."

Her heart pounded in her chest. "Oh, that's wonderful! I thought they would!"

"Are you free now?"

"Yes!" She tucked the cards into the metal box.

"Our reservations for dinner are for six o'clock. We could have a drink first. Can you meet me there at five?"

"That's perfect."

"Do you have the tickets?"

"Yes. Concert's at eight."

"Sounds like a wonderful evening."

"I'm very happy for you, Richard."

"Thank you."

There was silence on the line as they both seemed to wait. Then Richard said, "I'm leaving the office now. We'll talk later."

They both hung up.

Jean-Claude, the maître d' at Francine's, near Dupont Circle, took Lillian's lightweight coat.

"Will it be vermouth, Lillian?" Richard asked. She nodded. Richard asked for a vermouth, and a whiskey and soda for himself.

Jean-Claude signaled for their waiter as he took Richard and Lillian to their table. He smiled as he gave them the heavy, embossed menus. They were a handsome couple, he thought. They had come to Francine's for over two years now. He had always prided himself on being able to imprint the names and faces of his clientele into his memory, but these two had been simple. He could not tell exactly what race they were, only that they seemed too tall to be Japanese. Both were slender, pale-skinned, supple like reeds, moving with grace as he escorted them to their table. The woman always dressed in the Western style, with sophisticated elegance, usually in shades of blue-reds and black, which complimented her coloring. He admired the Oriental hair. She wore hers slightly waved, pinned up, revealing the high cheekbones and slightly shortened profile. Oriental women were as chic, as feminine as French women, he thought. Well, almost.

The Oriental man was always polite, speaking in a low, well-modulated voice. He ordered the meal and wine with assurance. His manner was not so suave as to be continental, or pompous, like an American aspiring to elegance. Jean-Claude conceded that he had an understated style all his own.

Jean-Claude knew Richard as Mr. Peng, and Lillian as Miss Chin. He gathered they were not married. They did not seem like the sort to have the usual married life, children. They appeared too serene, too contented with the way they were. Perhaps they were past the age. But perhaps they would marry and have children one day, Jean-Claude thought, returning to their table to take their order. They would have beautiful children with beautiful manners. Perhaps they would even bring their children to lunch at Francine's.

He was most pleased when they had accepted his recommendation of the sole and the sweetbreads in champagne sauce, and he now went to report to the kitchen with a light heart. The wine captain came to fill the couple's glasses.

Lillian raised her glass. "Congratulations again, Richard. I'm very happy for you."

Richard smiled, and the two sipped their wine.

"What did Christensen say? And Eric Johns? What was his reaction?"

"Everyone seemed very pleased. Peter told me later the vote was unanimous. That surprised me, somewhat."

"Why?"

"Well, I've always felt restraint from Christensen and Johns. Perhaps _restraint_ is not the word. It's hard to describe. They're always polite, of course. But there's something visceral. They would like to like me, but they don't. They would like to trust me, but they can't bring themselves to, totally, especially nowadays."

"How can you be sure? How is it you've come so far in the firm, then?"

"I think they know I do certain things very well," he said. "Prepare briefs. Do research. Write reports. They didn't expect I might be good at other things, such as handling cases face-to-face with the clients themselves. I don't think they like ambition in people they think ought to stay in certain positions."

"So you think this promotion . . ."

"I don't know," Richard said. "I'm going to wait a few months to see. It's too soon to tell."

The waiter came with their appetizers. Richard had ordered sautéed soft-shell crabs, fresh from the Chesapeake. He cut into the soft bodies, squirting butter along the edge of his knife. Lillian had ordered an artichoke with hollandaise as her appetizer, and was now pulling each leaf off one by one, carefully biting and scraping the fleshy part of the leaves with her teeth. As she pulled each leaf she told herself to accept the tone of the evening. She could see Richard was pleased with the promotion but apparently not certain of the motives behind it. He was still not free. But he looked to be in good spirits, smiling, chatting about the concert they were to attend later in the evening. He offered her a bite of crab. Later, when the waiter came to take their appetizer dishes away, he poured more wine into her glass, loudly clinking the rim of her glass with the lip of the wine bottle. She struggled with herself, striving to be generous in spirit, wishing to match her mood to Richard's. Still, she wished they were talking about other things, pending things. She reached for another sip of wine.

At the end of the main course, Jean-Claude came to ask them if they wished dessert and coffee. Richard explained to him that they were on their way to a concert, and asked for the check.

"We can stop for coffee later, if you like," he said to Lillian.

The check arrived and Lillian watched as Richard pulled out his wallet. He drew out three twenty-dollar bills and waved them gaily at Jean-Claude. Lillian felt a pang of irritation. Had Richard had too much wine to drink? She had never seen him behave in as undignified a manner. She put her hand on his arm. "Are you all right, Richard?"

"Yes, yes, quite all right."

She saw that his eyes were glittering with an unnatural brightness. She saw that it was not from the alcohol. She realized suddenly that his chatter throughout the evening, his gay behavior, stemmed not from the wine, but from nervousness.

She looked at him closely. He was perspiring.

"Richard?"

He was looking toward the front of the restaurant, where Jean-Claude had gone to get her coat. Then he turned to face her.

"Lillian," he said.

She waited.

"Do you have a free weekened in the coming month?"

She thought for a moment but found that her mind had gone blank.

"I'm going up to New York soon to bring the final papers on the new store for my mother to sign." He hesitated. "Would you come with me?"

Lillian had asked Richard about his mother, but he had not told her much, only that he was her only child and that they had come to

America from China, alone together. Lillian knew the strength of the bond between Chinese mothers and their first, only sons.

"Wouldn't you rather conduct your business alone with her?" she said.

Richard shook his head impatiently. "That will take a few minutes, at most. No, what I want, really . . . what I meant, really, is for you to meet her."

Lillian began to smile.

"What I meant was, I would like for her to meet you. Whatever is most proper," he added, muttering. At that moment Jean-Claude arrived with Lillian's coat. Richard rushed out, saying he was going to hail a cab. Lillian bid Jean-Claude good night, thanking him for his special attentiveness. By the time Jean-Claude opened the front door of the restaurant for her, Richard had found a cab and was standing impatiently at the curb. Lillian got into the backseat. He slid onto the seat beside her, and told the driver to take them to the auditorium entrance of the Library of Congress. When he sat back again in the seat, she saw that he was pale, even with the wine he had drunk.

"Well?" he said, looking at her hairline. "Will you come with me? Next month?"

She laughed, suddenly feeling faint, knowing it was not because she had drunk too much wine. "Yes," she said.

O   O   O

Mei-yu sat at the table in her new kitchen and spread out sheets of writing paper. She put the date on the upper right-hand corner of one sheet and wrote in Chinese, beginning at the right side of the page and working her way down:

Dear Ah-chin,

We have been here for two weeks now and this is the first chance I have had to write to you. I feel so far away, as if I write to you from another country. How are you and Ling and Wen-wen? I think of you often, and of Bao. Has he taught you how to make his soybean and preserved mustard dish yet? Today I had the most powerful craving, just to smell that dish.

> So much has happened! Where should I begin? Our life is
> so different now. Our new home is a modern apartment that
> Madame Peng's son, Richard, was kind enough to find for
> us. When you come to visit, you will see how big it is. It is
> so big that for days, Sing-hua and I lost each other inside.
> Our entire place in Chinatown would fit into the kitchen
> alone! Bao would not believe the kitchen. I remember his
> refrigerator in the back of Sun Wah and how it would make
> great noises and how we were all afraid it might explode.
> The refrigerator here hums. It is so large that the food I buy
> for Sing-hua and myself fits all on one shelf.

Mei-yu reread this last paragraph and sighed. It was not good to crow
about one's good fortune to the friends left behind. She crumpled up the
sheet of paper and began the letter over again on a clean sheet. She copied
the first paragraph and, when she got to the second paragraph, wrote,

> Our new place is clean and modern, but far too large for
> Sing-hua and myself. You will see when you come to visit. It
> is a shameful waste of space. I imagine it will be very expen-
> sive to heat in the winter.

She reread the paragraph with satisfaction. The letter was headed in
the right direction now; at least it would not cause her friends to feel
envy. She knew Ah-chin would show it to everyone she knew. She
continued to write,

> I was very relieved when I received permission to bring Sing-
> hua to work until school begins in the fall. She brings paper and
> crayons and draws and learns words and numbers while I
> work. When I have a lunch break, we walk and explore the
> area around the shop. We found a place that cooks an Amer-
> ican dish called a hamburger, which Sing-hua likes very much.
> They are small, about the size of Bao's meatballs, but squashed
> flat, and cheap, costing a dime apiece. She can eat three or four
> of them for lunch. Soon I hope to find someone who will be able
> to stay with her at home. Remember how we used to help each
> other with our children, Ah-chin!

Mei-yu sat back from the table and read what she had written. It
seemed to her that the more she wrote, in her attempt to close the

distance between herself and her friend, the farther she drew away. How could she describe to Ah-chin the feeling of riding in the swift, shiny black car, of having a bathroom right in their home and of being able to draw enough hot water to fill the tub—of marveling at the smoothness of the cool ceramic walls of the tub before slipping into the water? How could she describe to Ah-chin her new friend, Kay Lynn, who bought small things with delight, at a whim; barrettes, plastic measuring cups and spoons, decorative glass figurines to put on her windowsills? Mei-yu recalled how, in Chinatown, Ah-chin had stood for long moments in front of a basket of bitter melons, picking up and pinching each one. She had muttered, "We can't afford this," repeatedly, until she finally put them all back in the basket and turned away, glaring at the waiting merchant. What would Ah-chin think of Kay Lynn?

Kay Lynn had driven her and Fernadina to the new shop on that first day. She chattered on about her new purchases and how she had learned to make orange juice from pulp frozen in cans. Mei-yu listened with half an ear but stared out the window, wondering, every time the car stopped, if they had arrived at her new workplace. Finally Kay Lynn stopped the car. "This is Clarendon Shopping Center," she said. "This is where new shop is."

Mei-yu wondered why the sign in the window of the shop said Modern Hong Kong Tailors, since none of the people she knew who would be working there were from Hong Kong. Later, Kay Lynn told her that Americans believed that the tailoring from Hong Kong was superior, and cheap, and that Nancy Gow had chosen the name for those reasons. Inside, she saw how it lived up to the "modern" part of its name. She ran her hand over the smooth surface of the front counter, and looked up to see eight panels of lights suspended above. Good for the eyes, she thought, better than the single light bulbs that had dangled from the ceiling in the sweatshop where she had worked in Chinatown.

Nancy Gow, the manager, shook her hand, and seemed brisk, pleasant. She spoke English very well, and wore bright blue glasses whose plastic rims swept up at the outer tips, as if in imitation of her eyes, which were slanted even more so than Kay Lynn's. She proudly showed Mei-yu the back section, which was divided into three different sewing stations. Each station was outfitted with a factory sewing machine, ironing board, table for cutting fabric, and a model form for fitting. Mei-yu also noticed the assortment of boxes full of pins and multicolored spools of thread.

"You will oversee the other seamstresses," Nancy Gow said. "They will be arriving later this week. It is your responsibility to see that each gets her fair share of work, that each does a good job. And here," she said, pointing to a station at the back, "is your place."

Mei-yu stared at the long wooden table, the drawing board, the sewing machine, and the three different-sized pairs of professional shears. She picked up the largest pair of shears and worked them, hearing the snick of the blades as they slid closed, smooth and firm.

"These are the styles of clothes we offer to our customers," she said, flipping through a ring-bound notebook of several pages. Mei-yu saw pictures of dresses, jackets, skirts, blouses, formal gowns, and even delicate lingerie. Some of the styles she had not seen before. "We also offer cleaning services, pressing, and alterations. Kay Lynn will show you the rest. Do you have any questions?"

"No," Mei-yu said. She looked around, seeing that Fernadina was walking around the different sewing stations, inspecting the shiny machines.

"We have a fitting set for this afternoon, here," Kay Lynn said. "Then we have to drive to three ladies' homes later to show them our styles."

"Yes, yes," Mei-yu said, her thoughts whirling.

"Kay Lynn!" Nancy said sharply, becoming suddenly agitated, "you didn't tell me Mr. Peng was coming today!"

Kay Lynn turned around to face the front of the store, equally surprised. Richard had come through the door and was looking around the counter, appraising the appearance of the store. Nancy bustled forward to meet him.

"Ah, Nancy," Richard said when he saw her. "Things look very good. You have done much since last week!"

"Thank you, Mr. Peng," Nancy said. "Do you like the Formica countertop? And the chairs, don't you think they add a special touch?"

"Yes, they do. Did the men from the factory set up the machines properly?" He began to move toward the back of the shop. "Are you satisfied that everything is in working order?"

"Yes, yes," Nancy said, following him. "They came last Thursday and did all the work. I checked the machines myself. Oh, Mr. Peng"— Nancy pushed Mei-yu forward gently—"this is Wong Mei-yu. She arrived on Friday."

Richard and Mei-yu shook hands, formally. "Welcome, Mrs. Wong," he said, smiling. "I came hoping to meet you today. My mother wrote to me and sang your praises, both of you and your work. I hope you will like working here. And this is your daughter?"

He waited for Fernadina to come and shake his hand. Mei-yu was glad to see that he did not impose himself on her daughter, as other adults had done. "Why, doesn't she like people?" some had said when Fernadina hung back from them. Richard smiled at her daughter, then turned away to look at the rest of the shop. Mei-yu saw how her daughter looked up at his face with interest.

He had a northern face, Mei-yu thought, stealing brief glances at him as he joined Nancy and Kay Lynn in their inspection of the new machines. She did not want to stand and stare as they continued with their business matters. She went to her station and began to try out her new shears on pieces of scrap fabric, looking up occasionally as they made their rounds. He did not look at all like she had imagined; he did not look at all like the son of Madame Peng. His was a lean face, not bony or overly fine, but hard, rather closed in expression. His brow was high, his hair thick, parted on the side. When Nancy explained something about the machines to him, he appeared to listen intently, looking directly into her face, giving quick nods of acknowledgment. When they moved to another station, Mei-yu saw that he carried himself gracefully, but with a certain tension; shoulders held square, head thrust slightly forward. He certainly did not appear to have his mother's sense of ease. She noticed how Fernadina followed him as he made his way from station to station. Mei-yu replaced the shears in their case and called her daughter back to her. "Don't tag along, Sing-hua," she said, bending down to smooth her daughter's hair. She waited while the others consulted with one another and made their final comments. Then she became aware that Richard was walking toward her.

"I'm glad to have met you, Mrs. Wong," Richard said. He did not smile, but his eyes were kind. "I am certain you will like it here. Kay Lynn will take good care of you. If you have any questions, or need anything, she will see to it. And, yes, I almost forgot. It is a bit early yet, but I want to invite you to a special event at the Chinese Embassy, set for June. You will receive an invitation in a week or so." He turned to see that Kay Lynn had joined them and was now looking at him expectantly. "Of course," he went on, "I am hoping to see you there, Kay Lynn, and Nancy, as well." He faced Mei-yu again. "Many of the Chinese community will be there. Perhaps it would be a good opportunity for you to meet them, then. The Embassy is a famous gathering place."

"Oh, I hear much about it, very fine food!" Kay Lynn said.

"Then we will see you there?" Richard said, looking at Mei-yu.

Mei-yu was thinking that she had never been to an embassy. She had heard of the one in China, where diplomats, statesmen, actors and actresses, people of influence and wealth had gathered. She had never imagined herself in such company. She became aware that both Richard and Kay Lynn waited for her reply.

"Yes, thank you," she said. "I would be honored to attend."

"Good," Richard Peng said. He smiled at Fernadina, then, after stopping briefly to speak again to Nancy, left the shop.

"Fine man, Mr. Peng," Kay Lynn said, pulling back a strand of hair that had fallen into her face and reclipping it. "He seem cold, like businessman, but he is very kind. Ask Nancy. He help her when she first come here from New York eight year ago with husband and children. First he find job for husband at pharmacy downtown, then send her to dress shop in Chinatown. They save up enough money to buy house near here."

Mei-yu nodded politely but was thinking to herself that she had made a poor impression on Richard. She had hardly said a word. She wondered what Madame Peng had said in her letter to him. Again she found herself thinking how the son was so unlike the mother, in looks, in personality. "Have you ever met Madame Peng?" she asked Kay Lynn.

"No. But Nancy told me about her. Nancy work for Madame Peng in Chinatown, like you, many years ago. She say Madame Peng sacrificed much to bring her son to this country, to send him to best schools. She endure much hardship. But she proud mother now, mother of rich American lawyer. He very good son to her. Take care her business here, new shop, and visit her in New York. Now we all wait for him to marry and have many children!"

"He is not married?" Mei-yu said. She was surprised to hear it. He appeared to be in his thirties.

"He marry American woman before, when very young. Some people say he marry her to become American citizen. I don't believe that, why he do that? Why they stay married if they not love each other? They divorce three years ago. No children. Very sad."

Kay Lynn shook her head. Then she added, in a conspiring tone, "But wait you see his new lady friend, Lillian! She very beautiful, very smart, very modern. They marry soon, I bet!"

"Is she American, too?" Mei-yu asked.

"No! Lillian Chinese, born in Taiwan. She went to college this country, then went back to parents in Taiwan. Now she has important job at Embassy. She speak like you, no accent!"

"I would be interested to meet her," Mei-yu said. She could not think why, but later that day, and even into the evening, she found herself thinking about Lillian, imagining what she looked like, sounded like.

Mei-yu forced her thoughts from Lillian and Kay Lynn and looked down at the letter in front of her. She was dismayed to see how short it remained; her writing covered barely a page. What else could she tell Ah-chin? How had they so much to talk about during their days together in Chinatown? Ah-chin had always talked about the price of food, of Mrs. so and so's sore foot, or how she and Ling could not make Wen-wen eat meat. She had talked mostly of Wen-wen, and herself of Sing-hua. Mei-yu picked up her pen.

"Sing-hua is learning English and is eager to go to the American school in the fall," she wrote. "There are many other children in the place where we live, and a playground near the buildings where she can play."

Mei-yu got up from the kitchen table and went to Fernadina's bedroom. Looking out the window there, she saw her daughter on the swings, swinging high. Twenty feet away, in the sandbox, other children were playing, digging holes, carrying bucketfuls of sand from spot to spot. Mei-yu thought at first that Fernadina remained oblivious of the other children, swinging with her head back, reaching with her feet for the sky. But then Mei-yu saw her daughter turn her head to watch the others in the sandbox.

Would she ever learn to play with white children? she thought, listening to the happy shrieks of the children in the sandbox. Two weeks ago she had heard different sounds. She had been cleaning in Fernadina's room when she heard cries outside. She looked out the window and saw Fernadina faced with another girl about her age, though taller. The other girl, who was white, stood with her back to the swings, holding her arm out, blocking Fernadina's path to them. Mei-yu could not hear the girls' words but could hear the passion in their high-pitched voices. She saw Fernadina reach out and push the girl. She shouted at them from the open window. She saw how Fernadina turned her face toward her but did not step away from the other girl. Then Mei-yu saw a woman running toward the girls from the side of the building. She left her place by the window and hurried out of the apartment.

The woman was shaking Fernadina roughly and screaming at her when Mei-yu, still yards away, shouted for her to stop. The woman dropped Fernadina's arm and grabbed her own daughter.

"Your girl pushed my Karen, I saw her," the woman cried.

Mei-yu held Fernadina close and soothed her. Fernadina's face was dark, hot, dry.

"Your daughter would not let my daughter play on the swings," Mei-yu said. "I saw her stand in her way."

"Who are you?" the woman demanded. She had reddish-blond, tightly curled hair. Her face was white, freckled, now blotched with anger.

"I am Mei-yu Wong. This is my daughter, Fernadina. And you? You must be Mrs. Simpson."

"Who told you that? Your friend, that China laundry lady?"

Mei-yu felt her face growing hot. "I was told that all children may play here. Your daughter had no right to stop mine from using the swings."

"So? She had no right to hit mine, either." She jabbed a finger at Fernadina.

Mei-yu saw how Fernadina continued to glare at the other girl. She knew, in spite of the anger she felt on behalf of her daughter, that Fernadina had been wrong to use force.

"Sing-hua," she said.

Fernadina, who was holding her mother's hand, pinched her palm fiercely.

"She should apologize!" Mrs. Simpson said.

Mei-yu saw her daughter's pain, yet persisted in the lesson she felt she needed to teach. "Sing-hua," she repeated, trying to sound stern.

Fernadina looked up at her mother's face. Mei-yu saw how her daughter pleaded for fairness.

"Sing-hua," she said softly, prying open her daughter's fists, stroking her fingers reassuringly, "perhaps, if you apologize to Karen, she will apologize to you for being unneighborly. Will you do that?"

Mei-yu was not certain if she had meant for Mrs. Simpson to hear, but the woman said, "What! You have some nerve!" She yanked her daughter back close to her side.

Mei-yu clamped her teeth together. She saw there was no reasoning here. She took Fernadina's hand and began to walk back to the apartment building.

"You're the ones that oughta apologize for even coming here!" Mrs. Simpson shouted at their backs.

Mei-yu took Fernadina back to their apartment and poured cold tea for her to drink. Her hands shook as she poured. What had she done?

she thought. She did not want trouble with neighbors. What had come over her, that she had spoken to make Mrs. Simpson even more angry with her and Fernadina? She felt her heart beating heavily in her chest as she watched her daughter sip from the dragon teacup. She knew she would somehow have to bear the looks of hatred from people like Mrs. Simpson, but what of her daughter? Should she continue to teach Singhua to turn her face, her back, to keep going, and hope that people with hatred would not follow? She realized now how she had lost faith in that lesson, how she had failed to teach her daughter that lesson by her own behavior that afternoon. What other lesson could she teach her, then? She watched as Fernadina put her teacup down and stared at the kitchen table, her eyes clouded with fatigue. Mei-yu took her to her room, lay down on the bed with her, and stroked her temples until they both fell asleep, shivering with a strange kind of exhaustion.

Mei-yu was glad the next day was Sunday and that she had the entire day to spend with her daughter. They went past the swings in the back of the apartment building and continued walking to the elementary school yard beyond the post office. They inspected the blacktop and the game fields and guessed what kind of games were played there. They picked dandelions in the fields. Mei-yu rubbed some of the tender, spiky leaves between her fingers and nibbled at them, finding that they tasted peppery but sweet. She decided to try stir-frying the greens, and raced with Fernadina to see who could gather the most to bring home for supper.

Later, Mei-yu sliced some Chinese sausage to fry with the greens. At the dinner table she began to tell Fernadina about the games she had played with her schoolmates in China; games played with small rubber balls, sticks, jacks. She began to describe a game played with a spindle and a length of string when they heard a knock on the door. Both stiffened. Mei-yu found herself listening for angry voices. For an instant the thought crossed her mind that she should have sought permission to pick the dandelion greens. Had they broken the law? When the knock came again, softly, she stood up and went to open the door. A white man and a woman stood there with uncertain smiles. Two children stood close to them, behind their legs. The woman held a plate with a tall white cake on it, while the man held out his hand.

"My name is Don Johanssen," he said. "And this is my wife, Bernice. This is Ronnie, our son, and this is Sally. We're your neighbors from down the hall."

"We just wanted to say welcome," the woman said, holding up the cake for a moment, then lowering it again, laughing nervously.

"Ah, yes," Mei-yu said, then saw how her visitors continued to wait, expectantly. Mrs. Johanssen was holding the cake out to her. "Please, come in," she said, taking the plate and standing aside. "Thank you very much. You are very kind. Come in. Fernadina!"

The American family came through the doorway, the children crowding their parents' flanks like newborn calves. Mei-yu saw that the girl was a little older than Fernadina, the boy somewhat younger. They had shiny brown hair, like their parents. She showed them into the dining room and they sat around the table, staring at Fernadina, who fixed her eyes on the cake in the middle. Mei-yu did not have enough plates, but the Johanssens accepted their pieces of cake in the palms of their hands, nodding and smiling as if they always ate cake that way. At first there was little talk. Mrs. Johanssen, Bernice, told Mei-yu that the cake was called an angel food cake. Mei-yu tasted it and found it sweet, with a spongy texture. There had been a cake with a similar texture in China, she remembered, an airy cake that she had eaten on special occasions. It was an expensive cake to make, requiring many eggs, much sugar. She smiled to Bernice with appreciation. Don Johanssen chatted on, saying that he worked for the government, downtown, and took the bus to work every morning. Mei-yu watched as the children devoured their chunks of cake and smiled when Ronnie, the boy, began to tease his sister, all the while throwing looks in Fernadina's direction to see if she was watching. Mei-yu saw how Fernadina eyed them both.

Then Don Johanssen said to Mei-yu, "We're sorry about what happened yesterday afternoon. Bernice saw it from our bedroom window."

Mei-yu looked up to see Bernice smiling at her with sympathy.

"You must not think Mary and Joe Simpson are bad people," Mrs. Johanssen said. "Joe lost a brother in Korea. He and Mary just don't understand anything anymore."

Mei-yu looked at her new neighbors. She could see that both the Johanssens had at least made an effort to understand. They did not, altogether, of course; neither did she. She could not see how anyone could understand why men died at the hands of other men, nor could she see that there could be anyone who could forgive the act. Still, she felt no more pity for the Simpsons than she felt for herself. She remembered the face of Mary Simpson's young daughter and how her face had taken on her mother's look of rage. Hatred was even more grotesque on the face of a child, she thought. Then she turned to Mr. Johanssen. "I wish to live here peacefully," she said. "Mr. and Mrs. Simpson must understand that. Neither my daughter nor I want any trouble."

Don and Bernice Johanssen nodded as they stood up and gathered their children to leave. They were certain the Simpsons knew that, deep down, they said. The Simpsons were good people. They hoped there would be no further incidents.

Days later, Mei-yu had watched from the window as both Fernadina and Karen Simpson approached the swings. Neither girl had acknowledged the other, and both selected swings at opposite ends. They both swung fiercely, the chains of one's swings screeching and groaning to drown out the other's. The pattern continued through the week, into the second week; Mei-yu saw it would never change.

Now she watched as Fernadina sat in the swings alone, watching the other children play in the sandbox. Children were strange, naked in their passions, she thought. She knew that being forthright that way and strange in the eyes of others, Fernadina would take many bruises, she would hurt. But her daughter was also strong, upright, like a little column of stone. She would be able to withstand the bruises, the hurts. *My little stoneface,* Mei-yu thought. *If only I could teach you to bend a little, life would be kinder to you.*

She returned to sit at the table in the kitchen.

"Sing-hua and I have many adjustments to make," she continued in her letter to Ah-chin. She had decided not to tell Ah-chin about the incident with the Simpsons. Why give her friend cause for worry?

> *But the future here looks promising. We have no com-*
> *plaints, except that we miss you. Please write to us soon,*
> *and tell us all about the goings-on in Chinatown.*
>
> > *Yours with affection,*
> > Mei-yu

Mei-yu reread her letter and sighed. It was a difficult trick, telling the truth, but not the whole truth, like walking a wire. She folded the single page and slipped it into an envelope. She addressed it to Ah-chin's and Ling's bakery on Canal Street and put a stamp on it. She wondered how her friends were and what was happening now in Chinatown.

○ ○ ○

Kay Lynn paused to look at her husband as she carried the dinner dishes into the kitchen. Tim had set up the ironing board in front of the television set in the living room and pulled a damp shirt from one of the canvas bags he had brought home from the laundry. He spread one sleeve on the board and watched the screen of the television as he waited for the iron to heat up. A weekly variety show had just begun. Kay Lynn had watched it with him before and had laughed at the different acts that had appeared. There had been acts with dogs, jugglers, people who talked through dummies held in their laps. Almost as amusing as the acrobats in the circus in China, she thought, putting the dishes in the sink and running water over them. She went back into the living room. Ting was ironing, laughing at a man dressed up as a fat lady.

"Don't you think Mei-yu is looking better these days?" Kay Lynn said to her husband in Cantonese.

"Hah?" Tim said, staring at the screen, ironing, his left hand manipulating the shirt on the board as deftly as a blind man.

"I told Mei-yu to fatten up a bit, to fill out. She looks better than she did a month ago, don't you think?"

Her husband chortled as the fat lady's wig fell off, revealing the man's bald head underneath. Kay Lynn went back into the kitchen to wash the dishes. She had invited Mei-yu and Fernadina over that evening to try a tunafish and cheese casserole for which she had found a recipe in her ladies' magazine. Mei-yu said she had found it to be a tasty dish. Mei-yu was always polite. Fernadina had asked for soy sauce. What did the child know? Anyway, Mei-yu must have taken her advice, eaten more fats, butter, onion cakes made with lard, Kay Lynn thought. She was looking almost sleek, her skin taking on the sheen of good health. Now she needed to improve the way she dressed, to add color to her drab wardrobe. Kay Lynn wondered why Mei-yu always wore her gray and black skirts and blouses, those flat shoes from China. She looked like a refugee. Kay Lynn had tried to coax her into choosing colors: pink or a light blue. "How you expect be pretty, the way you dress?" she had said to Mei-yu. "You not be widow forever." They had been going through the inventory of fabric at the shop. "Are you wearing refugee skirt and blouse to Embassy? Everyone in community be ashamed to have you in same room! Here, see this." She pulled out a roll of silk the color of a dark rose. She pushed Mei-yu along to a mirror at one of the sewing stations. "Hold up to your face, see how pretty!" She saw how Mei-yu lowered her eyes at the sight of the fabric draped around herself. "Make yourself dress with this," Kay Lynn said, rolling out four full yards of the fabric. It made the sound of wind as she swiftly unfurled it onto the cutting table. Mei-yu held the stuff between her fingers. "Listen," Kay Lynn teased her, pinching her arm, "you be meeting many good bachelors at Embassy. They say this party bigger than one at New Year, maybe. You see many bachelors, good ones, good catches. Eh, maybe you meet Chung, professor at American University, graduate from best school, I hear, Harvard! He's one for you!" She circled Mei-yu and flicked her fingers at the wisps of hair at the nape of Mei-yu's neck. "And your hair, so old-fashioned! Why don't you get haircut, modern style, permanent? Here, try one of my lipsticks!" Mei-yu had finally laughed and pushed her away. Kay Lynn backed away but shook her finger at Mei-yu. "I only try to help," she said. "You don't want to miss chance."

Kay Lynn heard the roar of the television and Tim's yip of laughter in the living room. She placed the dish she had washed in the drain board and went to see what her husband was laughing at. A commercial flickered onto the screen. A cigarette box with legs was dancing.

"Tim," Kay Lynn said, watching her husband's shoulders move rhythmically as he ironed the tail of a shirt. Five shirts lay on the sofa, neatly folded and ready to be bundled up in brown paper. "Do you remember Dr. Chung, who gave that talk at the community meeting few week ago?"

Her husband grunted and flipped the shirt to iron the other sleeve.

"Don't you think he and Mei-yu would suit each other?"

Tim glanced over his shoulder at his wife. A smile lingered on his face, left from something funny he had seen on the television. Now he gave her a look of disapproval. "Stop your busybodying," it said. "Stop matchmaking." Kay Lynn knew that look. She sighed. Perhaps she was feeling something in the air; it was the month of May, after all. She would wager that even Richard Peng had gone off to New York to show his future bride to his mother. He had stopped by the shop on Friday, bringing papers for Nancy Gow to sign. He had been cheerful, even teasing Kay Lynn over her new red shoes. Kay Lynn had looked out the shop window and seen Lillian sitting in the front seat of Richard's car. She waved and Lillian had waved back. A good match for Richard, Kay Lynn thought. She had met Lillian only once before but had admired the way she looked, the way she carried herself, like a lady out of a magazine. She also had a warm laugh. She would make life happy for Richard, who seemed too serious to Kay Lynn. When Richard had gone from the shop, Kay Lynn and Nancy Gow looked at each other knowingly. Perhaps Richard would have good news to announce soon.

Tim bent down to pull another shirt from the canvas bag on the floor. Kay Lynn reached over and took it from him. "Here, let me," she said. She placed the shirt on the board and began to press. Tim put his hand on her hip. "Well, don't you think Mei-yu looks better these days?" Kay Lynn said. "My recipes are fattening her up, aren't they? Don't you think Dr. Chung would like her?"

"Shh, shh," Tim said, pointing to the television. The show had resumed. Kay Lynn looked and saw four musicians with hair shiny with what looked like pig grease singing and moving about onstage. "What's wrong with them?" she asked, setting her iron upright, astonished at the gyrations of the musicians.

"Shh, shh," her husband said in English, placing both his hands on her hips and standing very close. "Nothing wrong. Listen to music. Listen to drums. Do you like music, shall we buy a record player next, Kuei?"

Kay Lynn watched the musicians with her arms crossed. The iron gave a hiss from the board. "I don't know," she said, shaking her head, picking up the iron again. "Something wrong with them." She began to press the iron back and forth over the shirt on the board. Below, next to her own foot, she saw Tim's foot begin to tap to the rhythm of the music.

Later that same evening, in the building next door, Mei-yu wrapped the towel around Fernadina as she climbed out of the bathtub. She rubbed her dry and then waited as her daughter pulled on her nightshirt. She looked into the mirror over the sink, remembering what Kay Lynn had said about her hair. She turned her head to her left, then to her right, imagining what she would look like with short hair. She felt Fernadina's arms wrap around her legs.

"Don't cut your hair, Mama," she said.

Mei-yu laughed and bent to kiss her. She was getting too big to pick up now. "Auntie Kay Lynn told me I would look more American with short hair," she said in English. "Don't you want your mother to look American?"

Fernadina pictured Kay Lynn with her headful of barrettes and colorful rubber bands. "No," she said, frowning.

"We can learn much from Auntie Kay Lynn," Mei-yu said, following her daughter into her small bedroom. She drew the new drapes she had made, then pulled aside the matching bedspread for Fernadina to slip into bed.

"I hate tunafish!" Fernadina said.

"You weren't very polite tonight," Mei-yu chided her gently.

"American food is awful!"

"Not all American food is like tunafish, Fernadina. You must learn to like sandwiches, because you will be bringing your lunch to school in the fall."

"You won't make pork bao for me to take to school?" Fernadina looked up with dark eyes.

Mei-yu shook her head, smiling. "No, I am afraid I will be too busy to make pork bao. But you must promise me you will try to be nice to the other children in school, and be polite and respectful to your teachers. You must promise me that, Sing-hua. It is very important."

Fernadina buried her head in her pillow.

"Soon, in a few months, I must take you to the principal to enroll you."

Fernadina looked up from her pillow.

"Will you be home when I get back from school?"

Mei-yu sighed and stroked the bath-damp hair from Fernadina's face. "I will try. I have spoken to Mrs. Johanssen, and she said if I am not able to get back, that you can go to her house for the afternoon."

Fernadina sat up. She thought of the girl, Sally, whose eyes were blue, and the boy, Ronnie. The last time their mothers had brought them together to play, they had smelled of peanut butter. How could she spend entire afternoons with them? she thought. She pulled the blanket over herself.

"Are you sure you want this?" Mei-yu said gently, taking hold of a corner of the blanket. "It is very warm tonight."

Fernadina held on to the blanket with one hand tucked tightly under her chin.

"Very well," Mei-yu said, and kissed her gently under her ear. Fernadina did not move.

Mei-yu left the bedroom door slightly ajar and went down the hallway into the dining room. There, on the table, she had laid out the four yards of silk. She had decided to cut it into the style of the traditional Chinese dress, the close-fitting cheongsam with the high collar, frog closing, and slit up the side. She had enough fabric to make a jacket as well. She smiled as she remembered Kay Lynn following her about in the shop with her many suggestions and comments. She had been grateful that Kay Lynn had taken her in hand, showing her the workings of the new apartment, introducing her to the shopkeepers in the little center down the street from where they lived. She had even driven Mei-yu into Chinatown on H Street when Mei-yu had told her she had run out of certain Chinese groceries.

"Ai yah," she had said when she started the big car with a roar, "why you want to go to Chinatown for? It very small, very poor. You should shop here, in supermarket. They have everything you want."

"I couldn't find the kind of soy sauce I wanted, or fresh bok choy, or bean sprouts, or ginger, or hoisin sauce," Mei-yu said. She sat quietly while Kay Lynn drove, thinking of her first visit to the supermarket alone. Kay Lynn had taken her there once, but she had been mesmerized by the variety of foods and the brightly colored packages lined up high in the aisles surrounding them, and had not paid attention to Kay Lynn's instructions and helpful hints. Later, when she had gone alone, she had walked down each aisle slowly, picking up cans, reading labels, selecting boxes and packages to shake and weigh in her hand. In the meat section she was dismayed not to find fresh meat. All meat and poultry was sealed up in packages of cellophane, or frozen. Mei-yu could not smell the meat to see if it was fresh, or see all sides of the meat to make sure there was the proper amount of fat. Americans were either not very choosy or very trusting, she thought. She remembered the sides of pork and beef hanging in the butcher shops in Chinatown in New York. There, she could point to exactly what she wanted and tell the butcher where to cut, how deep, how far. Surely that was the best way to buy meat. Also, in Chinatown, butchers left the heads of the pigs intact, for some people bought the ears or the jowls. Mei-yu had passed many an upside-down-hanging pig and stopped to ponder the smile on its face.

In the American supermarket she walked down an aisle where there were packages of rice, dried beans, and peas, all piled up neatly on the shelves. She stopped and picked up a package of split peas. The package cost twenty-three cents. It was so simple to shop here, she thought. She was about to put the package of peas back on the shelf when suddenly she thought of Hsiao Pei, her amah. As a child she had gone shopping with Hsiao Pei many times before. Hsiao Pei had taught her everything about food; how to pinch and tap vegetables and fruits to make certain of their freshness, how to look into the eyes of a fish to determine how many minutes it had lain lifeless. She wondered what Hsiao Pei would think of this supermarket. She wondered what she would say if she could see how easy it was to buy a package of peas nowadays. Hsiao Pei would probably laugh scornfully, and recall the days of the Japanese Occupation when food, even peas, was scarce.

During those days Mei-yu had watched Hsiao Pei slip out of the household and come back, many hours later, pulling out small sacks of grain and dried beans from a pouch hidden in front under her shawl. She had been like a fox, stealing back with food from the hunt to her den. Mei-yu missed going out with her amah, and begged with such persistence that finally her amah relented and told her she could go too, but only if she promised to stay close. Even then Mei-yu had to run to keep up with her amah, who walked with her tiny, rapid steps, hugging close to the many walls and alleyways that were laid across the City of Peking like trails in an elaborate maze. Some of the alleys, or _hutungs_, were so narrow that no vehicles, not even ox-drawn carts or rickshaws, only people alone on foot, could pass.

At that time, during the Occupation, Mei-yu had seldom left the courtyard of her home except on her way to and from school, and even then had stayed on the larger avenues. Now, on Hsiao Pei's secret route through the back ways, Mei-yu saw the most narrow _hutungs_ in Peking for the first time. The houses bordering these alleys were smaller. The people standing in front of the houses watched them pass without a word, and Mei-yu noticed the roughly patched clothes, the bare feet. For the first time she saw beggars leaning against the walls, holding out their rice bowls for food. She and Hsiao Pei stepped over trenches filled with sewage, and her amah yanked her hand hard when she nearly stumbled against a large bundle of rags covered with flies lying against the doorway of a house. She turned to look, but Hsiao Pei pulled her hand again and hissed under her breath for her to hurry.

Hsiao Pei looked to her left, right, and behind her as she pushed forward urgently. She knew Japanese soldiers usually patrolled the larger streets only, stopping citizens to take food from them, but were known to look down the length of a _hutung_ on occasion. She carried no string shopping bag that would give her away; whatever they managed to find had to be small enough to slip inside the pouch underneath her shawl. She held on to Mei-yu's hand tightly. Whenever a Japanese soldier turned to look down through the _hutung_ they were in, she would immediately slow down and lower her head. Mei-yu instinctively did the same.

After what seemed to Mei-yu at least twenty different turns and duckings into smaller and smaller alleyways, they finally reached a neighborhood at the end of the city. The houses here were wooden shacks that leaned against and supported each other in slanted, haphazard rows. There were no courtyards. The doors opened from the interiors of the shacks directly into the *hutung*. Mei-yu saw no one. Hsiao Pei walked up to a plain wooden door in the middle of the *hutung* and, after looking around a final time to make sure no one watched, knocked. After several moments, a man opened the door a crack. Hsiao Pei showed him her thick roll of paper money. He took the money and disappeared, closing the door. Judging from the thickness of the roll, Mei-yu expected to receive large bags of rice, and wondered how they were to carry them back without being noticed. Then the man opened the door and held out his hand, opening and closing his fist impatiently. Hsiao Pei reached into her skirt and held out a ring Mei-yu recognized as her mother's; a piece of coral carved in the shape of a beetle, set in gold. The man took the ring. He disappeared back into the darkness for a moment, then came back. He opened the door wider and gave Hsiao Pei a small sack of dried peas and a tin of dried fish. He closed the door quickly. Neither he nor Hsiao Pei had said a word.

The *hutung* was still empty of people. Facing the wall, Hsiao Pei quickly slipped the small bag of peas down into her pouch and tied the tin under her apron. Mei-yu could not tell that Hsiao Pei had food hidden on her but saw the sweat gathering on her amah's upper lip. As they turned to leave the alleyway another woman suddenly appeared at the far end. She stopped abruptly on catching sight of them. Then, seeing that they were leaving, she slowly approached the wooden door.

After what seemed to be more than twenty twists and turns in a totally different direction, Mei-yu found herself back at the rear entrance of her father's house. Hsiao Pei brought the food to Mei-yu's mother in the kitchen, where she sat alone.

"No one saw us," Hsiao Pei said, setting the bag of peas and the tin on the table.

Ai-lien refrained from exclaiming with disappointment at the pitiful store of food. She had heard what it was like on the outside. She reached out and placed her hand on her daughter's cheek.

"Were you frightened, Daughter?"

"Yes, Mama."

"Did you see any Japanese soldiers?"

"Yes, Mama."

Ai-lien stroked Mei-yu's face. "You need not be afraid now. We are safe here." Mei-yu's father had been in prison for a year now and the Japanese soldiers no longer came to their house. She looked up at Hsiao Pei. "From now on, Hsiao Pei, you must go alone. I would go, but I would only be a burden." She looked down at her feet. Then she looked up and took the bag of peas. "I will put these on to soak," she said.

Mei-yu put the package of peas into her cart. She pushed her cart down the aisle of the supermarket and turned the corner into another aisle, where boxes of detergent and household cleansers were piled high. She could not remember where Kay Lynn had said the tinned goods were. The brightness of the lights and the colors in the store oppressed her. The smell of disinfectant rose from the polished linoleum floors. More people were around her now, rolling their carts along the aisles, turning the corners and narrowly missing other carts. Mei-yu brought her cart to the front of the store and gave a quarter to the clerk. She watched him put her package of peas into a paper sack. _See how simple it is now, Hsiao Pei?_ she thought as she took the sack and two pennies change.

On the day of their trip to Chinatown, Kay Lynn had parked the car on H Street and waited there while Mei-yu went down the stairs below street level into the Mee Wah Lung grocery store. It was a tiny, dark place, and she stood inside the doorway awhile to allow her eyes to adjust to the dimness. She caught the familiar, slightly putrid smell of dried fish; of roast pork, which hung in strips in a small plastic-walled cubicle in the center of the store. Against the wall she saw the large glass jars filled with candied ginger, jujubes, sour plums, dried plums, star anise, dried tiger lily buds. She picked up a shopping basket, smiled a greeting at the middle-aged Cantonese woman sitting at the counter trimming bok choy, and scanned the shelves for her brand of soy sauce. She brushed past another woman who was inspecting thousand-year-old eggs packed in a barrel full of sawdust. Mei-yu found her soy sauce, and next to it, hoisin and brown bean sauce. _This is where I will come to shop,_ she thought. _I recognize and can touch and smell everything here._

Kay Lynn had clucked her tongue when she saw Mei-yu come out of Mee Wah Lung with two large shopping bags. "You never become American," she scolded, starting up the Ford violently. "How you ever learn, if you never try? You stay refugee all your life!" She turned her head to look for oncoming traffic as she backed the car out of the parking space, and scowled at the grocery bags on the backseat. Mei-yu felt Kay Lynn's disappointment keenly but said nothing, looking out the window instead. As they left Washington's Chinatown, all two or three blocks of it, Mei-yu felt her spirit sink. Here, on H Street, there was no crowd of people pressing along the sidewalks in front of the aging buildings, no vendors, no noise. Besides Mee Wah Lung, there was one other grocery store, and three restaurants with tattered awnings. She saw two elderly Chinese gentlemen standing in the sun on the sidewalk, leaning on their crooked canes. Because of the heat of the day, they had taken off their padded jackets and stood now in their shabby, though freshly pressed cotton shirts, silk vests, and shiny-bottomed trousers. They stood on the sidewalk and watched the sky with the wisdom of old monkeys. Where were the families, the children? Mei-yu wondered. Were they at the Community Center, a tiny storefront place a block away, or had most of them fled Chinatown to settle in the suburbs, as Madame Peng had said? In China, Mei-yu had passed through villages such as this one, villages that had been deserted as its people hurried off, fleeing approaching armies. How had these old gentlemen of H Street, and the few women of Mee Wah Lung, been left behind? As the car took them farther and farther away from the failing village, Mei-yu turned to watch the old gentlemen, who remained standing, squinting in the sunshine. She wondered where the others had gone, and why they had not taken their grandfathers with them.

Mei-yu was not certain she wanted to know these people of the new community, the ones who had moved out into the suburbs. Kay Lynn had told her the success stories of the Wan family, who had made their fortune in the restaurant business and were now living in Chevy Chase, and of Professor Chung, formerly of Harvard. Kay Lynn told her of the spectacular modern house the Wans lived in, and of how the professor was in demand as a speaker at colleges and universities throughout the country. These were the members of the new community. These were the proud Chinese, the successful Chinese, in America. "These will be your new friends," Kay Lynn had said.

How would she appear to these people and the people at the Embassy? Mei-yu thought as she stood over the folds of silk lying on her dining room table. Both groups of Chinese appeared to have grown accustomed to the richness of America. They had struggled for and successfully acquired its ease. How would she fit in with them? She felt particularly reluctant to meet the Taiwanese in their own Embassy. How could she feel otherwise, when she knew she was unable to give wholehearted support to Chiang Kai-shek's government in Taipei? It was not that she was pro-Communist, for she had never forgotten the acts of Mao's Liberation Army when she had boarded the last boat to escape them. How could she enter a political arena bearing no loyalties? "Don't worry," Kay Lynn had said. "No one at Embassy will talk politics to you. You not business, military. You only people. Same as me. We go to have good time, eat good food!" Still, Mei-yu could not rid herself of her unease at joining such company.

She had never been at ease among strangers. She had always relied on Kung-chiao to coax her along, to gently force her to face people, to go places. She fingered the silk before her. She had never worn a silk dress in America. There had never been reason to look fine. In Chinatown, in New York, she had worn her dark cotton skirts or trousers. Kung-chiao had never seen her in fine traditional dress here. Perhaps he would have liked this silk, this color, she thought, smoothing the cloth out on the table. But he never seemed to have minded the clothes she wore, never seemed even to have noticed what she wore. Kung-chiao had always looked at her, not her clothes. She began to weep, then, remembering she had left Fernadina's door ajar, held her breath. She wiped her eyes with the back of her hand, stepping back from the table to avoid spotting the silk. She focused her eyes on the fabric, releasing her breath slowly. After several moments, she reached into the pocket of her skirt for her box of pins. They were not there. Thinking she had left them in her bedroom, she walked softly down the hallway, then turned on the light in her room. The box of pins was on her dresser. She slipped it into her pocket, then sat on the bed. She took a corner of the bedspread and pressed it against her eyes. After a few moments, she reached under the bed and pulled out the cardboard box of photographs. She opened the lid and saw Kung-chiao's face staring at her. He looked out from a picture of him and Tsien-tsung, his friend, standing in front of one of the buildings of Yenching University. Mei-yu laughed, shuddering, seeing Kung-chiao smiling at the camera, his hands in his pockets, leaning a little toward Tsien-tsung. His spectacles were set slightly crooked on his face. Tsien-tsung stood with his arms crossed over his chest, looking dour as always. Mei-yu stared at Kung-chiao's face until she no longer saw it. Then she shuffled quickly through the other photographs, catching sight of herself and Kung-chiao standing on the banks of a lake, sitting in a park in Peking. Then she replaced the lid of the box and began to slide it underneath the bed. She wanted to push it far back, farther than she could reach, when she felt it bump against another object. She moved her hand and felt another box. She pulled it out and suddenly realized what it was, realized that she had forgotten to give it to Richard Peng. It was the cedar box that Madame Peng had given her to give to him. She held it and dusted it off with her hand. It was light. She shook it gently. There appeared to be nothing in it. She could have lifted up the lid and looked inside, easily. She held it up to her face, as if to peer through it. Then, as if with sudden resolve, she took the box with both hands and slid it back under the bed, next to the other one. She would have to remember to give it to Richard Peng, she thought, straightening her back. When? It would not be seemly to carry it to the Embassy and then give it to him in front of all the people there. Should she bring the box to the shop in hopes that he would come by someday, and give it to him then? He didn't appear to know about it himself, at least he had not inquired of it. Madame Peng had not said it was an urgent matter. Mei-yu decided she would think about the box later. She patted the pocket of her skirt, hearing the reassuring rattle of the box of pins, and got up from the bed to turn out the light in her room.

The yards of silk waited for her on the dining room table. She did not want to look fine for anyone, she told herself, picking up one end of the silk and smoothing it out. Kay Lynn's talk of bachelors was shameful. She did not want to meet anyone new, she thought. Kung-chiao had not been dead a year. She closed her eyes, seeing in her mind the photographs of Kung-chiao, herself. She thought of staying home, of not attending the reception. Then she realized how dishonorable it would be to refuse the personal invitation of Madame Peng's son. She knew she must attend. Then, further, she knew Kay Lynn had been right; she could not go dressed in her black shirt and trousers, or plain cotton skirt. She would have to go attired properly, spendidly. When she opened her eyes, the silk lay there, shining and soft. It was a deep color, not bright; she would not call attention to herself in a dress made of such fabric. She would cut it in the simple Chinese style. She would go to the reception and leave early. She smoothed out the length of the silk on the table. Then she took her shears and began to cut, catching the folds of silk in her fingers as they fell away from her shears like petals dropping.

O O O

The weeks passed quickly. Business at the Modern Hong Kong Tailors shop had grown brisk, and by the first week of June, the women found themselves behind in their orders for three entire wedding ensembles. Mei-yu had begun to bring work home, staying up late to sew beads onto bodices, lace onto trains. Sometime during the second week, when Kay Lynn approached her and asked her if she had finished making her dress for the Embassy reception, she looked up, startled. She had to admit that she had stitched the dress together but had not finished the hem or attached the frog closings. "Ai, ai, ai," Kay Lynn cried. "What you doing here, then? Embassy party tonight! If you dress like refugee, I not go with you! Tim and I drive alone! You take bus to Embassy!" Moments later she threw a package of embroidered frog closings onto Mei-yu's table. "Nancy say, go home and finish dress," she cried. Mei-yu laughed but bowed to the command and left the shop to take the early bus back to her apartment.

She had not been deaf to the excitement growing in the shop. She had heard Nancy Gow and Kay Lynn talk of what they had heard about the Embassy parties, of who they would see there. Their voices had taken on a conspiratorial tone as they whispered the hope that the announcement of Richard Peng's engagement to Lillian Chin would be made that evening, for everyone in the Chinese community knew by now how Richard had taken Lillian up to New York to meet his mother. Richard had chosen the right path, the right woman, now, everyone said. Before, he had been a reckless youth, had fallen in love with a white woman and suffered the consequences of an ill-made marriage. Now, a mature man who enjoyed professional success and good standing in the community, it appeared that at last he had found the right partner, as well. Good fortune would bless him with many fine children, an heir. Both Kay Lynn and Nancy anticipated that moment when eyes at the Embassy would grow wide with astonishment. Those in the tight circle of the Embassy, who were often preoccupied with the international diplomatic process and unaware of what went on in the Chinese community in the Washington area, evidently had not an inkling of what was to come. They cast their eyes afar but missed what rustled about in their own nest. How would they react? Would the announcement of Lillian's engagement to an American citizen, a non-Taiwanese with unknown political leanings, create an embarrassing situation at the Embassy? Would the Embassy officials become tight-jawed, speechless, or would they be able to cover the entire situation with the aplomb developed over decades of diplomacy in Washington?

When she got home, Mei-yu found Fernadina playing with Ronnie Johanssen in the backyard of the apartment building. They had taken their toy shovels and were now digging near the hedge at the far end of the yard. The two had become good friends, grown accustomed to spending quiet afternoons together. They scarcely noticed when Mei-yu came out to tell Fernadina that she had come home early and would be inside.

Mei-yu was grateful to be able to leave Fernadina in Bernice Johanssen's care. She had been ashamed at first, reluctant to confide in Bernice about her work, her lack of time, of how she had had to leave Fernadina in the shop with Nancy and the other seamstresses. Clients were clamoring for her now and she had had to leave the shop often to go with Kay Lynn to do fittings. She saw how Fernadina's eyes followed her whenever she left. She also knew Nancy and the seamstresses were too busy to look after her daughter properly. She was afraid Bernice would think her a bad mother, for Bernice stayed at home, baking cakes, fetching her children in from the yard, wearing her crisp apron. But Bernice had listened and seemed even eager to help. She agreed to take Fernadina into her house during the day. She even asked Mei-yu what Fernadina's favorite lunch foods were. On that first day when Mei-yu brought Fernadina over, she handed Bernice a brown paper sack. Inside was a container filled with the cold noodles and leftover chicken she had meant for Fernadina to have for lunch. The next day, Fernadina asked her for a sandwich, saying that Ronnie had given her a part of his that had been made with a delicious kind of meat called bologna. At first Mei-yu wondered if her daughter had been ashamed of her lunch of leftovers, but she began to make bologna sandwiches for Fernadina in the mornings before she went to work. Perhaps it was a good sign, she thought, perhaps her daughter was beginning to bend a little.

Inside the apartment Mei-yu brought her dress to Fernadina's bedroom in order to work by the light of the window and to be able to see her daughter playing at the same time. She carefully rolled the edges of the silk and began to hem with tiny, precise stitches. She had only the bottom edge of the dress to finish, the frog closings to sew on. She began to think of the evening ahead, of the people she would meet. Contrary to what Kay Lynn had thought, she had known the Embassy function was tonight. She had only childishly held on to the hope that if she did not finish her dress, she would have a good enough reason not to attend. Her unease had hardly diminished at the thought that she would be meeting the successful Chinese of the community, who would no doubt be examining her, assessing her future, her place among them. Would they smile at her as Roger, Kung-chiao's second cousin, had? Then she remembered the excited voices of Nancy and Kay Lynn as they had talked of the evening ahead. She began to draw a certain sense of reassurance from the feel of the lovely silk dress in her lap. She even began to feel a certain pride in that Madame Peng's son had extended her his personal invitation. Her feelings gradually expanded beyond those even of obligation now. She gave herself over instead to her curiosity, her secret wish to look into the fabled world of the Embassy, and began the last stitches of her dress with quick fingers.

At six o'clock Fernadina came in, asking for her supper. Mei-yu wound the thread around her needle to make the last knot. She carefully laid the dress out on the sofa, then went into the kitchen to fix Fernadina a bowl of noodles with fresh tofu and vegetables. She had just finished chopping the bok choy when Kay Lynn knocked on her door and came in.

"Postman put wrong letter in my box," she said, handing Mei-yu an envelope. "Too bad. Tim and I wait for letter from uncle in San Francisco, but we get nothing."

Mei-yu looked at the envelope and saw who it was from. She wanted to open it but waited politely, though impatiently, for Kay Lynn to leave. Kay Lynn handed her a small pouch.

"I bring makeup over for you," Kay Lynn said. "Look inside. You see eyeliner, eyebrow pencil, rouge, powder, lipstick. You make yourself pretty for tonight."

Mei-yu opened the pouch and saw the assortment of tubes and small pots and pencils. She began to hand it back to Kay Lynn, but Kay Lynn waved at her impatiently.

"You use makeup! You know how, eh?" She gestured at the dress lying on the sofa. "Dress ready?"

Mei-yu nodded, bemused at Kay Lynn's fussing.

"We leave at six thirty. Tim not want to miss appetizers at Embassy."

Mei-yu waited until the door had closed behind Kay Lynn, then opened the letter.

"Dear Mei-yu," the letter began.

> _Thank you for your letter of last month. I am glad to hear that you are pleased with your new home and your work. Nancy Gow has told me that you have been doing very well at the shop and that the customers have increased their orders from you tenfold. This, of course, is of no surprise to me._
>
> _This letter will be short. My hands have grown stiff . . . the pen is an ache in my fingers. I am writing to ask if you have kept your promise to an old mother and given the cedar box I left in your care to my son, Richard. If you have not_

done it, then I beg you, do this for me without further delay.
You are young; time flows through you. I am old, and feel
time drying out my bones.

Chinatown is changing, though not all for good, as I had
hoped. No doubt your friends will tell you. It is beyond me
now. A pinch on the cheek to the girl.

Affectionately,
S.L. Peng

Mei-yu read the letter twice, then folded it and tucked it under her sewing box. She felt a sudden shame for not having done the old lady's bidding long ago. She went to fetch the cedar box from under her bed, resolving to speak to Richard Peng about the matter later that evening. Perhaps she could arrange to bring it to his office the next day. She resisted shaking the box or putting it up to her ear again, but put it on her dresser and put a clean cloth over it. Then she hurried back into the kitchen to boil the noodles for Fernadina's supper, for it was already close to the time when she had agreed to bring her daughter to Bernice's for the evening.

The Embassy was ready, Lillian thought as she walked through the foyer, making her final inspection. The tall ceremonial vases in the foyer were filled with white- and salmon-colored gladioli and sprays of yellow forsythia, tuberoses, tulips. Lillian breathed in the fragrance of the flowers, noting with satisfaction how the light of the rose-shaded lamps on the walls lent the room a feeling of softness and warmth. She knew she had done her job well. Guests coming through the entrance of the Embassy would enter and surrender the day, leaving behind all that had been ordinary. Here, in the soft light, the heady fragrance, people would let drop their various armor and don veils.

Lillian walked through the foyer into the anteroom. The rugs had been returned from the cleaners that afternoon, and she saw that the colors of the wool looked deeper, richer now beneath her satin shoes. In the main room black lacquer vases filled with purple, green, and white snapdragons were placed on the mantelpiece. Lillian moved the vases farther apart, studied the effect for a moment, then continued through the short hallway into the dining room, where she inspected the decanters of sherry and the sherry glasses lined up on the table. Ivory-colored napkins were arranged, fanlike, at the opposite end. Beyond the swinging door to the far right of the table was the kitchen, where Lillian went to check with the chefs who were busy directing the preparation of the appetizers. Assistants were chopping fresh shrimp and water chestnuts, adding scallions and beaten egg to form a puree. Into this mixture they splashed soy sauce, sherry, sesame seed oil. The puree was then spread onto diamond-shaped pieces of stale bread. Lillian knew that the shrimp diamonds would go into the hot fat only when she gave the chefs the signal that all the guests had arrived. The head chef came to acknowledge that everything was also ready for the buffet, which would be served at eight o'clock. Deliveries of fresh duck, chicken, beef, vegetables, fish, and fruit had arrived earlier in the day, and everyone in the vast kitchen stood ready to perform his appointed task. The chefs' report to Lillian was merely part of the vast ritual. The entire Embassy staff had rehearsed and performed its duties many times over, and was now an experienced, polished company.

Satisfied that all was in order, Lillian left the kitchen and walked back through the fireplace room, across the foyer, and into the drawing room, to the left of the entrance. Here, she gave the final instructions to the other Embassy staff: the guard who would keep watch over the belongings of the guests; the persons who would make their way through the crowd, silently stealing away stray used napkins, half-empty, abandoned sherry glasses. The ladies' powder room was at the end of the drawing room, where she went now to stand before the mirror.

Here, she carried her inspection over to herself. She had done her makeup well and it appeared fresh still, her brows arcing delicately over her subtly lined eyes, her cheeks powdered and rouged to look like early peaches. She knew her dress, a cheongsam made of delicate silver silk brocade, suited her perfectly, fitting her closely, shimmering. Why, then, did she feel unable to face the evening?

The feeling of doubt, of unease, had begun weeks ago. It had begun the moment she had entered Madame Peng's parlor. In that moment, when Lillian met Madame Peng's eyes, she saw judgment so swift, so final, that she felt faint. She managed to seat herself in another chair, removed from the sofa, where the old lady sat, and Richard's chair, opposite it. She dared not look at the son, or face the old woman, who spoke to her in soft, polite tones. _This is what a bird feels like, stunned before the weaving head of the cobra,_ she thought. She did not remember much of the conversation, only that the old woman had inquired of her birthplace, her birthdate, and if her parents were yet alive. She remembered answering, her throat feeling parched. The woman had rung for tea and savories. Then Lillian had allowed her eyes to look about the room, to probe into the darkness. She heard the mother and son speaking about business matters. She felt her jaws moving about a dry-crusted pastry. She sipped the tea. Then, after what seemed like endless, empty minutes, Richard rose to escort her from the room. She stood waiting in the hallway while he went back to speak to his mother. When he returned, ten minutes later, she saw how his efforts to smile failed. His lips had remained white, pressed tightly together. The old woman's eyes had seemed to follow them. Lillian could feel their gaze shifting between her and Richard, long after they had left her apartment in Chinatown.

In the car, riding back, Lillian asked why. Richard said that his mother was old, getting strange in her ways. He gave a sharp laugh. He insisted that it did not matter what his mother thought, but Lillian heard the anger in his voice. She wondered, during the four-hour ride back to Washington, what kind of man he was to hate his mother so.

But then his anger continued to burn in the weeks following, as well. He was abrupt, aloof, and told her he could not call her, that his work at the firm demanded all his time. She turned away and worked on the details of the Embassy schedule. She was determined that the evening of the tenth of June would go perfectly. She told herself that whether or not Richard came was of little consequence to her. She told herself that what was most important was that the people, the right people, came to greet the Minister of Finance and pledge support to the Taiwan Government, and to enjoy the hospitality and ambience for which the Embassy was famed.

But now, as the first guests began to arrive and as Lillian took one final look at her face in the mirror in the powder room, she knew that what weighed most heavily on her mind was that she feared to see Richard, feared to know what she would feel for him.

Richard stared at the keys in his hand as he stood outside his car door. It was already six thirty. The sky was still light, evidence to the contrary that the evening had begun. He put his hand on the handle of the car door but did not pull on it.

This is what it is like, not being able to move, he thought. First had come the invisible, swift strike, without warning, as if it had come out of the bush or the sand. Then the numbness, beginning in the extremities, spreading up the trunk of the body, seizing the spine, the nerves, and finally the heart and brain. *I am being killed,* he thought, then laughed coldly, as he knew he was still alive, healthy, perfectly able to move. He got into the car and turned on the ignition.

He had been astonished, at first, at how much his mother had aged. She had seemed to puff herself up with gaiety when he had come into the room, but he could see that it was with tremendous effort that she kept herself so. Her breathing came in little shallow gasps. He had thought to speak to Dr. Toy about her health. It could not be the usual thing, asthma, or even her gallstones. But as old and ill as she had looked, he could feel the strength coming from her and, when she grasped his arm that day, was amazed at her grip.

He had been prepared for his mother to act coolly toward Lillian, but he was totally shaken when her eyes narrowed the instant Lillian was introduced. It was then that the numbness began to spread through him. He had been unable to speak, or even return Lillian's startled looks in his direction. But his mind continued to work and grow hot with anger at his mother's judgment. When Lillian was gone from the room, he faced his mother and told her, in hoarse tones, that Lillian was the woman he had chosen. She shook her head once, then closed her eyes and settled back against the cushions of her sofa, looking almost flat, spent. Then she told him about the cedar box she had given to Mei-yu Wong. "What box?" he said.

"The family box. The box I give to you to keep, you, the last of us," she replied.

"What is in the box?" he asked.

She did not answer. She looked shriveled, asleep.

"Mother," he said, alarmed in spite of himself, taking up her hand with the many rings.

She opened her eyes. "The box," she said, and pushed him away.

Richard drove onto the Whitehaven Parkway, north of Dumbarton Oaks. He would reach Massachusetts Avenue and the Chinese Embassy in a matter of minutes. He had committed himself to the evening, after all, had promised Lillian to introduce members of the Chinese community to those at the Embassy, to act as the oil between the gears. But as to Lillian herself, he did not know. The numbness had spread to the center of him now. Perhaps seeing her would finish him, he thought, feeling almost relieved at the thought.

"Ai, Mei-yu," Kay Lynn said when Mei-yu opened the door at six thirty. "You look so pretty! See, Tim, see how she looks!"

Both Tim and Mei-yu ducked their heads from each other. Kay Lynn reached out to touch the hem of Mei-yu's silk jacket, still staring at her with admiration. She saw the touches of makeup and nodded her approval. "She alive again, Tim," she said, laughing, giving Mei-yu a push out the door.

They reached the Embassy in twenty minutes. Driving past the circular driveway of the chancery as they looked for a place to park, they saw the line of long black limousines idling, pulling up to the entrance in turn to discharge passengers dressed in evening clothes. Mei-yu could not remember where they had finally parked, or how many blocks they had walked to the Embassy. She remembered only Kay Lynn's excited voice chattering in her ears and the feeling of tension that seemed to fill the air of the warm night, like electricity gathering before the storm.

Kay Lynn stepped on Mei-yu's heels as they approached the portico of the Embassy. "Oh, smell the flowers!" she said, pointing to the magnolia blossoms and laurel on either side of the entrance.

"I smell shrimp toast," Tim said.

Mei-yu let her friends go by, wanting to gather her wits, to breathe deeply before entering the Embassy. She saw how the pale, waxy magnolia blossoms had begun to fold for the night.

"Come on, Mei-yu!" Kay Lynn whispered to her impatiently from the entrance.

Mei-yu entered the foyer of the Embassy and found herself deep among a crowd of strangers. Kay Lynn and Tim had promptly disappeared. She saw Chinese faces, American faces, and lowered her eyes whenever any of them, several, turned to regard her. An official approached her and asked to see her invitation. He stood aside, smiling, when she showed him the embossed Embassy card.

Mei-yu walked slowly through the foyer, finding openings through the groups of people that led her to the small anteroom to the right. These were business people with interests in Taiwan, she realized, hearing snatches of conversation about textile quotas, cheap labor. She saw the photographs of Chiang and Madame Chiang on the walls. She stared at the portrait of Chiang, trying to summon deep within her sympathy for the general's present position. Again she felt the pang of hypocrisy as she stood in the Embassy representing him, for she could not bring herself to believe in him now.

On those summer evenings in Peking when she had hidden below the window of his study, she had often overheard her father talking to his colleagues about Chiang and the Kuomintang government, how he thought their aims were noble, but that they could not but succumb to the overwhelming combination of adverse elements: the aggression of the Japanese; the persistent opposition of the Communist Chinese; and the nation of China itself, crippled with ancient beliefs, a complicated and divisive language system, and lack of contact and transport between the naturally bounded provinces. Her father had also said that he thought Chiang's stubborn military posture and dependence on old ways of thought outmoded, inadequate to deal with China's problems in the modern world. At that time, she had sat under his window, dreaming in the light of the moon and hearing his words without truly understanding the weight of their meaning. When she was older, however, she realized that her father's assessments had proved to be prophecy.

Now Mei-yu was aware of the reports in Washington that the aging Chiang still sought to retain American interests in his Nationalist island government. He continued to fend off reports of corruption and mismanagement within his enclave, and claimed, in a bid for sympathy and support from the Western nations, that his government was the only true China, fiercely opposed to Communism. He still had Washington's ear, but for how long?

Mei-yu turned away from the portraits and pushed past the clusters of businessmen on her way back toward the main hallway. And what of the Communists? she thought, noting that even here in the hall were photographs of Chiang. The Communists had commanded the attention and support of the masses, certainly, through bloody revolution. Now it was to be seen what they could do to alleviate the hunger and misery in their huge country, to enlighten the peasant economy. No Chinese she knew here talked much about the Communists or about the bloody acts. No one had heard any news of or from family back on the mainland. People were still waiting to see; Mao's programs of reform were still to be implemented. Mei-yu thought of her parents, her brothers, and Hsiao Pei in Peking. She wondered how they had been treated by the Communists. She wondered if they had enough to eat, if her father lived, still.

Feeling suddenly saddened and even more alienated from the people talking loudly behind her in the foyer, Mei-yu walked over to the glass display cases against the wall of the hallway and leaned over to look at the odd collection of cricket cages and cups. Her brothers, Hung-bao and Hung-chien, had kept crickets. The drinking cup in the corner of the case was similar to the one Hung-bao had carved out of bamboo. She moved along the case, admiring the exhibits, shutting out the noise and presence of the crowd, when Nancy Gow came up and took her arm.

"What are you doing here, pretending to be a ghost?" her friend said, laughing.

Mei-yu was glad to see her. Nancy had on a turquoise-colored silk cheongsam and wore bright splashes of matching eye shadow. She peered at Mei-yu from behind the upswept rims of her glasses.

"Why look so glum?" she said, giving Mei-yu's arm a gentle shake. "There are many interesting people here. Come, I'll introduce you to my friends in the drawing room."

Nancy gestured to the doorway of the large room to the left of the hallway. Mei-yu could see a group of Chinese women standing there, each dressed in shimmering silk and satin cheongsams and carrying on animated conversation with one another. Nancy saw that she hesitated. "Don't be shy, now. Come, it's time you made some friends."

"Are they Taiwanese?" Mei-yu asked. Immediately she felt ashamed, for Nancy shook her head in mock dismay.

"Is that what you are afraid of? No, they are not. They are from all over the mainland. One from Shanghai, another from Soochow, one from Hankow. Silly girl! I promise you nobody here, not even the Taiwanese, will ask you to pledge allegiance to one government or the other. We have not come here for political reasons. After all, we do not live in Peking or Taipei, so who are we to judge?"

Nancy saw how Mei-yu continued to watch the group of women. "Come," she said, pulling on Mei-yu's arm. "They are like you and me. All have left families behind. Some have lost parents, brothers and sisters. We all have sadness in common, but this night, tonight, is not a night to sigh and pine for what is lost. We meet tonight to make friends in order to be able to keep going here, in this country. Smile, Mei-yu, I will not let you sour the evening with your long face!"

Mei-yu followed Nancy into the drawing room and smiled when the women turned to greet her warmly. Nancy introduced her to the five women, all who seemed to have had similar backgrounds to Mei-yu's, having come from the educated, upper middle class in China. They gathered around close to admire Mei-yu's dress and to draw her into their circle of talk. They all spoke Mandarin, although each spoke with the accent of her particular city and province. Mei-yu found herself answering their questions about her work, about her daughter, how different she found life outside of Chinatown. She was glad to see that the women listened with interest, sympathy. Nancy must have told them about Kung-chiao, for all discreetly avoided asking her about her husband, even though they all wore wedding rings. One woman, Yolanda Eng, took a pen and wrote her name and phone number on a piece of paper to give to Mei-yu. Then Mei-yu noticed that Nancy seemed to shift her stance and look away from the group toward the far end of the drawing room. Mei-yu followed her glance and caught sight of a slender woman dressed in silver making her way through the crowd.

"That's Lillian Chin," Nancy whispered. The women of the group continued to chat, but eyes turned to dart in Lillian's direction.

Lillian Chin radiated the aspect of an Embassy hostess, not only in her dress, but also in her bearing, Mei-yu thought. She knew how to tilt her head, to move without seeming to move, to receive the admiring glances of all around her with utter poise. Mei-yu watched as Lillian stopped to speak to a group of people, then laugh. Her voice carried through the crowd, high, musical.

Someone tapped Mei-yu on the shoulder and she turned around to see Kay Lynn, who was holding a glass of sherry in one hand and a napkinful of shrimp toast in the other.

"Hurry, or there be no more left," she said, indicating the appetizers. She eyed the other women in the group with uncertainty, although they all smiled at her. None of them spoke Cantonese, it seemed, except for Mei-yu and Nancy Gow, who had now gone to speak to another group of people across the room. She was relieved to see that something else had caught their attention across the room, and turned to see what it was. The woman in silver immediately caught her eye. She could hardly contain her excitement, whispering loudly to Mei-yu, "I wonder where Richard is? Why aren't they together?" She craned her head above the crowd, looking around the drawing room, apparently forgetting the group of women behind her. Then she pinched Mei-yu's arm. "I see him, there!"

Mei-yu followed her eyes and saw Richard standing in the doorway of the drawing room. He was looking about the room, apparently searching for someone. She was startled when his eyes stopped to rest on her face. She immediately shifted her gaze, pretending to find interest instead in Kay Lynn's sherry glass.

Kay Lynn, meanwhile, had returned to watching Lillian. "The lovers play game," she said happily. "They don't want people to know about engagement, so they stay apart. They wait, to surprise everyone at end of party."

Mei-yu thought of Kay Lynn's and Nancy Gow's speculation of the past weeks. She looked up in Richard's direction again and saw that he had disappeared.

"Eh, you try sherry, shrimp toast, Mei-yu?" Kay Lynn asked her, holding up her half-empty glass. "Better hurry, many people in main room, appetizer almost gone." She gestured for Mei-yu to follow her. "Maybe I find Professor Chung for you," she continued, winking. Mei-yu had never seen her friend behave in such a manner. She suspected she was the tiniest bit drunk.

In the main room people were standing in line to meet the Ambassador and the Minister of Finance from Taiwan and his wife. Kay Lynn and Mei-yu went to the end of the line. Mei-yu heard the clink of sherry glasses, smelled the delicate aroma of the shrimp toast, and realized all at once that she was hungry. Kay Lynn beckoned to her husband across the room. Persons of the Embassy staff had been threading their way through the crowd, bearing trays of sherry and baskets of shrimp toast bedded in napkins. Mei-yu watched with a smile as Tim whisked an entire basket from a passing tray and brought it over to them. She picked up a toast diamond with the tips of her fingers and bit into the hot, crisp crust, being careful not to burn her lips. The salty-sweet flavor of the juicy shrimp burst in her mouth. Tim handed her a glass of sherry. She took a sip, savoring the nutty taste. Perfect with the shrimp, she thought. She was beginning to feel quite happy.

The reception line moved slowly, steadily, and as Mei-yu moved along within it, sipping her sherry, she wondered what she would say to the Minister of Finance. Most people, she saw, merely murmured a greeting and shook his hand and bowed to his wife. The Ambassador stood next to the Minister of Finance at the front of the line and welcomed the guests of the evening. Lillian Chin stood at the minister's left, introducing him to some of the more important-looking business people. Richard Peng stood on the other side of the minister and introduced him to the members of the Chinese community. Neither Lillian nor Richard acknowledged each other but performed their social duties with dreamlike motions, nodding and chatting and shaking hands.

Then Mei-yu saw the moment when the minister met an American man of particular importance and began to chat with him at length. The entire reception line seemed to stop in its tracks. In this instant Mei-yu saw how Lillian turned to look at Richard, as though she sought to meet his eyes. Mei-yu saw pleading, desperation on the hostess's face. Richard did not see her look. He was looking around the room, frowning, seeming to be lost in thought. Perhaps Lillian was exhausted from the strain of hiding their secret, Mei-yu thought, looking back at the hostess. Perhaps, in seeking contact with him so openly, Lillian had decided to drop the game.

Then, in another moment, Mei-yu became conscious of someone watching her, and was startled again when she looked up to see that Richard's eyes had focused upon her. In the instant their eyes met, Mei-yu could see, even at that distance, that Richard's eyes did not express any of those qualities that indicate a person's warm interest in another, a man's interest in a woman, for instance. His eyes were filled instead with confusion, anxiety. Then he looked away. Before she could think, something, an impulse, caused Mei-yu to look again in Lillian's direction, and she saw that the hostess was now staring at her as well. Mei-yu felt as if her face had been struck on both sides. She lowered her eyes. In spite of her own shock, she thought she had seen pain and confusion on Lillian's face, as well. She heard Kay Lynn say something next to her but attended the thoughts in her own head instead. What was happening? What games were being played that seemed to involved her, yet were games she knew nothing of?

As she drew closer to the head of the line, Mei-yu felt increasing anxiety. The feeling of relaxation and relief she had experienced before in talking with the women in the drawing room had disappeared. As she drew within three people of the head of the line, she heard Lillian's and Richard's voices clearly, one high, one low, as they introduced the guests to the Ambassador and to the minister. She heard the name of the important American guest, Henry Campbell, who now stood to Lillian's left to help her introduce other business people to the minister. Then she found herself faced with the Ambassador himself. Richard Peng came forward and introduced her to all those in the immediate circle as a new member of the Chinese community in Washington. Mei-yu smiled briefly in Richard's direction, then fixed her eyes on one of the buttons of the Ambassador's dress shirt. The Ambassador bowed to Mei-yu and thanked her for her presence. Mei-yu bowed in return, remembering to smile, then moved on automatically, bowing to the Minister of Finance. She sensed Kay Lynn following close behind her. Then she felt Lillian Chin's eyes on her face.

"I welcome you to Washington, Mrs. Wong," the Embassy hostess said.

Mei-yu saw that Lillian had regained her air of self-possession and grace. In the face of such control Mei-yu sensed the conflicting voices within her grow silent. "Thank you, Miss Chin," she said. She realized she no longer pitied Lillian but admired her, envied her, and it seemed strange to her that she read the same thoughts regarding her in Lillian's eyes, as well.

The two women continued to stand, facing each other, smiling uneasily, until Kay Lynn pushed forward and complimented Lillian effusively on the success of the evening. Mei-yu left the line in relief. She took another glass of sherry from one of the silver trays and walked out through the foyer onto the portico to breathe in the cooling night air, to try to make sense of what she had seen and felt in the main room.

At eight o'clock a gong sounded. By this time the last of the guests had made their way through the reception line. When the last vibrations of the gong had died away, two uniformed Embassy staff members came to take hold of the massive doors to the buffet room and pull them open slowly. Guests gathered immediately around the doors, craning their heads to see, raising their eyes to the ceiling at the smells that wafted out. Mei-yu came in from the portico, wondering what the stir was about. She watched as the Ambassador escorted the Minister of Finance and his wife through the doorway, then turned and called out to the company before him, "Please, everyone, to the buffet!"

Kay Lynn spoke of the buffet for weeks afterward. She described in detail how the guests had approached the enormous round table slowly at first, admiring the dishes placed at the outer edge with an intensity bordering on reverence. She described how the staff people stood at various points around the table next to the hot and cold dishes, ready to help serve, their pride obviously showing. The food represented all that the earth could give, she said, fish from the sea, birds from the air, meats from the land, vegetables of every color, shape, and texture. The table glistened from the sparkling gelatins of the cold dishes and the shiny, hot-oil sauces of the hot dishes. The Ambassador, in a good humor, urged the company to begin, passing out the heavy Embassy plates himself , posing for the photographers, joking that no leftovers were allowed.

Kay Lynn described how the guests had approached the buffet, selecting first from among the cold appetizers of cracked radishes dressed in soy sauce, vinegar, and sesame seed oil; sliced jellyfish, eggs that had been hard-boiled in black tea, thin slices of boiled beef shank whose edges shimmered with brown gelatin, and spiced soybeans. Farther down the line had been more cold dishes: A shiny bean-thread noodle, cucumber and shredded chicken salad, slices of barbecued pork, and curved pieces of fish smoked in anise sauce arranged to look as if they leaped around the edges of the plate. Then came the hot savories, dumplings steamed and fried, stuffed and puffy with shrimp, pork, shredded black mushrooms, and vegetables. Steamed rolls stuffed with barbecued pork and red bean paste, stamped with red dye, came next, and farther along were flat, crackling chewy onion cakes. "I had to get two, three plates!" Kay Lynn exclaimed, remembering. "My chopsticks were shaking! I couldn't decide, so I took little of everything!"

Tim teased, "She took a lot everything. She left nothing for anyone else, and didn't eat for three days afterward."

"Why be proud?" Kay Lynn replied, "I not naturally dainty like Mei-yu, who came to table late and then only nibbled at this and that, like palace pet. You worried about getting gravy on your dress, eh," she teased Mei-yu, but Mei-yu replied that she had been preoccupied by her thoughts, quickly explaining that she was probably only stunned by the very bounty of choices before her. "Oh, but the dishes that followed!" Kay Lynn went on, dismissing Mei-yu's daintiness. She went on to describe platters of rice, noodle ribbons mixed with seafood, bok choy and baby corn, scallops the size of the fleshy part of one's palm, shrimp cooked to curl just so. Sweet and sour beef ribs, pork ribs in black bean sauce, crackling roast duck, squid with garlic, eggplant with dried shrimp, and more. "I have forgotten," Kay Lynn cried in dismay.

"Remember the bean curd and swimming soybeans dish?" Tim prompted her. "The creamed Chinese cabbage that looked like wet white jade? Remember how the chefs kept coming and coming with beautiful plates of food, how they had even wiped the gravy from the edges of the plates?"

"Yes, yes," Kay Lynn recalled, and then continued to describe the rest of the buffet, going around the table until her eyes glazed with the memory.

For dessert there had been slices of fresh pineapple, orange, and steamed sticky sweet rice with preserved dates and red bean paste. Mei-yu had eaten some of the roast duck and creamed cabbage and now, relaxed, feeling pleasantly but not overly full, carried a small plate of sweets and a cup of jasmine tea through the drawing room, looking for her new friend, Yolanda Eng. By now the evening appeared to have reached a natural lull. People who had formerly been standing were now sitting, quiet, sipping their tea. Women whose lipsticks had gone pale from eating were now too sated to dash off to the powder room to effect repairs. Men who had been discussing business and political strategies were now talking about golf, or looking at their watches. Mei-yu had decided that Yolanda and her husband had already taken leave of the party and was considering seeking out Kay Lynn to see when they would be leaving, too, when she suddenly saw Richard approaching her. Impulsively she looked around for Lillian but did not see her. Richard seemed to move stiffly. Unlike the flushed, slightly perspiring faces of all the other guests, his seemed pale, cold. Mei-yu wondered if he had partaken at all of the buffet.

"Good evening, Mei-yu," he said in English. His voice sounded strangely hoarse, she thought, but then, he had been talking all evening, introducing different persons to one another.

"Good evening, Richard."

"I am glad I have a chance to talk to you at last." He stopped abruptly, then explained, "I have never been faced with so many people!"

"But you and Miss Chin handled your duties very smoothly, I thought," Mei-yu said, hoping he would smile and relax somewhat. She knew instantly that her words had caused exactly the opposite effect, for she saw the muscles of his jaws tighten. Then he seemed to regain his composure.

"I wanted to speak to you about a certain matter, Mei-yu. Forgive me for not waiting until tomorrow, but I feel as long as you are here . . ."

"Not at all. Please, what is it?"

"When I was in New York, my mother mentioned that you had a box."

"Oh, yes! I wanted to speak to you about it myself, but I thought the reception line was hardly the place to mention it. Forgive me for not having given it to you sooner, but we have been so busy at the shop, and I have been concerned about my little girl . . ."

"Please," Richard said. He looked exhausted, Mei-yu thought. "Please don't apologize. I fully understand your reasons, whatever."

"I had thought to ask you if I could bring the box to your office tomorrow. Or perhaps, if you were planning to come by the shop, you could pick it up then," Mei-yu said.

Richard looked down, then up, straight into Mei-yu's eyes, and said, with great effort, "This may sound absurd, but I was wondering if, only when you are ready to leave, of course, I could drive you home, and take the box from you then?" He rushed on, seeing the startled look on Mei-yu's face. "I know it seems an impulsive act. It's just that, and I am somewhat embarrassed to have to admit this, I received word from my mother today. . . ."

"Did you? I did, also!" Mei-yu said.

"Really?" Richard seemed scarcely surprised. "She often exaggerates the importance of certain matters, but she did sound very anxious that I have the box in my possession as soon as possible."

"Yes, I was alarmed myself at the urgency of her letter. Is Madame Peng . . . is your mother well, Richard?"

Richard laughed sharply. "My mother would like people to think that she is old and ill. It is a kind of game she plays. Actually, she is very strong." He looked at Mei-yu closely. "She was very kind to you, wasn't she?"

"Yes. I owe my new life here to her."

"And you feel a sense of duty toward her? Loyalty?"

"Yes. I feel I will never be able to repay her for her kindness toward me."

Mei-yu wondered what lay behind Richard's smile. It was not a smile of gladness, of relief, of any feeling she knew. It was more like a smile of self-mocking anger.

"Would you do me . . . us . . . this favor, then?" Richard asked Mei-yu. His voice was soft, tired. "May I take the box tonight?"

"But what about Lillian?" Mei-yu wanted to say. How could she and Richard simply leave the Embassy together? Wouldn't people notice?

He seemed to read her mind. "Please don't worry," he said. "If you will leave quietly now, I will follow in a few minutes. I plan to return immediately to the Embassy afterward. No one need know that I was even gone."

"But Kay Lynn, I came with Kay Lynn. . . ."

"If you wish, I'll arrange to have someone on the staff give her a note saying that you were taken ill and that I offered to drive you home. If she is still here when I get back, I shall tell her the same thing myself. Surely she would see nothing wrong with that."

Although she remained reluctant, Mei-yu could see no further reason to resist. In going along with Richard's plan, she would only be complying with the wishes of Madame Peng. However sudden Richard's request, however strange the circumstances and conflicting her feelings, Mei-yu felt she had no right to deny them this now.

"All right," she said. "Ten minutes?"

"Less. Wait for me in the parking lane, to the right as you leave the Embassy."

Lillian could not deny it. Throughout the evening she had sensed that what had come between Richard and herself had settled to rest with finality. As the hours passed, as the buffet table had become spattered, the dishes of food gouged and dispersed, she felt her hopes diminish. Richard had spoken to her but once, in formal, curt greeting. Later, she had given him opportunity to speak to her, but he had shifted away. The anger and hurt she felt she managed to convert into energy that enabled her to become the vivacious hostess. She had been especially witty that evening, particularly high with color. She knew the people of the community were watching her and Richard, but she also knew that the buffet had served as a great diversion, and was glad to sense, after all the guests had finished their piled plates of food, that the issue of her romance with Richard had faded from their minds.

Now she felt a crushing fatigue come over her, and excused herself from the minister's group in the buffet room to walk outside for fresh air. As she passed through the main room she noticed Richard standing there with his back to her, talking with a group of American men. She continued quickly on her way to the foyer. There, at the doorway, she stopped, seeing the woman in the dark red dress, Mei-yu Wong, putting her jacket over her shoulders. Lillian drew back from the doorway and watched as the woman, who was still unaware of her presence, fastened her jacket, then stepped out onto the portico. Strange that she had not thought to bid the Ambassador or herself good-bye, Lillian thought. A beautiful but shy, awkward young woman. Someone she had seen Richard watch all evening. It seemed odd to her that she would take leave of the Embassy alone. Hadn't she come with the Woos, Kay Lynn and Tim? Lillian decided not to go outside and run the risk of meeting the young woman again, but went to the powder room in the drawing room instead. She was relieved no one else was there. She let cold water run on her wrists and closed her eyes. She felt a great pressure swelling inside her. She knew the feeling, had fought it the entire evening. A few more hours, she must keep tight control of herself for a few more hours, she repeated to herself. Then she became aware of the sound of the water running over her wrists. She turned off the tap and dried her arms with the linen towels. Fine linen in the powder room, she thought proudly to herself. That had been her idea. What other Embassy in Washington could claim that touch? She looked in the mirror, re-arranged a curl of her hair, and stepped into the drawing room. There, through the doorway, she saw Richard standing in the foyer, looking at his watch. He did not see her. She did not know how long the woman in red had been gone, and she did not need to guess why Richard was standing there now. In another instant he, too, was gone.

Lillian looked down to see the fabric of her dress move over the beating of her heart. She watched, counting the beats, listening to them in her ears until finally they subsided. Then she breathed deeply. Someone called her name from the main room. She waited, counting imperceptibly some other beat within herself, then went toward the voice, smiling, tilting her head.

Mei-yu picked up the box and held it for a moment before turning off the light in her bedroom and returning to the living room, where Richard waited. He rose from the sofa and held out his hands. He took the box, carefully avoiding touching her fingers.

"Thank you, Mei-yu," he said, tucking the box under his arm. She had hardly dared hope he would open it in front of her. "Good-bye."

He had been gone several moments before Mei-yu realized that she remained standing with her hands lifted in front of her, as if she still awaited the removal of the box. It was as if it had evaporated, leaving only a slight feeling of dust in her hands. She lowered her hands, rubbing her fingers together lightly, absently. Scenes from the evening continued to shift in her mind, colliding, leaving nothing clear. Her thoughts returned again to the box. She had only been its deliverer, she told herself, but the urgent tone of Madame Peng's letter, the look in Richard's eyes, continued to weigh on her. She wondered what forces worked between the mother and the son.

Mei-yu felt suddenly very tired. She was relieved the box was no longer in her hands, glad that she had not looked inside it. She wanted to think nothing more of it. She thought of her daughter instead, opening the door to go down the hall to the Johanssens' to bring her back. Sing-hua must be sleeping deeply now, she thought. She hoped she could carry her from the children's bedroom and back to her apartment without waking the child.

○ ○ ○

In mid-morning, the next day, Saturday, Kay Lynn knocked on Mei-yu's door.

"You okay?" she said, peering at Mei-yu closely. "We all wonder why you left like mystery last night. Richard said you not feel well. Too much sherry, you think?"

"Perhaps," Mei-yu said. "But I feel much better today."

"It also strange that Richard and Lillian say nothing last night. Nancy said she felt something wrong between them. You think so, too?"

"Yes, I thought so." Mei-yu thought Kay Lynn was looking at her rather slyly. Had her friend seen the glances between Richard and herself, come to the wrong conclusion about their departure? She decided she would have to tell her the truth. She wanted to confide in someone about the evening, anyway. She indicated for her friend to come inside.

"Oh, no, Tim and I must go now." What Mei-yu had seen as Kay Lynn's sly look had disappeared, replaced by a sudden shy manner. "We go to see doctor today."

Mei-yu was alarmed at first, but then saw that Kay Lynn had begun to smile broadly.

"We think we have baby!"

"Oh, how wonderful, Kay Lynn! Do you take the test today?"

"Yes, yes. I go now. Wish us good luck!"

"I will!"

"Oh!" Kay Lynn had turned to go but now faced Mei-yu again and shook her finger at her. "You not meet Professor Chung last night! I told him about you and he wanted to meet you. We looked for you, but poof, you gone! You both have dinner at my place soon, eh?"

"Maybe," Mei-yu said, laughing, thinking with relief that perhaps Kay Lynn had not suspected anything of her and Richard after all. She decided it had only been her own uneasiness that had made her think Kay Lynn had been suspicious.

She watched as her friend walked with exaggerated care down the apartment stairs. She was happy for the Woos, knowing how long they had waited for their child, how much they had wanted it. She was about to close her door when she decided instead to go check her mailbox on the ground floor. She heard a door slam down the hall and saw Ronnie Johanssen run down the hall toward her.

"Is Dina home?"

Fernadina, who had been practicing writing her letters at the kitchen table, came out at the sound of Ronnie's voice.

"Can I go, Mama?" she asked Mei-yu.

"Yes. Wait for me, I'll go downstairs with you. How are you today, Ronnie?"

"Fine, Mrs. Wong," he said. "C'mon, Dina!"

Before she could stop them, the two friends were pounding noisily down the stairs.

American children were so casual, exuberant, Mei-yu thought to herself as she unlocked her mailbox and pulled out a letter. Ronnie had been good for Fernadina, although she was not certain about the nickname he had given her daughter.

She saw with delight that the letter was from Ah-chin. She had wondered when her friend would write to her. She hurried back up to the apartment, tearing open the envelope as she went.

"Dear Mei-yu," Ah-chin's letter began. Her friend wrote in Chinese.

> I am sorry not to have written sooner, but Wen-wen has been sick (imagine, in the middle of summer!) and Ling and I have been very busy at the bakery. I am glad to hear that you are happy in your new home. I dream of the day when we can come to visit you and help you fill your house, even if for only a few days. Ling and I have applied to move into a bigger room, but we will simply have to wait and see. I

*think more and more people are coming into Chinatown.
Housing is very tight, as always.*

*Before I forget, Bao told me to tell you that he thinks of
you every day, and that he has sent you a special box of
sauces and spices that he thought you couldn't get there, in
Washington. I told him to write to you himself, but you
know how bad he is at that sort of thing. Incidentally, don't
tell him I told you this, but I know for a fact that he, our
Bao, is thinking about sending away for a bride from Hong
Kong! I went to see him the other day and found him in his
kitchen, poring over a Hong Kong magazine with advertisements for young Chinese women seeking husbands here in
America! He hid the magazine when he saw me, but I knew
what he was up to. I can understand that he is lonely, without a wife too long, but imagine, a bride from Hong Kong!
What if they get the pictures mixed up, and the wrong bride
shows up? How is one to prove such things? I don't even
know if such things are legal. Do you think I should discour-
age him from going on with this scheme? I have introduced
him to women here in Chinatown, but he says they are
as appetizing as three-day-old leftovers . . . toothless old
spinsters, women with withered limbs. He says all the
good women are taken. What are we to do with him,
Mei-yu?*

*And now, here is the most important news from
Chinatown. Colonel Chang is dead. He died three days ago,
two weeks after he entered the hospital. Apparently, he
claimed his innocence up to the very end, but then he was
also said to have been raving, only semiconscious most of
the time. Yung-shan has not been seen or heard from since
he first left. Rumors are that he has gone to try to find proof
of his father's innocence. People need something to gossip
about, after all. I think the general feeling here, though, is
that the matter is closed at last. I hope this news brings
peace to your heart, Mei-yu.*

At this point in Ah-chin's letter Mei-yu closed her eyes and became
still. Images of Colonel Chang flashed in her memory, then faded. She
was relieved that she felt only dullness and fatigue within her. She did
not feel peace, but neither did she feel anguish. She had prepared herself well. She picked up Ah-chin's letter and continued to read.

I saw Madame Peng the other day, walking down Mott Street on her way to the Union. She looked very well, I must say, though she walked with the help of a bamboo cane. She stopped at the corner to scold some teenaged boys lounging about, and when one talked back to her, gave him a clout on the back with her cane. I hope I am as good an example to the youth when I am her age. I worry about the youth here in Chinatown. More and more are dressing like Americans, wearing grease in their hair, growing it long in back and combing it constantly, as if they had nothing better to do. They wear black boots with thick heels, suck on toothpicks, and make insulting remarks to old people when they walk by. Used to be they worked hard for their parents. Now they stand around on the street corners, saying they are Americans and want better jobs than washing dishes and ironing clothes. Can you imagine, being ashamed of the sweat of their parents! They have been left alone too long while their parents work, so they join these gangs. I am watching Wen-wen closely, even though he is young. He says his American name is Jack. Already my son is a gangster! President Leong has set up programs at the Union for the youth, but they say his programs are old-fashioned, no fun. No fun? Life is fun? Parents worry that soon there will be more crime here from these youth. We had just begun to enjoy the freedom in the streets . . . at least no more of Colonel Chang's men hanging around. Now we have these youth gangs. What to do?

That is about all, Mei-yu. I don't wish to bore you with how long I waited in line for a special catch of sea bass, only to find that they had run out when it was my turn. Wen-wen misses Sing-hua. We miss her, and you, too, Mei-yu. I wish we could stand the two of them together to see if Wen-wen has caught up to her in height. Maybe it would be better for him to wait just a little longer. Ai yah, he still refuses to eat meat, only noodles, noodles. How will the boy grow, on a diet of noodles?

Ling sends his best. I am sending you some black bean cakes in the next mail. Write again soon.

Your friend with affection,
Ah-chin

Mei-yu folded the several pages of Ah-chin's letter and went to get paper and pen to write a reply. Ah-chin sounded the same, she thought. In spite of the changes in Chinatown, the hardships remained the same. Mei-yu imagined the strand of hair hanging down in Ah-chin's face, her look of exasperation. She found herself wishing that all her friends could come to Washington. She wanted to show them life here, how much easier, how much better it was than in Chinatown. Perhaps Ah-chin and Ling could start a bakery in Washington. She went into her daughter's bedroom to find paper, and heard the children's voices in the yard in back. She would tell Ah-chin that life for the children here was better, too, and that if they came, they could feed Wen-wen bologna sandwiches. Surely he would grow then, as tall and fat as the American children.

○ ○ ○

The late morning sun had singed through the fog by the time Yung-shan Chang turned the corner of Grant Avenue and Sacramento Street. He stopped to remove his jacket, turning back to look down Grant Avenue. Even though he had not been back in more than fifteen years, the main artery of San Francisco's Chinatown seemed somehow unchanged to him; perhaps only slightly busier, dirtier now, noisier. The shops and the people remained the same. He could almost hear the rattle of abacus beads along with the clang of the old metal cash registers as merchants tallied up their take; the clatter of heavy ivory mah-jongg pieces as they were piled up on tables lining the street. In his youth Yung-shan had gone to sleep and woken to the sound of the thick game tiles being tossed and clicked one upon the other. In his sleep he had dreamt of thousands of tiny tusked animals doing battle.

He had been reluctant to return to San Francisco. It had been here, in 1930, that he had been brought as a young boy, here that his father had begun his attempt at a new life. Yung-shan had never known his mother, who had died giving birth to him in China. He did not remember the long voyage across the ocean, or how his father had managed to elude the officials in San Francisco who kept watch for illegal persons such as they. He did not remember how his father had found the avenue direct into the heart of Chinatown, where he began his new business, and rose to challenge those merchants who had already established territory there. It had been here, in San Francisco, where his father had waged the first wars with the other powerful merchants from Canton, and where, because of the deadly nature of the wars, his father had feared losing his greatest fortune, the life of his only surviving son. This son, Yung-shan, was kept in hiding, spending his days living in one strange dark household or another, kept out of sight like a talisman wrapped in velvet.

Finally, in 1940, even though the wars in San Francisco had long subsided, Yung-shan's father told him that he had decided to move the business to New York. They moved when Yung-shan had just turned fourteen years old.

There, in New York, Colonel Chang began to teach his son his new business. Yung-shan learned to take numbers from people who lined up in his father's office or who called on the telephone. He learned to wield the numbers in magical sequences that resulted in profits for his father's business. All along he remained protected, watched over carefully by his father's men. When he reached eighteen years of age, he began to question the columns of numbers, to yearn for walks where no one accompanied him. He began to loathe the crowded streets of Chinatown. When he reached twenty-five, he decided that he would leave Chinatown but found himself unable to tell his father. He despised himself for fearing the wrath of his father, for fearing the curses Chinese fathers heaped upon disloyal sons. He cursed his own feelings of obligation toward his father, his guilt. Although he remained with the business, he managed to convey his intentions to his father by refusing to undertake certain duties, by avoiding the company of his father's men. By the time he was twenty-eight and reaching the point of desperation, he and his father were barely speaking.

Now his father was dead. Yung-shan knew that he, the son, stood to inherit his father's debts and the grievances held against him these many years, both in New York as well as San Francisco. But he also knew it was unlikely that any of his father's enemies would recognize him here on the West Coast; he knew he was in no real danger. No one fought to the death anymore; at least, the older merchants no longer seemed to have the spirit for it, and the laws forbade it. But still, he knew word might have spread that he was here. He knew to be careful.

Yung-shan looked at the address written on the paper he held in his hand. The cook in Chicago had said he had sent Wo-fu to this address. Probably the address of yet another cook. Every other man in

Chinatown was a cook, he thought, continuing to walk down Sacramento and then turning right onto Waverly Place.

He had begun his initial search for Wo-fu in the Chinatown of Toronto, spending weeks there going from restaurant to restaurant, shop to shop, street to street. He had kept an account of all the places he visited and the people he talked to, especially those who thought they had seen Wo-fu, but after several weeks, he began to wonder if he were being misled, or if Wo-fu had simply vanished, for he saw no sign of him. Then one day, passing a crowded teahouse during the noon hour, he caught sight of Wo-fu inside, waiting on tables. Astonished, forgetting caution, Yung-shan entered the restaurant. He had made his way halfway across the room toward Wo-fu's table when the waiter saw him. They both froze, but in the next instant Wo-fu had abandoned his tea cart and was making his way toward the back of the restaurant. Yung-shan followed, pushing both waiters and customers out of his path. When he finally reached the rear entrance, he stepped out to find himself in an empty alleyway. Wo-fu had disappeared. Yung-shan searched the alleyway, the street in front of the teahouse, and the streets surrounding the area for several blocks. He berated himself bitterly for having acted impulsively when he should have remained calm, knowing he should not have tried to confront Wo-fu until after the lunch hour had ended and the crowd had gone. Finally he returned to the teahouse, following his last hope that Wo-fu might have left clues there as to where he might have fled. One of the cooks overheard him questioning the other waiters and came over, saying that Wo-fu had talked to him of having a cousin in Chicago who had begun a successful wholesale business. He complained that Wo-fu had talked him into giving him over fifty dollars, promising that he would invest in the cousin's business for him. "Find the cheat and make him give me back my money," he shouted after Yung-shan, who was already on his way out the door.

In Chicago, Yung-shan spent another several weeks tracking down Wo-fu's cousin. He knocked on the door of a Southside tenement and was confronted moments later by the landlord, who came out of the apartment next door and complained that the tenant and another young man had left long ago without paying the rent. "Look how they left the place," the man, who was white, said, showing Yung-shan the ten-by-twelve room, bare except for a rusty sink attached to the wall, a two-burner hot plate, a metal-frame bed, and piles of wadded-up newspapers that might have been stuffed into clothes for warmth. The room was dank, cold. "Smell the stink," the landlord went on. "I can't rent the place no more. Your friends was always cookin' stink, eatin' stink. Everybody else in the building was always complainin'. What do you Chinks eat, anyway?" Yung-shan glanced sideways at the landlord. The man's head was bald, with a brow like a wooden bowl and a nose that looked to have been broken. Yung-shan stared at the newspapers lying about, guessing that the Chicago cold had driven out Wo-fu and his cousin. The landlord, who had been looking at him with suspicion, seemed suddenly to brighten. "Hey, you one of them agents from Immigration?" he asked. "You gonna catch 'em, send 'em back to Hong Kong on a leaky junk?" Yung-shan looked at the man, considered giving him a knife-hand blow to the throat. He gave him twenty dollars instead. "Whatever you know," he said, watching the man stuff the bills into his pocket. Then the landlord admitted having seen letters sent to the cousin with a return address of San Francisco. He had kept the return address, thinking it might come in handy if he ever decided to report them to the Immigration Bureau. "You sure you're not from Immigration?" he asked Yung-shan again. When Yung-shan gave him no sign, he shrugged and went back into his apartment. Moments later he reappeared and gave Yung-shan a scrap of paper with an address written on it. "Even if you ain't with Immigration," he said, spitting on the floor of the hallway, "you look like you could find those scum faster 'n they could, anyhow."

Yung-shan checked the address the man had given him again and found himself standing in front of the How How Noodle House on Clay Street. It was approaching the noon hour; Chinese men were pushing past him through the door. He decided to go in, choosing a seat in a small booth near the kitchen. Seconds after he had seated himself, a waiter set a steel teapot and a thick china cup in front of him, then slapped down a pencil and piece of paper. Yung-shan chose his lunch from the menu suggestions written in Chinese on strips of paper taped to the wall, and wrote it on the piece of paper. Scarcely ten seconds later the same waiter, bearing a huge tray stacked with empty dishes, picked up the paper on his way back to the kitchen.

While he waited for his lunch Yung-shan watched a worker eating at the table next to him. Noodles and dumplings slid down his throat as quickly as fish down a pelican's gullet. He hardly seemed to chew. Then he picked up the bowl with the remaining soup and gulped it down noisily. He put the bowl down with his right hand while his left hand reached for his wallet. His entire lunch had taken less than ten minutes. Yung-shan wondered if the noodles wriggled in the man's stomach.

The waiter brought Yung-shan's order of shrimp dumplings and noodles in broth and set it down in front of him. Yung-shan picked up his broad-headed soup spoon and stirred the dumplings around, for the broth appeared to be boiling hot. As he stirred he watched the four cooks working their frantic pace in the kitchen, which was separated from the dining room by a low partition. They appeared to be standing in a cauldron of steam as they tended the pots of boiling noodles and dumplings all around them. One cook was stretching out fresh noodles, pulling them apart and separating them into individual strands. The noodles vibrated like harp strings between his arms as he pulled, promising elasticity and chewiness when they emerged from their broth bath. Meanwhile, amidst the din of crashing plates and voices raised in Cantonese chant, the waiters continued to trot back and forth between the tables and the kitchen. That was one thing he had never had to do in Chinatown, wait on tables, Yung-shan thought. He watched as they came bearing their enormous trays, wondering how they were able to carry dishes between splayed fingers without mishap. He had seen as soon as he had entered that Wo-fu was not among them.

He knew Wo-fu would be watching for him now. He also knew Wo-fu could be anywhere on the streets in San Francisco, staying just out of sight, working, scraping up enough money to buy a ticket elsewhere. He had looked for him long enough now that he no longer needed to refer to the one photograph he carried of him to show strangers. Now Wo-fu's face was before him, always.

Wo-fu had one of those faces that looked eternally young, smooth, without even a sign of whiskers, although Yung-shan knew he was at least twenty-five years old. He had the fine features of a girl: large soft eyes, a small nose, an almost delicate chin. At first Yung-shan had thought the man too soft, too weak to be of any use to his father. But after he had watched him on the streets of Chinatown in New York, at the request of his father, he discovered that Wo-fu blended in well among those on the street, speaking a slangy street English picked up, no doubt, in Hong Kong. He also saw that he was quick, and seemed to possess an intuitive street sense of knowing what to do and where to be next. Yung-shan decided to approve Wo-fu's initiation into his father's company as a street man; someone who could listen and watch for any news that might prove to be of use to the old man. It wasn't until afterward, when it was too late, that he saw that Wo-fu had in fact been an ambitious, hungry, even greedy person; someone who could be bought.

Had he been more thorough, had he spent more time following Wo-fu, Yung-shan told himself, he would have seen that the man was not trustworthy. However, his father had been impatient, had wanted a new man quickly, and so he had approved Wo-fu. The decision, the mistake, rested heavily upon him now. He knew he should have taken more of an interest.

Yung-shan looked to the table next to him and saw a different man sitting there, slurping soup. He noticed now that new customers were seated at every table opposite the wall where he sat in his booth. His waiter brought him a fresh pot of tea and the grease-stained check, scurrying by, too busy to look disapprovingly at the way he dawdled over his bowl. He calmly returned the stares of the other customers as they looked at him over the rims of their bowls, reading contempt in their eyes at the way he sat at leisure. To them, he probably looked like another shiftless bachelor out of work. They all looked like they had other mouths to feed; wives who toiled long hours or who stayed in their rooms, tending babies. Yung-shan looked around him and noticed there was not a single woman in the restaurant. He thought suddenly of Mei-yu, as he always did when he thought of women. How was she managing now? he wondered. He hurriedly took a mouthful of noodles, feeling shame overwhelm him. He had been the fool with her from the very beginning. How had he dared hope to win her by threatening her husband? How had he thought to win her love by scheming to entrap it? He cursed his own weakness. Hers was a face that remained with him, reminding him of his shame, his foolishness. Now he had his name to clear with her, as well. He shook his head to escape memory of her. He looked up to meet the eyes of the men who had finished their lunches and were now on their way back to work. He saw it was obvious to them that he was not a working man, that no hot iron waited in a cramped spot for him.

His thoughts returned to his father and the last day he had seen him in New York. Two days before that, Fong had come running to his apartment and told him what he had heard Lee tell the police at the Fifth Precinct. Yung-shan knew he must move quickly, but he knew also that he must see his father once more. He had attempted to approach his father before, right after he had heard the police had captured Lee, weeks earlier, but the old man had insisted they remain apart. "That is exactly what the police want, to trap us together," his message had said. But now that Lee had agreed to talk, Yung-shan knew he must consult the old man a last time. He moved into a vacant room above the Hong Hing Trading Company on Park Street and waited for two days, thinking that his father might send for him, preparing himself for his next move. Fong reported to him daily, bringing him food and the news that the police had searched his apartment, and that they had decided they would settle for the arrest of the Colonel alone. With that latest news, Yung-shan knew he could wait no longer.

He found his father sitting up on the couch, attempting to button his shirt. He held his head up stiffly, prevented by the large bandage on his neck from looking down at the buttons. He cursed as he fumbled with trembling hands. Yung-shan came forward to help him, but his father pushed his hand away angrily and then, exhausted from his efforts, feebly stuffed his shirt, unbuttoned, into his trousers. Yung-shan saw how the trousers were now loose and shapeless on his father's wasted body. His father was glaring at him with what he thought was his impatience and exasperation of old.

"I told you not to come! You've come to watch me die, is that it?"

Yung-shan refused to rise to his father's bait. "We haven't much time," he said. "Fong is downstairs watching for the police. He thinks they will be here any moment."

"Hah!"

Yung-shan watched in alarm as his father shuffled his feet about the base of the couch.

"What are you doing?"

"My slippers!" The old man groaned in rage. "I can't find my slippers!" He shuffled his feet furiously. Yung-shan found the worn black slippers and, grasping his father's ankles, put them on his feet. He was shocked to feel how thin the ankles were, as fragile as the wrists of a woman.

"They won't find me here, stuck like a rat in a hole!" his father was saying, trying to rise. "I'll have dinner at Quon Luck's, as usual, and if they want me, they'll find me there, waiting for them."

"Wait, Father," Yung-shan said, holding on to the old man's arm and pulling gently. The old man collapsed against his arm and fell back onto the couch. Yung-shan feared he had fainted. Then he saw the faint glint of his eyes beneath the hooded lids.

"Father," he said, listening at the same time for Fong's shout of warning, for already precious moments had passed. "Tell me once more. Did you send Lee and Tam to kill Wong Kung-chiao?"

His father's eyes turned to him slowly. They shone with contempt. "Weren't you the one who counseled me against such antics?" he said.

"Yes," Yung-shan said.

"Then you believe the father betrayed the son, in the same way the son betrayed the father?"

Yung-shan bowed his head to the sound of bitterness in his father's voice. He knew he could never make his father understand his reasons for wanting to leave the business. He resisted the urge to throw his arms around his father's knees, to beg for forgiveness. "You must believe me," he said quietly. "I never betrayed you."

They were both still for several moments. Yung-shan thought his father had sunk into a stupor when he felt the old man's hand tighten on his arm. He bent nearer to his father's face, catching his breath at the sour smell of illness.

"What is it, Father?"

The Colonel's eyes suddenly opened wide. "I have many enemies, but only one had the power to do this to me," he said. "But you must find proof! You cannot fail me in this!"

"Who was it, Father?" Yung-shan said, reaching into his pocket for a handkerchief to wipe the spittle from his father's lips.

His father appeared not to hear him. Instead, with great effort, he raised himself up. He beat his fist feebly against the body of his son. "You must find Wo-fu. The truth lies with him. Find him, make him tell you and everyone else the truth!"

He appeared to be raving. Yung-shan tried to press his father gently back onto the cushions of the couch, but the old man resisted vehemently, struggling against him with surprising strength.

"Find Wo-fu! Bring him back!"

Yung-shan saw how his father's eyes looked wildly beyond him now. He could see that the old man had forgotten him altogether. The fear that this was the last vision he would have of his father alive seized him. Yung-shan took his father's hands, pressed them together against his own chest, then left the room.

Fong was waiting at the bottom of the stairs. The police were still nowhere in sight. "Go now, there is nothing you can do," Yung-shan told him, and watched as the trusted man slipped out of the building and disappeared down the street. Yung-shan walked rapidly through the darkening alleyways of Chinatown to the room above the Hong Hing Trading Company and began to gather his things, his mind whirling. One by one he envisioned the faces of his father's enemies as they had struggled against him for more than a decade in Chinatown, each accusing the other of undermining business and the well-being of the community. Why would any of them go to such extremes to trap Chang now, when his power was obviously on the wane, when it was apparent to everyone that the entire structure of business in Chinatown was changing, giving over to new blood from Hong Kong, to the new generation of American-born Chinese? Who had wanted Chang the most?

Whoever had struck at the Chang family had struck at the wrong heart, Yung-shan thought bitterly. He knew he had hardly kept it a secret in Chinatown that he had yearned to leave his father's tradition of business, that he had felt suffocated by the shadows created by his father and that all the maneuvering and scheming related to the family business had always been repugnant to him. Perhaps his father's enemy had counted on this reluctant nature of his, calculated that he would not pursue the trail of any who attempted to ensnare his father. An enemy as arrogant as this must be taught that they had made a terrible mistake, that they had underestimated the son's sense of duty toward the father, Yung-shan thought. He vowed to show the enemy how the son would exact payment for the treachery done to the father. His father's words rang again in his ears. Find Wo-fu, he had said, the truth lay with Wo-fu. Here, at least, was the beginning of the trail. Even if the truth did not end with the waiter, Yung-shan felt in his bones that it began with him. Where to find Wo-fu, then, where to look? He could begin by questioning the other waiters who had worked alongside him at the Sun Wah Restaurant. Perhaps even ask Bao, the cook. The cook was a cagey fellow. Even if he did not know where Wo-fu had gone, he could still piece together an intelligent guess. He could also be counted on to remain quiet. Yung-shan knew he was too clever and cautious a man to begin telling a story before he knew the ending.

Yung-shan looked up to meet the eyes of his waiter, who had taken his bowl away and was now wiping his table with a wet rag. He gave him two dollars out of his wallet. He noticed that the place was almost clear of people now. The cooks in back were eating their own lunch. Two were sitting at the table nearest the kitchen, the other two standing up, sipping from their soup bowls. Yung-shan walked over to the cooks and nodded to them casually. They nodded in return but concentrated on their lunch. Yung-shan addressed the cook nearest to him in Cantonese. The man, who still wore his apron, looked as though he might have worked at the noodle house the longest.

"Good place, good food," Yung-shan said. "Been here long?"

The man shook his head. Then, between gulps, said, "Two months only."

Another, younger cook looked at Yung-shan with suspicion. "You from Immigration?" he asked.

"No. I'm looking for a friend. I owe him money. I have enough to pay him back now but can't find him." He pulled out the photograph of Wo-fu standing in front of the Sun Wah Restaurant along with three other waiters and Bao the cook. He pointed to Wo-fu. "Have you seen him around?"

The younger man glanced over his bowl, seeming to consider, then lowered the bowl from his mouth. His lips were shiny with soup. "Friend, you say? Sure. You pay him back, he pay me back. He worked here for a couple of months, then moved over to the Golden Lotus café on Washington Street. I went to collect what he borrowed from me but found out he left there, too."

Yung-shan turned to the others, showing them the photograph. "Any of you seen him?"

The others shrugged, then turned their eyes to the bottoms of their bowls.

Yung-shan went back to his table to leave a tip, then continued on his way out of the restaurant. The bright afternoon sun struck him full in the eyes. He took out a small notebook from the breast pocket of his jacket and squinted at the address he had taken from his father's ledger. It was the address of a close business friend, someone the Colonel had relied on before. This someone knew the entire network of business in Chinatown in San Francisco and was aware of the comings and goings of every new face in the area. Yung-shan had waited to call on him until after he had exhausted his own information, for he knew to call on this man, even though he was a friend of his father's, would be to announce his presence in San Francisco. He had hoped that would not have been necessary. Still, this man would know if Wo-fu remained in San Francisco, or if the waiter had gone on to Los Angeles, Vancouver, or even back to Hong Kong. Yung-shan saw from the address that at most it was only a four-block walk. He turned north and began walking.

○ ○ ○

Mei-yu had had scarcely the time or energy to think of anything other than her work during the weeks following the evening of the reception, for business at the shop had reached its peak season. When she opened the door that Saturday afternoon, a month following, and found herself face-to-face with Richard Peng, she felt a great shock. She had not expected to see him again. She realized suddenly that she had hoped not to see him. She regarded him with a stunned wariness, even though she sensed his calm, his cordiality. Finally her sense of propriety roused her and she stood aside to invite him into her living room. As he stepped past her, she ran her fingers through her hair, realizing that she had not bothered to pin it up that morning; that it lay on her shoulders like a sheath, thick, heavy. She tried to keep her voice calm as they walked into the living room, exchanging pleasantries. After she invited Richard to sit down, she asked him if he cared for a glass of iced tea, excusing herself in the same breath to flee into the kitchen. There, standing at the sink, winding her hair up onto her head and breathing deeply, she asked herself why he had come.

Minutes later, composed again, she returned to the living room, bringing a tray with two glasses of iced tea. Richard turned and smiled pleasantly. He had been looking out the front window. He seemed changed from the last time she had seen him, she thought, setting the tray down on the table in front of the sofa. Instead of the dark business suit, he wore a plain blue cotton shirt and dark slacks. He seemed younger, less severe, less like her employer. But when he sat down at the far end of the sofa, remarking how pleasant he found her living room, Mei-yu noticed the deliberateness with which he moved, heard the measured tone of his voice, as if everything he did and said had been predetermined and was now only unfolding according to design. His plans, she thought to herself, whatever they were, had been carefully laid. She sat back at her end of the sofa, assuming a calm pose, but readied herself, turning her face full toward him, attuning herself to his every nuance.

Then Fernadina came out of her room, looking questioningly at her mother when she saw the two of them sitting there.

"Say hello to Mr. Peng, Sing-hua," Mei-yu said, indicating for her daughter to greet their guest. Fernadina came forward reluctantly. "Sing-hua and I had planned to go on an outing this afternoon," Mei-yu said meaningfully.

"It is a beautiful day for it," Richard said, smiling from mother to daughter. "I'm sorry to have intruded. I promise I won't keep your mother long, Sing-hua."

Fernadina stared at their guest for a moment, then went back down the hallway into her room. Mei-yu reached for her glass of iced tea and took a sip, waiting.

"I apologize again for surprising you like this," Richard began. Then he laughed. "But I couldn't call you; you don't have a phone."

Mei-yu laughed also, out of politeness, thinking to explain that she did not think she had enough reason to have a phone, that she thought phones too expensive, but she changed her mind. She did not want to appear frugal, backward.

"Since you have made plans," Richard said, smiling in the direction where Fernadina had gone, "I will say what I have to say quickly. The reason why I came," he said, placing his hands carefully on his knees, "is to ask you if I may call on you sometime."

Mei-yu felt suddenly cold. Why was he, a man thought to be engaged to another, asking her this? What did he want from her? She saw that he looked at her calmly, yet she sensed that he guarded himself. His voice had been even, yet she had heard the tension in it.

"Mr. Peng," she said, then stopped, searching for the proper words. He was her employer, after all; there was much at risk. "I am very flattered, indeed, but I do not think I can . . . go out, socially. I am very busy at the shop. Which is a good thing, of course," she added hastily. "And my daughter sees me too little as it is." She stopped, seeing that he did not react, then went on, hearing her words tumble out. "Fernadina will be going to school soon, and I feel I must spend as much time as possible with her in order to help prepare her. It has been a difficult adjustment this past year, for her as well as for myself." She stopped abruptly again, ashamed and angry at the fear she heard in her voice. Why should she tremble before a man who, for all she knew, had dishonorable intentions? "Why, why are you asking me this?" she blurted.

Richard sat back, seeming to gather himself. "I have been clumsy and abrupt, I see," he said. "Please forgive me. Let me explain, for I think I know what you are thinking. What I want only is . . . what I hope only is to know you better. I am free to say this, as I am not obligated to anyone. I am not engaged to Lillian Chin. That will soon be apparent to everyone in the community. It is true, we had thought to marry, but we were fortunate in realizing that our marriage would not have worked. I will not burden you further with that story, only that as proof of what I say, you will soon learn of the news that Lillian is planning to return to Taiwan within the coming year. I, of course, am committed to my work and the community here."

Mei-yu waited while Richard reached for his glass of iced tea and took a sip. He put the glass down and met her eyes. "You need not worry that I have any plans to take advantage of your position at the shop. First of all, you must believe that I have no plans to take advantage of you in any way. Second, your position at the shop is secure. If you do not accept my word on it, then accept my mother's word. For it was she who sent you here, and you know that the trust between you and her remains inviolate."

At the mention of Madame Peng's name, Mei-yu began to feel her fears slowly recede. She began to see sincerity in Richard's eyes. He continued to regard her quietly. She realized finally what he was asking. She felt her face grow hot, and picked up her cold glass, resisting the urge to press it against her cheek.

"Forgive me, I see I have made a mistake," Richard said, rising from the sofa.

"No!" Mei-yu looked at him, startled. Then she laughed, nervously. "I mean, yes, you did take me by surprise. I'm afraid I don't know what to think."

"Perhaps it would be better to wait," Richard said. "There is no hurry, after all."

Mei-yu stood up. They faced each other awkwardly for a moment. Then Richard said, "Perhaps it would be a good idea for you to have a phone, don't you think? Then, in a month's time, if we decide to talk again, I won't have to surprise you like this." He pointed to the end table at her side of the sofa. "Right there would be a good place." He smiled at his own presumptuousness.

Mei-yu laughed, charmed at his gesture in spite of herself. "All right. Perhaps it is inevitable, a telephone. It will save Kay Lynn many steps, at least, when she wants to talk with me."

They both moved toward the door. Richard asked Mei-yu about Kay Lynn, when she was due to have her baby.

"She's doing well; the baby's due in March, I think," Mei-yu said. They both talked freely now, relieved to have something to talk about other than what truly occupied their minds. Then she stood, holding the door open, aware of his closeness.

Richard stepped beyond the threshold of the doorway, then turned. "May I call you, then, in a month?" he said.

Mei-yu nodded. "Yes."

Immediately after she closed the door, Mei-yu ran down the hallway and called for Fernadina to ready herself for their outing. She changed her shoes, her blouse, moving with light feet, giving Fernadina's braids a playful tug as she passed her in the hall. Fernadina ran after her and pulled open the door.

"Wait a minute," Mei-yu said, going over to the table in front of the sofa and picking up the tray with the iced tea glasses. She carried the tray back into the kitchen. She took her own glass and filled it with water, rinsing it quickly under the tap. Then she picked up Richard's glass. Uncertainty and a strange kind of exhilaration suddenly rushed through her. She put the glass in the sink, then, giving herself a little shake, ran to join her daughter.

Two weeks later, in the shop, at around five o'clock in the afternoon, when all the seamstresses had gone home and only Mei-yu, Nancy Gow, and Kay Lynn remained, cleaning up and discussing the order of work for the following day, Yolanda Eng, whom Mei-yu had first met at the Embassy, hurried in to pick up the silk blouses and dress she had ordered.

"Ai, these are beautiful, superb, Mei-yu!" she said, holding the blouses up to her body and inspecting herself in the mirror. Mei-yu saw how the blouses, American-styled with ruffled fronts and sleeves, suited Yolanda's feminine appearance. Her new friend wore her blue-black hair in an elaborately braided chignon. She wore makeup, even in the daytime. She looked very much the well-groomed young Chinese matron, Mei-yu thought, even with the new Western-styled clothes. When Nancy and Kay Lynn came to admire her new clothes, Yolanda set the blouses aside and, cooing, gave Kay Lynn's growing belly an approving pat.

"Children are life's only true joy," she said knowingly. "May your first be a boy, Kay Lynn!"

"We don't care," Kay Lynn murmured. "We've waited so long, all we want is for it to be healthy."

"Hah," Yolanda retorted, "your husband may pretend not to care, but believe me, you will be much happier and relieved if the first is a boy. My husband would have divorced me had I not had Ming, and right away, too! By the way, Nancy and Mei-yu," she said, turning to the other women, "Ming is having his seventh birthday in two weeks and I want to invite your children to his party. He has invited some of his American friends from school, but I want him to meet Chinese children, too. Do you know that he has practically forgotten how to speak Chinese? We can hardly get him to speak it at home at all now." She looked at Nancy. "Are your children the same? Doesn't it seem like all they can do is pick up rough playground language? And at such an early age! That's what it comes to, sending your children to American schools."

"My husband and I speak Chinese to our children at home," Nancy said. "If they don't talk to us in Chinese, we don't respond. Simple."

"Oh, we have spoiled our children, I'm afraid," Yolanda said. "Both my boy and girl just chatter on in English. My husband and I can hardly keep up with them. Perhaps I have an excuse, being a housewife, but my husband is a chief engineer with the power company!" She turned to Kay Lynn and wagged a finger. "Let that be a lesson to you, new mother!"

Nancy took the blouses and dress and began to wrap them. "Any news, Yolanda?" she said, folding the clothes between layers of tissue. "I missed the community meeting last Saturday."

"None of you went, did you?" Yolanda scolded. "And you, Mei-yu, I haven't seen you there in weeks!" She sat down next to the sewing table where Nancy was folding her purchases. "Well, you missed some very interesting news, I must say," she said.

"What? What did we miss?" Kay Lynn asked, drawing up a chair.

Yolanda waited until Nancy had finished wrapping her things and the rustling of the tissue paper had stopped. "I saw my friend Jacqueline Yee there. Jacqueline writes for the community newsletter, you know. She was at the Embassy to interview one of the attachés there. She says the Embassy invited her there because it wants to strengthen its ties to the community here. Anyway, guess what she found out?"

"I bet it has something to do with Lillian Chin," Kay Lynn said.

Yolanda looked crestfallen. "Who told you?"

"Nobody! Go on, tell us!"

"Well," Yolanda said, her enthusiasm somewhat diminished, but renewing rapidly as she continued, "Jacqueline says that Lillian Chin is transferring back to Taiwan. She will be training her replacement for the next six weeks, and then, after that, she will be gone. What do you think of that?"

The women were silent for several moments. Then Kay Lynn stood up. "I'm not surprised, from the way she and Richard Peng acted at that reception at the Embassy. They had a falling out and now she can't bear to stay here."

"How do you know?" Nancy said, frowning. "Maybe she decided that her position at the Embassy was more important to her. Maybe Taiwan called her back."

"No, I can't believe that," Kay Lynn said. "You even told me, Nancy, how certain you were that she and Richard would announce their engagement and that Lillian would stay here. No, something happened between them."

"What do you think, Mei-yu?" Yolanda asked. "You've been pretty quiet, here." When Mei-yu gave her no answer, Yolanda muttered to Kay Lynn, "Mei-yu's above all this, I can tell. Look, she's not even listening."

"I wonder what Madame Peng thought of Lillian?" Nancy said quietly, as if thinking out loud.

"What did you say?" Mei-yu said, looking quickly at Nancy. The other two women were talking and had not heard Nancy's remark. Now Nancy appeared not to have heard her.

"Well, I guess we'll all have to look elsewhere for something to gossip about," Yolanda said, turning back to Mei-yu and Nancy.

"Who do you think Richard will court now?" Kay Lynn said.

They all sat in silence for a moment. Then Yolanda stood up and picked up her parcel. "If I weren't married, I would offer myself," she said. "Oh, I was only joking, Nancy, you're always so serious!" Then she turned around, looking at Mei-yu. "Here is the likely one," she said slyly.

"Oh, no, not her," Kay Lynn said. "I already have someone picked out for Mei-yu. She and Professor Chung are having dinner at our place tonight, right, Mei-yu?"

"Yes!" Mei-yu said, jumping up with apparent relief. "I almost forgot! We'd better hurry, Kay Lynn."

"I've got to go," Yolanda said. "Please send me the bill, Nancy. And don't forget about Ming's birthday party!"

The three women at the shop watched Yolanda leave.

"Our best customer," Nancy breathed, beginning to write out the bill. "What has she ordered so far?"

"Four dresses, a robe, two blouses, and a jacket," Kay Lynn said. "Her husband must run the power company."

"Kay Lynn, I'll meet you at the car, I just want to make sure I have everything," Mei-yu said, walking back toward her table.

"Oh, look how late it is!" Kay Lynn cried. She picked up her purse and keys and left the shop, walking in her already heavy way.

Mei-yu watched until Kay Lynn had gone, then approached Nancy, who was still writing out Yolanda's bill.

"What did you say again, Nancy, about Madame Peng and Lillian?"

"What?" Nancy did not look up but continued to write.

"You said something about Madame Peng and Lillian awhile ago," Mei-yu persisted.

"Yes." Nancy stopped writing. "It was only a thought. I was just thinking, you know, how some mothers think the women their sons choose are never good enough. Well, Madame Peng could have found something wrong with Lillian."

"With Lillian? I find that hard to believe. And you think Richard is the kind of son who would yield to his mother's wishes on a matter like that?"

"All I know is that the two are extremely close," Nancy said. "When I was working for her in Chinatown, Madame Peng once said to me that she would give up her life for her son, and that she felt he would do the same for her. I believe she may feel that way about Richard, but only Richard could tell you how he feels about his mother in that regard. Why are you so interested, Mei-yu?"

Mei-yu shook her head, feeling suddenly as if she had revealed too much. "Nothing, Nancy. The whole affair is curious, that's all. I'll see you tomorrow," she said, turning and walking toward the door.

That evening, Mei-yu sat where Kay Lynn had seated her, next to Professor Chung, and marveled at the flatness of his nose as he droned on about political theory and the future of Taiwan and United States relations. He certainly seemed an erudite and culturally polished person, she thought. Earlier in the evening, the professor had asked her if she ever attended the concerts given by the Budapest String Quartet in the Library of Congress auditorium, and she confessed that she had never heard of the group or their concert series. _He's dismissed me as a musical illiterate,_ she thought, almost gratefully, yet listened politely as he returned to his favorite topic of strained international relations. Kay Lynn, the proper Chinese hostess, kept jumping up from the table to tend to her cooking. Her husband, Tim, contentedly ate whatever his wife brought to the table and left all the polite questions to ask of Professor Chung to Mei-yu. During one of the professor's longer explanations of why it was inevitable that the United States recognize the government in Peking, Mei-yu suddenly found herself thinking of Richard, comparing him to this flat-nosed man who was boring her to tears. There was no comparison, really, she found herself thinking. She knew Richard was intelligent, cultured, yet she had never seen evidence of him flaunting those qualities. Then she remembered Nancy's words about Madame Peng and Richard. She realized again how she had always thought it strange that the mother and son were so different, so unlike each other in personality and type. Strange, also, that he, said to be so closely tied to his mother, and she herself had never shared fond remembrances of the old lady with each other. But then, Mei-yu realized, she and Richard had not spoken much to each other at all. She found herself curious about the relationship between the mother and the son, about what effect, if any, Madame Peng had had on the relationship between Richard and Lillian Chin. When would Richard call her? she wondered, thinking of the new telephone she had had installed the previous week.

She smiled at the professor, hearing the echo of his inquiry as to whether she had as yet visited the National Gallery of Art. "Wonderful exhibit of Degas watercolors there now," he said. Afraid that he would ask her to go see them with him, Mei-yu said that she had already enjoyed seeing them.

"Really, when, Mei-yu?" Kay Lynn said, huffing to the table with a steaming plate of stir-fried shrimp and snow peas.

"Just a few days ago, last weekend," Mei-yu said.

"You didn't tell me!" Kay Lynn said.

"Oh, I don't tell you everything, Kay Lynn!" Mei-yu said sweetly, laughing.

Professor Chung called Mei-yu the following Sunday, to ask her if she would like to attend the Budapest String Quartet concert scheduled for Monday evening.

"Oh, I'm afraid I can't," Mei-yu said, "I promised to watch my neighbor's children while their parents go to a preschool meeting."

The professor then invited her to come to his lecture on tungsten production and the economic impact that industry had on China–United States relations the following Saturday afternoon at American University.

"I'm terribly sorry," Mei-yu said, astonished and irritated at the man's persistence. "I'm taking my daughter to a friend's birthday party that afternoon." When she hung up, she was relieved at not having to lie to the man but found herself thinking of other excuses to give him should he call her again. She stared at her new black telephone with distaste, wondering what other annoying elements it would bring into her life. It seemed to read her mind, for it rang immediately again.

"Hello!" she said, meeting the challenge.

"Hello, Mei-yu?"

She recognized the voice instantly. "Richard?"

"Yes. Have I called at an inconvenient time?"

"Oh, no, no!"

"Shall I call you back another time?"

"No, please, Richard. I just had an annoying call, that's all."

"You did?"

She found herself surprised, then gratified at the sound of concern in his voice. "It was nothing, really. The telephone is still new to me, that is all."

"Are you sure?"

"Yes, yes, quite sure."

"Well, then." There were a few beats of silence. "How have you been?"

"Very well, thank you. And you?"

"Quite well. And your daughter?"

"Very well, thank you."

Neither of them spoke. Mei-yu listened to the faint electrical whisper of the instrument in her hand and felt suddenly self-conscious, as if something, someone, were listening in on their conversation. Then she heard Richard's voice again.

"Mei-yu, I think you know why I am calling."

"Yes."

"Have you had enough time?" She heard the hesitation in his voice.

"Yes." She felt suddenly overcome with awkwardness, uncertainty. She was glad that at least he could not see her face.

"I thought it might be a nice idea if you would allow me to take you and your daughter on a drive to see a little bit of Washington. There are beautiful parks, and interesting, wonderful things to see. Fernadina might enjoy the monuments, or the Smithsonian, for instance. What do you think?"

Mei-yu breathed with relief. It was a nice way to begin, she thought. "I think we would both enjoy that very much, Richard," she said.

"Good. Shall we say next Sunday, then? Mid-morning, around ten o'clock?"

"That would be fine."

Mei-yu hung up the phone but seemed still to feel the current of Richard's voice coursing through her hand. Again she chastised herself for not having said more, for not having been more responsive. She felt like a peasant girl from the country whenever she spoke to him. He always seemed so certain of what he said, while she struggled just to clear her mind, as if her shyness with him had stricken her dumb. She suddenly thought of her mother's words of advice on womanly behavior toward men. "Be gentle, kind, serene, and quiet; be compliant," her mother had said. "Dress beautifully, groom yourself with care, and strive to please in voice and manner, always." She thought of the way her mother, and even modern women like Yolanda Eng, presented themselves. Her mother would have approved of her shy manner to-ward Richard, Mei-yu thought, only her mother would not have known that her manner with Richard was a manifestation of her real shyness toward him, and not a deliberate act.

She had not been that way with Kung-chiao, Mei-yu thought. In fact, Kung-chiao had been even shyer with women than she with men. It was she who had been the bold one between the two of them, she who had engaged his eyes. This feeling of awkwardness with Richard was new to her. Perhaps it was because it had been so long since she had been approached by a man she had been impressed with, or per-haps that she had grown accustomed to her role as widow. Or perhaps, she told herself, it was because of the kind of man Richard appeared to be.

When Mei-yu told Fernadina later that week that Richard would be coming by on Sunday to take them on an outing, her daughter looked at her mother with alarm.

"Why?" she asked.

"Because he thought it would be nice for us to see Washington, to explore a little. Aren't you excited, Sing-hua? I think it was very nice of him to suggest that, don't you?"

Fernadina shrugged, then slipped off her mother's lap and went into her room.

The cicadas were already trilling their dry song at full volume when Richard drove into the parking lot in front of their building on Sunday morning. Mei-yu dressed Fernadina in light cotton and tucked scarves in her purse for them both to wear later for protection from the sun, which promised to be searing by noon. Mei-yu walked out of the apart-ment building and was struck immediately by the waves of heat that rose up from the asphalt of the parking lot. August in Peking was like this, too, she thought. The humidity made the air feel thick, and she felt moisture gathering above her lip, under her eyes. Richard opened the back door of the car for her daughter while she slipped into the front seat. Fernadina had obediently repeated the friendly greeting Mei-yu had rehearsed with her earlier in the morning, and seemed content to sit perfectly still while Richard drove.

They opened the windows on both sides of the car and turned their faces to the breeze as Richard took them across Key Bridge, then en-tered Rock Creek Parkway. Here, the air seemed cooler. Trees shaded the areas on either side of the road. Unprotected areas of grass had been scorched by the sun, as were the uppermost leaves of the trees, but underneath, near the ground, lay pockets of forestlike greenery, with ferns and vines looking cool, dark. They came upon the point where the creek itself passed over the road, and as they drove slowly through the water, Fernadina tapped her mother's arm and asked to be let out to walk in the water.

"I'm sorry, we can't stop now, there are cars behind us," Richard said. Fernadina leaned out of her window as far as she could to catch the water as it sprayed out behind the tires of their car.

"We'll go to the zoo another day," Richard said, driving north past the entrance of the zoological park. "I'd like for you to see the parks and the reflecting pool between the Lincoln Memorial and the George Washington Monument." He turned around to Fernadina. "There's a wonderful pool of water there, Sing-hua, if you want to get your feet wet."

Fernadina laid her head on her mother's shoulder and looked out the window as they drove through the white-stoned city. The sun was so bright now that they could only squint, and grow sleepy.

Minutes later Richard was circling around the Ellipse in front of the White House.

"This is where the President lives, Sing-hua," Richard said.

"Do you think we could find a place and get something cool to drink?" Mei-yu asked, tying a scarf around Fernadina's head.

"Certainly. Let's see. Perhaps we can do even better than that."

Richard parked the car and they got out to walk. The day was so warm that even the tourist crowds had thinned, and those who had braved the heat walked slowly, holding tour programs over their heads as shields against the sun. Richard walked up to a vendor who stood in front of a white box on wheels and bought what looked to Mei-yu to be candies made of ice.

"These are called Popsicles," he said. "Here, pick one, Fernadina."

Fernadina picked the cherry-flavored one. Mei-yu took the grape and Richard the lime. Mei-yu thought hers more refreshing even than watermelon. She watched, laughing, as Fernadina licked at her rapidly melting stick, her tongue turning a bright red. Richard bought her another when that one had disappeared.

"Come, let's walk to the pool," he said, leading them toward a vast grassy area surrounding a long rectangular pool of water. Mei-yu saw how the pool, still as glass, reflected the image of the Lincoln Memorial at one end and the Washington Monument at the other. Fernadina ran to the pool, drawing close to a group of children who were sailing toy boats in the water. She promptly took off her shoes and socks and, sitting down at the edge of the pool, dipped her feet into the water. Mei-yu and Richard walked over to a stone bench underneath a tree nearby to sit and watch.

"She is enjoying herself very much, Richard," Mei-yu said. "Thank you."

"Not at all," Richard said. He pointed to the pool. "Look how she splashes the other children!"

They sat in silence for several moments. Mei-yu saw how Fernadina's shirtfront was now stained bright pink from the Popsicles. She leaned back on one arm, feeling the rough stone of the bench against her hand. She felt relaxed to the point of drowsiness. Richard sat not far from her, his back slightly bent, his arms resting naturally on his thighs. Then he turned to look at her.

"How do you like Washington, Mei-yu? It's very different from New York, isn't it?"

"Yes." Mei-yu laughed. "Everything is different. The feeling of space, of distance between places . . . and the people. We are leading a completely different life now, Sing-hua and I."

"Do you think it is mostly because you no longer live in Chinatown?"

Mei-yu thought for a while. "Yes. I think coming here finally made me realize what it means to be in America. Here, I've finally seen Americans, white people, I mean, and how they live. Compared to Chinatown, compared to my life in China the past few years . . ." Mei-yu searched for the words. "It is difficult to believe sometimes how people live here, how they think. Everything is so fast, so efficient and modern."

"Are you comfortable?" Richard asked. Mei-yu saw interest and concern on his face. Again, she thought of how much younger he looked now, without his business suit. "Do you feel comfortable around Americans?" he said.

Mei-yu shrugged, looking down into her lap. "Most people near where we live seem to have gotten used to seeing us. But I'm not always certain what they think of me. My neighbors, for instance. There is one neighbor who avoids me at all costs. I was hanging clothes out on the line in the backyard the other day and happened to see her come around the corner of the building with her basket of clothes. When she saw me, she turned back. She would rather have wet clothes than join me or have her clothes on the same line with mine. Even my other neighbor seems uncomfortable in my presence, although on the surface she is friendly and has helped me in many ways. I feel it from other

Americans, too. Have you ever felt this way? Have you ever felt that the two people, white Americans and Chinese, have their own distinct surfaces? Even beyond physical appearance, I mean. That our Chinese surface is one of politeness, and the American surface that of friendliness? That one surface only reflects the other surface, like two mirrors facing one another, and that we are blinded by this, made unable to look any further?"

Mei-yu saw how Richard nodded, his eyes searching her face, encouraging her to speak further. The words seemed to come to her tongue in a forceful stream now, as if they had been waiting there all along to be released.

"The strangest thing," she continued, "is that when I go to the grocery store, or into the shopping center, and see all these American faces, I find myself beginning to act and speak just like them, to the point where I think that I am like one of them. And then, when I come home and see my face in the mirror, I am shocked, just as if I were they, looking at me. Then I begin to feel afraid that I am in danger of losing myself, that part of me I have always been. And what's more, I realize that even if I lost all of that part of me, that doesn't mean that I will ever truly become one of them. Oh, I probably don't make any sense." Mei-yu paused, then went on, speaking softly, as if to herself. "I feel as if I've swum too far out to sea and now find myself far from any shore. And all I can do now is to keep swimming and swimming, at all costs." She looked at Richard, seeing that his eyes were still intent upon her. She looked away, suddenly embarrassed that she had spoken so freely. "I suppose you are used to hearing this kind of talk, from those newly arrived," she said, smoothing her skirt.

"No, not at all," Richard said. "I've never heard anyone express themselves the way you have, although I feel certain that many must feel as you do. I myself, for one."

Mei-yu looked up in surprise. "You? Forgive me, it's not that I don't believe you, but you have lived here many years. You seem like an American. At least you seem totally at ease here in this country."

"I may seem to be. But living here a long time doesn't necessarily make that much of a difference. My face will always remain the same to me, as it does to you. The mirror doesn't lie to me, either."

They were both silent for a moment. Mei-yu watched as Fernadina pushed a toy boat toward the middle of the pool.

Then she asked, "Do you feel this way, even at work?"

Richard laughed sharply. "The feeling is strongest where I work because the people there pretend it does not exist. They prefer the calm-ness of the surface. They do not acknowledge the presence of the undercurrent."

Mei-yu heard the bitterness in his voice.

"I have one friend there, Peter, who is at least honest with me," Richard continued, looking away from her toward the street, where a busload of tourists had stopped. "The others pretend to appreciate my work and reward me in token ways. I accept what they give me and act grateful. No, I must say that I am grateful, that despite the hypocrisy and deceit, I am thankful to have work, good-paying work. And that is what gives me the sense of loathing, for the situation, for myself. I play along with them, on the surface. If I were truly brave, I would leave the firm and establish my own office." He stopped, noting Mei-yu's inquir-ing look. "Yes, I have tried," he said. "I have applied for loans at banks in order to have the capital to start my own office, but the banks have always looked askance at the applications of non-whites. They turned me down." He shrugged. "In that way, in terms of acceptance in this country, there is very little difference between those in the Chinese community who work in the restaurants and laundries and tailor shops, and those like myself. It is only the arena that is different. Those in the Chinese community choose to work among people like themselves. They are protected that way, to a degree, but insulated and oppressed economically as a result. I may be doing better financially, working among whites, but still, that feeling of isolation remains, that real divi-sion persists." Richard paused, tilting his head as if to listen to the thrumming of the cicadas in the trees overhead. "I suppose I could sell my interest in the apartment building, borrow money from my mother, but I find myself wondering if it's worth it. Perhaps I am being overly cynical." He turned to Mei-yu. "At least, those in the community can work hard, hoping and believing all along that their patience and sacri-fices will enable their children to live better lives than they do. And that is not only true of the Chinese, Mei-yu. I know that other immi-grant people have similar dreams for their children, as well. It is only in the matter of style that the Chinese and other Orientals differ from other groups, say the Italians, or the Irish. Among other things, the Chinese remain very quiet and modest about their dreams, the Chinese remain true to their surface. They don't want trouble, above all. What do you think, Mei-yu? Is it because I have no children to dream for that I am cynical? What are your wishes for you and your daughter?"

Mei-yu shook her head, now following Richard's gaze across the parched grass to the line of tourists that wound around the Washington

Monument. "I hardly know how to answer you," she said. "I know I would perhaps have given up long ago if it hadn't been for my daughter. I knew I had to be strong for her. I worked for her, I still do. Only, I don't think of it as a sacrifice. I think of it as love. I do not want her to feel beholden to me. It is not her fault we must live how and where we live. That is just the way things are."

Silence fell between them. They both looked away, suddenly embarrassed at how they had revealed themselves to each other. They both watched another line of tourists following their guide up to the Lincoln Memorial. Bright spots of light glinted from their camera lenses as they turned this way and that, looking to either side of the pool below them.

"Have you had any word from Madame Peng?" Mei-yu asked, then immediately laughed, realizing how she had referred to his mother.

Richard smiled. "No, I heard from Dr. Toy, who says she is managing well, but nothing from her directly."

His voice sounded controlled, flat now, Mei-yu thought. "When did you and your mother come to this country, may I ask?" she said, allowing her curiosity to gain hold of her.

"In 1924."

Mei-yu hesitated, then continued. "It was unusual, wasn't it, for a Chinese woman to come to this country alone at that time?" Richard turned to look at her, searching her face. "I'm sorry. I have intruded," she said, turning away. She sensed that Richard continued to look at her. When she looked toward him again, he had turned his face. A moment later, he stood up and moved away a short distance, kneeling in the grass at an angle to Mei-yu so that she saw only part of his profile. "It's a long story," he said finally. "I'm not certain you would want to hear it now."

"But I do," Mei-yu said, stopping short, wondering again if she had gone too far.

Richard seemed to study the ground in front of him for several moments. When he did speak, his voice was so low that she had to lean forward to hear. "Actually," he said, "our arrival and stay in San Francisco is very vague in my memory. I remember feeling sad; I guess I was about seven at the time."

"Why did you leave China?"

Richard turned and smiled at her. "You are very direct," he said, holding his hand up to indicate that he did not mind. Then he was quiet again. Mei-yu thought he stared at the reflection of the monument in the pool ahead of them, but then realized that his stare was blind, and that he looked inward, searching his memory.

"In those days, back in China," Richard began, "we had been living from village to village, in the delta land near Canton. My father was a warlord. He was one of many struggling to control the roads then, for with the end of the reign of the Manchu Emperor, many years before, there was no one left to govern the vast territories. Warlords roamed the countryside, raising their own armies from among the peasants, fighting battles with each other, taking what they needed from the surrounding villages. My father and a rival warlord fought to keep control of the northern road into Canton. Control of that road meant control of all the trade in that sector. Sometimes, on certain campaigns, my mother, sister, and I, along with other families, followed close after, setting up camps just hours away from the men." Richard shook his head. "It is hard for me to believe now that my father was such a warlord, especially since I grew up and received most of my education here in America. America has an infant's history compared to China's. It is difficult for people here to grasp that the feudal system remained so long in effect in China. In fact, even when I talk about my father now, it is almost as if I refer to a legend, someone who was mythical, not real."

Mei-yu nodded. "I'd heard of the warlords. My father told me about them, although by the time I was old enough to think very much about them, most had been absorbed by the rising political parties or had been driven from the countryside."

Richard seemed to think for a moment, then continued. "On one campaign, after an entire day of bitter fighting, my father was taken captive by the other warlord. We waited in our camp, my mother and sister and I, for word of my father. We wondered if he was alive or dead. We wondered if the enemy would bargain for his life. Then night fell." Richard paused. "That night," he continued, his voice low, "what I remember most about that night were all the campfires. My mother and my sister and I were sitting next to our fire, not too far from the road, and I remember seeing, in the distance, the campfires of the enemy, a whole circle of them, small, bright. I imagined that my father sat, proud and erect, dressed in full armor, in the very center of them. Can you imagine that sight, a warlord sitting in the middle of a circle of fires!"

Mei-yu nodded. "What happened then?"

Richard seemed to rouse himself from deep thought. "It got to be very late. I remember the darkness. Things began to get very confusing; people were moving back and forth, running everywhere, shouting, crying in panic, saying my father was already dead. Then I remember two of my father's men running to my mother, one, then later, another, bringing her messages from the enemy camp. My mother read the messages by the light of the fire. I remember looking at her face, how it seemed to be on fire, too. Red sparks flew up into her face, but she did not seem to notice. She shouted for someone to bring her paper and pen. She scribbled a reply, gave it to the messenger, then grabbed me and held me to her. I remember her fingernails digging into the back of my neck. I thought she would smother me. Then she dragged me and my sister along and shouted for everyone in the camp to get back on the road. I remember wagons, horses, people on foot, hurrying back and forth. It was as if a whole village were moving. Shadows cast by the fire-red light danced everywhere. I remember my sister and me being put on a wagon, and my mother running alongside, shouting, telling people what to do. Everyone obeyed her. She was terrible that night. . . . I remember I was frightened to look at her, her hair was wild and I saw her teeth in the dark as she screamed. I watched people stamping out the fires, watched as the smoke rose, white like ghosts in the dark. Then I must have fallen asleep. I must have ridden in the wagon all night. When I awoke, I heard water rushing, and when I looked out I saw that the wagon had stopped by a river. Our people were setting up another camp. New fires were being made, only, in the light of the sun, which was just beginning to rise, the fires looked pale and small. Perhaps the wood was wet with dew."

"What happened to your father?" Mei-yu asked softly.

"My mother told me later that he had been taken away. I myself believe he had been hanged that very night. At least that is what I heard my father's men saying, days later."

Mei-yu remained silent. Richard plucked at the grass at his feet, held some in the palm of his hand, then tossed it into the air. "Do you remember what I said before, about sacrifice?" he said.

"Yes," Mei-yu said.

"One of the messages my mother received from the enemy that night was a note demanding ransom for my father. The note demanded that she send them gold."

Mei-yu waited.

"My mother knew it wasn't only the gold they wanted," Richard said, "for they had demanded that I deliver the gold. I, the son of the warlord."

"So your mother refused?" Mei-yu said, her voice dry with disbelief. "Your mother sacrificed your father for you?"

"Yes. She knew there was no bargaining with the warlord who held my father. She knew he would have killed me, as well. She realized then that we had no chance other than to flee."

They were both silent for a moment. "But, the other message from the enemy camp," Mei-yu said, "did you say there had been two?"

"I never found out the content of the second," Richard said. He looked at her. "It hardly seems to matter now, does it?"

Mei-yu remained still, unable to find words.

"During the next few weeks," Richard went on, "we traveled from village to village. We finally arrived at my mother's parents' village near Kweilin, farther to the north. My mother left my sister and me there with our grandparents while she journeyed to my father's parents' village a hundred miles away, to settle family affairs there. Food was scarce. I remember our old grandparents giving us what little rice they had. Once I saw my grandmother putting straw into her mouth. Then disease swept through our grandparents' village. We were all taken sick, all four of us. I went into a deep sleep. I remember waking one day, feeling very hot and weak, and seeing my mother kneeling in front of my bed, weeping. She told me a neighbor had sent word to her to hurry back, but it had been too late; my grandparents and sister died soon after she arrived.

"My mother and I had nowhere to go then, you see. My father's family had given her money but had refused to take her into their house, now that their son was dead. The men in my father's army had long since scattered to join other warlords in the south. My mother knew they had no loyalty remaining to her. She continued to fear for my life. The only hope she had left was an uncle who had gone to America long ago in search of gold. It was a wild hope, a faint hope, but the only one she had. She took me to Canton, then to Hong Kong. There, she wrote to her uncle, and worked as a seamstress and sold buttons while she waited to hear from him." Richard paused, then turned to look at Mei-yu. "It was not pleasant for you, was it, your arrival in San Francisco?"

"No. I have tried not to think about it."

"We heard from this uncle in early 1924, just before the Exclusion Act had been passed in this country. The Exclusion Act was the law that prohibited non-white people from immigrating into this country. This uncle wrote saying that if my mother wanted to come legally, she would have to hurry. He said that if she could get herself across the ocean, he had a friend in San Francisco who was willing to help her get into the country, who was willing to claim her as his wife, as that was the only way. But this friend had a price, he said."

"What was this price?"

"That she promise to marry him."

"And your mother agreed?"

"You must understand, Mei-yu, that she herself, a woman, was the most priceless treasure a man could bring into the country in those days," Richard said. "Most of the men who had come to this country in hopes of finding work had been unable to bring their wives and children with them. The whites had restricted entry quotas; they did not want an increase in the Chinese population here. As a result, there was a terrible shortage of Chinese women; one for every five hundred or more Chinese men. Families were broken, men were forced into bachelorhood. Many men went back to China, rather than live separated from their families. Others could only afford to work here and send money back. Then there were still others—" Richard stopped. Mei-yu saw a dark look flash across his face.

"Others?" she said.

"Those who managed to enter the country illegally, in spite of the Exclusion Act, which remained in effect until 1944." Richard looked at Mei-yu, hesitating. "Colonel Chang was one. He arrived in this country six years after we did, in 1930."

Mei-yu looked away. But then her curiosity compelled her to ask, "How did he do it? How did this country let him in?"

"No one knows for sure," Richard said. "There are many stories. . . . In fact, the method of his entry into this country had been a favorite topic of speculation in New York. One version is that when his boat drew close to the bay at night, he jumped overboard and swam ashore, somehow managing to avoid the landing officials altogether. Another story is that he entered through Canada, and came down the coast to San Francisco. Stories of his feats, both his manner of arrival and his reign in Chinatown in San Francisco, preceded his move in New York, where he began to make trouble for my mother and the community."

Mei-yu wiped her forehead with her scarf. And now he was dead, she thought. Then she realized that Richard had not finished his own story. "But please go on, what happened to your mother and yourself, then? She agreed to this scheme with this man, and found a way for you both, across the ocean?"

"Yes," Richard said, leaning back with both hands on the grass behind him. "We boarded a boat. In order to protect herself, my mother pretended she was a man. She smeared her face with oil and soot. She bound her breasts. She told me I was to act like her younger brother, and that I was not to speak to anyone. She told me to be brave, but I was afraid, and I could sense her fear, too."

"And in San Francisco?"

"Her uncle's friend came forward with false papers and claimed her as his wife, and I his son. He was a wealthy merchant, already an old man. The Immigration officers must have seen through the ruse, but perhaps money passed hands. In any case, they let us in."

"It was a terrible risk she took!" Mei-yu said. "What if her disguise had been discovered on the boat? What if the officials had sent her back?"

"She took the risk because there was that small chance that the scheme would work. She had seen others in China who had been more desperate, who had lost everything, including the hope of ever seeing their families again, who had thrown themselves over cliffs, into wells. She decided to take this one last chance. If the scheme hadn't worked, if she and I had been sent back to China, then she probably would have killed herself. And I probably wouldn't be here speaking to you today."

Mei-yu shuddered. "And then? Your mother kept her part of the bargain?"

"Yes. She married the old man. We lived very well after that, at least we always had enough to eat. We lived in a large apartment above his dry goods store in Chinatown. He never spoke to me. He wanted his own son. His first wife and children had died long before in China and he had hoped to begin a new family here. He was an old man with an old man's delusions. He died three years later."

"And that is when your mother brought you to New York, and set up her own business?"

"Yes. She took the money her old husband left her, began her tailoring business, sent me to the best schools, and saw to it that I had everything."

Mei-yu suddenly remembered Madame Peng's words to her that one afternoon in Chinatown, when she had said, "You have not known true suffering." The words struck her now with the painful clarity of their meaning.

"So, you see," Richard said, standing up, for they both saw that Fernadina was running toward them now, "I am beholden to my parents, and especially to my mother, for she made the ultimate sacrifice for me. It is beyond duty, what I feel, beyond love. There is no word to describe what I feel. Only, whatever it is, it is absolute. And binding."

Mei-yu looked up at Richard, but he had moved away, walking toward Fernadina. Fernadina slowed when he drew near and veered away when he reached out to her. Mei-yu felt a pang, watching them, wishing Fernadina had allowed Richard to come close to her. Her daughter then rushed at her, panting from the heat.

"Where are your shoes and socks?" Mei-yu asked her. Fernadina pointed back to the pool. Mei-yu saw that Richard was walking back toward them.

"Shall we go soon?" he said. "You both must be hungry. I know where we can get some lunch. Or would you rather I take you home?"

Mei-yu gave her daughter a gentle push in the direction of the pool. "Go get your shoes and socks," she said, watching as her girl walked back with her child's gait, leading with her stomach, bobbing her head, swinging her arms loosely at her sides. She turned to Richard.

"I'm sorry about Sing-hua," she said, getting up from the stone bench.

Richard smiled, shaking his head in a gesture that indicated he accepted the child's behavior.

"Yes, let's have lunch," Mei-yu said, beginning to walk toward the pool. She saw how Fernadina had found her shoes and socks and was now sitting on the grass, putting them on. "Give her time," she wanted to say to Richard, who had joined her, but shyness prevented her. _He has revealed himself to me,_ she thought. She glanced at him quickly but saw that he looked straight ahead. He looked quiet now, thoughtful. _His nature is like mine,_ she suddenly thought to herself, and, shocked at this realization, began with a start to run away from him, toward her daughter.

○   ○   ○

At the end of August, when Fernadina turned six years of age, Mei-yu took her to the elementary school registrar to enroll her.

"Didn't you get our notice not to teach your daughter to read and write?" said the registrar, a trim middle-aged woman with iron-colored hair. She showed Mei-yu a copy of the School District Manual. "See, this is the 1955 edition, brand-new. It says that parents should not teach their children to read or write." She tapped emphatically at the front page with her finger. "This outlines the new methods of teaching children on the elementary level. We want to make sure our children learn to read and write the proper way, from the very beginning."

"I never received the notice," Mei-yu said, suddenly worried that the school might not accept her daughter. "I did teach her to read and write a little, but I only taught her so that she might have a good start."

Despite her concern, she looked on with pride as Fernadina sang out the names of the letters, wrote her name, read, and even added figures on the test the registrar gave her. But her fear returned when she saw the dismay plain on the registrar's face.

"She's ahead, but she'll have to enter the first grade in any case, because of her age," the registrar said, frowning, stapling the results of Fernadina's tests together and putting them into a manila folder. "I'll tell Miss Lamston, who will be her teacher, to put her in the Bluebird reading group. That's the fastest level," she explained to Mei-yu.

School began in September. In the mornings Mei-yu put a sandwich in a brown paper bag and gave it to Fernadina before she went down to join Kay Lynn, who waited for her in the car. "Walk with Sally Johanssen," she instructed Fernadina as she hurried down the stairs. "Listen to your teacher, don't talk back, concentrate. I'll be back this afternoon."

Fernadina walked with Sally Johanssen, Ronnie's older sister, for the first few weeks. Sally was one grade ahead of Fernadina and walked very quickly, tossing her brown ponytail as she turned her head from side to side, as if watching to see if anyone were looking. Fernadina skipped to keep up with her, wondering why Sally was not nearly as friendly to her as her brother. One day when she went to the Johanssen apartment to meet Sally, Mrs. Johanssen opened the door and stared at her in surprise.

"Didn't Sally and Karen come by for you? I told them to," she said, wiping her hands on her apron. Ronnie came running up behind her. "Hi, Dina!" he yelled. "You coming here after school?"

Mrs. Johanssen looked down at Fernadina, who was already walking away. "I'm sorry, Dina, I'll speak to those girls when they come back this afternoon."

When Fernadina left the apartment building, she saw the two older girls several blocks up ahead. They walked next to each other, their ponytails, one blond, one brown, swishing side to side in perfect unison.

After that day, Fernadina waited in the apartment until she was certain Sally Johanssen and Karen Simpson had left the building and were well down the street. Then she left the apartment, making sure the door was latched. She walked in the direction opposite the school to the nearest intersection, where she crossed with the light, remembering her mother's warnings about traffic, then walked back in the direction of the school on that side of the street, walking slowly enough to be certain she didn't meet up with the two older girls later at the intersection closest to the schoolyard.

In class Fernadina sat behind a girl named Linda Hancock. She stared at the white-blond hair on the girl's head and arms, at the pinkness of her scalp and skin. Linda's fine hair spun down in tubelike curls, while Fernadina's own hair, now worn in two pigtails, was straight, stiff as the bristles of the paintbrushes standing in the little pots next to the jars of tempera paint in the back of the room. Linda came to school smelling of peppermint and had a red plaid lunchbox with a thermos. She had a different dress for each day of the week. She knew the answers to the teacher's questions, too, and waved her arm in front of Fernadina's face as she called out "Me! Me! Me!" whenever Miss Lamston asked for someone to answer a question. To Fernadina, Linda Hancock seemed perfect. Whenever Miss Lamston walked through the rows of desks, watching them write out their A's or B's, remarking on Linda's neatness or the speed with which she made her letters, Fernadina would feel a strange pang inside her. For even when Miss Lamston praised her own letters, Fernadina thought her voice not as warm, the time spent near her desk not as long. She began to write bigger letters, faster, and found herself dreaming of taking Linda's perfect blond curls and clipping them off with her paper scissors.

In the Bluebird reading group Fernadina stared at the pictures of the boy, Dick, and the girl, Jane, and their pets, Spot and Puff. "Run, run, run, see Spot run," she called out before the teacher turned the page. She didn't know what made her do it, except that, among other things, she wanted to see the pages turn faster, wanted to see Spot run faster. Miss Lamston had asked her to wait quietly while the other children pondered the large-lettered words, but finally, after two warnings, she sent her to sit in the corner as punishment. Here at least Fernadina could press her hot cheeks against the cool walls, stare into the darkness of the corner, and imagine that she was far from the torments of school and with her mother, instead.

But the worst time for Fernadina was recess, when all the children in the class walked in single file behind Miss Lamston on their way to their designated play area outdoors. As soon as the doors opened, the children seemed to rouse with their sense of freedom, like little animals released from their cages, and even while forced to move in single file, they would roil past Fernadina, shouting, "Mudface! Itty bitty slitty eyes! Ching Chong Dina Wong!" She would whirl about, her braids whipping straight out from her head as she turned to face the one who had yanked them last. Once Miss Lamston saw who had shouted at Fernadina and scolded him severely, saying, "We don't talk like that to our friends and classmates, Bobby!" Then she gave Fernadina a squeeze on the arm and appeared about to say something, but became distracted by a commotion at the head of the line. Fernadina, who had begun to feel as if her heart would burst with misery, watched Miss Lamston with gratitude as she waded into the sea of second- and third-graders that churned onto the playground. But moments like those were rare, and though Fernadina tried to keep Miss Lamston in sight, tried to stay close, she would more often find herself separated from her teacher, kept away by the children with louder voices.

Whenever she heard Miss Lamston's whistle blow, signaling the beginning of play, Fernadina would climb the dusty hill to the patch of trees at the far end of the playground and wait there until recess was over. Here she walked on the huge exposed roots of the trees, balancing, inspecting the network of smaller roots, waiting, until Miss Lamston blew her whistle and it was time to go back in again. Here, from the top of the hill, she would watch the groups of children play, watch Linda Hancock run from her group to join Karen Simpson and Sally Johanssen, jumping rope.

Sometimes Miss Lamston would come to the base of the trees and coax Fernadina into playing with the other children. Sometimes the entire class would play a game called Red Rover, where two lines of children linking arms would form, one line opposing the other across a field, and where, following the chant, "Red Rover, Red Rover, send _____ over," the child whose name had been called would run across toward the opposing line and try to break through the barrier of linked arms. Fernadina enjoyed this game, for she loved the sound of wind whistling in her ears as she ran as fast as she could, loved the feeling of breaking through the barrier of arms. The moment she heard her name called from across the field, she felt her heart jump and begin to beat faster. She began to walk to school every day with the hope of playing Red Rover, her head filled with visions of herself running as swiftly as the wind.

Still, there remained the days when the class split up and the girls played their games and the boys played theirs. It was on these days that Fernadina sensed trouble, for it was then that Miss Lamston could not watch everyone but could only walk back and forth to oversee each group in turn. It was at this time that Linda Hancock took over the play of the girls.

One day during the last part of October, when the air was cool and the ground covered with frost, Linda Hancock led the girls out onto the blacktop, carrying the big red rubber ball they used to play squareball. Two other girls carried the jump rope. Fernadina followed in the line and watched as the boys headed out toward the kickball field with Miss Lamston following, blowing on her shrill teacher's whistle.

"You stand here, and you stand over there, Tilly," Linda said, taking her place in square one. The area was divided into four equal squares with one girl standing in each square. Fernadina took her place in the third square. The object of the game was to keep the ball bouncing between the four squares until one girl missed, either by failing to bounce the ball or by bouncing the ball out beyond the boundaries of the chalked squares. Linda began the game by bouncing the ball smartly into Tilly's square, who bounced it into Renee's. Renee bounced the ball into Fernadina's square, and Fernadina bounced it back into Tilly's. Gradually the pace of play began to pick up and the bouncing became harder, more sharply angled. The girls in the squares began to let out sharp little grunts with each bounce and those watching began to shriek. Fernadina felt the excitement rising around her but kept her eyes on the ball. When Tilly shoved the ball toward her so that it bounced up hard against Fernadina's chest, she managed to get both hands in front of the ball and bat it sharply away, in Linda's direction. The ball bounced off the girl's ankle and out of bounds. Linda was out.

"C'mon, your turn, Dee-Dee!" Renee yelled to the next girl in line, moving around the square to fill in Linda's spot.

Linda brushed at the spot on her white anklet where the ball had bounced. "Fernadina's a show-off," she said.

Fernadina moved silently around the square behind Renee.

"Fernadina's a show-off, and she doesn't have a father, either," Linda taunted.

Fernadina threw herself on Linda and grabbed her wrist. She heard the girls screaming for Miss Lamston but heeded more the pain as Linda grabbed one of her pigtails and pulled on it with all her might. Fernadina brought Linda's wrist up to her face and sank her teeth into it. Linda screamed. Then a whistle blew shrilly close to Fernadina's ear. She felt someone take both her arms and pull her up off Linda. "Come with me, Fernadina," she heard Miss Lamston say. Her teacher was squeezing her arm tightly now. Her voice quavered strangely. "I'm afraid we're going to have to go to the principal's office."

Fernadina hung back, but she could not resist the strength of Miss Lamston, who pulled her away from the blacktop toward the school building. She looked back to see the girls clustered around Linda, who, though tended to now by another teacher, continued to weep over her wrist.

Fernadina had heard Miss Lamston say before, "You must behave, or you will have to go to the principal's office," and had often imagined, with no little fear, what the principal's office was like. Her class passed that office on its way out to recess every day. Its location in the hall was marked by an enormous American flag that hung from its staff over the door. As the children made their way down the wide linoleum-floored hallway, pausing often in their lines as other classes came out of their rooms, they had full view of the flag, and had ample chance to wonder what exactly went on in the principal's office. Fernadina had often found herself stopped in line directly in front of the door underneath the flag. The lower part of the door to the office was wood, the upper part made of a kind of bubbly-looking glass. She had looked at the glass part more than once and seen shadows within the office, shadows that appeared to wave within like the seaweed in the fishtank in her classroom. She hardly dared to wonder what happened to the children who were sent there. No one in her own class had been sent there; Miss Lamston had threatened only her. Mrs. Douglas, the principal, a large woman with thick legs, had often come to their classroom to make speeches and to talk to Miss Lamston. She had seemed nice enough then, but Fernadina wondered what she was like, waiting in her office for the bad children who were sent to her.

Now Miss Lamston escorted her under the flag and turned the doorknob of the wavy-glass door. No water rushed out to engulf her, no giant Mrs. Douglas waited to gulp her. The room in fact turned out to be a smaller version of her own classroom. Here, Fernadina saw another, smaller flag hanging over a plain-looking wooden desk, a world globe on its stand in the corner. The smell of freshly sharpened pencils seemed especially strong. Fernadina sat where Miss Lamston indicated, in a chair in front of the desk. Mrs. Douglas, who looked smaller now that she was seated, looked at her sternly but without meanness. Fernadina stared at the squares of linoleum under her feet as she listened to Miss Lamston tell Mrs. Douglas what had happened on the playground, and then the sound of the telephone dial whirling and clicking as Mrs. Douglas made a call. As soon as Fernadina heard Mrs. Douglas say, "May I speak to Mrs. Wong, please?" she stiffened.

How many times had her mother told her to obey her teachers, to obey the rules of the school? She had told her mother of the teasing, of the boy who had pulled his upper lip back and squinted his eyes to make a buck-toothed, squirrely face at her. "He is only teasing you, you don't look like that, Sing-hua," her mother told her. "No matter what they say or do to you, you must remain strong, you must not fight or be mean in turn. It is true, we are different. We are like guests. We must prove ourselves to be worthy guests, guests who want no trouble. We must work hard, instead, to prove ourselves, to be able to live life peacefully. Do you understand, Sing-hua?" Fernadina had always understood, but she still did not like being a guest; she hated having to be polite when others were not.

"Your mother is on her way, Fernadina," Mrs. Douglas said, hanging up the phone. "Would you wait here, please, while I speak to Miss Lamston outside?"

Fernadina nodded, watching as Miss Lamston opened the glass door and stepped out into the hallway with Mrs. Douglas. Miss Lamston looked unhappy and worried now, very much like her mother, Fernadina thought, although her teacher was not nearly as pretty as her mother. Miss Lamston had a long, thin nose and very crooked teeth, which Fernadina could see even when her teacher had her mouth closed. Her teeth gave her a sad look, even when she smiled, Fernadina thought.

She had not heard her mother's voice on the other end of the telephone but imagined her face; the tiny furrows between her eyes that appeared whenever she was worried or angry, the brows that lowered when she frowned. Fernadina always longed to put her hands to her mother's face to smooth the lines away, to make her face clear of worry, to make her smile. But it seemed now that more and more things had gone wrong, and that no matter how hard she tried, everything she did made her mother unhappy. That she had cried because she was no longer allowed to go to work with her made her mother unhappy. That she hated school made her mother unhappy. But the one thing Fernadina suspected that made her mother the most unhappy was also the one thing that frightened Fernadina the most as well; this was that there was someone else now who had come to demand her mother's time and attention, someone else who had command of her mother's smiles. This person was Richard Peng.

Fernadina had seen him the first time he had come to see her mother. He and her mother had sat in the living room far apart from each other. His stay had been brief. Then quite a long time seemed to have passed, several weeks, at least, and Fernadina thought he would not come again, but he did, and this time he took them places in his car and bought her cold, sweet things to eat. Her mother had told her to be nice. She had been polite, but she could tell that Richard Peng did not notice, that his attention was given to her mother. She had eaten the cold ice and played in the long pool of water, but she saw all the while how Richard Peng talked with her mother, how close he sat to her. And after that day, Richard Peng came every week, and every week he would charm her mother, and try to charm her, too, but she resisted. Sometimes when he came, he would try to speak to her, but she would not answer him. She would hide in her room and remain very still, listening to her mother's voice as she sat talking with Richard in the living room. Once, recently, she had come out and seen that they were sitting close to each other. Her mother had jumped up when she saw her and, after kissing her and smoothing back her hair, brought her closer to Richard Peng, urging her to smile and tell him about what she had learned in school. But Fernadina had remained mute, and she had felt Richard's eyes go cold.

Even as she sat in the principal's office, knowing that her mother was on her way to her that moment, Fernadina missed her, missed the touch of her as she missed her father. She wanted to beg her mother's forgiveness, promise her she would be good in school, good everywhere and all the time, if only her mother would not leave her. Should she tell her mother that it wasn't her fault, about what had happened on the blacktop? Should she tell her what Linda Hancock had said about her father? Fernadina knew that Linda and Karen Simpson had been talking. She thought of them with hatred, for it was not true that she did not have a father. No one could take her father away from her.

The door opened and her mother came in with Miss Lamston and Mrs. Douglas. Fernadina had resolved not to cry, but the moment she saw her mother she felt her mouth begin to tremble. Mei-yu came and touched her daughter's cheek, then sat down in the other chair in front of the principal's desk. Mrs. Douglas took her place behind her desk and Miss Lamston stood leaning against the door. Everyone seemed to wait. Fernadina held her breath.

"Well, Mrs. Wong," Mrs. Douglas said finally, "I am sorry to say that we think Fernadina is not very happy here at Thomas Jefferson Elementary." She looked over ruefully at Fernadina, who had fastened her eyes on the paperweight on the principal's desk. The paperweight was a flattened globe of glass containing many different-colored flowers that seemed to spiral around inside. "Miss Lamston has told me that your daughter has disrupted her reading group a number of times," Mrs. Douglas continued, "and that she walks around the room during naptime. We asked you to come today because she bit another little girl on the playground."

"Ah." Mei-yu sighed, shaking her head. She looked across at her daughter, whose tears were now making large wet spots on the front of her dress. Mei-yu took out her handkerchief and gave it to Fernadina.

"We often have children who have difficulty adjusting to the first year at school, Mrs. Wong," Mrs. Douglas went on. "But we find that most children adapt and take to school fairly happily, given time. Fernadina, however, seems to have a different set of problems than most other children. We wanted to talk to you today to try to find a way to help your daughter."

"Mrs. Douglas, may I?" Miss Lamston said, leaning forward from the door. The principal nodded.

"Mrs. Wong," Miss Lamston said, "some of the children here at school have been teasing Fernadina, as I'm sure she has told you. Some of the teasing is harmless, some of it isn't. I'm sure Fernadina thinks her schoolmates are cruel and mean to hurt her, and she reacts to defend herself. I sympathize with the way she feels, although I think we need to find a solution so that she doesn't feel compelled to fight the other children. I've been thinking about this for a while. . . . " She hesitated, looking over at Mrs. Douglas, who gave her a nod of encouragement. "My idea is that if the other children knew more about China, about Chinese culture, about how you live, perhaps they wouldn't think to tease Fernadina as much." She paused. "What do you think?"

Mei-yu thought for a moment. Then she said, "Perhaps you are right, Miss Lamston. But children only mimic their parents. If the parents speak badly of Chinese at home, how can you expect the children to behave any differently?"

"Could we just try one thing?" Miss Lamston persisted. "It might not make any difference, but how would you feel about coming to our class one day to talk to the children about China? Perhaps you could bring something from China, wear a Chinese dress, teach us a song, teach the children something about Fernadina's heritage so that the children, that we, could learn about China, and think of it and the Chinese more in terms of friendship, rather than strangeness."

Fernadina looked at her mother proudly, hopefully, thinking that none of the other children had a mother who was as pretty or who could sing as beautifully as hers. Let the others see how wonderful her mother was, she thought.

Mei-yu had not missed the earnest look in Miss Lamston's face. She saw now how her daughter watched her. She thought of what dress she would wear, what song she would teach. "I think that is a very good idea, Miss Lamston," she said. "I would be glad to try."

Fernadina saw that Miss Lamston had regained her smile. "Could you come next week, then, Mrs. Wong?" her teacher said. "I could show the children where China is on the map, beforehand, to prepare them a little. I'm sure they will be very excited when they know you'll be coming."

Mei-yu agreed to come during the next week. The tension in the room seemed to ease. Then Mrs. Douglas turned to Mei-yu once again.

"Mrs. Wong, before you go . . ." The principal hesitated, then continued. "Perhaps, even though it appears we might have found a solution to this one problem, there still remains another problem that we feel we need to talk to you about." She glanced at Miss Lamston, who leaned once more against the door, her eyes lowered. Mei-yu looked back at the principal, waiting. "We think that Fernadina is, well, lonely, perhaps depressed. We know you must work every day, but is there anything you can do, are there any relatives living close to you with children Fernadina's age, perhaps, who could spend time with her while you're at work?"

Mei-yu knew what the principal was trying to say. "My daughter misses her father," she wanted to say, but found herself unable to. She looked at the two well-meaning women, wondering if they had a proposal to solve that problem, as well. Then she stood up. "I am most grateful for your concern," she said, gesturing for Fernadina to come to her. "I look forward to visiting Fernadina's class next week. But as for this other problem, I can only say that Fernadina's loneliness grieves me as well, and I am doing my best."

"Mrs. Wong," Mrs. Douglas stood up. "We didn't mean—"

Mei-yu shook her head. "No, please, I understand. We are both very grateful. But for Fernadina and myself, it is a matter of time. Things will change for the better, soon. Please be patient. And I will speak to her again, I promise."

Mrs. Douglas looked at Miss Lamston, who said nothing, but moved away from the door as Mei-yu took Fernadina by the hand and reached for the doorknob.

"Please, a little more time," Mei-yu repeated, then closed the door after Fernadina and herself.

"What do you mean, Mama?" Fernadina asked as they walked down the wide corridor of the school on the way out.

"Shh, shh, I need more time, too, Sing-hua. We will talk later, eh?"

Then she stopped and took Fernadina by the shoulders. "Promise me that you will never fight again, never. You make me feel sad and ashamed when you fight. You should feel ashamed, too. Promise me, Sing-hua!"

Fernadina promised, feeling that she would rather die now than have her mother feel ashamed because of her. She looked up and saw that her mother, though looking tired, smiled at her now.

"Now what do you want to do, we have the rest of the day," her mother said. "Shall we go visit Ting at the laundry? Or would you like an ice-cream cone?" She looked down at her daughter, who only held her hand tighter, as if to say anything at all was fine with her now. Good, let the afternoon go, Mei-yu thought. She was grateful for the time to think, to search for the words to explain to her daughter the many changes that were about to take place in their lives.

○ ○ ○

Changes took time, Mei-yu told herself as she walked the one block from the shop to the bus stop on Washington Boulevard. It was snow-ing. She had waited throughout the fall, then through the winter months, watching the progress of her daughter. Things had improved, but the time was still not right, not yet.

She joined the small group of people waiting at the bus stop. A month before, during a similar snowfall, a man Mei-yu had come to recognize as a regular passenger on the same bus had flapped his arms and commented cheerfully that snow was good for a person, that it cleansed the soul. Now Mei-yu saw how the snow had settled onto his thick overcoat, in his hair and mustache. He stood, hunched among the others, looking like a great sad beast peering out from under his wool. She turned, searching in vain for the bright lights of their bus, then, shivering, joined the heat of the huddle.

She thought of Kay Lynn, who was at home with Fernadina. Who was caring for whom? she thought a little ruefully. Kay Lynn was now in her ninth month. Her doctor had forbidden her to drive a month ago, and now she had asked to stay home from work. Nancy had chided her, saying she had gone soft. "Women of your stock pull soybeans in the fields right up to the minute they give birth," she said. "And after-ward, they go right back, with no complaint. What do you mean, your legs are swollen, your back hurts, you can't sit still?" Nancy had been too severe, Mei-yu thought. Kay Lynn did indeed look woeful now; her face had grown puffy with the rest of her, and her eyes were red-rimmed from weeping. "Was it like this for you, Mei-yu?" she had cried, wiping her face and hoisting herself up in her chair with a groan. They had been sitting in her kitchen. "It will be over soon," Mei-yu told her. "Think of the child you will have. Always think of that. This is a small price to pay. Here, drink some milk."

Mei-yu strained to see through the thickly falling snow. Cars continued to churn by slowly, but there was still no sign of the bus. At least Fernadina was warm now, Mei-yu thought, curling her toes inside her boots. Her daughter had recently begun to go over to Kay Lynn's apartment after school to help her clean house, run errands. Or sometimes she would simply sit with her auntie while the latter watched television and shifted her weight and sighed. Mei-yu imagined the two of them back in Kay Lynn's apartment now, her friend propped up, looking like one of her huge foam-stuffed pillows, and her daughter, sitting beside her, ignoring the babble of the electric box, bent over a book.

Fernadina behaved like a different child now, Mei-yu thought. She complained less and less about her schoolmates teasing her, now only moaning that one of them, a bespectacled boy named Sam, followed her home from school every day. She brought home a new vocabulary of American smart talk she had picked up from a new circle of friends. Dee-Dee, Tilly, Elise, or Patsy said this, did that, she would recount at the end of the day. She had brought home a note from Miss Lamston that told them about the public library near where they lived, and that said her daughter could borrow books there to supplement her reading in the Bluebird group. Then there were the songs she had learned in class, songs she sang softly to herself before she fell asleep at night. Had the solution been that simple? Mei-yu thought, remembering the day she had visited Miss Lamston's class.

She had worn a simple blue silk cheongsam. The children of the class had rustled like anxious chicks, murmuring excitedly when they saw her. Mei-yu had walked to the front of the room and nodded a greeting to Miss Lamston. She set the box she had brought on Miss Lamston's desk, then, looking up, smiling, greeted the class in Chinese. Some of the children burst into excited giggles at the singsong speech; others fell into an imitative chatter of their own. But they all fell quiet when she began to draw from the box, one by one, the articles she had brought. Carefully she set the wooden figure of the Chinese peasant on the front edge of the desk. The three-inch figure carried a pole from which dangled two little buckets filled with fantastically tiny carved vegetables. "Don't touch," Miss Lamston called out as the children rushed from their desks to line up to examine the figure more closely. Mei-yu took out the bracelet with the carved ivory beads, Fernadina's jade pendant, the books of poetry. "Look, they write backward, upside down!" one boy exclaimed, pointing to the poetry volume. Later, Mei-yu taught them a Chinese nursery song, a simple song based on the five-note scale about children riding in a boat down the river. Then she wrote Chinese words on the blackboard, showing them how some words were like pictures. She drew a horse, then the word _horse,_ showing the children how four strokes of the character depicted the legs of the horse. She drew a tree, then wrote the character _tree,_ showing how the branch strokes depicted the limbs of the tree. Throughout her visit she felt the children's eyes on her face, her dress. She saw how her daughter watched with shining eyes, and how, when she stood in line with the others to look at the articles from the box, she had proudly told a classmate next to her, "This was from my uncle Bao," pointing out the jade pendant. Toward the end of her visit, Mei-yu wrote the name Sing-hua in characters on the chalkboard, and Fernadina stood up to explain the meaning of her name, "new flower." Some of the children tittered, but Mei-yu was glad to see that Fernadina did not respond and sat down quietly again in her seat.

Mei-yu had been amused and pleased by the kind of questions the children asked her. One child asked about her family back in China. Another asked if people really ate dogs in China, and a boy asked her why the Chinese language sounded so funny, so much like singing out of tune. At the end of the visit Miss Lamston led the class in applause, and walked with Mei-yu toward the door at the back of the room.

"Thank you so much for coming, Mrs. Wong," Fernadina's teacher said. "The children loved every minute of it."

Mei-yu turned to look back at the class. Most of the eyes in the small faces remained fixed on her. Fernadina had turned to look, too, then had quickly turned to face the front of the room. Mei-yu could tell, though, how pleased her daughter was.

"I enjoyed it, too," Mei-yu said, shaking Miss Lamston's hand. "Thank you for inviting me, for suggesting this."

Miss Lamston opened the door for Mei-yu. "I think, I hope, we'll see a difference from now on," she said. "Good luck, Mrs. Wong."

"Here it is, finally!" the man standing next to Mei-yu exclaimed. She looked up to see their bus slowly approaching around the bend of the road. Inside the lighted bus she saw people standing, packed together. When it pulled up to their stop, Mei-yu gave her quarter to the driver and made her way to the middle of the bus. After several more people boarded and pressed their way toward the back of the bus, she found herself wedged between two men carrying briefcases. One held a newspaper up to his face, reading in the greenish light. Probably one of the government workers, Mei-yu thought. Probably one of the many who left their homes at seven in the morning, were at work in their offices by eight, and shuffled papers there until it was time to go home. People riding the bus always seemed so intent on their own thoughts, busy, anxious, Mei-yu thought as she looked down through the bus. Several other people were attempting to read, too. No one talked. The air in the bus was close, smelling of bus fumes, wet paper, wet wool. She gripped the metal ring above her head as the bus moved forward in the line of traffic, hesitating on the ice-covered road, testing its way like an old horse. What was normally a twenty-minute ride could now take an hour, she thought, looking at the man in front of her, who held his paper close to his face.

By the time she got off at the stop in front of her building, forty minutes later, Mei-yu saw her daughter's face at the front window of their apartment, anxiously looking out. Mei-yu hurried up the front walk, up the stairs. She opened the door of the apartment and gratefully inhaled the smell of rice cooking. Fernadina came to help brush the snow off her coat. She pointed to the kitchen. "Look what I've done," she said proudly. She had set the table, taken the meat out from the refrigerator that Mei-yu had chopped that morning, cleaned the vegetables. "Thank you, Sing-hua," Mei-yu said, smoothing the hair of her daughter's braids. "You've become so responsible. You've grown so. How was school? How is Auntie Kay Lynn today?" She took down the wok and set it on the stove.

"School was okay. We did art and painted things. I painted a bird and a house. Auntie Kay Lynn said her legs hurt and asked me to rub them. She's so fat, Mama!"

Mei-yu listened to her daughter chatter on while she prepared their dinner. *She has grown, changed so,* she thought again to herself as they sat down to eat. Kay Lynn had remarked the same thing, as had Richard.

"She seems much happier, Mei-yu," he had said. He had begun to come for supper on Saturday evenings. On this Saturday evening, two weeks ago, they had just finished eating, and Fernadina had brought her plate into the kitchen. Mei-yu noticed that even while Fernadina spoke to Richard now, answering all his questions politely, she always rose straight after they finished eating, cleared the table, then went into her room. She saw how her daughter avoided Richard's eyes when she came back to take their rice bowls out into the kitchen.

"Thank you, Sing-hua," she said. "I'll finish here. It's time for your bath."

"I took one yesterday!" Fernadina said.

"Don't argue with me, Sing-hua. Go on, run the water."

"No, please, Mama!"

"Do as your mother says," Richard broke in. His voice seemed to startle Fernadina, who gave him a quick, defiant look, then turned to stare questioningly at her mother. Mei-yu repeated her gesture toward the hallway. Fernadina made a small, squeezed noise of protest, then turned and stamped down the hall into the bathroom. Soon there was the sound of water running into the tub. Mei-yu looked at Richard, feeling confused in her reaction to his intervention. She had been re-lieved, in a way, but she had also felt a twinge of resentment. Then she immediately felt abashed, for she did not think resentment was the proper feeling, either. She stood up to put more water on for tea. Richard followed her into the kitchen.

"Does she talk back like that often?" he said.

"No," Mei-yu said, putting the kettle on to heat and then turning to face Richard. He was leaning against the refrigerator across the room from her. "She's just begun it recently. She went over to one of her friends' houses and saw how she behaved with her parents. She says all her friends can do more than she can, that they have more freedom. Can you believe that, from a six-year-old?"

"From an American six-year-old, yes, from a Chinese child, no," Richard said, shaking his head, smiling ruefully.

Mei-yu fixed her eyes on the boxes of cereal placed on top of the refrigerator in back of Richard's head. She saw the colorful pictures of tigers and kangaroos eating the cereal, the advertisements urging chil-dren to send away for baseball cards, special prizes. She knew what Richard was thinking, that her daughter was becoming spoiled. She knew he thought she was too lenient with Fernadina, that she indulged her child as though she were an American parent. Although she knew he was probably right, she wanted to explain that she felt her daughter had known enough sorrow, that she wanted her to be happy now, and free. She also wanted to explain that with Fernadina, it had always been her father, Kung-chiao, who had been the disciplinarian, Kung-chiao who had assumed that role, in the way of all other Chinese fathers. But she kept silent. The fact that Richard had seen the many ways Fernadina continued to need her father and the ways she herself continued to need her husband made her feel strangely ashamed. It was as if he had seen and recognized this most intimate truth of their lives, as if he knew that all she provided for herself and her daughter was still not enough.

He followed her as she carried the tea tray into the living room. Down the hall, the sound of water running had stopped. They sat down on the sofa and listened to Fernadina splashing in the tub. He waited while she poured the tea.

"I have made a decision, Mei-yu," he said.

She looked up.

"I have decided to quit the firm and set up my own office."

"Richard!"

"I know. I have thought about this for a long time. I know how things stand at the firm now. I know I can't stay there, because I know I'll never be able to do what I want."

"But what about the expense of setting up your own office? Have they changed their minds at the bank, about giving you a loan?"

Richard shook his head. "No. But things are easing, I can tell. Things have become fairly quiet in this country now, for everyone. Everybody is more relaxed. They just want to keep peace, to make money, to live well after all those years of war. People are beginning to think more about their own lives and have become less concerned, less suspicious about what their neighbors are doing. I have seen, in the community, how more and more of our own are being hired as technicians and research people. I also see that American business is becoming less wary of foreign-born people starting businesses, especially the Chinese, because our businesses, like our restaurants, don't threaten anyone. We provide a kind of amusement, diversion, so we've proved ourselves to be harmless, even desirable, in American communities. And after all, money is money. Do you remember Wan, the restaurateur in Maryland?"

"Yes."

"He recently got a loan to start a new restaurant in Alexandria. He even found American businessmen to invest in it. But he'd already proven that he could be successful. I think, if I can get started and prove that I can attract clients, then I can apply to the banks again when I am ready to expand. I've decided to sell my interest in the apartments here. If I add that with what I have in savings, I'll be able to open an office. It will be modest, at first."

"Where would you locate it?"

"I haven't decided . . . either in Washington or here, in Arlington, but I want to make sure I make myself accessible to both Chinese and American clients."

"Have you told anyone at the firm of your decision?"

"Not yet. I wanted to talk to you first."

Mei-yu looked up at him quickly. His eyes were searching her face. He was looking into her again, she thought. She took her teacup and leaned back against the sofa.

"Mei-yu," he went on urgently, "it's everywhere. In New York, Washington, the West Coast; everyone is buying, building. Offices, businesses, houses, roads are starting up all over. This is what happens when the world is at peace. This country has never been richer. Do you see it? Do you feel it?"

Mei-yu thought of the bulldozers that were clearing ground for the new apartments in back of their own yard, of the new stores being added to the shopping center. She thought of the things she had bought: Fernadina's bicycle, a radio, a used sewing machine, even two pairs of shoes.

"It's there for everyone, for people like us as well," Richard said. "We must also take the opportunity to build."

She looked at him, knowing the meaning of his words. She struggled to look away from his narrow black eyes, which held her with their intensity. She tried to think of herself and Richard together. She searched within herself for feelings she might have toward him, feelings she had once known and garnered for someone else. The words *respect*, *friendship*, and *gratitude* formed in her mind, but her heart, in spite of all her searching, yielded little more than sympathy. Suddenly she thought of her old amah's words, of how Hsiao Pei had once explained to her how parents in the olden days chose husbands and wives for their children. "They had to make certain that the two would work well together, like a matched pair of oxen, Mei-yu," Hsiao Pei had said, "for they knew that what they were to face most in the world was work. If one had strength and stamina, then the other must have common sense. If one was able to pull to the right, then the other must be able to pull to the left. They needed to be harmonious in nature. And they both needed to be healthy, of course, able to have many, many children." Hsiao Pei had laughed when Mei-yu asked how the partners in such pairs felt about each other. "Oxen don't ogle each other when they work side by side, Mei-yu," her amah had said. "They concentrate on moving together, in finishing their task. They feel grateful in having their hay at the end of the day, in having a place to rest. That is how they feel, Mei-yu."

Mei-yu looked at Richard. *Here is strength of will*, she thought to herself. *Here is knowledge, experience, guidance.* She was drawn to that core, that presence, but saw that it was also self-contained, impenetrable. "Please tell me about your wife," she suddenly heard herself saying softly.

Richard looked startled at first but recovered quickly, reaching for his tea. "She was very pretty, intelligent; she came from a fairly wealthy American family," he said. "Her father had his own hardware business. We married very young, while I was still in graduate school."

"Where did you live?"

"In Boston. We had very little money. My mother had disapproved of our marriage and had cut off all my funds. Ruth—that was her name—worked as a librarian at the university."

Mei-yu waited. Richard turned his empty teacup around and around in his hand, staring at it. "We could not have children," he said at last. "Ruth could not." He turned the teacup a final time, then set it down on the table in front of him. "When I think back, I am almost grateful. A child of mixed blood would have suffered terribly in this society then, even more so than a child of wholly Chinese blood, like Fernadina." He looked up at Mei-yu briefly, then looked away again. "Anyway," he continued, letting his breath out in a loud sigh, as if he wished to expel the memories of his story, "we stayed together for much too long a time. I was ashamed to admit to myself, and to my mother most of all, that I had made a terrible mistake. But after a while, our divorce became inevitable."

Mei-yu saw how his eyes moved sideways, away from her. It was an instinctive movement, like the movement of the second eyelid that she had seen in certain animals, that milky membrane that slid over the eye and prevented further glimpses into that eye. She always felt, in such animals, that they could see her from within the opaque lid, even though she could not see them. She wondered what Richard was thinking now.

"When you said you wanted to build," she said hesitantly, "did you mean that you wish to have children?"

He looked at her. For an instant Mei-yu thought she saw a flash of his innermost self, that self within the core he had kept so carefully hidden from her. In that instant she saw pain, his need. "Yes," he said. "I want, like everyone else, to continue, to renew. I want you. I want a family. I want a son."

○ ○ ○

"You're not eating, Mama," Fernadina's voice interrupted Mei-yu's thoughts. "You're not listening to me."

Mei-yu stared across the table at her daughter. Fernadina had finished her supper and was now staring at her with mock disapproval, imitating the way she herself often looked.

"Never mind, Sing-hua," Mei-yu said, picking up her bowl. "Don't wait for me. You may leave the table if you wish." She watched as her daughter took her bowl and chopsticks into the kitchen and put them in the sink. She ate some of the stir-fried beef and Chinese celery in her own bowl, but the food was cold. She put her chopsticks back on her plate. Fernadina had gone to get her book and was now in the living room in her favorite reading position. She had taken one of the large cushions leaning against the back of the sofa and placed it flat on the seat. She propped her book on the cushion, and, kneeling in front of the sofa with her elbows supporting her head, was now absorbed in her reading. Every so often she would call out to Mei-yu, "Mama! What does E-A-G-E-R mean?" Mei-yu would answer, and continue to watch her from the dining room, smiling at how her daughter's sharp shoulder blades and behind moved in rhythm to the words as she read aloud to herself. If Sing-hua was spoiled now, as Richard had said, Mei-yu thought, she was nevertheless still happier now than she had been a year and a half ago. Perhaps such happiness was worth the sacrifice of a few principles.

And at least her daughter was not as spoiled as Yolanda Eng's children, Mei-yu thought, remembering the birthday party given in honor of her friend's son, Ming. Ming had torn open his presents and put on his new cowboy hat and holster with two shiny pistols loaded with caps. He had run about shooting his pistols, filling the room with noise and the smell of sulfur, then poked among the shredded paper of his gifts to look for the model battleship he had wanted. When he discovered he had not received it, he began to whine, so the other mothers in the room began to shift uneasily in their chairs, scold their own children, and send Yolanda anxious looks. "My children get books for their birthdays," Nancy Gow had said, frowning at the huge stack of gifts. Her two children sat stiffly in their chairs lined up against the wall, blinking at the other children tussling in the paper. Mei-yu sat among the other mothers, listening with half an ear as they compared their children. She thought of how she and her brothers had played in their father's courtyard, spinning tops and inventing ingenious games of their own, using two wooden sticks and a rubber ball. Childhood had been simple then. She watched as her daughter played quietly with two other girls in a corner, then looked up as Ming began to gallop around the room again, brandishing his pistols, his spiky black Chinese hair mussed by his new cowboy hat. She remembered thinking how odd he looked. She also remembered thinking how grateful and proud she was that her daughter was neither a spoiled little tyrant nor a child trained to be as obedient as a chair.

Now she shook her head of memories of the party, rising to take her own dishes into the kitchen. Her daughter still needed to know that she lived in a Chinese house, she thought. She needed to be taught to accord the proper respect to others; her elders, for instance, her teachers. She had tried to teach Sing-hua these things herself, but she knew deeply within herself that such discipline was the role of fathers. Such had been her own father's role. Mei-yu realized the logic, the perfect sense of Richard's proposal. A balance was needed, a balance that she alone had been unable to provide.

She looked at her daughter again. Sing-hua was sleepy now. Her head drooped onto the sofa, but she still struggled to keep her eyes open to read. Mei-yu began to feel an ache inside her. Could she accept Richard knowing how her daughter responded to him? "Parents don't consult children," Richard had said. "Children obey their parents. That is the way." Richard's way was so simple, so clear, Mei-yu thought, searching within herself, listening to the various voices, sorting them. She longed for things to be simple and clear again, for someone to say to her, "This is the way." Richard had said there was no hurry. But she saw how he intended to wait until she consented. *Why not go his way?* Mei-yu asked herself. Her mind told her there was every reason to, yet her heart remained caught. What was it deep within her that prevented her from yielding, from allowing herself to be swept along with the current that seemed to flow with such certainty and force? Mei-yu did not know, but she knew she could not give Richard an answer until she felt wholehearted, until her heart, as well as her mind, was free of doubt.

Four days later Tim, in a panic, called the shop to tell Nancy to come hurry and take them to the hospital, that Kay Lynn's time had arrived. The whirring of the sewing machines stopped as Nancy shouted for Mei-yu to stay and watch things while she hurriedly put on her coat and left. Mei-yu told the other women to keep at work but found herself hovering near the telephone for the remainder of the afternoon, twisting the ends of her tape measure, which was still draped around her neck. Twelve hours later Tim called her while she slept at home and, in the voice of one who was stunned, or dreaming, told her that his wife had given birth to a healthy seven-pound girl.

"What name have you chosen, Ba ba?" she asked the new father the next day as they passed through the lobby of the hospital and entered an elevator. Tim looked up at the numbers above the door of the elevator that lighted up, showing the level of floors as they ascended.

"I thought we have boy," he said. "I no choose girl name."

Mei-yu looked at Tim closely, but he avoided her eyes. The elevator bumped slightly when it reached their floor. She followed Tim as he headed toward the nursery where the newborns were looked after, and pressed her face against the glass as she looked at the rows and rows of babies all sleeping in their cribs. Then she saw the tiny dark face with the long black hair.

"There she is!" Mei-yu said, pointing through the glass. "Look how long her hair is, look how beautiful she is! Sing-hua was nearly bald when she was born!"

She looked at Tim, who seemed to gaze at his daughter uncomprehendingly. One of the nurses inside the nursery smiled at them and went over to pick up Tim's daughter. Mei-yu pulled his arm.

"Come, she's going to bring her to Kay Lynn's room now."

The two of them continued down the hall and entered a room shared by four women. Kay Lynn lay with her eyes closed in the bed closest to the window. Mei-yu went up to her friend and touched her gently on the arm.

"Eh, new mother, how do you feel?" she asked, feeling proud herself, then suddenly like weeping, remembering the elation and relief she had felt when she had delivered her own daughter. "Not so bad, was it?"

Kay Lynn smiled weakly. "I fell off my father's buffalo once, on hard ground. This was much worse."

Mei-yu patted her arm, laughing. "I saw her, just now. The nurse is bringing her in. She's beautiful, Kay Lynn."

"Tim?" Kay Lynn asked weakly.

"He's here."

Mei-yu turned away from the bed as Tim came forward. The nurse brought the infant into the room and laid her in Kay Lynn's arms. Its eyes were closed in sleep. Mei-yu marveled at how tiny it was, how the hand with the perfect fingers clutched at the edge of the blanket.

"Have you decided on a name, Kay Lynn?" Mei-yu asked.

Kay Lynn turned her head to regard her husband. "I've been thinking of the name Dorothy, Tim. Dorothy is modern American name, pretty, to go with Woo. Dorothy Lee Woo. Do you like it?"

Tim shrugged.

Kay Lynn's face twisted. "Tim is disappointed he doesn't have boy," she said to Mei-yu. Mei-yu saw the tears of fatigue and hurt in her friend's eyes. She turned to Tim and saw the same look on the man's face.

"Shh, don't quarrel now, Kay Lynn," she said, stroking her friend soothingly. "Tim is a new father. He doesn't know what to think. Kung-chiao was the same."

"Really?" Kay Lynn looked up at her as her tears spilled down her cheeks.

"Yes," Mei-yu said. It was a lie, but she could see how her friends needed time to adjust to their new infant. "Soon, too soon, you will be very jealous at how close father and daughter will become."

Kay Lynn looked down at the tiny face on her arm. "Eh, her father poor stupid laundryman, Mei-yu, he want son so he can brag how son will make him proud someday. Come here, laundryman," she whispered hoarsely to Tim. Tim came forward, hesitating. "You look at her," Kay Lynn said, "you look at your daughter, Dorothy. You will see how she make you proud someday."

Tim reached forward and touched his new daughter's cheek. Mei-yu turned away from her friends and walked over to the door, where a nurse waited.

"It's her feeding time," the nurse said. She went over to Kay Lynn's bed and took the infant in her arms. Mei-yu wondered if this was the modern way of caring for infants, for she had nursed Sing-hua herself. They took care of everything in these American hospitals, she thought, watching as the nurse carried the baby back down the hall to the nursery. She looked back at her friends. Tim was sitting on the edge of his wife's bed, stroking her forehead, murmuring close to her face. Kay Lynn had her eyes closed, but Mei-yu saw how she gripped her husband's hand.

As she walked back from the bus stop on her way home from the hospital, Mei-yu thought of Kung-chiao, remembering how he had reached out to hold their new daughter, how he had given her both her Chinese and American names. Now Kung-chiao was a ghost. Was he watching her now? she wondered. Did he know she thought of taking another husband? *Forgive me*, Kung-chiao, she thought, addressing her husband's spirit. *You have not come this far, so you cannot decide for me this time. Because you have not come this far, I alone must choose for our daughter, who needs, in spite of all that I have tried to give her in your name, a father's voice and hand. You must know that if I choose to take another in your place, it is not to betray your memory, for you live, to me, still.* Mei-yu stopped in the middle of the sidewalk, heedless of whether anyone saw how she behaved. *Kung-chiao?* she said, half aloud. She stood perfectly still. *Do you forbid me this choice, Kung-chiao?* She listened, but she heard nothing. Kung-chiao's ghost did not speak.

Later, when Mei-yu got back to her apartment, she found a letter in her mailbox. It was an aerogram, blue, light as tissue. She saw from the stamp that it came from Peking. She brought it up to the apartment, where Fernadina greeted her from her reading spot at the sofa. She went into the kitchen and sat down at the table, staring all the while at the name printed neatly on the back of the aerogram. The name was that of her brother, Hung-chien. She slipped her finger in between the glued edges of the thin paper and pulled the sides apart carefully, fearing all the while she would tear the words. The paper trembled in her hand as she read.

"Dear Mei-yu," the letter began.

> I wish, after all these years of silence between us, that I would be able to break the silence with good news. But I have only sad news. Our father is dead. You knew, when you left us, that his health had already been destroyed by his term in prison. Last night, after supper, he went to bed, and in the morning our mother found him gone. I write to you now only to tell you the news, and to ask that even if you and he parted with bitter words, that you find it within yourself to honor his memory.
>
> Beyond this sad thing, we all greet you with fondness. Mama is in fairly good health, although she grieves. Hung-bao is working in the countryside. I have my duties in the Party. Hsiao Pei is still with us, getting old but still managing to do the cooking and shopping. Since space is so precious now, we have given up the main portion of our house to share with four other families. Mama, Hsiao Pei, and I live in the two rooms that used to be our parents' room and our father's study. The kitchen is shared by all. We feel it is our duty as patriots to do whatever is necessary in order for the new programs to succeed.
>
> We hope you have fared well in your new country and in your new life.
>
> Your brother with affection,
> Hung-chien

Mei-yu reread the letter, noting that it was dated more than two weeks ago. She turned the letter over in her hand, looking for signs of tampering, knowing how little word came out of Red China these days. Had Hung-chien spoken freely, or had he spoken what he thought censors would have allowed? What did he mean, that Hung-bao was in the countryside . . . Where in the countryside, doing what? What were his own duties within the Party? Was he involved in the new Communist bureaucracy now? How was her mother, really, and how stooped, how much smaller had Hsiao Pei become? The only simple fact in the letter had been the news of her father's death. Mei-yu thought of that last day she had seen him, that day he had turned away from her. He had become a ghost to her then. Now the ghost was dead as well.

Had her brother's letter come as a sign? As she carefully refolded the aerogram she became increasingly aware of a new feeling growing within her. Along with the news that this final link to her father, her father's ghost, was severed now, the letter had brought home the realization that those who were still alive, her brothers, her mother, and Hsiao Pei, could no longer hold her; that they were far away, locked in what seemed to be another world, another time. All that remained of her family now were her memories of them as they once had been. Mei-yu then suddenly recognized the real effect of the letter; that it had finally set her free of all ghosts, set her free at last to embrace her future in this country.

Had she not already seen this future all around her, as Richard had described? Had she not already witnessed one part of the future in the form of Kay Lynn's infant, just hours ago? Had she not already experienced it herself when she had addressed Kung-chiao's spirit, asking for forgiveness for looking beyond into a future that could not include him?

Mei-yu put her brother's letter in a drawer, then remained still for several moments. She thought of Richard, hearing again his words to her, the urgent tone of his voice. She thought of her own need, of Fernadina's need. She knew it no longer mattered what lay in her heart. She knew the way was clear now.

Richard put the car in neutral and let it idle as they sat in the choked traffic of Canal Street. It was already late afternoon. They had left Arlington at twelve and driven north on Interstate 95 through New

Jersey, across the George Washington Bridge into Manhattan. Richard had urged Mei-yu all morning to hurry in her packing, repeating that they would surely hit the worst traffic in Chinatown unless they left well before noon, but she kept remembering things she had forgotten to do, changing her clothes repeatedly and dashing this way and that. Fernadina waited impatiently also, wondering what possessed her mother, what caused the nervous shine in her eyes.

Now they sat in the traffic, feeling the warm air of the summer growing hotter inside their car. Fernadina, in the backseat, rolled down her window and stuck her head out. A slight breeze wafted her way, bringing street smells intensified by the afternoon heat; sea brine and spilled fish gut from the fish stalls, old cabbage, hot fat, garlic.

As their car slowly approached the intersection of Canal and Mott Streets, Fernadina looked to her right and saw the crates. Although the vegetables and fruits had long been put away in the shops, arranged in neat pyramids on the wooden shelves, the crates themselves remained on the sidewalks, cracked open like empty crustacean shells. Shards of yellowing vegetable leaves and stalks hung limply from the splintered slats. Chinese people made their way in a vast procession around the crates, hurrying home from their shopping, carrying string bags bulging with green globe melons, yellow onions, plastic bags sagging with squid. Fernadina watched the people make their way through the wreckage of the crates, remembering the time when she and her mother had been among them.

Finally, after what seemed like an hour of crawling along the streets, moving more slowly than all the pedestrians who hopped over the curbs on all sides of them, Richard found a parking space near Columbus Park. Fernadina saw how her mother fumbled around in the shopping bag full of gifts she had brought, checking and rechecking each parcel. She watched as she checked her makeup in the car mirror, smoothed the skirt of her suit, and smiled in a quick, twitching way at Richard. Then her mother turned to her and, reaching out, said, "Come, Sing-hua, don't hang back so." Fernadina saw the flash of the new ring on her mother's hand and decided, even though she considered Richard to be her mother's accomplice, to walk on his side.

They found their way back to Canal Street and the entrance of the bakery. Ah-chin saw them before they saw her. They had barely opened the door when she shrieked and rushed from behind her glass counter to greet them. She showed all her gold rimmed teeth as she smiled, reaching out to pat Mei-yu on the cheek, exclaiming loudly how well she looked. She bowed shyly to Richard, then turned to Fernadina with a shout, giving her a hug so fierce, she picked her up from the floor. Her auntie still smelled of flour and eggs, Fernadina thought, accepting the custard tart Ah-chin offered her and going over to sit on the wooden ledge near the window of the shop.

"Congratulations, Mei-yu," Ah-chin said, wiping her hands on her apron. "We were so happy to hear of your marriage." She looked out the window anxiously. "Ling said he would be here. He must be with Wen-wen somewhere. He'll be back soon."

Fernadina saw how the adults seemed to laugh after every sentence, how her mother's eyes darted about the tiny cramped space, never settling on Ah-chin's face for long. She saw how thin her auntie was, how she had flour in her hair, and how, even though she wiped her hands on her apron, her hands remained covered with a dried, cracked kind of paste. Then her mother pushed the bag of gifts toward her auntie, who rolled her eyes as she hefted the bag and laughed. Her mother and Auntie Ah-chin spoke in that other language, the same one she heard her Auntie Kay Lynn and Uncle Tim speak to each other while they were at home. She had never heard Richard speak that language. She saw how he leaned against the glass counter, smiling slightly, watching the two women. She saw how her auntie Ah-chin kept her arms crossed tightly against her chest, how she kept raising one hand to flick her hair out of her face and nodding her head quickly in answer to everything that was said.

"And you, Sing-hua, eh, how do you like your new life?" her auntie said, turning to look at her. "You look so fine in your new dress, your new shoes!"

Fernadina shrugged, then bit into the remaining half of her custard tart. She saw how her auntie stared at her, then turned again to talk to her mother. Fernadina wondered how her auntie would have reacted if she had told her she did not like her new life at all; that she did not like the fact that Richard was now living with them, that her mother had changed toward her, that she found the new house they would be moving into too large, too cold. She thought of how she hated the new rules, of how she could not talk at the dinner table but must remain quiet while her mother and Richard Peng spoke to each other. She thought of how she hated not being allowed to enter her mother's room any longer; how the door was now closed to her at night.

Her auntie had noticed her new dress, her new shoes. She did have many more things, that was true. There had also been new books, a record player. But she did not care about the new things. She cared more that the life she and her mother had was no more. She had asked her mother why she had done this, why she had brought them this new life. She had asked her mother about Ba ba. She told her mother Richard was not like Ba ba and that she did not want him to be living with them. Her mother had only answered her with tears, kissing her and promising her that their new life would be better. Fernadina sensed her mother was not lying to her, exactly, but she saw the same look on her face that she had seen on the faces of other people who had lied to her. When her mother held her and said to her, "You'll see, Fernadina, our life will be better," Fernadina thought her voice sounded higher, louder, like the voice of the school nurse who had swabbed her arm on vaccination day and come toward her with the needle, saying, "Now, this won't hurt a bit." Fernadina heard the difference between their voices, though, heard the pleading in her mother's voice, and for this reason did not align her mother with the school nurse altogether in thinking she betrayed her. Still, that begging quality in her mother's voice made her feel all the more angry toward her. There was no way to explain to her auntie how she really felt, Fernadina thought. She looked out the window of the bakery and chewed her custard tart instead.

The two women had grown quiet. Ah-chin's life had not changed at all, Mei-yu was thinking, feeling conscious of her new linen suit. She felt foolish, knowing how she had fussed at home in her wish to impress Ah-chin. There had been no need for that, she saw now. Her friend stood covered with flour, her hair hanging in her face as usual. Mei-yu felt such shame that she moved over to the window, pretending to look out, and said, "I hope Ling and Wen-wen get here soon. I wanted to go to the Sun Wah before Bao got too busy with the dinner hour."

Ah-chin shook her head. "Ai yah, ai yah," she said, "Bao isn't here, Mei-yu. I told him you were coming, but he said things had already been arranged and that he had to leave."

"Leave?" Mei-yu stared at Ah-chin. "Where did he go?"

"To Hong Kong. To fetch his bride."

Ah-chin clucked her tongue and went behind her counter to look for something. Richard asked Mei-yu what was wrong, but she only shook her head.

"Here, look," Ah-chin said, bringing them a magazine. "That crazy man. This is the one he said he picked."

Fernadina jumped off the ledge and came over to look at the magazine, but the adults shooed her away. She retreated back to the window ledge and began petulantly to sweep crumbs from it onto the floor.

"She's so young!" Mei-yu exclaimed.

"Bao's bride?" Richard said. He read the words underneath the photograph aloud: "Twenty-three, an experienced waitress and hostess in Hong Kong, healthy, looking for husband in America."

"I told him he was crazy, that he was better off with a widow here in Chinatown," Ah-chin said. "At least a widow would have been grateful to have him, at least she probably would not try to run away. And even if she did, he would have a better chance of catching a woman nearer to his own age than a girl like that! How long do you think a person as young as that will be content stay with him, eh?" She slapped the magazine against the counter. "I told him she and others like her are only looking for paper husbands, a way to get into this country. But did he listen to me?" Ah-chin gestured toward the ceiling with disgust.

"So he is in Hong Kong now," Mei-yu murmured.

"He said he was sorry he could not be here to greet you," Ah-chin muttered, "but what good is that, the foolish old buzzard."

Ah-chin turned as the bells above the door sounded and Ling and Wen-wen came into the bakery.

"Hoy, Mei-yu!" Ling said, coming forward to shake her hand. Fernadina looked at Wen-wen, who avoided her eyes.

"Eh, Wen-wen, you remember your girlfriend Sing-hua?" Ling said, shoving his son toward Fernadina, who pressed closer to the ledge in back of her.

"Look!" Ah-chin exclaimed, clapping her hands. "He's as tall as she is now!"

Ling pushed the two children together back to back. "Yes," he said, placing the palms of his hands on their heads to show that they were even, "Wen-wen has finally begun to eat pork these days. See how it makes a difference?" He cuffed his son affectionately on the back of his head. Fernadina turned to glance at her former playmate before she took her place back at the window ledge. She recognized the round face, the stubborn cowlick in back. At least he didn't look as if he would cry. In that way he had changed a lot, she thought.

Richard bent and whispered something into Mei-yu's ear. Mei-yu turned to Ah-chin.

"We must go now to see Madame Peng," she said. "Shall we meet later for dinner?"

"Yes, yes," Ah-chin said, turning to Ling, who nodded assent. "But not at Sun Wah. Bao left everything up to Shen while he is away, and the poor boy is barely managing things. I hope he doesn't lose all of Bao's customers! No, let's go to the Four Five Six; they have wonderful seafood."

"Six o'clock, then?" Mei-yu said.

Ah-chin looked to Ling again, who nodded, even though he seemed to be preoccupied with the teasing of his son. "Hey, Wen-wen, I mean, Jack," he said, prodding his son in the back, "how come you don't greet your girlfriend?"

Jack made a grimace and walked away from Fernadina, taking a stand behind his parents' counter.

"Never mind," Mei-yu said, taking Fernadina's hand. "They'll get to know each other again at dinner. Good-bye. Until six, then."

Fernadina followed her mother and Richard as they left the bakery and continued along Canal Street.

"I can't believe Bao went to Hong Kong," she heard her mother say to Richard, who walked ahead of them. They had to walk single file because of the crowd all around them. Richard walked quickly. Fernadina had seen how relieved he had been to leave the bakery, how he had had nothing to say to her mother's friends. She had seen how he had feigned interest in the rows and rows of moon cakes and fried rice squares in the glass counter behind Ah-chin.

"I wanted to see Bao so much," her mother repeated. "I thought he would have waited for us."

"Perhaps it was beyond his control, as Ah-chin said," Richard replied, talking loudly above the noise of the crowd. Fernadina saw her mother's mouth twist in that way she had when she did not understand something.

Ya-mei, Madame Peng's old servant maid, opened the familiar red door. "Ah, ah," she said, smiling broadly, beckoning for them to enter. She reached out and ran her wrinkled finger along Fernadina's neck as she passed. Fernadina heard the yapping of the pug from the kitchen and was about to push open the swinging door to play with him, as she had always done in the past in her visits here, when her mother took her by the hand and pulled her along the hallway toward the drawing room. She saw the dark long-legged table against the wall, the lamps that were always on, even in the light of day. She had come this far before, but had never entered the drawing room, for that had always been the room of the adults. She looked back toward the kitchen, where she knew the dog would be, but Ya-mei was following her closely and blocked her view. In the next moment she found herself standing in the dark chamber.

"Come closer, come closer!" came a cracked voice from the sofa in the middle of the room. Fernadina went toward the lamplit area in the room where she saw Madame Peng. The old lady was sitting up from her pillows, holding out one arm to her.

"Go, go," her mother urged. Fernadina obeyed, approaching the old lady, who grasped her and held her close. Again Fernadina felt the cool satin of the old lady's bedjacket against her face, smelled the overpowering scent of camphor and sandalwood.

"How she's grown," Fernadina heard the voice in the throat above her head.

"Mother," Richard said, coming forward, lowering his eyes as he drew near.

Madame Peng nodded to her son, then squinted past him. "And here is your exceptional bride," she cried, "how glad I am for both of you!"

She pulled Fernadina onto the pillows next to her, nodding with approval as Richard and Mei-yu seated themselves in the chairs in front of the sofa.

"An imperial-looking pair, I must say," she said in her high-pitched voice. "I am so pleased. She suits you well, Richard. And you, Mei-yu"—the old lady looked closely at her—"I am glad to see you looking so well. You cannot imagine what joy the sight of you together brings to my heart."

"Thank you for your blessing, Madame Peng," Mei-yu said. Again she experienced that familiar unease, knowing that the old lady studied her. Then the feeling that had always been peculiar to that room returned to her suddenly, as if a dark curtain had dropped upon her without warning. Even though the furnishings and the closeness of the room were familiar to her, the sensation of finding herself back in the room itself was strange. It was the feeling that she had come full circle, as if she had followed a mysterious summons back to the room, like a migrating bird that had heeded the call to return to its point of origin. She felt this powerful sensation take hold of her, and then, seeing the look of approval and satisfaction on Madame Peng's face, was suddenly struck with the realization that the old woman herself was the source of this summons, that it had been the old woman who had directed her course. Could it be, she thought to herself, feeling cold begin to spread within her, that Madame Peng had intended her marriage to Richard all along? In a rush she thought of how Madame had encouraged her to go to Washington, D.C., of how Richard's engagement to Lillian Chin had ended after their visit to his mother. She turned to look at Richard, sitting next to her, but Madame Peng's voice interrupted her thoughts.

"Yes, I confess," the old woman said, laughing. "I am so happy now that I can freely admit that I was guilty of matchmaking, Mei-yu."

Mei-yu turned to stare at Madame Peng. Had her suspicion been so plain on her face that the old lady had read her mind? She could not tell what Madame Peng was thinking. The old woman seemed only to gaze upon her and Richard with affection and pleasure.

"Yes, I sent you to my son, Mei-yu," Madame Peng said. "I hope you will forgive this act of an old-fashioned, overbearing mother who wants only happiness for her children. But you both took things in your own hands, did you not? You did choose to marry on your own, did you not? You were not forced to marry?"

Both Mei-yu and Richard were silent for a moment. Then Richard said, "No, Mother." Mei-yu looked at her husband and saw that his face was expressionless.

"And things have turned out well, have they not?"

Mei-yu saw how Madame Peng beamed at them. The pleasure of an old person, especially one who had suffered as Madame Peng had, was even more touching than that of a child, she thought.

"Yes, Madame Peng," she heard herself saying.

"Well, then, forgive me if I rejoice in my own wisdom!" Madame Peng said, nodding with satisfaction. "I knew widowhood would not suit Mei-yu for long, and I trusted my instinct that my son would recognize his bride when he saw her. Believe me, you both could not hope for a better match, for you are alike, you two."

Mei-yu heard Richard clear his throat.

"I myself avoided the matchmaker when I was young, Mei-yu," Madame Peng continued. Mei-yu saw how the old lady tilted her head back, as if to think back to the past. "Our backgrounds are very similar, did you know?"

Mei-yu looked at her in surprise. Madame Peng had never told her anything of her past before.

"I was born in Tientsin, not far from Peking," the old lady was saying. "When I was sixteen, I ran off with a dashing young man from the south, an officer in the army. Richard's father. Woe befell me the day I married this man, Mei-yu. Forgive me for saying this, Richard, I do not mean to dishonor the memory of your father, but it is true. If I had obeyed the will of my parents, who had consulted a matchmaker, I would have married someone within my own region, my own class, and not a soldier of fortune who roamed the hills, wandering from town to town. I would have made a marriage of comfort and security." Madame

Peng paused, then shrugged violently. "Pah!" she said, shaking her head. "The past is the past, and the only good thing is that I have learned from it! The lesson here is that the aged know what is best, hah? The important thing is that you, the next generation, learn and prosper from my experience. And so, my blessings to you again, children!"

Ya-mei entered the room, carrying a tray heavy with tea and savories. Madame Peng immediately began to fuss over the array of plates on the tray, acting the role of the solicitous hostess. Mei-yu looked again at Richard, who had not moved throughout the whole of his mother's recital. She had seen how he had greeted his mother when they had first arrived. The two had not touched each other, or hardly spoken. She had seen how Richard had not looked at his mother throughout the telling of her story but had kept his gaze fixed on an object elsewhere in the room; on the table between them and the sofa, on the lamp next to Sing-hua's head. She saw how he kept his hands very still on his knees, how he sat in his chair, tensed in his effort to look at ease. Was this how their love, their bond, was expressed? she thought, perceiving the invisible battle between the mother and son as one struggled to gain nearness and the other fought to retain distance. She did not understand such expression. But then how could she presume to understand their relationship? she thought. Even Richard had failed to define it.

Mei-yu also suddenly knew, as she continued to study her husband's face, that her suspicions of Richard's motives had been groundless. She had come to know the heart he protected within himself. He had, in fact, surprised her with his ardor, his sensitivity, the interest and concern he brought to their marriage. It was true she thought he was severe with Sing-hua, that the rules he demanded of their household suited adults more than children, but she also saw the signs that Richard and her daughter drew nearer to understanding each other. No, Mei-yu thought, feeling her suspicions fall away. Richard had been too much a husband for her to doubt him. He did not behave like a man who had been forced to marry.

Fernadina stared at the rings on Madame Peng's hands as the old lady slowly and painstakingly selected the best of the sesame seed cakes and lotus root buns for her guests. She was glad the adults seemed to pay very little attention to her. She watched her mother nibble at her cakes and lay them aside, casting glances at Richard. She heard the tone of Richard's voice as he answered his mother's inquiries about his new office, their new home, how he used the same tone that he used with her at home, that tone that was patient on the surface of it but impatient underneath. She saw how his hands kept his napkin tightly folded, and how, during those moments when no one said anything, he glanced at the doorway.

She jumped off the sofa when, after what seemed a long time later, Richard finally stood up, signaling the end of their visit.

"Forgive me if I do not come with you to the door," Madame Peng said. "My old legs are too slow to obey. And if you go to see Dr. Toy once more, Richard, snooping around for details about my health, I shall never forgive you. Give me the dignity of my old age, for that is what ails me, nothing more."

"Mother, Dr. Toy says the air here is bad for you, that you should go to a warm place with dry air. . . ."

Madame Peng waved her son quiet. "Nonsense. This is where I belong. I shall die here."

Both Mei-yu and Richard stood, waiting, for the old woman appeared to have something more to say. Mei-yu was aware that Madame Peng was looking at her again.

"I have waited long for this," the old lady said.

Mei-yu felt Richard's hand on her arm as he steered her out of the drawing room. Sing-hua was already waiting for them in the foyer.

"Good-bye, Mother," he said, not looking at the woman on the sofa.

"Good-bye, Madame," Mei-yu said, looking back, then at her husband.

"I expect to see you both again very soon," Madame Peng said. Mei-yu heard from her voice that she had leaned back in her pillows again.

"Richard? What did she mean by that?" she asked her husband after Ya-mei had closed the door behind them.

"What time is it?" he said, avoiding her eyes.

"Nearly six."

"We'd better hurry. We don't want to keep Ah-chin and Ling waiting."

At the Four Five Six, Mei-yu searched her mind for another topic of conversation. Their table had fallen quiet, becoming a strange, unnatural element in the roomful of tables where other families and parties of diners chattered and clattered away. She had been grateful for Richard's attempts to draw Ling out in conversation, but Richard knew very little Cantonese, and Ling very little Mandarin, or English. She had turned to speak to Ah-chin in Cantonese and was relieved when Ling joined them. She listened as her friends told her again about the increasing number of youth gangs in Chinatown, the worsening housing conditions, the price of flour, feeling acutely that she had heard all this before, and also that Richard remained isolated from the group. *This is a mistake,* she found herself thinking. The entire day in Chinatown had been one of terrible strain, of fighting to steer her way in the currents of feeling that had eddied all around her; within her, as well. She became aware of a painful throbbing in her temples.

When the waiters finally brought the platters of food to their table, everybody began to eat; the adults gratefully, because now they had an excuse for being silent, and the children eagerly, because they were hungry. Mei-yu observed how Ah-chin hid her own unease by fussing at her son. Her friend tucked the napkin under Wen-wen's chin and scolded him for picking out the pieces of beef from his noodles and hiding them under his empty shrimp shells. Later, she would talk to Ling about how much Mei-yu had changed, about how little they had to say to each other now beyond comparing how their children grew, or the price of food in Chinatown and in Arlington. She would confide that she thought Mei-yu's new husband aloof, cold, superior acting, like all the other Chinese who had become Americanized. "She doesn't want to offend me now that she's rich," Ah-chin would say to her husband. "She doesn't want to show that she feels sorry for me. How can I ask her how she is, knowing that whatever she says will cause envy to grow inside me? How can I ask her how she is without putting her in the position where she feels she is boasting? And how can she ask me how I am when it is plain how we are. It's all too plain, everything. It was foolish, this visit. We've lost her, Ling, and she is the lucky one."

Fernadina finished her dinner before everyone else and sat swinging her legs and looking around the restaurant. She sat next to the wall. Her former playmate, Wen-wen, now Jack, continued to ignore her. She did not care. She looked around at the circle of adults, wondering why they were so quiet. Where was Uncle Bao? Her mother had promised that she would see Uncle Bao again, but he was not here. Uncle Bao would have kept things lively. Her mother had told her another lie, she thought.

She stood up suddenly, ignoring Richard's frown. "Mama, can we leave now?"

The adults looked at her, the expression on their faces a mixture of consternation and shame, for she had voiced their own thoughts. But, being adults, they told her to sit down and behave, and without another word turned their attention back to their rice bowls.

O   O   O

It was not until Fernadina was much older, when she started to form her own adult relationships, that she began to comprehend how her wary alliance with Richard had come about and how it had evolved from the original truce that her mother had begged her to honor.

The terms of her mother's truce had been simple—that she be quiet, polite, and respectful to their guest. These terms had been easy for Fernadina to accept in the beginning, during the first of Richard's visits to their home, for she had regarded him as a stranger then and had always found it easier being polite to people she did not know or count on seeing often. Also, Richard had been polite in return, acting the proper guest. But it became an altogether different matter later when Richard came to live with them, when he began to assume the attitude that he belonged with her mother and herself. It was at this point that Fernadina closed herself up in her room and railed at what she considered the monstrous presumptuousness of the man. How dare he sit in her father's place? she cried to herself, aware that Richard sat with her mother in the dining room down the hall. How dare he pretend that he was more than a stranger, and how dare her mother treat him as more than an intruder? What right did he have to assume the place that was, as far as Fernadina was concerned, presently and forever taken?

It was not so much that Richard was physically different from her father that Fernadina found him hateful. It was true, though, that Richard's person gave her no feeling of comfort or warmth, as her father's had. Richard's was a bony lap, and when he stood up, he was tall, straight, his face remote from hers. His eyes looked down at her with an unvarying expression of sternness. He did not wear spectacles. In spite of all the physical differences, however, Fernadina sensed that it was Richard's behavior, his very nature, that offended her. She saw how he never seemed to move on impulse, as her father had. She never saw him gulp his food, scratch himself, or walk around in bare feet. He never stamped or swooped around the room, pretending to be this or that animal. He never mumbled to himself, or shouted with happiness or anger. He seemed instead to be thinking, thinking, always holding reins, considering the length and pull of them, moving in an exactly measured course. Fernadina felt the pull of the reins and, realizing that she herself had no power over the man, looked to her mother to blame.

Fernadina remembered how she had tried to punish her mother by avoiding her, by withholding what she had previously shared. She no longer went to greet her when she came home from work, no longer took part in their other rituals, refusing to help her comb her long, thick hair or run bathwater for her. She saw how her punishment took effect, how her mother ceased to plead with her, withdrawing instead into a pained silence. Her mother's withdrawal hurt her in turn, but still Fernadina could not loosen the grip she held on her own heart. She lay in her room in their new house at night and listened as her mother and Richard talked about her. She listened to the murmur of their voices far into the night, feeling misery in one part of her for causing such unhappiness, yet feeling a strengthening resolve in another part of her to preserve her loyalty, to resist the lie.

In looking back at this period, Fernadina could not remember exactly when things had shifted, when she had begun to look at Richard differently. Perhaps it had come about as gradually as when her shoes had begun to feel too tight, or when her wrists had begun to show beyond the sleeves of her jacket. She did remember, however, the feeling of loneliness that had come upon her during this time, how she missed her mother. She remembered the feeling of anger, as well, anger directed at everyone and herself. But she remembered the feeling of surprise, most of all, when Richard began to show that he understood and accepted her anger. She noticed how he began to sit on the sofa, not too close, when she read her books. She learned how he had an answer for every question she found in her books; she saw how he put down his newspaper to look into her face while he explained the meaning of a word or an idea to her. She found that, even as she answered his questions about her day in school in monosyllables, he persisted, gently, and persuaded her to talk to him about her teachers, her homework. And in spite of herself, she found that she began to wait for him to come into her room at night to smooth the edges of the blanket around her. Then, one time, she did not remember when, she found herself beginning to sob when he came to her room one night and asked her to be a daughter to her mother again.

From that moment, Fernadina decided that Richard was not an enemy. It was as if she, like an animal in the wild, had recognized Richard's claim to the territory next to hers and, after discovering that he did not bring any threat to her boundaries, had agreed to a truce. Still, she watched him warily all the same, keeping her distance, averting her head as she watched. She allowed him to approach her but did not draw close to him herself. But although it had been the issue of her mother's pain that had brought her and Richard together in their truce, Fernadina soon discovered that the issue itself had gone beyond her control; that her relationship with her mother grew only worse. It grew worse not because she fought Richard's explanation that her mother had always had her interests first at heart, that her mother had worked hard, suffered, and now needed her help and acceptance. It was not that her heart had hardened into a bitter nut, that she had closed it to understanding. It was that just as she had begun to see why her mother had done what she had, she learned that her mother had done something that she regarded as yet another, even greater act of betrayal.

Fernadina had watched her auntie Kay Lynn swell and turn into another being, someone she could no longer recognize. She had touched the hard, taut-stretched skin of her auntie's belly and felt the kick of the live thing inside against her palm. Later, she had touched the soft head of the infant as it lay dark-faced, wrinkled, and squalling in the arms of her auntie, and seen how it had commanded all the attention of the adults, how it held all the power in the room. Now she saw her own mother swell month by month, and she felt the sympathy and understanding she had begun to feel smother, in the same way she felt herself being squeezed out from the space in her mother's heart. She began to see the power of the little being take effect, even as it lay inside her mother, for she saw how Richard seemed to change. Although he continued to speak to her and come into her room at night to press the edges of the blankets under her chin, she sensed his preoccupation, his growing distance from her. Fernadina could do nothing but retreat in the face of what she perceived as this new threat, and threw herself into her books, her schoolwork, spending many hours alone in her bedroom.

When her brother, William Lien-sheng, was born, Fernadina witnessed the same fuss, the same focus of attention on him as she had seen with Kay Lynn's infant. She saw how everyone heeded the cry of the infant, how everyone in the household remained hushed, as if they feared provoking its power. She herself could not see the reason for such behavior. She looked at the tiny face of the infant and, although she tried, could not fathom any such power. She saw only fragility, from the transparency of the skin to the puniness of the fingers and toes. Everyone, from Auntie Kay Lynn and Uncle Ting to Richard and her mother, remarked how lucky she was to have such a lovely brother. She did not understand what they were saying.

One day, not long after the birth, her mother called her into her room. Her mother looked pale, smiling at her with trembling lips. The infant lay sleeping on her arm. Fernadina came toward her mother and allowed her to take her hand, then pull her close, pressing her face against hers in the same way she had seen her do with the infant. Fernadina was so close to the face of the infant that she smelled its milky smell. Then she heard her mother speak softly to her in her tired voice, heard her say how she loved her and knew that she would be a good sister to her new brother. For an instant Fernadina let her head rest against her mother's arm, marveling at the softness of it, the warmth of it. Then she pulled away, confused. The infant continued to sleep there, between them. She forgot her mother's soothing words, thinking instead of how the new infant commanded the household, how her mother's and Richard's eyes looked upon it with a gaze different from the one they fixed upon her. The world had changed. Where was her place in the midst of it? she remembered thinking.

At the end of Fernadina's second year in school, when William was three months old, the family drove up to New York again. This time Mei-yu packed the night before, carefully laying out their clothes: the new dress and new shoes she had bought for Fernadina, the new silk gown she had made for her infant son. They left very early the next morning, arriving in Chinatown well before eleven, before the onset of the lunch hour.

Fernadina had run ahead of the others and had been the first to enter the Sun Wah Restaurant. She immediately caught sight of her Uncle Bao, who was sitting in the kitchen with his back to her, smoking a cigarette and drinking tea. His apron hung from the refrigerator door behind him. He seemed to be staring at the tea leaves in his cup, deep in thought, and did not see or hear Fernadina at first. When she jumped into the kitchen, shouting his name, he started as if out of a trance and stared at her without recognition. Then, rising out of his chair, hurriedly stubbing out his cigarette in the same motion, he grabbed her by the shoulders as she threw herself at him. "Ai! Ai!" he said, rolling her between his hands as if she were a lump of dough. Then he looked up and saw Mei-yu with the baby, and Richard. On impulse, as he always did when he had company, he reached for his apron and quickly slipped it over his head, tying the strings behind him.

"Bao!" Mei-yu said, handing the baby to Richard as she came forward to greet her friend. "So you decided to wait for me this time!"

"Eh, Mei-yu," Bao said, taking hold of her hand, shaking his head, unable to speak further.

"Bao," Mei-yu said shyly, "this is my husband, Richard Peng. And this is our son. We have named him William."

"Ah, yes." Bao shook Richard's hand, bowing slightly. Then he turned to Mei-yu and said in Cantonese, "He probably doesn't remember. I watched him as a little boy when he used to accompany his mother on her rounds here in Chinatown." Bao held on to Richard's hand even as the other appeared to withdraw his. The cook seemed to search Richard's face. Then he turned again to Mei-yu. "I'm sorry I missed you the last time," he said. He hesitated, then added, as he reached over to poke gently at the blankets surrounding the infant William's face, "I can see you have made a successful marriage." Then he turned, smiling, seeming to have recovered from the shock of this surprise visit, and spread his arms. "Welcome to Sun Wah! Sit! Have some tea. Have you eaten yet today? Will you stay for lunch? Here, I have some fresh red bean buns I made this morning, I will put them on to steam."

Mei-yu watched her friend as he pulled out the chairs from around the kitchen table and gestured for them to sit. He flicked on the gas of his huge black stove, rubbing his hands as the burner in front ignited with a small explosion. All of his motions became familiar to Mei-yu again as she watched him pour water into the wok and place the bean-filled buns into the steamer. His movements were precise, deft as always, his expression concentrated. The cook remained the cook, she thought, but his look of fatigue and worry did not escape her eye.

Where was the wife from Hong Kong? she thought, turning to look back toward the dining room of the restaurant. She saw only the waiters whose faces she did not recognize, the few earliest customers who had just come in. Where was Shen? She watched as Bao adjusted the flame of his stove. _He looks older, so tired,_ she thought. Then she turned her attention to William, who had begun to whimper.

"There," Bao said, snapping the lid of the steamer into place. "A few minutes, now. Hai, Sing-hua, look what I have for you!" He brought over a tin of coconut candies. He took a handful of the candies, wrapped in different-colored paper, and spread them in front of Fernadina. Then he took one of her braids and hefted it in his hand. "How long has it been since Uncle Bao last saw you?"

Fernadina looked to her mother.

"Two years," Mei-yu said.

"Ai," Bao said. His voice sounded weary.

They all sat in awkward silence for a moment, then Bao jumped up again to bang the teakettle on the stove and start another burner roaring. A waiter trotted into the kitchen and called out an order for fried rice noodles with mixed seafood. Bao cursed softly, then went to the refrigerator, pulling out plastic tubs of freshly cleaned shrimp and squid. Mei-yu saw another waiter hurry in with another order.

"Bao," she said, standing up, "is no one here to help you today? Where's Shen?"

"Went to work in a new restaurant on the Bowery," Bao said, shrugging, chopping garlic and throwing it into his sizzling wok. His face was obscured by the rising steam as he threw a handful of shrimp into the hot fat.

"Then let me help you," Mei-yu said, beginning to roll up her sleeves.

"No!" Bao cried, setting his wok aside, coming over to grasp her shoulders and press her back into her chair. "You sit. These customers are early. After I fix their order, we'll have time to visit. Here, your bean buns are ready."

Mei-yu accepted the plate of steamed buns from Bao, then glanced over at Richard, who had been occupied with keeping William quiet. He saw her helpless look and shrugged.

A young woman appeared at the doorway of the kitchen. "Where you been?" Bao shouted, shoving his wok from the burner. After casting a quick glance at Mei-yu, he went over to the woman and pulled her by the arm into the kitchen.

"This is my wife, Rosalie," he said.

Mei-yu saw how Rosalie yanked her arm from Bao's grasp and moved a step away. She recognized her from the picture in the magazine from Hong Kong; a young woman with a round, impassive face, deeply set eyes, a rosebud mouth. She wore a pale blue cheongsam, black pumps. Around her neck she wore a gold necklace with a heart-shaped charm. Mei-yu saw how the expression on her face flashed from boredom to anger as Bao took hold of her arm again and pushed her across the floor to the rear entrance of the kitchen. The waiters came into the kitchen with more orders and circled around impatiently when they saw Bao had gone. Mei-yu turned the burners on low and scooped the finished noodle and seafood dish onto a serving plate for one of the waiters to bring out. Everyone in the kitchen pretended to ignore the shouting voices heard outside the back entrance, and all immediately fell to different tasks when Bao returned, his face red, his lips white with anger. Mei-yu dared not speak to him but took a place next to him as he replaced a wok on the burner and poured in more peanut oil to heat. She looked over at the kitchen table and was grateful that Richard pretended to ignore them, tending to William while talking softly to Fernadina.

"My wife is a spoiled, lazy child," Bao said to Mei-yu, turning his head so no one else could hear. "She came here only to play, to spend money. She heard that is what people do here in the United States."

"What will you do?" Mei-yu said, handing him a bottle of soy sauce, which he tilted into the noodles sizzling in his wok.

"I don't know. I don't know."

She heard the despair in his voice. "I'm sorry, Bao." She watched as he added sesame oil to the dish, searching her mind for words of comfort, finding none. She knew her presence was painful to him, but she did not want to leave him, either. She waited while he stirred the food in his wok with a great scraping sound. He kept his face averted, as if he hoped to conceal his humiliation from her. When the dish was finished, Mei-yu touched his arm and said, "We are going now. Let me know when to come see you again." He nodded, meeting her eyes briefly with gratitude, then, with head lowered, went out with the steaming dish in search of the waiter who had called for it.

Afterward, during the long ride back home on the interstate, Fernadina lay in the back of the car and watched the lights of the highway flash by through half-closed lids. She thought of how she had once again had to bid her uncle Bao good-bye, how this time he had not looked into her face but patted her awkwardly on the back all the way as she and her family walked out of the Sun Wah Restaurant. It was strange to her how adults kept coming and going to see each other even when the meetings always seemed to end unhappily. They had even stopped by the bakery on Canal Street to visit Auntie Ah-chin and Uncle Ling again. Auntie Ah-chin had not been there, nor Jack, only Uncle Ling, and although there had been the usual smiling and nodding of heads, she could feel how glad her mother had been to leave.

She had sensed, from the beginning, when she had watched her mother and Richard make their preparations for the trip, that this journey to Chinatown would be different from the one they had taken previously. Richard had been standing by William's crib while her mother laid out the clothes, and she remembered the way he looked at the infant, as if he could not take his eyes away. She remembered how he had told her that this trip was important because they were taking William to his grandmother to see for the first time. She had heard the sound of his voice, heard the feeling in it, and had seen how her mother had looked up quickly at him from her packing. Even though her mother told her later, in a reassuring tone, that they were also going to visit Uncle Bao in order to meet his new wife and to show him how much his favorite niece had grown, Fernadina had sensed that the presentation of William was really, what the trip was about.

She lay in the backseat of the car, fighting drowsiness brought on by the monotonous sound of the engine as they sped along the highway. She thought of how they had gone directly from the Sun Wah Restaurant to Madame Peng's, how Ya-mei had met them again at the red door. She remembered how she had ignored the yapping of the dog this time as she followed her parents into the darkened drawing room. She remembered how Madame Peng had pulled herself up from her place on the sofa, how, though she stood wobbling on her cane, she had cried aloud and flung out her arm to greet Richard, who came bearing his son. Even Madame Peng had seemed to feel the power of this tiny thing, for she gazed down at the infant with a look that seemed beyond that of love. She passed a trembling hand over the infant's face, pressed her wrinkled mouth to its forehead. Fernadina remembered how Richard had had to pull the infant away from the old woman's hands.

At the end of their visit Fernadina remembered how Madame Peng had looked at Richard and her mother with a smile she had never seen her smile before and said, in her hoarse voice, "Now I can die in peace." She saw how her mother had glanced again at Richard. It was then that she felt within herself a glimmer of understanding that somehow, with the presentation of this tiny infant, her half-brother, to Madame Peng, it was as if something very large and terrible had been concluded.

Now the infant lay asleep in the front seat, in the arms of its mother, her mother. It did not make sense, Fernadina thought, turning her face to the back of the seat, away from the flashing highway lights. She did not understand why all the adults behaved as though they had fallen under some kind of magical spell. The infant was so small, its voice so tiny. She closed her eyes. She was not bewitched, she told herself fiercely, just before she fell asleep. The infant was just like Kay Lynn's, a helpless thing, nothing more.

O   O   O

Fernadina watched her brother grow, watched him begin to speak, take his first steps, enter a phase where he tried to mimic all she did. During this time she kept close watch of the power he still seemed to exert over her mother and Richard, and even though she continued to assert to herself that she remained untouched by his power, she nevertheless began to realize that even she could not remain immune to his charm. Was it because he followed her all around their house? Was it because, in spite of being treated like a prince by his parents, he seemed to prefer her company, ignoring her scowls and hostile knees as he chose to climb into her lap and gaze adoringly into her face? Perhaps the seven-year gap in their ages enabled her to view him less as the brother who threatened her place in their household than as her special pet. But as they both grew older Fernadina realized how much a part of life he had become, how she found herself watching and waiting for him, feeling anxious for his comfort and happiness. She knew then that she had fallen under a similar kind of spell. Even so, she remained aware of the difference between how she viewed her brother and how her mother and Richard continued to view him, particularly in relation to her.

She often wondered, for instance, why certain rules in their household continued to apply to her but not to William. Even when he had grown old enough to join them at the dinner table, she wondered why it was still always expected of her to set the table, to fetch Richard a second bowl of rice, clear the table, and wash the dishes, while the boy was permitted to remain happily seated at his place, free to rattle a tattoo on his placemat with his chopsticks, or chatter away in his developing child's tongue. When she confronted her mother with this observation, her voice tinged with bitterness and envy, her mother explained that she was older, and was therefore expected to bear more responsibility. She also explained that table duties fell to girls.

It was then that Fernadina stared at her mother, realizing how her mother grew more and more like Richard every day, how she seemed to accept and embrace entirely his way in all matters of life. She had cut her hair; she wore colorful shifts and cocktail dresses when she accompanied him out to dinner. She had begun to cook Chinese food less, saying she was too busy to chop meat and vegetables. Fernadina began to notice strange foods appearing on the table: vegetables in creamy sauces that had been boiled in plastic pouches, orange and green Jell-O, large roasts of meat, frozen things for dessert. Her mother had even spoken of leaving the shop, of going to school to earn a degree that would enable her to set up her own retail business.

But even with all the changes that had taken place in her mother and in their household, Fernadina sensed that one thing remained the same: that Richard's will provided the structure underneath all, that it was Richard who saw to it that certain things would never change, that certain things would not be allowed to depart from tradition. It was in this structure that Fernadina recognized the role expected of her; that of compliant daughter at the dinner table, that of loving sister to the favored son. It was this structure that pricked her, like fish bones stuck in her throat. She stared at her mother, knowing how she accepted this structure, and realized that her mother had again chosen apart from her.

Although Fernadina recognized that her half-brother was the favored one, she grew less certain as William grew older that the role was an enviable one. For later, when William came of school age and brought home report cards with notes from his teachers saying that he did not work to his ability, or that he was unruly in class, Fernadina heard Richard scold the boy in the severest tone, more severe than he had ever used with her. She heard him tell William that he was to learn early on the importance of making the highest marks, and that he could never expect to achieve success in the world unless he did his homework faithfully and studied carefully for his exams. Fernadina knew how Richard stopped in William's bedroom every night. She often overheard the angry, tearful episodes as the boy defended his grades or his manner of working to his demanding father. She thought it strange that William was expected to bring home perfect report cards every time, whereas whether she brought home a perfect report or one blemished by a lesser grade or two did not appear to make any difference. Richard and her mother seemed to accept anything and all that she did without remark. By the time she reached junior high school, Fernadina began to realize that her mother and Richard would continue to view her achievements, no matter how outstanding, with a benign kind of detachment. This realization, together with her observation that her brother's achievements were taken seriously and even vigorously encouraged, confused her at first. But as she continued to win her place year after year on the honor roll, receiving recognition and respect from her teachers and classmates, she began to resent the attitude at home. Why wasn't she ever good enough? she would think to herself. She was as capable as her half-brother. Why the maddening difference? She decided, finally, that she would simply have to try harder, to bring home trophies so dazzling that none could ignore her efforts. In this way, Fernadina learned the meaning of hard work, of dedication, of competition.

At about the time she was preparing to enter high school, Fernadina discovered that she was not alone in having this compulsion to excel. It was at this time when Richard, who had been elected president of the

Chinese Community Association, began to organize the bimonthly gatherings for friends within the community to meet on a social basis. It was at these gatherings that Fernadina witnessed the true competitive spirit, of how members of the community competed among themselves as well as with their neighbors outside the community. Fernadina remembered how they would meet at one of the members' houses in Maryland or Virginia; how on these occasions she would meet twenty or thirty of her other "aunties" and "uncles." The gatherings always revolved around the community supper, of course, and it was here, in the judging of the food everyone brought, that the first competition of the day began.

Fernadina remembered the friendly argument as to who made the best pickled cabbage. Ten women had stood in her Auntie Mary's kitchen and squabbled over whether Auntie Gwendolyn or Auntie May had brought the best cabbage. It was decided that Auntie Gwendolyn's was best if one preferred cabbage more hot than sour, and that Auntie May's was best if one preferred it more sour than hot. Afterward, it was also determined, after much animated discussion, that Auntie Anna made the best smoked chicken, Auntie Yolanda the best red-stewed carp. Fernadina remembered how her mother won the accolade for making the best tea eggs.

The parties were always divided so that the adults were separated from the teenagers and the teenagers separated from the younger children. After supper, the men would retire into a separate room to smoke their cigars and begin their card games. The women, after cleaning up the tables and reclaiming their various dishes, would set up their mah-jongg tables in the kitchen. Fernadina roamed restlessly between the groups. She began in the kitchen, nibbling on a leftover chicken leg as she listened to the women in her mother's group talk. One woman lamented that her daughter was seriously dating a Caucasian boy from Princeton and that she was afraid she would marry him. Another woman proclaimed that she would not only box the ears of her son if he married a non-Chinese, but force his father to disown him, as well. Then the talk turned to their children's achievements, about whose child was attending which college, whose child had graduated with what honors, whose child had won this or that job. Fernadina listened carefully to the chatter of the women, which jumped back and forth randomly between Mandarin and English. Their voices were cheerful, light, happy from food and drink, but Fernadina heard the boasting, however artfully disguised, and was aware of the competitive currents crackling beneath the conviviality.

She did not linger long in the men's card room, as the smoke there was thick and the men seemed to talk only of sports or politics in a desultory manner. Some talked of Taiwan with nostalgia. Others talked in cautious tones about the Cultural Revolution that was taking place in Red China. She noticed how Richard remained aloof from the card game, how he sat by himself in a chair nearby, seeming to be lost in his own thoughts.

Fernadina passed through the younger children's room, where she saw William and his like-aged companions reading comic books spread-eagled on the floor among the empty plates and spilled food. Here also were the preteen children who were too young to congregate with the high school and college groups. These youngsters slouched around on the easy chairs, flipping through old *National Geographic* magazines, throwing bits of food at their younger brothers and sisters, or sighing with boredom.

Then Fernadina reached the teens' room. Here, she saw how everyone seemed to wear glasses, how they all seemed to fit into one of two subgroups: those who were quiet, shy, keeping to themselves, playing games of Go and chess in the corners of the room, and those who were aggressively holding court. She recognized Stephanie Ning, who, she had learned from the women's group, had recently won a national essay contest. Stephanie wore dark-rimmed glasses and a ponytail and spoke solemnly of Chekhov, Dostoyevski, and Nietzsche. Fernadina also recognized Hamilton Chiu, whose mother had announced that he had been accepted to Harvard. He stood among his admirers and told everyone his Scholastic Aptitude Test scores, his National Merit scores, and how he wanted to be a world-famous architect. Fernadina looked around the room, recognizing the faces of people her age who were less her friends than wary acquaintances: Roosevelt Hsu, Miranda Yap, Cecelia Chow. She found herself wondering why Chinese parents chose such grand, syllabically profuse first names . . . was it to offset the chop-chop of the last names? Had it been an effort to lend an immediate kind of distinction to their children? She thought of her own name and how she had begun to tell everyone that her name was Dina, Dina only, now. She was not alone; most of the young Chinese people in the community room referred to one another by their nicknames. She remembered that these youths, like herself, were children of the Chinese who had successfully assimilated into the affluent American middle class. Though some probably still spoke Chinese at home, all spoke only English here. Even so, given their affluence, their apparent ease in life, she noticed a pervasive tension in the room, a watchfulness. She listened to a discussion of the television show, the G.E. *College Bowl*, on which different teams of scholars from different colleges vied against each other to answer questions put to them by the moderator. She listened as the discussion turned into a who's who, what's what game of verbal sparring. As the game became more intense and turned into a series of arguments between Hamilton Chiu and another boy, she turned away, making her way toward one of the corners where two boys were playing chess. She remembered thinking how strange it was, being there, seeing Chinese youths like herself gesticulating and talking like Americans. She thought how different these youths were from their parents, playing cards and mah-jongg upstairs. She heard the jangling of the two voices, the two generations, the two languages. It made a strange kind of music, she thought.

She remembered thinking how different these Chinese community parties were compared to her high school classmates' parties. She noticed first of all how the American parents seemed much more lenient with their children. During Bonnie Breck's party, for instance, Bonnie's parents had fled next door to their neighbor's house. Ellen Hirsch had made her parents stay in the living room while her party went on in the rec room below. The people in Bonnie's crowd were football players and members of the Key Club, cheerleaders and Future Homemakers of America. They wore chino pants, madras shirts, shirtwaists, and Bass Weejuns. There had been dancing, and someone had brought beer filched from the family refrigerator. Fernadina didn't know if it was the rock music, which throbbed loudly and evoked mysterious impulses within her, the dimness of the lighting, or the smell of smoke as her classmates lit up their cigarettes and squinted through the smoke in adult fashion that brought on a curious loosening feeling within her. She remembered feeling faint with conflict; how the music made her feel like moving and dancing, yet how, when she peered through the darkness and saw how the boys clutched the girls and how the girls entwined their arms around the boys, she felt abashed. It was not as if she had not known of this kind of behavior, but that she could not imagine herself doing the same. She did not know what boys were about. She grew embarrassed at the thought that one should actually attempt to touch her, or that she should touch him. Her mother would have frowned on such behavior. Her mother and stepfather did not dance; she had not even seen them embrace one another in front of her. None of her teenaged acquaintances at the Chinese community gatherings danced. She spent most of her time at Bonnie's party carefully making her way from one side of the darkened room to the other, drawn and at the same time repelled by the murmurings that came from the corners.

At Ellen Hirsch's party she had listened to the twanging harangue of Bob Dylan's music and then the magical tunes of the Beatles. The people at Ellen's party were members of the Latin Club, the Philosophers Society, and the staff of the school yearbook. Although the lighting there was dim as well, people sat in groups reading poetry, singing along softly with John Lennon, or talking about the Vietnam War. Her classmates here concerned themselves with serious worldly issues. They were too sophisticated to dance, Fernadina thought. She saw how the clothes here differed from those worn at Bonnie's; how her girlfriends wore black leotards and skirts that seemed to have been cut from bedspreads imported from India, and how the boys wore black turtlenecks and corduroy jeans.

The main difference between the Chinese community gatherings and the parties given by her friends at school, Fernadina concluded much later, was that the community gatherings had been centered on the families themselves. Every member of each family attended, every member was accorded his or her place in the proper subgroup. She went to the community gatherings because her family went. Always, while there, she felt the keen sense of connection between the parents and the children, even as they separated into their different groups in different rooms. For even while the adults chatted or played their own social games, Fernadina saw how the aunties and uncles kept eyes and ears out for the younger generation. And she also saw how the younger generation, while sporting American styles and speaking slang, tested the tether to their parents but ultimately respected the strength of it. Fernadina knew that young Chinese like herself always remained aware of how they had been stamped. She never forgot, as she was sure they never forgot, that they were all expected to uphold the honor and dignity of the family, and to contribute to the status of the family in the community.

In contrast, her friends at school always seemed to strain against their family ties. For them, it was a constant effort to assert independence, to express their individuality beyond the family sphere. Fernadina found herself prowling the periphery of both groups. Perhaps she did not feel at ease at the community gatherings because she was estranged from her only true link to the community, her mother and Richard. Perhaps she did not feel at ease at her classmates' parties because, in spite of her estrangement from her mother and Richard, she nevertheless remained tied to the moral and social structure they had provided for her. She decided she was a misfit, a failed social creature. She often talked to her best friend, Ellen Hirsch, about her unease.

"A misfit!" Ellen snorted. "What are you talking about? Just because you've got more than one world?" They were walking home from Edison High, nearing the playing field fence, which ran the length of the school property. Fernadina shrugged.

"What are you, bragging or complaining?" Ellen went on. "You're lucky to be what you are. You're different." Ellen returned Fernadina's quick look with a wince. "No, I don't mean just that you're Chinese. Well, maybe I do. Like, you should be glad you're not like everybody else, you know?"

Not like everybody else. Every day, in the mirror, Fernadina saw how she was not like everybody else. Some of the differences she could think of, shamefully, for instance, were the fact that her hair was grass-straight and would not tease into the bouffant styles of the day; that her nose was short, her nostrils round, like a tiny dragon's; that she lacked the folded lids above her eyes and could not paint a rainbow of eye shadow on them. It was in the girls' bathrooms at school that she saw the differences, that she chided herself on her impossible vanity, that she stifled her interest in the way the American girls teased, sprayed, painted, and smudged their way to beauty.

She knew, however, that Ellen did not refer to her physical differences as much as her cultural and social ones, even though at school, students hardly thought to make distinctions. Fernadina thought of the widely held notion among her classmates and even among her teachers that Chinese, or all Orientals, for that matter, were naturally smart, quick, gifted. She had also not been unaware of the notion that Chinese were thought to be like Jews; that their families shared similar values, such as the mutual recognition of the importance of education, and that both encouraged, even pushed their children to be high achievers. She had also heard the whispers that the Chinese were money pinchers like the Jews, that they were devious and cunning in the same way, and that they grabbed and scrabbled for every bit of advantage. Fernadina wondered how such notions came to be. It was true that her closest friends were Jews. She thought of Ellen, Frieda Stein, Larry Parkin, Eddie Shapiro. She remembered their hours together in the library during what was supposed to have been their study time; their jokes, their spirited discussions of the stories of Nathaniel Hawthorne, predictions of what everyone in their group would become later in life. They had decided that Ellen would become a world-renowned genetic research scientist, that Frieda would change her name to Melanie Matthews and make it on Broadway, that Larry would become a surgeon, and that Eddie would grow up to be a clown. Her friends determined that Fernadina would become known professionally as the Inscrutable One or the Quiet Wonder. For that was the difference between them. Her friends were vivacious and visible, whereas she was the shadow, quietly waiting to place her quip. Perhaps the other students in the school thought that of the group, the "Brain Gang," as they called them, she was the least threatening. Perhaps inscrutability bought respect. Still, Fernadina wondered if it was out of respect that girls like Bonnie Breck invited her to parties.

Ellen suddenly stopped walking. They had reached the midpoint of the school property fence. "Do you know that man across the field there, Dina?" she said. "He's been watching us."

Fernadina looked to her left and saw a dark-haired man in a business suit standing beside a car parked on the street opposite the field. He was too far away for her to distinguish the features of his face, and when she looked toward him again, she saw that he had turned away from her and gotten into his car. In another moment he had started the engine and was driving away.

"Are you sure he was watching us?" Fernadina asked Ellen.

"Sure seemed it. Maybe not." Ellen shrugged.

The next day Fernadina stayed after school to work on a school newspaper article. It was almost four thirty before she finished her first draft and began to walk home alone. She was walking along the school fence, thinking of her article, when she gradually became aware of a car driving slowly behind her. She was not concerned at first, thinking it was only someone from the neighborhood driving slowly, watchful of the young children who lived there. But when the car persisted in its slow pace, sounding as if it were directly behind her, its engine idling with a panting sound, Fernadina turned. As soon as she turned, the car lurched forward slightly, as if the driver had been startled, and sped up. As the car passed her she looked, meeting the eyes of the driver for the briefest moment before he turned his face and continued down beyond her street. He was Oriental, middle-aged. He had thick hair, a regular, handsome, though somewhat heavy, face. There had been nothing especially threatening about him, although there had been something in the way he had met Fernadina's eyes that had startled her; as if in that one quick glance he had conveyed his recognition of her. She herself had never seen him before; not at the community gatherings, not among her stepfather's clients who sometimes came to their house. She thought it unusual that an Oriental man, especially one she did not recognize, should drive through this white middle-class neighborhood. Hers was the only Oriental family in the area. Perhaps he was a new client of her father's, lost, looking for their home. She continued walk-ing in that direction, half expecting to see the stranger's car parked in their driveway.

When she arrived at her house, however, the stranger's car was not to be seen. She looked up and down the street once again and, seeing nothing, decided that the incident with the stranger had probably meant nothing. She checked the mailbox, as was her custom when she came home from school every day, and found two thick manila envelopes from colleges she had written to requesting catalogs and application forms. She saw that one was from Barnard College, in New York City. This was the one she had been waiting for. She raised one knee to balance her books on and tore open the envelope. She pulled out the material: the catalogs, financial information, the application form. She read the ques-tions on the form quickly, stopping when she saw the requirement for the personal essay. This was the kind of challenge she looked forward to. In another instant she gripped the envelope and papers between her teeth, hoisted her books, and opened the door to go inside the house to begin work on her essay. The stranger was forgotten.

$$\bigcirc \quad \bigcirc \quad \bigcirc$$

"Come in, Steven, she'll be with you in a moment." Mei-yu ushered the young man into the living room and invited him to sit in the chair closest to the window. Her daughter's friend seemed to sidle over to the chair she indicated and sit down, arranging his elbows and knees awk-wardly, like a spider folding up. Young men were the same everywhere, Mei-yu thought, feeling bemused at first, then suddenly old. She sat down in the chair opposite him and looked into his face.

"Fernadina said you were going out to see a movie tonight," she said.

"I guess so," the young man said, shifting in his seat.

Steven had sandy hair and large round hazel eyes. He was pleasant enough, though clumsy, Mei-yu thought, smiling as the young man scrambled to his feet when Richard entered the room. Her husband's evening habit of going back and forth from his study to the kitchen to pour himself cups of tea was a familiar one. Now she watched Richard shake Steven's hand and sit down on the sofa near him, asking him in a friendly way about his interests outside of school and what his plans were for after graduation. Upstairs, they could hear Fernadina's footsteps hurrying from her room across the hall to the bathroom, the faint buzz of the hair dryer, the slam of the medicine cabinet door.

As Mei-yu watched her husband chatting with their guest, she thought back to the young men who had come to call on her in Peking, during those days before the arrival of the Japanese. She thought of the Chou brothers and how she had thought they had been so elegant and worldly. Then she recalled how they had sat gripping their knees also; how, when she had come into the reception room to greet them, they rose eagerly from the scrutiny of her father, who had been keeping them company. What must her father have been thinking? Mei-yu thought, glancing over at the young American boy, Steven, who sat examining his knuckles while mumbling replies to Richard's questions. At least her father had needed to concern himself only with the class of family she associated with. The families in Peking knew each other, and all of them, the young men, herself, the parents on both sides, knew what was expected. The rituals, the rules, had been clear. But that had been in China. What was she to expect here, in America? Who would her daughter marry here, in America? Someone like this round-eyed boy? She looked sharply across the room at him. Steven's feet were already longer than Richard's, and his jaw showed signs of further growth. It was thick of bone, promising what, solidity? Stubbornness? Mei-yu shuddered. Rapidly her mind skipped to the future. She imagined her daughter in college, pictured her bringing home a tall, big-boned young man such as the one before her and announcing that this was who she had chosen to marry. She imagined her daughter's wedding, the church, saw Richard walking down the aisle next to Fernadina in that solemn, stilted walk she had seen in American weddings. She could hear herself sobbing aloud at the vision of her daughter dressed in a cloud of white, and then, suddenly, she heard the voice of her friend Cynthia Yang, who came running down the aisle, shrieking, "Stop the wedding! Stop! It is illegal! Chinese and whites cannot marry here!" She felt Cynthia's hand grabbing her arm. "Remember what happened to my daughter and her young man from Princeton," her friend said. In spite of her horror Mei-yu laughed, for she saw on Cynthia's face, even in the midst of her distress, the pride, the boast, that a white man from Princeton had wanted to marry her daughter. Then Mei-yu turned to see that the pastor who was to conduct her own daughter's wedding, who waited in front of them at the altar, was holding up his hand. "What that woman says is true," he said, tilting his book at Cynthia Yang without taking his eyes from its pages. "Lift up your veil," he said to Fernadina, who stood before him. As she did so

Mei-yu felt her heart stop. Her daughter's face, whose happiness had shown through her veil, was now bare, growing tight with alarm. She was staring at her young groom, who seemed to grow taller, larger, his face disappearing in the heights of the church. The pastor closed his book. "It is against the law in the state of Virginia," he pronounced, looking at the space above Fernadina's head. "You and he cannot be joined here." Then he turned to leave them standing there in their shame and confusion.

Mei-yu looked up to see her daughter coming down the stairs. She was dressed in a pink blouse and a short blue skirt. Her hair was long and loose about her shoulders. She wore stockings. Mei-yu thought of the times when she and her friend Wen-chuan and the Chou brothers had gone out arm in arm into the evenings of Peking, to sing songs together, to visit classmates, to sit and watch the moon. They had shared simple pleasures. Then, when she had felt daring, she had worn a ribbon in her hair. Now she stared at her daughter who stood before her, seeing her suddenly as someone apart from her, fully grown, her heart-shaped face no longer childish. Fernadina stood taller than she, looking down from legs and a body that had straightened and grown long and strong on the diet of milk and meat. Mei-yu thought of how her other Chinese friends had clucked their tongues at the growth of their children, how they had taken to the plenty of their new country and grown taller, broader, hairier, towering over their wiry parents. She knew how they moved with their arms and legs flying, like birds; she knew how free they were. Too free. What were the pleasures for these young people? she thought.

"'Bye, Mama," Fernadina said, sounding too bright, too happy. The boy Steven had risen and was going out the door with her.

"Be back before twelve!" Mei-yu snapped, turning away from the sound of her own voice and the look her daughter threw her before she closed the door.

"What's wrong?" Richard asked when she rejoined him in the living room.

"I don't like him. Steven," she said, sitting down heavily.

"He seems nice enough to me," Richard said, sipping from his tea. "He seems serious. He said he wants to be a doctor."

Mei-yu laughed. She saw Richard's look of surprise and waved it away. She remembered the words of the pastor in her daydream. "Partake all you wish, but you may not become one of us." Wasn't that what he was saying? Was he, were the people who made the law, afraid of the color of her blood? That the children of a union between her daughter and a white man would have blood the color of mud, or perhaps more terrible, skin the color of mud? She remembered what her friend Cynthia Yang had said on the occasion when her daughter had finally wed her young man from Princeton. She had been standing in the reception line in a small church in Washington, D.C., where such marriages were legal, accepting the well wishes of her friends.

"It worked out well, even so," Cynthia had said to Mei-yu. "It's cheaper here in Washington, D.C., so our daughter's wedding was a bargain. It's because of the black people," she added, whispering. Then she laughed uneasily. "Look, the other side of the family!"

Mei-yu looked across the room at the young groom's family, the Robert Harrises, who sat clustered at their table apart from the others, looking like stranded missionaries. Not far away, their son sat among his new black-haired family, looking quite like the oversized lark that had been mistakenly hatched in a nest of sparrows. Mixing blood was not good, Mei-yu remembered thinking. Like the wild cats she had seen roaming the alleys near the wharf in San Francisco, cats that had mated randomly, bringing forth litters of kittens with mixed colored eyes, the left side blue, the right side brown; kittens that seemed mad compared to their parents, possessing a queer wildness born of the confusion in their veins. People were not cats, Mei-yu told herself, but still she could not forget Cynthia Yang's lament: "Hope that your daughter chooses one of her own kind, mother!"

But what if her daughter did choose otherwise; would the laws be changed by then? Mei-yu wondered. Richard had said it was a matter of time. Richard, who always believed in this country, who now considered himself an American. Was it because he had not spent all of his childhood and young adulthood in China that he could feel a citizen of this land? Mei-yu thought. Was it because Fernadina had that which she could not, altogether? Was it because of those memories of China that had taken root in her heart, like tangled vines; the fragrance of certain fruits she had not been able to find here, the constant, familiar song of her family language? Or was it more a matter of the laws of this still-strange land, the written ones as well as the unwritten ones, where white people still did not look upon her with the respect they accorded their own kind?

Mei-yu watched her husband as he sat on the sofa not far from her. He was sipping his tea, organizing his thoughts before he went back to his study to work. Twelve years they had shared, Mei-yu thought. They had plowed a long, straight row together in that time. Daily she felt his warmth, the weight of his shoulders against hers. She knew she continued to take comfort knowing that each day would be the same, that each day was assured. He did not seem aware that she watched him now. It was true what Hsiao Pei had said, Mei-yu thought; oxen did not look at each other. She and her husband rarely looked at each other, relying instead on their knowledge of each others' bodies and minds, knowing the precise measure of what each had to do. But she saw now that he had gotten older. Lines had appeared between his nose and cheeks, on his forehead. His hair had grown gray at the temples, thinner at the crown, but still shiny, still vigorous. His face, bent in the steam of his cup, belied no thought. She knew that look on his face, the blank face; the half-smile, the slight upturn at the outer corners of his eyes. This was the face presented to strangers, clients, all white persons, the face that enabled them to gain their quiet place in the community. She knew how she herself had adopted this face, how together she and Richard had fashioned their front. And even more success was promised ahead: the new clothing business that she was to open in the coming year, Richard's new office in Washington. The blank face had become his only face, Mei-yu thought, looking again at her husband. She had seen it presented to Steven, the boy, had felt the way Richard had probed the young man behind the polite and friendly front. "Who are you, do you mean well or ill? Can we trust you with our daughter? Are you honest, are you generous, how far dare we admit you?" The young man had not seen; no one could see beyond the blank face. Was she herself able to see into Richard more than any other? Mei-yu wondered. She had woken often in the night and looked over at his face, expecting to see its true expression of fatigue, of wavering hope. She had wondered if she would at least hear the sound of a sigh escaping. But Richard lay perfectly still. The blank face was necessary for survival, he had said to her once, half-jokingly. Neither questioned what he said, for during those rare times when they stood face-to-face and looked searchingly into each other's eyes, neither was certain of what they saw, beyond what they already knew, that they were a good team. All her Chinese friends told her how fortunate she was to have a husband like Richard, who was successful, who could pass virtually unnoticed throughout white society, and who remained respected and honored among his own kind. Be grateful, they had all said. Mei-yu stopped wondering about the blank face. For it was true; gratitude was what she felt most for her husband, and she knew it was no small feeling.

She looked away when Richard glanced up from his cup.

"Don't worry about Fernadina," he said, smiling, standing up. "Steven is a nice boy. He'll bring her home on time."

Mei-yu watched her husband move across the room and then heard him put his teacup and saucer into the kitchen sink. She looked up and smiled when he came back and put his hand on her shoulder.

"We must begin to let go," he said. "She goes away to college next fall."

Mei-yu shrugged. She felt his fingers squeeze her shoulder gently, then drop from her. Her husband waited a moment by her chair, then turned to go to his study.

Richard has accepted the ways of this country, Mei-yu thought, going over to stand at the front window of their house. He had already surrendered their daughter. He would not wait up for Fernadina, as she would. She looked out into the night and thought of her daughter and how she would be going away soon. She had already gone far, she thought. Fernadina was hardly recognizable to her in the way she came and went so easily, in her choice of friends who lured her farther and farther away. And her voice, her language, English now, frightened her, for it was always so precise and scientific and knowing. *Sing-hua has forgotten her native tongue,* she thought to herself. She and Richard had tried, she remembered, speaking to their daughter and son in Mandarin, refusing to respond when the replies came back in English. But then silence entered the house, and then sound worse than silence surrounded them when their children's friends came over to chatter on in English. She and Richard sat enveloped in their cocoon of silence until they grew to know they must yield to the flow of language around them or be separated from their children forever. So Mandarin, which had been for her the language of music, of the earth and animals, of humor and grace, fell away from their house.

But it was more than that, Mei-yu thought, searching the darkness beyond the window. Her daughter had a quality she had never recognized in herself. For it was beyond ambition, the way her daughter spoke of going to college, of learning, of beginning a career. It was the way she spoke of who she wanted to be. "What do you mean?" Mei-yu had asked. "You are who you are." "But who am I to be?" Her daughter repeated, her eyes burning. Mei-yu shook her head, thinking only that her daughter asked questions beyond her.

Who was this daughter who had grown so strange, who asked such questions? Mei-yu thought. Who was this daughter who possessed two faces: the face with the dark-shadowed brow, the face that brooded, concealing behind it the burning that prompted the questions; and the other face, innocent, clear, waiting to be written on. She remembered thinking, when she had given birth to her, when Kung-chiao had held her for her to see for the first time, *Could she be mine? Could this squawl-*

ing, tiny being be mine? She looked out again into the evening, remembering the sight, moments ago, of Fernadina coming down the stairs, remembering how she had thought, _Could she be mine? Could this tall bright girl with the flying hair be mine?_

"But why Barnard? Why New York City? There are so many other excellent schools you could go to," Mei-yu insisted. The same discussion seemed to have gone on for weeks now. She, Fernadina, and Richard were sitting at the dining room table. Supper dishes had been pushed aside; piles of catalogs and application forms now lay strewn before them.

"Barnard and Columbia are among the top schools in the country," Fernadina said, exasperation sounding in her voice. "And Columbia University is an outstanding graduate school, as well. I don't see why you're so against me going there."

"But they're in New York City!" her mother said, looking over to Richard for help.

Fernadina thought of a similar session she had had with her advisor at school. "Your father had gone to school in New York, hadn't he?" Mr. Bolton had said. She had looked up and seen in her advisor's face that he had already spoken to her mother and stepfather. "Won't you consider these other fine schools?" He went on to tell her about colleges in Massachusetts, Connecticut, Pennsylvania, and Ohio. "New York is a dangerous place," he said. "And Barnard is close to Harlem, you know, the worst section in Manhattan. It's too distracting there, you wouldn't have a real campus life. Here. Look at this campus." He pushed a catalog from a college in Vermont. "Four hundred thirty acres. Isn't it lovely? And listen. Their academic program is among the most rigorous in the nation. You would receive an excellent undergraduate education there."

Fernadina had stood up. "I'm going to Barnard," she said before she left.

"What are your reasons for wanting to study in New York City?" Richard was asking her now.

Fernadina stared at the table in front of her. She knew he would be the one paying for her college education. "Everything's in New York," she said. "Museums, music, dance, theater. All kinds of different people. People who are with it. It's a whole other education besides the academic one. Why wouldn't anyone want to go there?"

"Everything you've just listed sounds like extracurricular activity to me," Richard said. "Wouldn't you find that distracting?"

"No." Fernadina sighed loudly and tilted her head far over the back of her chair.

Showing nothing but contempt, Mei-yu thought, staring at her daughter, then at her husband. How was it that he remained so patient with her? she thought. Even now, after all these years since he had legally given her his name, she still refused to call him Ba ba. Always Richard, as if he were a stranger. Why did she persist in the memory of her father, dead for thirteen years now? Was that why she held on to this notion of going to New York to study, to be nearer somehow to this memory? Mei-yu remembered the night she had entered Fernadina's room and found her sifting through the contents of the old cardboard box she had dragged from the attic. It had been she, Fernadina, who had insisted many years ago on carrying the box from their apartment on Washington Boulevard to their present house. Yellowed and cracked photographs, letters, and documents lay carefully stacked in piles on Fernadina's bed. From the vantage of the doorway, Mei-yu saw the photographs of Kung-chiao and herself in the park in Peking, in front of their school. *We looked like children then,* she thought to herself, thinking that the girl next to the thin boy in the picture could not have been herself. "You may keep them," she had told her daughter. She saw, however, by the way her daughter held the photographs, that her offer had been meaningless; Fernadina had not been about to surrender them.

"Well," Richard was saying, picking up the Barnard application, "if you are so set on going, Fernadina, then I see it is pointless for us to resist. I am glad to see that you are applying to two other schools as well, though."

The phone rang. Richard stood up to answer it in the kitchen. Both Mei-yu and Fernadina turned to look at him when they heard the tone of his voice suddenly change to that of alarm. Fernadina could not see her stepfather's face, but she saw how he held the telephone cord, winding it repeatedly around his hand until his skin turned white. He was speaking rapidly in Mandarin, asking questions, listening briefly, then speaking again, urgently. Then he hung up. He turned to face them in the dining room.

"That was Dr. Toy," he said, his voice gone hoarse. "My mother has had a stroke."

"Richard!" Mei-yu said, standing up. "Is it bad?"

"Yes. I have to get to New York. I'm taking the next shuttle flight."

"When did it happen?"

"An hour ago." Richard shook his head. "I'll call you as soon as I know more. You may as well be prepared; we may all have to go to New York."

Fernadina watched as her mother hurried into her bedroom to pack for Richard while her stepfather called for a cab. His face was blank, but she saw how he gripped the receiver of the phone, how the cord shook. William came into the dining room.

"Is it true what Mama said, that Grandmama's sick?" he asked.

"Shh, shh," Fernadina said. "Yes. We might have to go to New York to see her. Have you finished your homework?"

Her brother nodded. Richard hung up the phone. In another moment Mei-yu reappeared carrying a small traveling bag.

"Shall I pack you something to eat?" she asked, looking at him helplessly.

"No. The cab will be here any minute."

The four of them went to wait in the living room. No one said anything. Richard checked his wallet, walked around the room, looked impatiently out the front window. Moments later the cab arrived, and Richard left.

Madame Peng lay in a private room at Columbia Presbyterian Hospital, where Richard had, in spite of the advice of Dr. Toy, brought her as soon as he arrived in New York. Fernadina and William waited nearby in the hallway outside the room while her mother and Richard conferred with the doctor.

"We can't tell right now," the doctor said. His face looked pallid in the light reflected from the pale green walls. "She's very weak. What medication did you say she had been taking?"

Richard's mouth twisted in exasperation. "She'd been under the care of a doctor in Chinatown, an herbalist. I don't know what he gave her. Perhaps some dried ginseng combined with other powders, I don't know. She was very stubborn, she refused to see any other doctor."

"Her heart is severely damaged. Did you know she'd suffered from rheumatic fever? The X rays also show scars on her lungs."

Richard shook his head.

The doctor hesitated. "I know this is difficult for you, but I must be honest. She has been very sick for a long time, perhaps years. I'm afraid she may succumb to this latest attack."

"Yes. I understand what you are saying," Richard said.

"She is not conscious, but you may see her if you wish. There is a nurse call button near her bed if you require assistance."

Richard nodded. The doctor left them in the hallway. Fernadina and William started when they saw Richard beckon to them. Then, reluctantly, they made their way across the threshold into Madame's room.

Fernadina realized, as soon as she entered the room, that as far as she could remember, she had never seen Madame Peng anywhere other than in her dark parlor. Here, perhaps due to the overhead light, the room seemed unnaturally bright, stark. Madame looked so unlike herself.

They stood near the door, as if afraid to approach the bed. Then Richard moved forward and sat down in the chair next to the bed. Mei-yu went to stand close behind him. A plastic tube connected to a bottle of clear liquid suspended from a stand next to the bed was taped to Madame's arm. Another pair of tubes had been inserted into her nostrils. A machine hooked up to wires disappearing under the sheets near Madame's chest beeped faintly.

"Is she dead?" William's voice quavered in the room.

"No, shh!" Mei-yu reached out to her eleven-year-old son. "See, she's breathing. She's resting."

Fernadina saw how flat Madame was, how perfectly white she looked lying beneath the sheet. Only her feet rose up in little mounds farther down the length of the bed. Fernadina saw the old arm with its slack skin, the blue veins looking startlingly dark against the pale skin. Every time Madame inhaled there was a sound like jujubes rattling inside a jar, and when she exhaled, her chest seemed to sink deeper each time, staying flat for a longer length of time. In a flash Fernadina thought of a film she had seen in science class, in which deep-sea divers in a special diving bubble had gone down into the black depths of the ocean where the sun's rays did not penetrate and brought rare specimens of pale, luminous fish up to the surface. She had seen the fish, stricken by the change in pressurization and light, flatten and fall apart in the divers' hands. She looked at Madame Peng lying before her now and imagined she saw the same kind of death. She looked to her mother in terror.

"Shh, shh, you two may go now," Mei-yu said, seeing the faces of her children. She held the door open for them and pointed to the lounge at the other end of the hall. Then she returned to Richard's place beside the old lady's bed.

How had Madame hidden her condition from them? she thought to herself. They had visited her only months ago, in the fall, and she had seemed fairly well then, although unable to rise from her sofa as usual. Had Dr. Toy known about her illness, had he helped her conceal it from them? Only a change in weather, perhaps a change in place, was all she needed, he had said. The old lady had scoffed even at that. Mei-yu stared down at the small body. The doctor here had said the stroke had affected her right side. She saw Madame's right hand trembling slightly, the index finger wagging in an irregular rhythm.

"Look," Richard said.

Madame's eyelids had begun to quiver. Both Mei-yu and Richard waited as the tremor passed, then leaned forward as the lids slowly raised to expose slits of the pale brown irises of the eyes. Then the mouth, previously slack, seemed to spread in what looked to be a smile, but then stopped, closing firmly. Richard knelt closer, as if readying himself to listen to what his mother might have to say.

Mei-yu looked at the old woman's face. She had never seen it in repose before, without makeup. It no longer looked like the face of the woman she had respected, admired, even feared a little. Now the eyes were closed again, the mouth still. The sparse eyebrows were all but invisible, the cheeks sunken and colorless. Madame's face had become masklike, as if made of clay, revealing nothing.

The next day, as Richard and Mei-yu sat by Madame's bed, they heard loud voices outside the room. A nurse came in to say that someone wished to visit Madame. "Do you know this man?" she said as old man Leong, the President of the Union in Chinatown, pushed his way past her into the room. Mei-yu was surprised at first when Richard nodded and shook the old man's hand in the greeting of an old family acquaintance. "Mr. Peng," Leong said, bowing formally, then, turning to Mei-yu, keeping his eyes lowered, he greeted her: "Madame Peng," he said. Mei-yu looked at him sharply, but the old man kept his face averted. She looked over at Richard, but Richard had turned his attention to his mother. Of course, Leong was right, Mei-yu told herself. In all respects she was Madame Peng now. But still, that Leong had conferred the title upon her came as a shock; it seemed a title from a generation long past, not one she felt suited her. She watched as Leong slowly approached the bed, peered at the still face, then went to sit in a chair against the wall. He gave no further sign that he was aware of her presence, seeming only to stare at the sheet-covered figure on the bed. No one said anything. Several minutes went by. Finally the old man stood up and beckoned to Richard, who accompanied him to the door.

Outside, in the hallway, Leong said, "There's nothing anyone can do, I can see that." He shook Richard's hand. "Come see me soon. She has left a will."

The old woman died two days later. She had not opened her eyes again or spoken. Mei-yu had seen how Richard had remained by the bedside, leaning forward a little, as if hoping to receive her last words. "Take the children home, they must not miss any more school," he told Mei-yu when the hospital orderlies came to take the body out of the room. His face had been drawn, his voice flat. He walked with her to the door. "Don't worry about the arrangements," he said. "I will tend to everything."

The train car swayed from side to side, unlike the bus that had rocked her back and forth that first time out of New York. Mei-yu listened to the rhythmical clicking of the train wheels moving over the tracks, the muted hoot of the whistle as it sounded at the approach and departure of every town. She looked out the window and saw the back lots of Baltimore, the plank-sided houses set too close to the tracks. She had thought the bus trip she had taken from New York years ago had been the final one. She had not known then that she would have had reason to return. This time she had bid farewell to a generation; this time there would be no one to summon her back. She looked at Fernadina and William, her children, the next generation, who sat in the opposite seat, facing her. Her daughter would be returning to New York, she knew. Neither she nor Richard could prevent her from seeking whatever she sought. That was the sorrow of parents, she thought, that of always being left behind.

Fernadina, as usual, was not aware that her mother watched her. She turned the pages of her book, impatiently, reading on, oblivious of the motion of the train, trusting that it would take her to her destination. Did her daughter know where she was going? Mei-yu wondered. She remembered how she had carried her, first under her heart, then in her arms, then on her back, tied in a shawl. She knew now she could carry her no longer; her daughter's path had become separate from her own. Fernadina had gained a certain determination, a confidence, the kind born of youth, of not knowing. She was like a young horse in a field that dashes first in one path and then another, whose head faces one way, toward the wind, yet whose legs carry it wildly in the opposite direction. She appeared to know where she was going, but did she? Mei-yu leaned back in her seat, exhausted, imagining the young horse galloping farther and farther away. She knew there was nothing more she could do for her daughter, for she had already given over everything. It was up to Fernadina now, she thought.

PART THREE

NEW YORK, SEPTEMBER 1968

The city was an assault to all sides, Fernadina thought. She was walking up the steps of her dorm. Behind her, beyond the quadrangle of the campus, she could hear the roar of the buses laboring up Broadway. Pigeons flapped close to her head, swirling soot into the air with the sound of pinion feathers crackling. She ducked, holding her breath as she hurried past the other students into the building.

She breathed easier when she reached her room on the second floor. Her roommate was not in. That morning, the first day of classes, she had awoken before her alarm and sat up to see Debbie Mitchell already standing before the bureau on her side of the room, taking the curlers out of her hair. Both had arrived days ago in time for the Orientation Weekend. Richard had said good-bye to Fernadina at the front of the building, whereas Debbie Mitchell's parents had climbed the stairs and waited about the room while their daughter unpacked her trunks. Debbie's mother sat on what was to be her daughter's bed and clucked with disapproval at the lumpy state of the mattress. She held the blue-and-white striped pillow on her lap, plumping it, picking out stray feathers. Debbie's father had greeted Fernadina awkwardly with a nod of his head and then gone back out into the hallway, where he lingered with the other fathers. "I'm sure you girls will get along just fine," Debbie's mother had said, looking at Fernadina sideways. "Where're you from, where're your parents from?" she asked. Fernadina told Mrs. Mitchell she was from the Washington area, although she guessed what the woman really wanted to know was what nationality she was. Most white people could never bring themselves to ask her directly, "What are you, what breed are you, Chinese, Japanese, Korean, Filipino?" So she added, after she told Mrs. Mitchell that she was from Washington, that she was Chinese. "Oh, isn't that nice," Mrs. Mitchell said to her daughter, who looked doubtful.

Later, after Fernadina and Debbie had been left alone and had eyed each other silently for several moments, Fernadina asked her roommate where she was from. Debbie replied that she was from Elyria, Ohio. She wore her hair in a bouffant style and wore pale lipstick, which made her look as if she had just kissed a chalkboard. When Fernadina politely asked her what her intended major was, Debbie shrugged and said she thought she wanted to teach college English someday. There was something in the tone of her voice and the way she sighed and looked away that made Fernadina's words stop in her throat. She asked no more questions. That night, she slept with her face to the wall so that Debbie would not hear her breathe. It was strange when she awoke early the next morning, forgetting, thinking she was alone in the room, then discovering that this other person went about her life on the opposite side.

Fernadina looked around the room they lived in. Her portable type-writer, dictionary, and alarm clock were in place, her bed neatly made up with her new set of blue sheets and navy blue wool blankets. Her side of the room looked practical, ready for work, she thought. On Debbie's side of the room there was the fat yellow quilt folded on the bed, the stuffed animals, the bag of pink foam curlers hanging from the bedpost. A set of framed photographs had been arranged on her bureau; Fernadina recognized the family resemblance in the faces of six brothers and sisters, parents, a set of grandparents. They were a close family, the Mitchells, she thought.

Her own mother had cried when she and Richard had gotten on the train in Washington. Fernadina had almost been relieved; her mother seemed to have been unable to decide all summer between scolding her or crying. First there had been the shopping trips to buy things for college, trips that had begun in excitement for both but which had ended in terrible quarrels in the department stores or on the way home.

"Make up your mind!" her mother had snapped when Fernadina hesitated between two blouses. "If you're going to be on your own, you've got to learn to decide. I won't be around to tell you what to do anymore!"

"I don't need that," Fernadina had said, regarding a skirt her mother had brought to her in the dressing room to try on.

"When you're at the point where you can buy your own things, then you can decide what you need or don't need," her mother said. She had pressed her lips together, forbidding any accusation from Fernadina that she was being unreasonable.

There had been the time her mother had come into Fernadina's room, stopping short, just beyond the doorway, and asked her if there was anything she wanted or needed to know about boys.

"No," Fernadina said, wondering if her mother was referring to what Ellen Hirsch and her other girlfriends had long whispered about.

"Well, I mean, you might meet someone who will want . . . I mean, who will like you very much," her mother said.

Fernadina shrugged, hiding the excitement and mortification she felt at the very thought.

"Just be responsible," her mother said helplessly.

Fernadina did not press her to explain. After an awkward silence, her mother frowned at her in a way to indicate that she hoped they understood each other, and left the room.

Just before she was due to take the train to New York, Fernadina found her mother crying in the kitchen. When she asked her what the matter was, her mother only shook her head and scolded her for leaving her room a mess. "How will people think I've raised you, sloppy girl?" she cried. "How can I let you go away from home like this?"

Even William, her brother, seemed to treat her differently, avoiding her. She thought it was because of the difference in their ages, or that he had discovered his own interests and friends. But she found the gifts he left for her on her desk and on her bed; packs of pencils, new typewriter ribbons, the new alarm clock. She went to thank him, but he would not allow it, refusing her entry into his boy's room cluttered with his rock collection, his planetary charts.

All Fernadina's friends had gotten into prominent schools. Ellen had been accepted to Bryn Mawr. At the end of the summer Ellen threw one last party for their group of friends. Everyone exchanged addresses, promising to write. They all agreed to meet again at Christmas. At midnight Ellen threw her arms around Fernadina and cried that she would never have another friend like her.

"Promise, promise you'll write."

Fernadina promised.

"Promise I can come visit you in New York. I'll probably die of cultural starvation at Bryn Mawr."

The two talked of the times they had shared, of what they hoped to experience at college. They talked of what they were leaving behind.

"My mother's getting weird, too," Ellen said. "Sometimes I think she's really glad to be getting rid of me at last."

"At least your mother's driving you to school," Fernadina said. "My mother's not even coming to New York. I think she's still upset that I'm going to Barnard."

"Try not to think about it," Ellen said. "It's your life." Fernadina nodded in agreement, but still, it cut her that her mother would not go.

It had been Richard who had explained things to Fernadina during their ride on the train together to New York.

"Try to understand your mother," he said. "She is unhappy because you have grown up. She didn't want to come to New York to give you away. Give her time. It'll be different when you come back at Thanksgiving; she'll have had enough time to get used to your being away from home then."

It had been Richard who had accompanied her to the registrar's office, studied the campus map with her, and helped her find her room within the complex of Brooks, Hewitt, and Reid residence halls. He had bought her lunch at a delicatessen near Broadway and 110th Street and watched her pick at her food and shred her napkin in excitement. After lunch, when they had walked back and were standing in the courtyard in front of her dorm, he gave her a check. "For you to see a little of the town," he said. They stood there silently for a while, then he said he had to catch the train back to Washington. When he turned to leave, Fernadina reached out awkwardly, taking hold of his jacket sleeve. She dropped her hand when he stopped, feeling suddenly shy. "Thank you," she said.

He smiled. "Write to your mother often. Let me know if you need anything."

"I will," Fernadina said. She felt her lower lip begin to tremble, and was glad when he left her.

Breakfast had been served that first morning at the cafeteria across the courtyard from Fernadina's dorm. She stood in line with her tray while students wearing hairnets handed out warped pieces of toast and spooned scrambled eggs onto plates. She found a table with two other girls who looked to be freshmen. One of them, who wore her startling red, frizzy hair combed straight back and tied so that the ends sprayed out behind her like the tail of a comet, joked that she was going to take her scrambled eggs to her biology class for analysis. Fernadina smiled at her over her orange juice glass. She learned the girl's name was Rhea Desjalb and that she commuted to school from Brooklyn. She was glad to discover they had been scheduled in two classes together.

Fernadina saw every kind of face in the large room of the cafeteria, East Indian, Asian, Hispanic, and black, among the white. Other young women wearing wire-rimmed glasses and a conspicuous ease (upperclassmen, Fernadina thought) sipped coffee and read pamphlets that had been scattered about the tables. On the way out Fernadina passed the bulletin board full of notices of meetings of different organizations and dates for antiwar demonstrations on campus. Someone stopped her, pressing a pamphlet into her hand. She took it but shook her head at the petition thrust at her, mumbling that she had classes to go to.

The first had been Political Science. She and twenty other freshmen sat in the lecture hall and listened while the professor introduced himself and described the format of the class. A graduate assistant handed out outlines and a reading list for the course. The professor then began to speak about the meaning of the term _commitment._ Fernadina heard the scrabble of paper and pencil as students began to take notes. "Commitment," the professor repeated, writing the word down on the chalkboard in front of the class. "Dedication, promise, a contract, written or unwritten, made between peoples, between nations, between generations." Fernadina looked up quickly, thinking the professor directed his remarks at her. But he continued to stroll back and forth in front of the board, talking, it seemed, to no one but the floor, gesturing with chalk in hand. Fernadina looked at the students around her who were writing furiously in their notebooks, acting as if they were hearing for the first time. She wrote nothing.

The next class, across campus, was Sociology. As she approached the quadrangle in the center of the campus, she saw a large gathering of students. At the southern end of the court a young man, probably from Columbia, on the other side of Broadway, stood on a wooden box and shouted through a megaphone. "Out of 'Nam Now!" he chanted, gesturing for all the students to join him. They pressed forward, united in a growing kind of frenzy. Young women with waist-length hair chanted with upraised fists. Young men shouted and cursed with voices already gone hoarse. A man making his way through the crowd handed Fernadina a leaflet announcing the formation of a new radical activist group on campus. Fernadina took the leaflet and stuffed it among her notebooks. She pushed her way through the crowd, finding a path through the bodies toward Milbank Hall, where her next class was. She moved as quickly as possible, fearing the expanding energy of the crowd, lowering her head as if readying herself for an explosion.

"Somebody's waiting for you downstairs," a girl from her floor told her.

"Thanks," Fernadina said. She had returned to her room to drop off her books before going back to the cafeteria for lunch. She thought the person waiting for her was Rhea Desjalb, who she had seen again in Sociology. She came down the stairs, looking for the cloud of red hair, but saw only a young Oriental man waiting by the desk.

"Hi," he said as she was about to walk past him. She looked at him, thinking he had made a mistake, but saw he was quite certain it was she he meant to address.

"You probably don't remember me. It's been a long time."

Fernadina stared at him. He was slightly taller than she. His narrow eyes looked even smaller behind the thick lenses of his glasses. His hair was long, falling over his forehead and hanging down almost to his shoulders. There was something familiar in the way he tilted his head as he spoke, Fernadina thought, but it wasn't until she noticed the cowlick at the back of his head that she knew who he was.

"Wen-wen?" she asked incredulously.

"Hah!" He laughed. "I hope not!" Then he nodded. "Yes. I was Wen-wen, then Jack. Now I use the name my parents gave me. Min. How are you, Fernadina?"

"Dina," she said, smiling, shrugging to indicate that if he could change his name, she could, too. "I'm fine . . . a little overwhelmed by all this." She gestured around her. "How did you know I was here?"

"Saw your name in the freshman directory. I didn't think there could be more than one Fernadina Peng."

"Are you a student at Columbia?"

"Yes. Second year. I commute from Chinatown."

"How're your parents?"

"Oh, fine. They're managing a restaurant in Fort Lee now, across the river. It's doing very well. They work with a good staff there so they don't have to work so hard, but still, it's every day, every week. I think they don't know how to live otherwise, you know."

"So." Fernadina looked around her, hoping to see Rhea appear. She was glad to see Wen-wen but felt suddenly shy, doubtful that they had much to talk about.

"Have you had lunch yet?" Min asked.

"No." Fernadina looked around a last time. Rhea was not to be seen.

"The food here is terrible, even for institution food. Come on, let's celebrate your first day. Let me take you to the Harbin. It's right down Broadway."

Fernadina heard the confidence in his voice, but when she looked at his face, she saw hope rather than expectation.

"Sure," she said. "Why not?"

The Harbin was a pleasant place, smelling, Fernadina thought appreciatively, like every other Chinese restaurant. They sat in a deep booth covered in red vinyl. Little lanterns with sides of patterned silk, dangling tassles, hung from the ceiling. Fernadina described her course of study to Min while their waiter set their places.

"Sounds like you're heading for a law degree," Min said.

"Could be," Fernadina said.

"So certain already?"

"You sound like my stepfather," Fernadina said, half-joking.

"Sorry. I didn't mean to." He turned to look at the menu. "Why don't you try the shrimp with garlic sauce. It's very good here."

She nodded and Min spoke to the waiter in Cantonese, giving him their order.

"What are you studying?" Fernadina asked when the waiter had gone.

"Psychology. Social work." He seemed about to say something further but changed his mind. They sat there in awkward silence. The waiter came back with a pot of tea and teacups, and Min poured for both of them.

"What are you smiling about?" he asked, looking up to find Fernadina studying his face.

"Oh, nothing, really," she said, looking away. "I was just thinking how different you are from when you were little."

"Thank God," Min said, rolling his eyes. "Maybe if I had cried when you saw me, you might have recognized me sooner. The stories my mother tells me of how I was!" He laughed, then stopped to study Fernadina's face. "You've changed a lot, too," he said.

Fernadina looked down into her teacup.

"You seem . . . Americanized. But then, look at me, I should talk." He laughed.

Fernadina nodded but felt Min's words touch a tender spot inside her. It was true, what Min said; they were American. But even though they both wore Western clothes and spoke English, she was aware of the difference between them. He seemed comfortable inside his skin. She knew he probably woke up mornings and did not give himself a passing glance in the mirror, whereas she woke up and looked into the mirror with surprise, even shock, at the face that confronted her there every time.

"What's the matter?" Min asked.

Fernadina hesitated. "I don't know. I don't know if you want to talk about it. I was just wondering how it was for you, growing up in Chinatown."

"Yeah," Min said, nodding. "We have come from different places, haven't we?" He seemed to think for a moment. "One of my first memories was of a very big, fat white man coming into my parents' bakery and asking for some pastries. I don't know what he expected, exactly, but apparently nothing my father gave him pleased him, because he started to shout obscenities. I think he thought our pastries were supposed to be like the French kind, you know, light and flaky, buttery. I think he was really grossed out by the bean cakes my father gave him. Anyway, I was about three or four then, and I was hiding behind the counter, and I remember feeling so scared that this huge man was going to flatten my father. I just remember how he stood there and shouted, how his spit hit my father's face, and how my father just kept nodding and bowing and holding his hands up like there was nothing he could do. From then on, or at least, for a very long time, until I was much older, I used to think all white people were big and fat and mean, and the best thing to do was to avoid them. At least you could always tell when they were coming, beforehand, like when they would drive down Mott Street in their cars, honking, or when they would come into the restaurants and expect to be served right away. Later, by the time I was going to school, I was sort of used to them. But I wonder sometimes about those memories, how many of them have stuck. I realize certain things nowadays, but sometimes the feelings of those memories remain. You know what I mean?"

"Yes. But go on. What was it like, in school?"

"Oh, our school was a dump. We were all mixed up. There were a lot of Chinese kids, some blacks, some Italians. The first day was the only day when all the kids showed up. After that, you never knew. Most of us worked, either in our parents' shops or in some restaurant, sometimes really late at night. A lot of us fell asleep in the classes. The teachers would go berserk. I mean, they'd face a completely different class each day, and during that class kids would sneak in and out. When I was in junior high, I went with a kind of gang. Belonging to it made me feel tough, I guess. Most of the kids in it worked throughout the afternoons and into the evenings, then went home to places where the parents weren't there because they were still at work. The only people at home were the grandparents or some great second aunt or uncle who did nothing but cry about the old days or complain about how everybody was too busy, that nobody was around anymore. So most of my friends would go out to hang around on the street. I guess the street wasn't as depressing. You could move around there, at least."

"How long did you stay with the gang?"

"I don't know, two years, maybe more. We had a kind of falling out. My parents still made me go to school every day. They really made a big deal about studying, about education. My father used to throw flour in my face and tell me if I didn't want to end up like him that I should go to school. My mother walked me there in the mornings and he came to pick me up in the afternoons. God, how we fought! But they didn't care how it looked, you know, me, a kid already taller than my mother, being dragged by the ear to school. And I remember those afternoons, coming out from class, dreading the sight of my father, who would always be waiting there for me, still wearing his apron. The guys in the gang used to stand around teasing him, calling him names like bean-face and paste-head. I didn't like that. Finally I told him, I said, Ba ba, don't come pick me up from school anymore, you don't have to do that. I told him I'd go on my own, and I did. I felt shame. I was ashamed of seeing my father waiting for me in his apron, but I think I felt more shame in being the one who made him do that. I think that's what split me up from the gang. I think the gang knew I felt ashamed."

Min refilled their teacups. Fernadina also saw that he had inherited his mother's gesture of raising his hand to sweep his hair back from his face.

"Did you ever go out of Chinatown?" she asked.

"Oh, sure. I'd take walks. I'd go down by the municipal offices of New York and look up and see these incredible buildings. That's where the administration of New York City takes place, on the far boundary of Chinatown. . . . You see Chinese people as far as Columbus Park, but few ever go beyond to the municipal buildings. I remember thinking how close the heart of the city was, but how far. It felt like it had nothing to do with us. Anyway, I began to take the subway farther and farther uptown. . . . I went to Macy's once to get my mother a birthday present. I wanted to get her something that wasn't made in Hong Kong or Taiwan. I got her a silk scarf made in Italy. She's so embarrassed I bought it that she only wears it at home, on her birthdays. Then once I went with a buddy to see a movie in Times Square. I never told my parents about that. Finally, while I was in high school, I met a student from Columbia who was tutoring English at the Union in Chinatown, and he brought me to see the West Side. That's when I first began to think about coming to school here."

"How do you like it?" Fernadina asked.

Min laughed, turning around to look out the window behind him at the people hurrying down Broadway. "It's crazy," he said. "But I like it. I like it a lot."

He leaned back from the table as their waiter brought their food. "How about you?" he said, lifting the metal covers from the hot dishes and sniffing the steam. "What was it like for you, growing up in the suburbs?"

Fernadina smoothed her napkin in her lap, thinking. "I suppose, after a certain point, we were comfortable enough. I mean, we had everything we needed. But I never felt a part of things. I was the only Chinese at school. The teachers thought I was smart, but the kids thought I was weird. I studied hard, like you. But most of the time I was just waiting, waiting to get out, waiting to find someplace where I could breathe."

"What about your mother? How is she . . . and Richard?"

Fernadina watched Min dish the shrimp out onto her plate and then onto his. She shrugged when Min looked up.

"They're fine," she said, looking away. "Busy making their way, busy keeping face."

Min said nothing but began to direct his attention to his food. Fernadina saw that he ate native style, holding his bowl up, quickly tapping the rice into his mouth with his chopsticks. He ate without self-consciousness, taking little heed of the grains of rice he flipped onto his placemat. She saw that his hands were slender. He looked up.

"Not eating?" he said. "Go on. It's really good."

He watched as Fernadina picked up a shrimp with her chopsticks.

"We hear a lot about Richard and what he's done for the Chinese community in Washington," Min said casually, setting his rice bowl down. "The community network needs more leaders like him."

Fernadina reached abruptly for the dish of chicken and peppers and began to spoon the gravy over her rice. Min observed her agitation quietly. When she spoke again, moments later, however, her voice was controlled.

"You're involved with community work? How do you manage it, I mean, with school and everything?"

"Living in Chinatown makes it easier," Min said. "I'm close to the community. I share an apartment with another Chinese student, right off Mott Street."

At the mention of Mott Street Fernadina looked up. Min saw the shadow fade from her face. She leaned back in her seat, seeming to think for a moment.

"Do you go to the Sun Wah anymore?" she asked. Her voice sounded wistful.

Min laughed. "Do I! I wait tables there three nights a week."

"Then you must see Bao!" she said. She was smiling now, and he was glad to feel the tension ease between them. "How is he?"

"Oh, as ever. No, better now, since his wife left him."

"What?"

"Sure, didn't you know? His wife ran off with a guy from Hong Kong a couple of years ago. He actually seemed relieved. Anyway, I work for him now. He yells at me, but I don't mind, we get along okay. The crowds keep coming. He's had three or four assistants in the past year; no one stays with him long. One of these days someone will take a cleaver to him." Min picked up his chopsticks. "Why don't you go see him?" he said.

Fernadina hesitated. "My mother said I shouldn't bother him with all the troubles he's had."

"He asks about you. He talks about you a lot."

Fernadina looked up.

"We're seeing more and more young Chinese-Americans wandering into Chinatown," Min went on. "You can really see the difference between them and the Chinese kids who were raised there. It's in the clothes, the way they keep looking around like they don't know what they're doing. Some come into the Sun Wah and ask for the English menu. Bao's pretty mean sometimes, pretends he doesn't know what they want. He'll throw the plates on the table and yell at them in Cantonese. I've seen them cringe, like they don't understand the language, but they get the point. I remember Bao and I talked about this one night, after a group of young Chinese-Americans had eaten dinner. Bao said some of them were totally Americanized and had lost the ability to see who they were. They were the ones who could come to Chinatown and breeze through it like the other tourists, like they didn't care about the conditions and how people were really living there. Then there were the others who were still tied to their Chinese-ness. I don't know what else to call it. He said these were the ones who would come back and try to work to improve the way things are in Chinatown. He said he expected you to come back."

"Me?"

"Yes. But there were other reasons, he said."

"What? What did he say?"

Min hesitated. "He said you knew."

Fernadina was still.

Min wiped his mouth slowly with his napkin and looked across at her, seeming to weigh what he was about to say next carefully. "You know, Dina, you and I are coming from opposite ends, in a way. I have to come uptown to find my way, and you have to go to Chinatown." He continued to look at her, hesitating. "Bao said that the task before you was more difficult, though, because of what happened to your father . . . your family there."

He saw the rapid blinking of her eyes, and went on hurriedly. "But he also said he was certain of you, that you would find whatever you're looking for."

"He said that?"

"Yes."

Fernadina wiped her eyes. "Did Bao send you to tell me this?"

"No." Min paused. "I had my own reasons for looking you up. I wanted to tell you about our service organization. I wanted to invite you to our meeting in Chinatown next week." He saw Fernadina's unease, how she shifted her gaze from his face and began to scrape her chopsticks slowly against the edge of her plate. He went on. "We are students and volunteers who are trying to provide services to the people in Chinatown. We want to provide companions and helpers for the elderly, day care, and information on health and education."

He waited, wondering if Fernadina was listening. She was staring at the table in front of her placemat.

"Let me tell you about Mr. Kam," Min said. The tone of his voice made Fernadina look up. "Mr. Kam is over eighty years old. No one knows when he came to this country, but we have seen the pictures of the family he left behind in China. Some of his old cronies say he came here to find work to send money back, but that he lost track of his family. They disappeared during the famine, the revolution, who knows. Anyway, Mr. Kam doesn't speak English, and he can't see to work anymore. He sits on a bench in Columbus Park and dreams. He sits there all afternoon until one of us goes to get him and brings him to a noodle shop where he gets his meal for the day. Then we bring him to his room, above the Phoenix Gift Shop, where he has a cot and a table and a sink. He still washes his own shirt. It's sad for Mr. Kam, but there are hundreds of Mr. and Mrs. Kams in Chinatown. It's not enough to feel sad. . . ."

"Min, stop this, I do want to help. . . ."

He did not appear to hear her. "Some of us have this feeling of"—he put his hand to his chest—"our heritage, I guess. Some of us feel gratitude, obligation, guilt, whatever. We're tied in that way, we can't forget what our parents and grandparents went through, what they did for us."

"I know," Fernadina said. Her voice sounded small. Min stared at her at length, then smiled.

"There's a girl in your dorm who works with us," he said. "Her name is Connie Wing. You could go with her to the meeting if you want. We've got a small office on Mulberry Street."

Fernadina nodded slowly.

He picked up the check. "It's easy to get to Chinatown from here," he said. "You just take the IRT to Forty-second Street, then change to the BMT downtown to Canal Street. You get out, and you're there. Simple. You remember my parents' bakery?"

"Yes."

"It's a take-out place now. Barbecue pork, duck. I hate walking by it every day on my way to the subway. I keep hoping to see the things my parents used to make in the windows."

After Min paid, they went out onto the street, where they began to walk toward the subway stop at 103rd Street. They walked the three blocks in silence. When they reached the stop, he turned to face her.

"Come to Chinatown," he said, smiling, backing away. He swept his hair out of his face. "Bao would love to see you."

Fernadina lifted her hand to wave. "Thanks for lunch." She watched as he ran down into the subway station. She remained standing there, hesitating, leaning forward, feeling almost as if her legs would carry her after him, but then turned her face toward the campus and began to walk away, uptown.

Fernadina thought of going to Chinatown every day. On the evening after her meeting with Min, she went to the phone in the lobby of her dorm and dialed the number of the Sun Wah Restaurant. The familiar voice answered, shouting, "Hah? Sun Wah!" like a curse. Fernadina hesitated, forgetting all words as she listened to the slamming of the pots and the sound of water running in the sink in the background. When Bao shouted into her ear again, demanding an answer, she hung up, trembling. A few days following that evening, while she was studying in her room, she heard a tap on the door. A Chinese girl poked her head in the room.

"Are you Fernadina Peng?" she asked.

"Yes."

"Hi. I'm Connie Wing. Min told me about you. He says you might be interested in coming to our planning meeting this weekend."

The door swung open. Connie saw Fernadina's roommate, Debbie, who sat on her bed, reading. "Oh, excuse me," she said.

"No, it's all right, isn't it, Debbie?" Fernadina said, addressing her roommate. Debbie looked up at the two of them, shrugged, then went back to her reading.

Connie shifted her books. "Look, I'm on my way back from class. Why don't you come to my room? I have some pamphlets there that describe our programs."

"Sure. Okay." Fernadina threw another look at her roommate as she closed the door, but Debbie did not appear to notice. The two Chinese girls went down the hall, then across the walkway to the east wing of the dorm. Connie opened the door to her single room and invited Fernadina to sit while she rummaged through a stack of papers on her desk.

"I have the pamphlets here somewhere," she muttered, pushing her glasses back up on the flat bridge of her nose. "Min said you grew up in Washington, D.C?" She looked up at Fernadina for an instant before she resumed her search. She had short glossy hair that swung forward at either side of her face.

"I grew up in Arlington, about eight miles from Washington," Fernadina said. She noticed the reproductions of Chinese paintings on the walls of Connie's room, the books of Chinese poetry on the shelf.

"We have a lot in common, I bet," Connie said. "I grew up in New Jersey. Is your father a doctor, too?"

Fernadina took the pamphlet Connie held in her hand. "No. My father's dead."

"I'm sorry. I didn't know."

"That's all right." Fernadina turned the pages of the pamphlet.

Connie began to speak rapidly. "The meeting this weekend is to organize work details to cover the different areas of need. I'm in charge of the tutoring program. We could use somebody to tutor English, if you'd be interested in doing that."

"I—I'm not sure about that," Fernadina said. "I really couldn't teach . . . I don't speak Chinese anymore."

"Oh," Connie said, then waved her hand to dismiss Fernadina's embarrassment. Don't worry about it. I hadn't spoken Chinese since I was little, either, before I joined the program. You'd be amazed how quickly it comes back to you. Let's see . . ." She shuffled some papers. "You could always do shopping for some of the elderly. That would be useful."

Fernadina tried to imagine herself back in Chinatown, bringing groceries to someone like old Mr. Kam. She pictured herself standing by his cot, looking down at the worn photographs of his family. She imagined herself seeing his freshly washed shirt hanging up to dry. Then she became aware that Connie was asking her a question.

"Excuse me, what did you say?" she said.

"I said, have you been to Chinatown recently?" Connie said.

"No. My parents visit there every year, but I stopped going years ago."

Connie nodded. "I was the same. I resisted going for the longest time. Maybe because it had turned into a tourist trap, maybe because I thought people there were on view, like animals in a zoo. But it's changed. It would be interesting for you to see how it's changed. Now that the days of the Old Heads have just about passed, people are beginning to be receptive to new ideas. That's why our organization started. We wanted to provide people with basic services, yet at the same time not threaten the traditional way of life that makes Chinatown Chinatown. It's been difficult. There's been a lot of resistance, but I think we've made a start. I know I've learned a lot, both about Chinatown and myself."

Fernadina looked at Connie's eager face and felt gladness, relief, even, that she was going to the meeting on Mulberry Street. She took the pamphlets with her and read them that evening with growing resolve. But then, when Saturday came, she found herself knocking on Connie's door and telling her, mumbling, that she could not go with her to Chinatown.

"Is something wrong?" Connie asked.

"No. No. I just can't go this week. Maybe next time," Fernadina said.

"Is it because of the language?"

"No. Yes."

"Look, I said not to worry about that because—"

"No." Fernadina was shaking her head, backing away. "I'm sorry. I just can't go."

Connie looked at her a long time. "That's all right," she said. "I know how it is."

"Maybe next time," Fernadina repeated as the door closed. Confusion and despair seized her. Why couldn't she force herself to go? she wondered. Was it truly because she had forgotten to speak the language, that she had lost the tongue of Chinatown; was it that she feared she would be looked upon as one of the hollow bamboo generation, those born in America who had become empty of the Chinese heritage and soul? Or was it, as Bao suspected, that she feared that the ghosts of her childhood still lingered there?

Why else had she come here other than to confront these fears, these ghosts? To her, the past was like a birthmark, never fading. She sensed that whatever answers she sought lay close by, in Chinatown, but knew that until she overcame her fears, or at least confronted them in her mind, she could not draw near, not yet.

It was as if the city knew Fernadina's uncertain state, for it seemed to clamor for her attention now, to flaunt its many forms of distraction. With her new friend Rhea, Fernadina began to explore the Upper West Side, walking, sifting through every block. The music of 96th Street engulfed her as she moved within the crowds of white, black, and brown-skinned people. Congas, trumpets, tin drums pounded and blared from radios amidst the whistling calls of the men sitting on benches who winked and beckoned to her. Rhea pulled her back whenever she raced ahead down Broadway. "What are you afraid of?" her friend would ask, laughing. "Typical out-of-towner—jumpy, shifty-eyed, dark under the eyes from lack of sleep." Fernadina, abashed, would slow her walk to her friend's pace but would still find herself swerving, jumping from the paths of people who seemed to come at her from all sides.

And in the day, during and between classes, the sound of the demonstrations and chanting reached her window. Leaflets continued to flutter like flags on the cafeteria tables. On some evenings, after study, Fernadina would walk, trying to shake the feeling that the city awaited her. Rhea tried to explain. "You're just getting used to being in the city. But you're right, I feel it, too. There is tension on campus. There's tension on every campus in the country. It's the war. Everybody's going crazy."

Even as Fernadina accepted her friend's explanation, she knew there was something else, as well. She could not imagine what it was, this impending feeling, but everywhere she went, every moment, she became aware that she waited.

One Sunday, early in November, she looked up from her desk, where she had been studying for exams. The sky outside her window was heavy-looking, gray, appearing as if to rain. She closed her text. She knew the material, she thought, and her eyes had grown weary from reading. In spite of the threatening sky, she decided to go to the Metropolitan Museum, which had become one of her favorite places. She took her umbrella and went across the quad to Broadway, where she caught the 104 bus down to 86th Street. There, she changed to the crosstown bus that went to the East Side.

Manhattan had that canopied look. While the bus moved through the near-empty streets, Fernadina looked out the window to watch people walking in the grayness, carrying the heavy Sunday _New York Times_ under their arms or standing out in front of restaurants where they had had brunch, trying to decide what to do next. As the bus passed through Central Park she saw that the trees were stripped of leaves and that the ground was covered in layers of yellow and brown. At 5th Avenue Fernadina got off the bus and walked the few blocks to the museum. As usual, crowds of people, New Yorkers and tourists alike, had taken Sunday refuge inside the lobby there and were milling around, their little Met button-clips twinkling from their collars.

Fernadina spent an hour at a special photography exhibit on the second floor, then moved on to the paintings, lingering in the room of the French Impressionists. She wandered through a hallway of Flemish paintings, stopping to peer at the shadows in the dark portraits. On the way out of the museum she took a wrong turn and found herself in the hall of Egyptian antiquities. She ran her fingers along the edges of the empty limestone sarcophagi and inspected the cat-headed idols standing like sentinels on either side of the archways. The feline faces appeared serene, but Fernadina wondered what stories of the past they had to tell.

It was dusk by the time she made her way down the steps of the museum and walked along 5th Avenue to take the crosstown bus back to the West Side. She noticed how the streetlights had come on. When she got off the bus at 110th Street and Broadway, she walked up a block and went into a delicatessen, where she bought a sandwich, an apple, a carton of milk. When she came out, it was raining. She opened her umbrella and was glad it was only five more blocks to the gates of the college.

She passed the darkened storefronts, tilting her umbrella against the rain. Few other people were walking on the sidewalk. This was typical on a Sunday, she told herself, looking behind and around her. She saw someone walking in the same direction on the opposite side of the street. She began to walk more quickly, fighting the light wind that pulled at her umbrella. She walked near the curb, staying within the light of the streetlamps. "Walk fast, act confident, and you'll survive this city," Rhea had told her once, half-jokingly. Fernadina was almost running by the time she reached the gate of the campus. She was glad to see the shadows of other students hurrying through the quad. She ran up the steps of her dorm. Inside the doorway she brought down her umbrella and shook it. The lobby was empty. That was strange, she thought, and what was even stranger, no one sat at the reception desk either; the red lights were blinking insistently on the switchboard. She walked through the dimly lit foyer, stopping to look in the student boxes to see if she had gotten any messages. Finding none, she began to walk through the lobby on her way to the broad staircase. Suddenly a man stepped out from the shadowed alcove behind the staircase. She stopped, shocked, then turned away, thinking to run. "Please don't," the man said. "I need to talk to you, Fernadina." He came toward her. When she began to back away, he stopped. "Please listen to me," he said. "Don't be afraid. Do you recognize me? You've seen me before, haven't you?" In spite of herself, Fernadina raised her eyes to look at the man as he drew nearer. She remembered him, then, as the man in the car who had followed her near the school field, months ago. It was the face whose eyes she saw recognized her again.

"Would it be all right if we sat there?" the man said, pointing to the group of chairs and a sofa across the lobby. Fernadina saw that there they would be in plain view of anyone coming in the front door or down the staircase. Out of the corner of her eye Fernadina saw the girl on night duty return to the reception desk, a cup of coffee in her hand. Reassured, but still wary, she nodded, standing back to allow the man to walk past her toward the group of chairs. She waited until the man seated himself on the sofa, then she moved toward a wing-backed chair opposite it. A table covered with magazines and newspapers separated them. A brass floor lamp nearby gave off a soft light. She sat down in the chair and waited, holding her bag of food and her damp umbrella in her lap. She twisted the pleats of the umbrella between her fingers. The man was still wearing his raincoat. He took out a packet of cigarettes. He offered her the packet, but she shook her head. She watched him light his cigarette, then lean across the table to pull an ashtray closer to him. He drew on the cigarette, looking at her, seeming to appraise her.

"My name is Chang Yung-shan," he said. "I am Colonel Chang's son. No doubt you are familiar with that name."

"Yes," Fernadina said.

"No doubt you have grown up hating the name."

Fernadina hesitated, looking to see what emotions flickered across the man's face, but she saw none. "No," she said. "_Hate_ is not the word."

"I see. Then perhaps that makes my task a little easier."

"What is it? What do you want of me?"

Yung-shan stared at her, seeming to consider something, drawing on his cigarette again. Then he leaned forward. "I have come to tell you that it was not my father who arranged your father's murder."

Fernadina stared at him.

"It was Madame Peng."

Fernadina felt the ribs of the umbrella beneath her fingers as she tightened her grip. She saw Yung-shan's eyes intent on her face. "Why should I believe you?" she said finally.

Yung-shan saw the confusion on her face. She was still young, he thought. He leaned back against the sofa. "Perhaps if you knew what Madame Peng's motives had been, you will find it easier to believe me." He waited, but Fernadina said nothing. "Madame Peng saw many opportunities in many things," he went on. "She had the gift of recognizing possibilities in people. She saw them immediately in your parents when they arrived in Chinatown. She saw that your mother, especially, would be useful to her. Your parents' arrival coincided with the time when Madame Peng began to sense her advantage in her long struggle for power with my father. She had worked long to establish an understanding with the Chinatown police, to infiltrate and control the channels throughout the community. When my father fell ill, she sensed the time was right for a trap. She lured my father's men away from him with promises of wealth and papers that would legitimize their entry into this country, and used these men to betray him. She laid the trap with your father's life."

"How do you know this?" Fernadina said.

"I found the man responsible for setting the trap. You probably don't know his name—Quan Wo-fu."

Fernadina remembered the name. She thought back to her childhood, recalling the whispers that reached her ears in the days following her father's death. She watched now how Yung-shan breathed deeply, wearily.

"I followed Wo-fu for eight years," Yung-shan said. "I followed him all the way to Hong Kong before I caught him and threatened to turn him over to friends of my father's who have their own operations there. It was then that he told me everything." Yung-shan paused. He looked at Fernadina, who had stood up from her chair. "But that is far from the end of it. You know you must know the rest, however terrible it may be, for you to be sure, don't you?" he said. His voice was gentle. He waited until she sat back down, then, slowly, continued to speak. "Madame Peng had, in particular, designs for your mother, as I said. With your father dead, she knew your mother would be at a loss to know what to do. So she took her into her own hands, guided her, nurtured her, and then, when she was well enough, sent her to her own son, in Washington."

Fernadina began to pluck at the tufts in the upholstery of her chair.

"You may suspect, as I think you do, the reason behind this," Yung-shan continued. His voice sounded drained. "Your mother was, unwittingly, to fulfill all of Madame Peng's wishes to perfection."

"You mean, by marrying Richard, by having my brother," Fernadina said, her voice barely audible.

"Exactly. Madame had her heir. The Peng family line was assured."

"My God," Fernadina said. She suddenly remembered the look on Madame Peng's face the day the old lady received her grandson. She looked up sharply when she heard Colonel Chang's son laugh. He made a short, hoarse sound, more like a cough.

"Madame had her satisfaction with all of us," he said, leaning forward, looking into her eyes. "Now, shall I tell you what her real triumph was?"

Fernadina turned her face from him.

"Yes, you know this much, you might as well know this last thing, perhaps her main motive for having undertaken the entire scheme."

Fernadina willed herself to look back into Yung-shan's face. She saw how his eyes stared at the space in front of him, focusing on nothing. "You knew, didn't you, that Madame Peng was a widow herself?" he said.

"Yes," Fernadina said. "When I was older, my mother told me stories of how Madame had been consort to a warlord, back in China."

"You heard how her husband had been killed by a rival warlord?"

"Yes."

"Then hear this. Sometime, much later, after she had come to this country, she learned that this same warlord, the one who had killed her husband, had also fled here. She learned that he had changed his name, begun a business in San Francisco, and later moved right into her own territory in New York. She could not believe her luck, that the man had come so close. She had the advantage, you see, because he did not know who she was; he had never seen the wife of the man he had killed, and she bore her maiden name, as did, and still do, all women in China, even when married. But she could not strike right away, for she knew the power of the laws in this land. She knew it was not the same as it had been in China, during the time of the warlords, when men made up their own laws. So she waited. She waited, patiently, for many years, increasing her strength, biding her time, weaving her trap. Then, finally, only when all the signs pointed in her favor, revealing her great opportunity, she struck."

Yung-shan turned his head to regard Fernadina with burning eyes. "It was her greatest triumph, her murder of your father, for it was in this act that she brought about the downfall of her greatest enemy—her husband's murderer, that warlord, my father, Colonel Chang."

O O O

Both Fernadina and Yung-shan looked up when they heard the front door of the dorm bang open and saw two students come inside, laughing, shaking the rain from themselves. Fernadina turned away from them, hiding her face behind the wing of her chair. Yung-shan sat back from the light of the lamp. The two students chatted briefly with the girl at the desk, then clopped over to the staircase in their clogs and made their noisy ascent, the hard wooden steps resounding loudly with each step. When she heard the steps fade down the hallway on the upper floor, Fernadina turned to Yung-shan.

"Is it for vengeance's sake, too, that you've come to tell me this?" she said.

Yung-shan lit another cigarette. "Vengeance," he said, savoring the word as he drew it into his lungs with the smoke. "No. It's too late for vengeance." He looked closely at Fernadina through the smoke. "It took me eight years to find Wo-fu, to prove my father's innocence. I don't regret those years. It is ironic, though, that even though I know the truth now, I cannot tell anyone, I cannot clear my father's name with anyone but you. That is why I have come. You are the only one with whom I can share this truth."

"Is that why you followed me before?" Fernadina asked.

"Yes. I wanted to tell you then; I thought you were old enough. But when I saw you, when I drove by your house, I thought, no, if I told her, she would tell her mother. I didn't want to take that chance. I decided to wait until you were alone, away from her." He paused, clearing his throat. When he spoke again, he spoke quickly, as if with some urgency. "The person I had wanted to be able to tell all along was your mother. If I had found Wo-fu earlier, found proof of Madame Peng's intentions, I could have warned her . . . everything might have turned out differently. But as it happened—" He stopped again, shrugging as if to say all such thoughts were meaningless now. He crushed his cigarette against the bottom of the ashtray and watched the last wisp of smoke curl into nothingness. "Your mother appears to have made her peace with her life," he said. "It would serve nothing for me to tell her what I know. It would only cause her more pain, and I believe she has suffered already." He turned to Fernadina. "It is you, I believe, who are chained to the past. You must be free of that past before you can begin life on your own. But that is not the reason why I have come to see you. I have a favor to ask of you."

Fernadina waited.

"I do not wish to have your father's murder case reopened in Chinatown," Yung-shan said. "Even though my business now is legitimate, I believe that my name, merely by association to my father and his dealings in the past, would fall under suspicion." He passed his hand over his eyes, looking suddenly exhausted, Fernadina thought. "I simply can't risk an investigation," he went on. "It would jeopardize the life I've managed to build for myself." He looked at her. "The favor I ask, then, is this: Drop the past. Don't arm yourself to pursue this end. Your father's murderer is dead. You know everything now; that should be enough."

"Are you talking about my studies here?"

"Yes. Isn't that your aim? To study law?"

"How did you know?"

Yung-shan remained silent.

Fernadina leaned forward in her chair, seeking his eyes. Why did she find herself believing what he said? Why did she feel this sense of trust? Was it that she sensed he bore the memory of his father as she bore the memory of hers, that they had this terrible burden in common? But she said, in spite of this feeling, "How do you know that I will be satisfied with your explanation of all of this, of what has been my life? How do you know that I won't need to prove the past for myself?"

"I don't know," Yung-shan said. "But there is one other person who knows what I know. Perhaps he can explain it better."

"Who?"

Yung-shan hesitated, then said, "Bao. Bao can confirm what I have told you."

Fernadina stared at Yung-shan. "Why didn't he tell me himself, before?"

"He had no proof. He only sensed what was happening. In his own way, Bao knows more than anyone what goes on in Chinatown. Besides, he knew it was not his place to tell you, a young girl, your own story. He waited for you to go to him."

"Then why didn't he warn my mother?"

"He wasn't certain, as I said. He respected your mother. And perhaps," Yung-shan said, pausing, "perhaps he sensed that your mother realized what course her life was taking all along."

"I don't believe that!" Fernadina said, rising from her chair.

"Only she will be able to tell you," Yung-shan said, meeting the challenge in her eyes.

There was a long silence. Fernadina felt Yung-shan's eyes studying her. She could think of nothing to say. Finally she saw him rise.

"I don't expect you to be able to give me an answer right away," Yung-shan said. "But I believe you will honor my request. I believe that you will see that silence, in the long run, is the best course. For everyone."

Fernadina saw that he was about to leave. She suddenly realized she did not want to be left alone with what she knew. "Is that it?" she asked, hearing the panic in her voice. "Will we talk again? Is there somewhere I can write to you?"

Yung-shan shook his head. "It's better you didn't." He began to move away, then stopped, seeing the stricken look on her face. "Wait a year. If you really need to find me, Bao will know."

He nodded to her, then walked out of the lobby.

A week later, Fernadina sat at her desk and stared at the sheet of paper in front of her. On it she had written her name, "Fernadina Peng." She scratched through the name "Peng" and wrote above it the name "Wong." She wrote the name again, "Fernadina Wong." She looked out her window and saw that outside, the dark November sky seemed to lie close to the ground, promising snow. Then she pulled open the drawer of her desk and took out the letter she had received from her mother the previous day. She unfolded it and read it again:

"Dear Fernadina," her mother's letter began.

This will be short because I have to pick up William to take
him to the dentist before going back to work. We haven't heard

from you in so long! Are your courses taking everything out of you? Has your Sociology professor gotten more "with it"? We are very eager to see you at Thanksgiving. I've invited Kay Lynn and Tim and their children to join us. I had been thinking of having turkey, but I think I will roast two ducks and serve pancakes with them, Peking style.

Your stepfather is looking forward to seeing you this weekend. I thought to bring William and go with him—it would have been nice for all of us to be together again, but he said the meeting of the Law Association would take only a day and that he would be back that same evening. I'll just have to wait until Thanksgiving. I hope you will make time to have lunch with him. Please be nice, Sing-hua.

Enclosed is a picture of William describing his science project to one of the judges in the regional competition. He won third place! We are very proud of him. Please write—

Love,
Mama

Fernadina refolded her mother's letter and slipped it into the drawer of her desk. She stared again at the paper on which she had written her name, thinking back to Yung-shan's words, thinking of the words she would say to her stepfather, to her mother. The words lay like stones within her skull, yet somehow her mind felt light, her thoughts raced.

Someone tapped at her door. Libby, the girl whose room was at the head of the stairs, poked her head in.

"Your father's downstairs, Dina," she said.

"Thanks," Fernadina said, not bothering to correct her dorm mate. She waited until she heard Libby shuffle back down the hall, then reached for her coat.

She saw Richard standing in his overcoat in the lobby as she came down the stairs. His face, although smiling, belied his concern.

"Hello," he said. "I got your letter. I told your mother I was at a Law Association meeting for the day. . . ."

"I know," Fernadina said.

Richard reached out to her, touching her wool scarf, then dropped his hand. He looked around the lobby. There were several girls sitting about, reading mail, chatting idly. "Shall we find a place to talk?" he said.

"There's a coffee shop down the street," Fernadina said, turning toward the door. Richard nodded, then followed her out of the lobby.

They went into a small shop on Broadway, near 112th Street. They sat in a booth and waited in silence as a dark-haired waiter poured them coffee into thick white mugs. Richard unrolled the paper napkin from around his flatware and smoothed it out on the table in front of him.

"I love your mother, Dina," he said, "and I want more than anything to preserve the life that we have together. Even if you believe nothing else that I say, you must believe this."

"I don't know what to believe anymore," Fernadina said. Tears filled her eyes. "How can it be, how can she not know the lie she lives? How can you allow her to continue living this lie?"

"Because the lie has become the truth," Richard said. "There is no other way for us to live now."

Fernadina wiped her eyes. "Have you known all along?"

Richard sighed. "I have known certain things, suspected others. Sometimes it's hard to know the difference. One thing is for certain, though. I had come to know what you know now only recently, after my mother's death."

Fernadina shook her head at the waiter who approached them with the menus.

"Please listen to me, before you judge," Richard said, after the waiter had gone. "If you mean did I know who killed your father before I married your mother, no, I did not know. I had no awareness of the nature of my mother's intrigues in Chinatown. At that time I had deliberately distanced myself from her." He stared at the coffee mug he held between his hands. "It is difficult to explain, our relationship, my mother and I," he said. "When we first arrived in this country, we were almost as one; she took me everywhere with her, afraid that she would lose me, too, as she had the rest of her family. Then she realized that in order to protect me from the struggles that went on between her and the other leaders in Chinatown, and in order for me to receive the best education, she had to send me away to school. I remember how those first few years away from her were agony. But then, as I grew older and prepared to enter college, I recognized the values of this country, and realized that in order to succeed, I must embrace them. It was at this point that I realized how much my mother and I had gone our separate ways, how I had become an outsider to Chinatown, while she had become more and more an important figure, an elder, there." Richard paused, sipping from his mug.

"While I was still very young, barely out of college," he went on, his voice low, "I married an American woman. I married for love, but I cannot deny that there was that element of rebellion against my mother. I was aware of her expectations that I marry a Chinese, return to Chinatown, take over her business. I was aware that she expected me to fulfill the obligations of the dutiful Chinese son." Richard's eyes flickered to Fernadina's. She thought she saw shame, regret in them. When Richard continued, he spoke haltingly, searching for words. "When my marriage failed, my mother called me to her, saying she forgave me, that she wanted us to be mother and son again. I knew I would always feel that bond between us, but I also knew I did not want to become involved in her business. So I moved to Washington, where I joined a prestigious firm. I resolved to be helpful to my mother in other ways, helping her with her new tailoring shop, seeing to her basic needs. Perhaps it was out of guilt from denying her my commitment to Chinatown that I became so deeply involved in the Washington Chinese Community Association. In Washington, perhaps because the community itself was so small, the problems were not political as much as social, economic. I felt I could work within the system there." Richard stopped. Fernadina saw what effort it took him to continue. She sought his eyes to encourage him to go on, but he stared only at the cup in his hands. Finally, still keeping his eyes fixed to the cup, he went on. "I met a woman at this time, a Taiwanese woman. Lillian . . . this woman, and I had planned to marry. I had thought to reconcile with my mother, to make things right with her at last, so I brought Lillian to meet her." Richard gave a sharp laugh. "I remember very well what my mother said after she met Lillian. 'I forbid you to marry her,' she said. Her reasons were that Lillian was too old to bear children, that her allegiance to Taiwan was all wrong. She was too modern. I cannot tell you how outraged I felt. I returned to Washington with Lillian. I kept telling myself I had outgrown my feelings of obligation to my mother, but I soon found that I hadn't; I found that I was bound. Perhaps you find that hard to understand." Richard raised his eyes to Fernadina's. Fernadina shook her head, not knowing what to say. "Anyway," Richard continued, "my mother told me to go to your mother, telling me she was her choice for me. She told me that your mother, whom I had only met once or twice then, had a message for me that my mother had sent with her in a wooden box. I had thought to ignore my mother's instructions, but I couldn't. I couldn't ignore my past, my obligations to my mother, everything. They gnawed at me, do you see?"

Fernadina nodded.

"I went to retrieve the box from your mother. I opened it when I got to my apartment. Inside, I found a scrap of paper that my mother had carried all the way from China. It was the last message she had gotten from my father before he was killed. She had saved it for just an instance such as this. She knew I was intent on pursuing my own happiness, that I wavered in my duty to her and the memory of my father. Sending me the scrap of paper was her way of telling me that my father had sacrificed his life for me, that it had been he who had actually commanded us to abandon him, not my mother, as I had believed all along. She knew the paper was her last hope of bringing me back to her, but she knew it would succeed." Richard wiped his face with his napkin. "The characters my father wrote were barely legible, but the message was simple: 'Avenge my death. Preserve our line.' I knew I was not great enough to turn away from these words. I knew then I had to accept my mother's way."

Fernadina studied her stepfather's face. "But it was not you who avenged your father's death," she said. "You said you had known nothing of the role Colonel Chang had played before your mother's death."

"Yes. That's true. I was a boy at the time of my father's death and never saw his murderer. When he came to this country, he changed his name, so I remained unaware of who he was. My mother also kept his identity from me, even though she found out who he was soon after he arrived in Chinatown. She told me this in a letter Leong gave to me after her death. She said she'd claimed to undertake my father's first command herself. I don't know whether she kept me out of her plans to protect me in case anything went wrong, or if she wanted the satisfaction for herself. Perhaps she claimed the first command for herself because it was plain the second part of it had been addressed to me."

They both remained very still, then Richard looked up. "Dina, I am appalled at what I know. I am appalled that what has happened, has happened. Sometimes, when I stop to think about my life, our life, I feel as if I stand inside it and see it as a great smoldering hole . . . as if everything I had known and been had been struck by lightning. I see devastation, and I feel anger and despair at having been struck." He paused, leaning back in the booth. He looked old, Fernadina thought. She saw the gray in the hair at his temples for the first time.

"Yet, I know I have a choice," he went on. "I can remain inside the hole and allow myself to turn into ashes as well, or I can pull myself up from the hole and face another way. I have chosen the latter way, Dina. I have accepted that I cannot withstand the force of lightning, nor understand why it happened to strike me. In this way, I can continue to live. Do you see what I am saying?"

"You are a coward," Fernadina said.

Richard said nothing. They sat in perfect silence until the waiter came and slipped their check on the table next to Richard's elbow.

"Please, think about what I've been saying," Richard said finally. "You have so much before you yet, you live in a time and place where there is so much opportunity. When you come home at Thanksgiving—"

"I'm not coming home," Fernadina said. Her voice was cold.

"What do you mean?"

"I've made other plans. I've decided to work for the committee on the antiwar demonstration planned on campus for December."

"But your mother—"

"What would I say to her?" Fernadina broke in, her voice rising. "That I'm grateful to her for living a lie? That I'm fine and happy as a result of it?"

Richard shook his head. His hands trembled.

"You needn't say anything," he said. "You could be, simply, grateful." He looked up to see that Fernadina was crying. "Dina," he said gently, holding out his napkin to her.

"My mother," she said, pressing the napkin to her eyes. "Do you think she knew?"

Richard was silent so long that Fernadina lowered her napkin to look at him. His face was pale.

"I believe your mother, like myself, may have suspected certain things," he said finally. "But in the end, I believe she chose not to know." He studied his stepdaughter's face. "Fernadina," he said, his voice low, "you must not judge what you have been given. The past is the past; you must look to your future now." He sought her eyes. "You may judge me however you will. I have been foolish and weak, although I have tried to do what is right. But please, don't disturb the truth as your mother knows it now. Don't judge her. Whatever she did, she did for you."

Fernadina covered her face with her hands.

There was refuge here, Fernadina thought. She sat in the library, at one of the long oak tables placed along the length of the main reading room. Her Sociology book lay open before her, but she could not read.

She glanced along the length of the table and saw other students study-ing for the exams to be held before the Thanksgiving break. Heads were bent under the soft light of the lamps placed at even intervals along the table and slight sounds were audible; pages turning, pencils scratching, chairs creaking discreetly. But Fernadina's thoughts were not on her exams. She kept thinking of her past, and how she had been made to choose, even from the earliest memories.

Bao had held a tangerine in one hand and a coconut candy in the other behind his back, and said, "Choose!" That had been easy. Either treat would have made her happy. The more difficult decision had been when her mother had left her with him at the Sun Wah Restaurant while she went to work, and Bao had said to her sternly, as she was about to cry, "Be happy or sad! Choose!" The choice had been be-wildering to her until Bao told her that crying and being unhappy were not allowed in his restaurant; that her mother would be back. Then it had been easy.

Was it that simple? Fernadina thought.

Someone tapped her on the shoulder. She turned and saw that it was Connie Wing.

"Hi," Connie whispered, sliding into the seat next to Fernadina.

"Hi," Fernadina said.

"You haven't been taking your messages. Min's left you a couple al-ready, and I have, too."

Fernadina shrugged. She had not returned Richard's calls, either.

"We wanted to let you know of our next meeting. You said you might come."

"When is it?"

"Next Tuesday, before Thanksgiving. Will you still be in town, or are you going home?"

"I don't know yet."

"We're meeting at the Sun Wah. Min said you knew where it was."

"At the Sun Wah?"

"Sure. We've done it before; Bao fixes us a great dinner, then we talk and plan afterward." Connie gathered her books. "Come if you can." Before Fernadina could answer, she was gone.

On Tuesday the snow was falling thickly. Fernadina and Rhea were coming out of Milbank Hall.

"God, we're free, no more exams!" Rhea said, tilting her head back to let the cold flakes fall on her face. "Come on, let's go do something outrageous. Let's go to Bloomingdale's, there's still time before they close." She looked over at Fernadina. They were approaching the quadrangle now. In spite of the weather, a group of students had set up a wooden table and were stopping people to sign a petition. One girl approached Rhea, who nodded and signed. When the girl showed the petition to Fernadina, she shook her head. The two friends continued walking.

"What's the matter?" Rhea asked. "I thought you supported the movement. I thought you were staying the weekend to work on the planning committee for the demonstration in December."

Fernadina looked at her friend. "I've changed my mind. It's more important for me to go home." She looked away. She knew there would be more demonstrations to plan for in the spring. She knew she could prove her loyalties there, later. "I've got to go home this time," she said.

"Are you all right?" Rhea said, looking into her face. "You've been awfully quiet these past few weeks. You've been holed up too long, that's your problem. I can't believe you've been studying all this time. You really need to get out." She gave Fernadina an encouraging nudge. "Come on, let's go to Bloomie's. You could get a real New York shirt for your brother, or something nice for your mother."

Fernadina hesitated. She pictured Bloomingdale's, the chic store where the escalators glided from one glittering floor to another, where elegant ladies passed out samples of perfume, and where the counters spilled with the latest fashions and fads. There was something new, fresh, magical about Bloomingdale's, Fernadina thought. She felt herself succumbing to its allure. "Okay," she said to Rhea. "But I want to make a phone call first." She started in the direction of Brooks Hall.

"Hurry!" Rhea called as she walked in a circle under the sky, catching snowflakes with her tongue.

In the lobby of her dorm Fernadina dialed the number she had found on one of the messages in her box. An unfamiliar voice answered.

"May I speak to Min, please?" she said.

"Min's not here. Can I take a message?"

"No, thanks . . ."

"You want the number of the restaurant where he works?"

"No, never mind. Thanks anyway." She hung up.

Outside, Rhea was waiting with a snowball. She lofted it at Fernadina, but it disintegrated in midair.

"Too soft." Rhea snorted, looking up at the sky. "It's the kind that keeps coming, though."

They walked on Broadway toward 110th. Rhea ran a few steps and slid on the snow-dusted sidewalk beyond where Fernadina walked. "C'mon! Race you to the station!"

Fernadina wrapped her scarf one more time around her neck and began to trot after Rhea. They went down into the 110th Street subway station, bought tokens at the booth, and pushed through the turnstile. As they stamped their feet of snow on the platform, craning their necks to look up the tracks, they saw the lights of the downtown train approaching.

"What do you know," Rhea said to Fernadina. She took off her gloves, flexing her hands. "God, it's been nearly a month since I've been to Bloomie's!"

Rhea held her hand over her ears as the train rumbled into the station, slowing down with a terrific squealing of brakes. She and Fernadina entered a car and sat on a metal bench. The doors closed, then slowly, after a few lurching starts, the train picked up speed.

Fernadina felt the bumping of the rails underneath the hard metal seat. She looked at the reflection of faces in the glass windows opposite of where they sat. She looked at Rhea's image; Rhea with the fair skin and red hair, who sat to her left, humming to herself, her gaze roving along the row of advertisements near the ceiling of the car. She looked at the reflection of the Hispanic lady who sat to her right, dozing. Then she stared at her own reflection, and realized suddenly that she looked at herself not with shock, but with recognition. She studied the face that looked back at her; the high cheekbones, the narrow eyes that seemed not to see, the still mouth. She thought of the approaching Thanksgiving weekend and of the faces she would see at home. She thought of her mother, who would have taken her woks and big steamer out of the attic and made enough dishes for an entire week by now. She thought of how she had helped her mother make roast pork buns when she had been younger; how she had been given the task of putting the right amount of pork filling onto each round of dough before her mother twisted the buns tight and placed them on squares of waxed paper for the dough to rise once more. She remembered how she had been the one to set the table, counting out the chopsticks, tapping them on end on the table to make sure each pair was of even length. She thought of how it would be her task again to set the table this coming weekend. A simple task, she told herself.

The train was slowing down with a deafening screech of brakes. Fernadina felt Rhea punch her lightly in the arm. "C'mon," her friend shouted. "I can't stand this noise. Let's get out and walk, or take the crosstown bus to Bloomie's." The train stopped. Fernadina saw "59th

St" painted on the posts of the station. She felt Rhea pulling on her sleeve.

"No, you go on," she said, motioning for her friend to get out of the car. "I've changed my mind. I've got to go somewhere today."

"Dina!" Rhea said, exasperation and disappointment sharp in her voice. She hung on to the rubber edge of the car door. "Where're you going?" The doors began to close and she hopped out on the platform.

"Some people I have to see!" Fernadina shouted. She hunched her shoulders in apology as her friend shook her fist and made a grimace at her from the other side of the window, running alongside a little way as the train pulled out of the station. There would be time for Bloomingdale's later, Fernadina thought as the train gathered speed. There would always be time for such things, later.

At the 42nd Street stop Fernadina got out and looked for the signs for the BMT line. She followed the crowds wending their way through the tile-walled maze to the downtown platform. After a few minutes' wait, the downtown local pulled into the station and Fernadina got on board. When she sat down, she saw her reflection again in the glass across the aisle. She stared at it. It stared back, confirming what she saw.

The train hurtled downtown in the dark tunnel, making stops at 34th, later at 14th. The car in which she sat became emptier. She became aware of other Chinese people around her; students carrying books, middle-aged men carrying empty shopping bags.

The train pulled into a station and Fernadina became aware of all the Chinese people in her car getting up to move to the doors. She looked up and saw the sign on the platform outside the window: Canal Street. She followed the people out of the car, walked down the platform, climbed the stairs. She came out into the street. People hurried by, people with faces she thought she knew. She walked along Canal Street, passing the stalls, the shops, hearing the barking speech, startled when she found herself recognizing a word here and there. She came to a corner. She looked right. At first she did not see it, as it was now almost obscured by all the new signs surrounding it. But then she saw it, halfway down the block, the sign of the Sun Wah Restaurant. She sensed the late afternoon lull that she knew would last the time it took to drink a cup of tea and smoke two cigarettes before the dinner rush began again. Then she began to walk up Mott Street.